About the Author

John Hughes was born in Sutton Coldfield, in the English Midlands, studied music at Royal Holloway College and has lived in Surrey for most of his adult life. He has earned a living in a variety of ways – selling pianos in Harrods, playing keyboards in a tribute band, editing a magazine, recruiting IT professionals and, most recently, managing in the NHS. He has written half a dozen non-fiction books but *Spitfire Spies* is his first published novel.

For Helen and Alice with love

John Hughes

SPITFIRE SPIES

All good wishes
to
Redhill Library readers!

John Hughes

AUSTIN MACAULEY
PUBLISHERS LTD.

A CIP catalogue record for this title is available from the British Library.

ISBN 9781785545627 (Paperback)
ISBN 9781785545634 (Hardback)
ISBN 9781785545641 (eBook)

www.austinmacauley.com

First Published (2016)
Austin Macauley Publishers Ltd.
25 Canada Square
Canary Wharf
London
E14 5LQ

Printed and bound in Great Britain

Acknowledgments

I would like to thank two people in particular for their cooperation in researching this story. Firstly, Miss Lettice Curtis (1915 – 2014), one of the first female pilots to join the Air Transport Auxiliary, who gave me useful information about life in the ATA, in particular relating to the de Havilland factory at Hatfield. In 1971 she published the definitive history of the ATA – *The Forgotten Pilots*.

Secondly, Alex Henshaw MBE (1912 – 2007), Chief Test Pilot at the Castle Bromwich Spitfire factory, who provided guidance about the scenes set in and around the factory and airfield (and who appears briefly in the story). He is believed to have test-flown 10% of all output at Castle Bromwich, sometimes up to twenty planes a day. He once famously flew a Spitfire the length of Broad Street in Birmingham at low level, and is also the only pilot known to have performed a barrel roll in a Lancaster bomber!

PROLOGUE

(Thursday 5TH March 1936)

For seven cold, muscle-aching hours the man had been squatting on the perimeter of Eastleigh Aerodrome, a sketch pad and notebook on his lap and a pair of powerful binoculars around his neck. He could see a crowd of people milling around the doors of the hangar-cum-workshop, some in overalls, others wearing suits or coats.

But there was still no sign of prototype K5054.

He was beginning to think the test flight had been postponed, or that the stupid bitch had got the date wrong.

She lay next to him, on a canvas groundsheet, polishing a lens for the hundredth time and fiddling impatiently with the settings on her two 35mm cameras. A competent photographer, she was nearly half his age, in her early twenties, blonde, with an appealing face and good figure. Despite a thick coat, head scarf and fingerless woolen gloves, she was shivering and her entire body was stiff from cold and inactivity. She reached for a thermos flask, poured steaming hot coffee into two cups and handed one across to him. He grunted by way of thanks, pulled out a hip flask and topped it up with a slug of brandy.

A few straggling bushes and a slight grassy mound hid them from view, though at a distance of several hundred yards from the aerodrome buildings it was unlikely they would be noticed. A month of hanging around English aerodromes and aircraft establishments had taught them that security was lapse – non-existent in places – which made their job that much easier.

Sipping coffee with one hand, he raised the binoculars with the other and panned slowly across the airfield just as he had done ten minutes before . . . and ten minutes before that. Nothing.

They had arrived in England four weeks earlier, not clandestinely but across land from Hamburg to the Hook of Holland, then by ferry to Harwich as ordinary fare-paying passengers. An extended holiday, he told the immigration officer, to study and draw British wildlife. The girl was his niece; she had come along to improve her English, photograph the birds he sketched, and keep her favourite uncle company.

Driving around in an Austin 7, they stayed in cheap hotels or boarding houses near RAF stations and aircraft factories, eavesdropped on conversations in pubs, chatted to workmen and picked up snippets of gossip from locals. Every morsel they gleaned found its way back to Germany via a postal address in Rotterdam.

They had only been introduced to each other a day or so before leaving Germany. At first she had been very quiet, speaking only when spoken to, nervous and unsure of herself; but gradually she began to relax and they soon developed a good working relationship. By the end of the second week, and not entirely to her liking, they became lovers.

She was good at her job and mingled easily in pubs, playing the demure young Danish girl on holiday in England staying with relatives. Pretty soon she was slipping in and out of restricted areas with the stealth of a seasoned cat burglar. Before long, with her disarming feminine charms well-nigh perfected, she could tease out more in an evening than the man could scrape together in a week. He hated her flirting with other men but knew it was necessary. He hated it even so. When she was out alone, he stayed in his room brooding and drinking. On her return there would be jealous cross-questionings, moody exchanges, and occasional violence, until she had assured him she had not been unfaithful to him . . . which wasn't always true.

Then she heard about prototype K5054.

The *Abwehr* – German Military Intelligence – had told them about the Supermarine Aviation Works at Woolston, a suburb of Southampton. The company had developed the S.6B floatplane, winner of the Schneider trophy back in 1931, the annual international air race between seaplanes that had become an excuse for a Government-sponsored research programme. When England won three victories in a row and the contest was over, the British could have created a new one in its place but chose not to. Why? All that research and development to produce a high-speed plane way ahead of its time ceased overnight? The remarkable talents of Supermarine's chief designer, R.J. Mitchell, left dormant? Unlikely. Which made Supermarine worthy of attention.

They drove into Southampton on the last day of February, settled into a hotel, sought out a pub close to the Supermarine works in Hazel Road, and spent the evening in the public bar, talking to each other superficially while listening to every scrap of conversation they could. The next evening, she appeared alone, looking awkward as women often do when walking into pubs unaccompanied. She told the barman her uncle was to meet her there, but he might be delayed. If he hadn't arrived by eight, she was to make her own way home.

A group of men were standing nearby at the bar. She was offered a drink and was soon engaged in conversation with them. Eight o'clock came and went, and no uncle. She stayed. The men all worked at Supermarine. They talked freely and she nearly went crazy trying to remember everything; in particular about the 'fighter' project, a revolutionary design, one of Mr Mitchell's. A genius, they all agreed. The 'fighter' was a new low-wing monoplane being built to an Air Ministry specification – and they'd be getting more than they bargained for, that was certain! A lot of names and jargon were bandied about, most of which she didn't follow. They referred occasionally to *Merlin* and she laughed when she realised it was an engine, not a person.

One conversation she remembered clearly; about the naming of the fighter. K5054 was just the registration number for the prototype. *Shrew* was bandied about as a possibility, so too was *Shrike*. But the most likely candidate was *Spitfire,* even though Mr Mitchell hated it. *Just the sort of bloody silly name they would choose*, he'd been overheard to say. Couldn't be called anything else, one man declared – you only had to look at it to see the name fitted like a glove. Whatever it was to be called, a decision had to be made soon. The test flight was only days away.

She was eventually given a lift home by one of her new friends, a chap in his early thirties, an engineer. In a quiet lane off Peartree Green, he stopped the car at the girl's suggestion. She let him kiss her, then steered his hands on to her breasts, and anywhere else he wanted. By the time he dropped her outside the large detached house in Southampton – supposedly the home of her uncle – she knew the date and venue of the test flight. She stood and waved as the engineer drove away, then walked round the corner to the boarding house where she and the man were staying. He was broody and sullen at first, but his mood didn't last long when she told him the news.

On the day of the test flight, they were in position by the aerodrome early. The one detail they didn't know was the time of the flight, so they had no choice but to sit and wait. By late morning they were cold, stiff and miserable, and by mid-afternoon they had convinced themselves that nothing was going to happen.

Then suddenly everything seemed to happen at once. A taxi plane landed, and a bulky man got out. The test pilot had arrived. The hangar doors opened; the propeller and nose of a plane were clearly visible as the prototype was wheeled slowly out into the open. Apart from the registration number and RAF roundels, it was unpainted and looked drab, but just one glimpse of its streamlined design was enough to convince them their wait had not been in vain. It was like nothing they had seen before. It had a long nose, very long, and the wings were unusual . . . sort of oval-shaped.

The girl knew nothing about airplanes, but you had to be blind not to appreciate such elegance. She focused her camera on its full length and through the powerful telephoto lens could see K5054 painted clearly on the side of the fuselage. She clicked away. They watched as the prototype's tail was lifted up and rested on an oblong trestle, so the fuselage was parallel with the ground – ironically for an official photograph.

The crowd around the hangar had grown. When the photographs were over and the trestle removed, the bulky pilot could be seen donning flying helmet and gloves. He climbed onto the wing of the plane and squeezed, apparently with some difficulty, into the confined space of the cockpit. The crowd drew back as the engine fired into life and the two-bladed propeller started to spin.

K5054 taxied slowly across the grass, turning westward to face into the wind. For a brief moment the plane stood motionless, as an athlete might before attempting a record jump. Then it began to edge forward, gradually picking up speed. The engine noise became louder as the pilot opened the throttle. The man followed its progress through his binoculars, the girl through her viewfinder.

K5054 accelerated as it traversed the field and lifted, a little shakily, into the air, then banked and turned to circle the aerodrome. They could see the whole of the underbelly and the unusual shape of the wings and fuselage. *The undercarriage farings are missing*, the man commented. The girl said nothing, too busy making the most of her precious few moments to take photographs. She cursed as a roll of film came to an end and switched hurriedly to her backup camera.

The display was brief – less than ten minutes. The plane disappeared from view for a while, then returned and, after several precision turns for the benefit of the spectators, the pilot brought K5054 gently back to earth and taxied towards the hangar. When he emerged from the cockpit, his face was all smiles; there were handshakes and slaps on the back, gestures and laughter.

The man at the perimeter lowered his binoculars and stood up, crouching as his aching limbs protested at the sudden movement. He packed away his unused drawing equipment and replaced the binoculars in their leather case. Within minutes they were in the Austin 7 heading back into Southampton.

A week later their report was in Berlin. The Chief of the *Abwehr*, Admiral Wilhelm Canaris, handed it personally to the German Air

Minister, Hermann Göring, who glanced briefly at the photographs then tossed them aside. He made a comment about Ernst Messerschmitt's new fighter being better than anything the British could ever dream up. He didn't appear to be interested in the slightest – though he kept the file containing the report.

Canaris left the Air Ministry angry and frustrated. Here was evidence that the British had a new fighter plane with the potential to out-fly anything the *Luftwaffe* had so far developed, and Göring dismissed it with little more than a cursory glance. Stupidity and blind arrogance! What was the point of running an intelligence service if reports were ignored, he asked himself, not for the first – or last – time.

Barely a month later, the man who had written the report was languishing inside a British prison awaiting trial for murder. The unreal, claustrophobic existence with the girl had eventually taken its toll; a combination of jealousy and an excess of brandy. One night, when she arrived back from a rendezvous too late for his liking, he smashed her head in with a poker for which he forfeited his life at the hands of the hangman.

Admiral Canaris was in no hurry to find new agents to take their place. Adolf Hitler had put a block on spying activities inside Britain which remained in force until September 1939, when war changed everything. By then R.J. Mitchell, the plane's designer, was also dead, from cancer at the age of forty-two. But his remarkable new fighter was already in service with RAF squadrons.

Apart from what could be gleaned at public air shows and pageants, and that it had indeed been christened *Spitfire*, the German authorities knew next to nothing about it.

Or the danger that it posed.

PART ONE

Chapter 1

(Tuesday 23rd April 1940)

Erich Schneider's feet slowly embedded themselves in the soft sand as he stood motionless on the brow of the dune, smoking a cigarette, staring into darkness, and wondering why the hell he didn't just creep out of Camp 4 that night and have done with it. One way, at least, of putting an end to the humiliation that bastard Ulrich so obviously revelled in dishing out.

Escape would be easy. The fences had been built more as a warning for outsiders to stay away rather than to keep trainees in. They stopped at the shoreline and he could swim round them in minutes. Nor would stealing a boat to get to the mainland be difficult.

He'd been at the camp a fortnight, but it seemed like a year on this bleak island with only the sound of the Baltic Sea for comfort. There were about a dozen trainees, all male and all there under coercion of one sort or another. He was the only Englishman; the others were mostly German, plus a few Scandinavians and Slavs.

He was learning to be a spy – or 'agent' as the tutors insisted. But he didn't want to be a spy; he was no good at it. He wanted to go home to his beautiful wife and his career, playing trumpet in the orchestra at Heidelberg, something at which he excelled. Back to those halcyon days before the war when life had been filled with music, love and happiness. Days when politics mattered little, before National Socialism became part of everyone's life whether you wanted it or not. Instead he was wasting his time learning to jump out of planes, make homemade bombs, and – he still couldn't truly believe it – how to kill.

The killing might come in handy one day if he got Ulrich alone for long enough. Schneider wasn't aggressive or malicious by nature, nor was he inclined to bear a grudge. He preferred to let bygones be bygones; people from the English Midlands are like that generally speaking. But with Ulrich he would gladly make an exception. Since day one at the camp Schneider had borne the brunt of the German's foul mouth and sadism, and now, with two days to go before returning to Hamburg, he could bear it no longer. He either fled or he retaliated. His mind was made up. Fleeing was not the answer.

"English pig!" Ulrich had hissed as they passed each other in a corridor for the first time. The next day he spat in his eye. On the second night Schneider had pulled back the sheets of the bed in his tiny wooden room to find them soaking wet and reeking of stale urine. There were elbows in the ribs, a head butt, and an extremely painful knee in the groin. In the past two weeks Schneider had turned the other cheek enough times to become eligible for Christian martyrdom.

He reported it all to the head tutor, who couldn't have cared less and told him not to behave like a runtish schoolboy telling tales to teacher. In other words, stand up for yourself, get even if you have to, but do something, anything, and don't show your weakness. He came away feeling wretched. But the tutor was right of course.

How the German knew his nationality was a mystery. His name was as German as Ulrich's own, albeit a working cover name. They all had one. Schneider's was Ernst. He spoke German like a native, devoid of any accent. His mother had been German and when he was a child they had spoken German at home in preference to English. He had a German wife and had lived for almost five years in Heidelberg, easily passing as a local. At nearly six feet tall with blond hair and blue eyes he even resembled the Nazi model of Aryan perfection. So how in God's name did Ulrich know he was English!

Schneider inhaled the last from his cigarette and tossed the end aimlessly into the sand. He watched the pale glow of the tip as it faded and died, then extricated his feet from the sand and shivered. It was time to go. As he plodded across the dunes, he puzzled over this fact yet again. Someone must have told Ulrich. Who . . . and why? He had thought long and hard about it, but reached no conclusion whatsoever.

Yet his decision was made. In the next two days, before he returned to Hamburg and the more sedate world of radios, codes and ciphers, he would teach Ulrich a lesson.

And Ulrich wasn't going to like it one bit.

Chapter 2

(Wednesday 24th April 1940)

Nobody, but nobody, could say that *Luftwaffe* Chief-of-Staff meetings were dull, thought Major Josef 'Beppo' Schmid – especially when Field Marshal Hermann Göring held them at Carinhall, his sumptuous hunting lodge north of Berlin. Schmid was currently being served coffee by a buxom, pig-tailed Rhine maiden as he sat listening to plans for the invasion of the Low Countries, codename Operation *Gelb*. Göring's ostentatious dress sense was well known, but only visitors to his home were aware that domestic staff were encouraged to wear equally bizarre costumes. Meetings often took place at Carinhall which had become something of a second home for the *Luftwaffe* High Command.

Schmid sat patiently, and anxiously, in his allotted space at the large conference table. As head of the *Luftwaffe*'s Intelligence Branch, his role at such meetings was to answer questions when called upon, quoting facts and figures either from memory or referring to the concise notes in front of him. That was all.

The subject of his anxiety was Göring himself, who was clearly a sick man. His concerns were shared by others around the table; he caught the lightening glances flashing between them from time to time – Kesselring, Stumpff, Sperrle, Milch, Udet, Jeschonnek, the cream of the German Air Force. Göring looked haggard. His behaviour was erratic, his reactions unpredictable. He was moody and his concentration was poor. "So let us move on," he would announce when he felt enough had been said on a particular subject. "What is next on the agenda?"

Operation *Gelb* was on at last. Norway and Denmark were virtually sown up already, in under two weeks. Holland, Belgium and Luxembourg would be tougher. For a start there was the huge British Expeditionary Force to contend with, spread with the French along the Belgian border ready to repulse an attacking force. Nobody was sure whether *Gelb* would turn out as the *Blitzkrieg* it was intended to be, or a replay of the trench

9

stalemate of twenty-five years earlier. Whichever, the Führer had now set a date and there was much to prepare.

It irritated Schmid to watch bad decisions being made before his very eyes by a man who was clearly not fit to run a kindergarten let alone the German Air Force. His carefully documented, painstakingly compiled reports on foreign air forces – their capabilities, strengths and weaknesses – were being ignored. Göring's arrogance blotted out anything he chose not to see.

The concern was not immediate; the air forces of other countries in mainland Europe were feeble at best. But if *Gelb* went according to plan and brought them within range of the British Royal Air Force, that was a different matter. Although his files weren't exactly brimming over with facts and figures about the RAF – relatively speaking they were a mystery – he knew they were a force to reckon with.

Everyone present knew what was really ailing their chief. This was no viral infection or nervous complaint, the usual blanket excuses proffered for his frequent absences from official Reich functions. It was the old problem.

Hermann Göring was a drug addict.

Morphia mainly, with a sprinkling of pethadine and paracodeine thrown in. Rumours abounded that he'd become hooked on painkillers after being shot in the balls during the Munich Putsch back in November 1923. Schmid never joined in such gossip mongering, and for good reason; he had been there on that fateful day and harboured vivid youthful memories of events. Besides, he knew it wasn't like that.

The discussion of Operation *Gelb* had ended with a reiteration of the projected date: Wednesday 8th May, precisely two weeks from today. Weather permitting. The topic switched to the next country earmarked for invasion, England, and eventually the whole of Great Britain.

"Dates," announced Göring with a flourish, "depend upon the speed with which *Gelb* succeeds. As already discussed, this should not take long – the armed forces of the Low Countries are insignificant. The only resistance will come from the British Expeditionary Force, but it will not be long until they are pushed back into their English Channel." This brought smiles to some of the faces around the table. "What will follow is in many ways regrettable." Nods of agreement. "I did not anticipate extending the borders of the Reich beyond France to the west – nor did the Führer. But the die was cast when Britain declared war on the Fatherland, and in a few short weeks we shall stand on the French coast surveying the cliffs of Dover without a doubt in our minds as to our next objective. When that time comes, we shall be ready for the challenge."

Schmid saw Commander Albert Kesselring stir uncomfortably in his seat. 'Smiling' Albert, as his friends had dubbed him, was not smiling at this precise moment. "We no doubt all share your resolve, Field Marshal," he said respectfully. "However, I feel it would be unwise to underestimate the defence capability of Great Britain."

Göring guffawed loudly. "Nonsense! The Royal Air Force is undermanned and flying out-of-date machines – just like every other air force in Europe. The *Luftwaffe* will slice through them like a knife through butter. I give them four days before they are wiped from the skies."

"I would not be so sure," Kesselring said plainly.

Göring raised an eyebrow. "Explain yourself. Tell us how the RAF is going to destroy the might of a modern, fully-equipped German Air Force. By magic?"

"Do not misunderstand me, Field Marshal." Kesselring chose his words carefully. "I merely point out that their capabilities should not be underestimated. British resources may not be substantial, but they are very well organised. Fighter Command has good planes – the Hurricane, and the Spitfire. The Spitfire in particular seems an impressive machine, so intelligence reports have been indicating for some time."

For four years to be precise, Schmid knew; he had the file details fresh in his mind, as did Kesselring who had ordered a summary report on RAF Fighter Command capability from him the week before.

Göring was unimpressed. "There is not a fighter in existence to compare with the Messerschmitt Bf 109. Your caution is unfounded, Kesselring." The tone was undeniably dismissive.

Your caution is well founded, Kesselring, thought Schmid, because you have read the reports and take note of your intelligence officer.

"I hope you are correct, Field Marshal," retorted Kesselring, who knew better than to pursue the subject. But he added: "Might I also mention at this point the important strategic differences that will exist between an invasion of England and anything we have so far tackled?"

Göring took the bait precisely as Kesselring had hoped. "Ah, you mean that it is an island? That had not escaped my notice." Laughs from around the table. "For that reason I expect the campaign will give the *Luftwaffe* an opportunity to demonstrate what it is truly capable of. Land forces will only be able to cross the Channel if they are free from harassment in the air, so it will be our proud duty to pave the way for them. In Norway and Denmark we supported the ground and naval forces. But when England's turn comes, the *Luftwaffe* will be at the forefront. This campaign will not be won on the ground but in the air."

An exclusive air strategy. What a brilliant notion, mused Schmid; and how like his own recommendation back in November.

November . . .

It had been a November day when, as a cadet at infantry school, Schmid had marched in full uniform behind Hitler and Göring as they processed through the streets of Munich in a vain attempt to seize control of the State of Bavaria. State police had blocked their way and opened fire, killing sixteen, injuring Hitler slightly and Göring seriously. The attempt at revolution had been a disastrous failure. Hitler ended up in Landsberg Prison where he wrote *Mein Kampf*. Göring was smuggled into Austria by his wife Carin and didn't return to Germany for three years. His wounds – actually to the thigh and groin – were slow to heal and Göring suffered much pain. Ironically, it was for arthritis rather than bullet wounds that morphia was initially prescribed.

Schmid's mind had been wandering. He began to focus again. The *Luftwaffe* High Command were developing their thoughts on strategic problems.

"If the attack on Britain is to be an exclusively *Luftwaffe* affair," said Hugo Sperrle, "we must not only concentrate on shooting down our opposite numbers but also destroying RAF airfields and maintenance depots."

There was a hum of agreement.

"Aircraft factories also," added Hans-Jürgen Stumpff. "The battle will be cut short if they cannot replace the aircraft we shoot down."

Göring turned to his chief intelligence officer. "Major Schmid, we shall be relying on you for accurate target details. What is the position?"

"Intelligence is poor, Field Marshal," reported Schmid truthfully, his broad shoulders rigid as if sitting to attention. "Established airfields and heavy industrial areas are well documented, but a great deal of change has taken place in Britain since September of which we know little."

"Why so?" demanded Göring.

"There is a limit to what can be learned from printed material, and the British have tightened up considerably in monitoring what is available. We need reliable, first-hand reports from agents, and the *Abwehr* has few in place. Details of aircraft production in particular are something we are lacking, location of new factories, output figures . . ."

Göring suddenly became animated. "Something must be done. I shall speak to Canaris. We cannot win an air war unless we know where to drop our bombs with maximum effect. This is a matter for concern." Then, without apparent reason, Göring reverted to discussing details of Operation *Gelb,* a shift of attention that puzzled some round the table and frustrated others. The older hands recognised it as a not uncommon tactic. Identify a problem with no easy solution, then change the subject.

Schmid felt a wave of despair flood through him. He found such capriciousness draining. He made no further contribution to the meeting.

As the chiefs-of-staff rose to leave, Göring called Schmid to one side. They walked into the garden and strolled around the immaculate lawns and flowerbeds.

"Let me know precisely your intelligence needs from inside Britain. I shall pass the details onto Canaris personally and put a red hot poker up his arse."

"That would be appreciated, Field Marshal," responded Schmid, the full implication of the remark lost on Göring.

"Tell me Schmid, do you share Kesselring's opinion about the Spitfire – that it is superior to any of our fighters?"

"He did not actually say that . . ."

"He implied it."

Fumbling for words, Schmid said: "In so far as I have certain specifications on file concerning the Spitfire's capabilities and can cross-reference them with those of similar *Luftwaffe* fighters, I would say the Spitfire should be regarded as a risk."

"Beppo Schmid," Göring said, almost affectionately, "you imagine that I never take the slightest notice of your intelligence reports." Schmid said nothing. He knew Göring refused to read anything more than four pages in length and so kept his reports brief. Even so, they rarely ever seemed to be acted upon.

"Well you are wrong. I do – sometimes!" Göring laughed aloud at his own witticism, his eyes gleaming. "I always have done, and when Jeschonnek did your job before you. But it does not mean I have to agree with them."

They had reached an ornamental pool. Göring sat down on a wooden bench, the dovetailed joints creaking under the strain. "Let me tell you, I know all about the Supermarine Spitfire. Canaris excelled himself and actually had an agent spying on the test flight back in thirty-six. He even supplied photographs. There were later reports on the first public appearance at the annual RAF display at Hendon the following year. With various modifications it eventually entered service in August a year ago."

Schmid was dumbfounded. It must have shown, for Göring was looking very pleased with himself. He stood up and began walking towards the house.

"So you see I do read the files and your reports. Remember I was once a combat pilot – and a fucking good one. I commanded von Richtofen's squadron, *Jagdgeschwader 1* no less, after the Baron was killed. But you know that of course. So from a flyer's point of view, I can hardly fail to be impressed with a development such as the Spitfire." He paused as they reached the terrace at the side of the house. "However, as commander-in-chief of the German Air Force I must ignore its technical excellence because it belongs to the Royal Air Force and not to us. Do you understand, Schmid?"

"Yes, Field Marshal," replied Schmid, struggling to understand at all.

"The Spitfire is only a threat if the British can produce them in large enough quantities, and that I doubt very much. You said earlier that you need more information about aircraft production. Very well, when I speak to Canaris I shall tell him to make Spitfire factories his utmost priority. Let's see what we can achieve for what it is worth."

"Thank you, Field Marshal." Thank God, sighed Schmid, he's actually going to do this!

Göring saluted stiffly and opened a door leading to a private part of Carinhall. "Leave it with me, Schmid. Before you know it there will be *Abwehr* agents coming out of the woodwork in Spitfire factories."

Schmid returned the salute and walked away.

He would believe it only when the facts started rolling in and not before. Was Göring really thinking ahead for once, genuinely engaged in dealing with this situation? Or was it the drugs? Either way, Kesselring would be relieved to hear it. Schmid hurried off to see if the others had left yet, but there was no sign of anyone. It was approaching lunchtime, he realised, and invitations to dine at Carinhall were rare. The generals would be halfway back to Berlin by now.

Chapter 3

(Saturday 27ᵗʰ April 1940)

For the first time since Alison had come to work for him, Lucas Kelly was worried about her. As he watched the Tiger Moth bounce gently across the parched New South Wales earth and rise into the air, a knot began to form in his stomach that normally only appeared when his other two pilots, both men, took off to perform their stunts.

If he had to trust his life to the skills of just one of his pilots, he would have chosen Alison every time. She was brilliant, the best female pilot he had ever seen, not that there had been many, and better by far than most men when it came to stunting. Kelly never used the word 'natural' to describe pilots; he knew too well the amount of hard work and determination that went into developing the skills required to control a plane. 'Naturals' were the ones who learnt fast, absorbed instructions first time, remembered everything . . . and didn't take risks. Alison fitted into that category. He knew because he had taught her every stunt she knew.

But something was wrong.

Yesterday she had made her first mistake in almost two years with the Flyers, miscalculating a 'falling leaf' manoeuvre – a series of half-spins, continually corrected, that sent the plane swaying backwards and forwards as it descended, like a leaf fluttering from a tree in autumn. She had levelled out perilously close to the ground, the tail skid raising a cloud of dust as it raked the parched earth. The crowd had gasped, thinking it was part of the show. It was not.

Whatever had caused the lapse of concentration might recur. And that worried Kelly.

For once it was not searingly hot. There was a patchy cloud base, at about five thousand feet, Kelly estimated, and it was a pleasant change not to have the sun beating down relentlessly. For New South Wales, it was a cool day. There was a slight breeze, nothing much. A perfect day for flying.

He was sitting on the roof of the loudspeaker van, his legs dangling over the edge, the heels of his dusty boots tapping occasionally against the metal side. Beneath him stretched a legend in letters two feet tall, bright red against a yellow background: *LUCAS KELLY'S CRAZY FLYERS*.

He watched as the Tiger Moth biplane – also yellow and red – gained height. In one hand he held a much-smoked cigar, in the other, a bulky circular microphone. Next to him on the roof was the speaker, crackling and buzzing, pointing away from him towards the crowds below. He liked being up there, nearer his pilots than the punters.

The joy-rides were over, the locals had had their spins around the field, and the real flying was about to begin. The Tiger Moth was levelling out beyond the perimeter of the field – hired from a farmer for the day – and banking back round towards the crowd.

He had spoken to her of course, debriefed her about the near miss and asked if anything was troubling her. Man trouble perhaps? The curse?

No! she had snapped indignantly, *nothing was wrong – she knew what she was doing thank you very much.*

Kelly was not convinced. Alison didn't make mistakes.

He tapped the edge of the microphone gently and began to speak, in his brash, matter-of-fact tone.

"G'day, ladies and gents, welcome to the show. My name is Lucas Kelly – no relation to Ned, not that I know of anyhow – and I'd like to talk you through the amazing and highly dangerous feats of crazy flying you are about to witness. Approaching us in the Tiger Moth there is Miss Alison Webb – she's from England but nobody's perfect!" Smiles from a few upturned faces. "Alison's going to start with some dangerous stunts, just to warm up – then onto the really perilous stuff."

All eyes were on the biplane as it began hurtling around the sky above their heads, plunging and turning, twisting and weaving. Gradually the manoeuvres became more and more complex, each more exciting than the one before. Kelly watched like a hawk. So far so good.

"Here's one that's guaranteed to make you gasp. This is called a 'loop' by those in the know." The plane approached the crowd from the left, flying straight and level at five hundred feet. Suddenly it flipped up and over, round in a perfect circle, then climbed away, turning sharply for a quick return. The crowd applauded loudly – some whistled, some cheered.

"We call this one 'The Spectacles'. Brings tears to your eyes when you're in that cockpit, take my word!" This time the Tiger Moth dived steeply before pulling up and over into what appeared to be another loop. But instead of completing the circle, it remained inverted at the top and dived in the opposite direction, then made the same manoeuvre again, only this time looping from the inverted position until it was back upright and flying in the original direction. An elaborate figure of eight.

The performance was faultless. Maybe yesterday's mistake was a one-off after all. Kelly began to relax a little.

The next manoeuvre was a bunt. The biplane gained altitude by flying a couple of circuits, then approached the crowd head on, dipping into a sheer dive. The engine noise rose in a rapid crescendo as the plane plummeted towards the ground. In the crowd fists clenched, hands gripped arms, teeth ground together. It was going to crash – they were convinced! Then, when it seemed beyond the last possible moment and a catastrophe was inevitable, the Tiger Moth flicked over ninety degrees and levelled out, flying upside down away from the audience, just sixty feet from the ground.

Kelly felt the relief pass in a wave through the people beneath him.

"Now the 'Falling Leaf'!" Kelly thumped on the side of the van with his fist and from inside a gramophone started to play. The strains of Tchaikovsky's *Waltz of the Flowers* crackled through the speaker. This was where she fouled up yesterday. He felt himself tensing up as Alison began the swaying routine that brought her in ever wider sweeps towards the ground. The plane was dancing to the music, so it seemed to the people in the crowd, unaware that a combination of engine noise and altitude meant the speaker was inaudible to the pilot. But the effect was impressive and raised an enthusiastic ripple of applause.

Kelly's fist tightened around the microphone as Alison reached the last twist of the manoeuvre. For Christ's sake watch your height, he muttered to himself through clenched teeth. *Don't screw up again!*

The last sideways twist, the last 'leaf', brought the plane to a point at the far right of the crowd. It hovered above the field, wings wobbling slightly as Alison corrected the controls. The Tiger Moth came ever closer to the ground, sinking the last few feet until the wheels were virtually touching the grass. Then they really were touching, as the plane dropped into a neat landing. Alison taxied past her audience, a gauntlet raised high in a jaunty wave. She had judged it to perfection.

"A big hand for Alison Webb, ladies and gents!" Kelly's voice displayed none of the relief that was surging through his body. As the Tiger Moth landed, another biplane, a Spartan C3, took off from another part of the field.

"Now it's Jeff Pickard's turn," announced Lucas Kelly. The second biplane didn't climb very high. Instead it flew away over some trees and turned at about two hundred feet. "Hey, ladies and gents, few of you could have failed to notice the portrait of dear old Adolf over there." Few could; it was in the very centre of the field, a crude caricature painted on a huge sheet of paper about twenty feet square and stretched out on lengths of

17

string between two poles. "Jeff here's going to do what we'd all like to do to the crazy bastard right now – excuse my language. Here he comes!"

The Spartan approached low and fast, careering towards the German leader whose face, for added ridicule, had been added to the body of Charlie Chaplin. The plane struck the image at eighty miles an hour, the propeller shredding the paper in an instant and scattering fragments in a miniature snow storm. The strings fell limply down the sides of the poles.

"If he could do that in real life, we'd all want to shake Jeff by the hand, right?" Heads turned upwards and nodded in agreement.

As the Spartan continued its routine, Kelly watched Alison out of the corner of his eye as she swapped from one Tiger Moth to another. It was painted in the same yellow and red and identical to the first in every way, apart from one. A spike had been fitted to the lower port wing tip, protruding about two feet and curving upwards slightly at the end. Alison climbed into the rear of the two cockpits, one of the engineers spun the propeller, and the engine burst into life.

Meanwhile, the Spartan had popped some balloons with its propeller, performed a sideways sweep with one wing almost brushing the grass, and flour-bombed the audience, waggling its wings as if chuckling at its own mischievousness. As it approached to land on one side of the field, Alison took off from the other.

"Thanks Jeff. Now, here's Alison again with a trick you won't believe until you've seen it with your own eyes. I won't say anymore, just watch the middle of the field . . . and don't blink or you'll miss it!"

As he spoke, one of the ground technicians ran out onto the field, pulled a large white handkerchief from his pocket and held it in the air for a moment to show the audience. Then he bent down and laid it on the ground, pegging all four corners lightly into the soil. He stepped back about twenty paces and stood and watched the Tiger Moth as it made its approach.

The plane was flying very low with its port wings dipped sharply towards the ground. It seemed to slow down and the engine sounded as if it might cut out at any moment. It was an ungainly sight, not at all part of the smooth, slick performance that had been witnessed so far. A murmur rose in the crowd, but not a single head turned away for fear of missing something. The plane continued its strange behaviour, flying with its port wings almost scraping the ground, and as it came within a hundred feet of the handkerchief it seems to slow almost to a halt, the engine sounding desperately close to stalling. The port side dipped even further.

Suddenly the Tiger Moth was pulling upwards, gaining speed and height, the engine racing, with the handkerchief impaled on the curved spike and billowing wildly in the slipstream. The starboard wings dipped and the port lifted to give the audience a better view of the spike and its prize. The plane banked round and flew over the heads of the cheering crowd. The wings rocked to and fro and the handkerchief slipped loose, fluttering slowly into the mass of people below. Arms stretched upwards to grab at the memento, and a friendly scuffle broke out as ownership was disputed.

Kelly saw none of this. He was watching the Tiger Moth.

Alison had banked round behind the van and was circling for a final low level pass across the field with a wing tip skimming the ground, just as Jeff had done earlier. Her control appeared immaculate and there was an even gap between her and the ground for the entire sweep. At the far end of the field was a tree; as it drew close, the plane flipped back to the horizontal and rose steeply to clear the top branches.

But not steeply enough.

The undercarriage whipped through the upper foliage, taking branches and leaves with it. The Tiger Moth rocked violently, seemingly out of control for a few seconds, then stabilised and moments later landed at the edge of the field, greenery still wrapped around its wheels. The crowd loved it; they thought this too was part of the show. It was not.

Jeff Pickard was back in the air now, climbing high in the air with a parachutist in the passenger seat. This was the climax of the afternoon. Kelly talked his audience through the thrilling sight of a man hurling himself out of a plane and descending to earth at high speed with only a few strings and sheet of silk between him and oblivion. When it was over, he announced the end of the show, thanked everyone for coming, and the crowd started to disperse.

It was another hour before autograph hunters and hangers-on had all filtered away. Kelly found Alison standing by one of the Tiger Moths, chatting to an engineer. He touched her arm and eased her away. "Ally, I want to talk to you."

Alison's face immediately set into a defensive frown. "I suppose you're going to tell me off for damaging the farmer's tree," she mumbled.

"No, I just want to know what's wrong."

"Nothing's wrong."

"Yes it is," insisted Kelly, his voice losing its Australian lilt as it always did when he talked to a Brit. "You hit a tree."

"So – no harm done."

"Ally, you never hit trees. Everyone else does once in a while – I do, Jeff does, but not you. You're too bloody good."

Alison stared across the field into the distance, gazing at nothing in particular. "It was bad luck . . . that's all."

"And you don't misjudge 'falling leaves' either."

She shrugged. "Another piece of bad luck."

19

Kelly deliberately walked into her field of vision and shook his head. "With your skill level, luck doesn't play a part."

She looked him in the eyes and shrugged again. "Sorry, Luke, that's all there is to it." She looked away, too quickly to offer assurance that she was speaking the truth.

Kelly backed off. He could tell she was not going to budge.

"Stubborn. You bloody Poms are all the same. I suppose it's where we Aussies get it from. Okay Ally, have it your own way." Kelly turned away. "Just come and talk to me when you're ready."

"Thanks," said Alison. "I will."

"Level with me and I'll level with you."

"It's a deal."

"Until then you're grounded."

Alison's jaw dropped. "But Luke . . ." she began.

"I'll do the stunts with Jeff until you get whatever it is off your chest."

"Luke!"

But Kelly was no longer listening. He plucked the remnants of a twig from the Tiger Moth's undercarriage and walked away.

Chapter 4

Camp 4 was run for the *Abwehr* by the *Luftwaffe* and situated on the island of Rugen, off the northern coast of Germany. In the wooden huts surrounded by high barbed wire fences and armed guards, trainees were shown the harsher aspects of being a secret agent, such as how to kill silently and quickly. At a nearby airfield they were taught parachute technique. The rest was carried out in Hamburg where Schneider would be heading back the next day.

He had worked out a plan for Ulrich, and because of his imminent departure it had to be carried out immediately. Tonight or not at all.

The day before, he had passed a note to one of the Scandinavians asking him to let Ulrich overhear that Schneider would be on the beach the following night at midnight, a sort of farewell nocturnal vigil before leaving the camp the next day.

At dinner that evening, the briefest nod told Schneider it had been done. Moments later Ulrich brushed past him as he carried his food to a table. Their eyes met, and the mutual agreement was there to be read, unspoken yet clear. Ulrich said nothing, but he knocked carelessly against the tray Schneider was carrying.

Schneider suddenly felt very scared, and his appetite vanished. He picked at his food without eating anything. He knew he had to do something. This kind of naked provocation had never happened to him before, and he felt instinctively that he must retaliate. They had trained him to be aggressive. He would now put it to the test.

But this was foolish behaviour. Ulrich was best ignored. Retaliation was what the German would relish; acknowledgement that all the goading had cut deep. What if his plan backfired? At best it would add to his humiliation, at worst he would probably receive a painful beating. The more he thought, the more he convinced himself to stay in his hut and sleep the night away rather than take risks for the sake of petty revenge. Sending Ulrich on a nocturnal wild goose chase would in itself be very satisfying.

His stomach felt less tense, and the desire to eat returned. Without glancing particularly at his plate, he stabbed at some food and raised it to his lips. His tongue touched the edge of the substance momentarily; it felt strange, and smelled disgusting. He looked down. On his fork was a piece of dog shit.

Schneider retched and pushed the plate away in disgust, wiping his tongue against his shirt sleeve. All thoughts of cancelling the midnight rendezvous vanished in an instant.

*

On the edge of the compound was a wooden tower, about ten feet high, from which trainees jumped to practice parachuting landings. To break their fall was a sandpit at the base of the tower, and it was here that Schneider had noticed a spade and a rake used to smooth over the sand. He stole the spade shortly after eleven, then crept through the maze of huts, safer than skirting around the inside of the fence where guards patrolled and spotlights shone. He made for the beach and the water's edge. Having chosen his spot carefully, he thrust the spade deep into the wet sand. There was a fat squelching sound, like a wet fart, as a chunk of sand came away. He threw it to one side, the beginnings of a considerable mound.

He dug for half an hour. There was an icy breeze blowing off the sea, and he welcomed the exertion to keep warm. Visibility was poor, but he could make out the sand beneath his feet. He made good progress. At one point he thought he heard footsteps further along the beach and stopped dead, listening intently; surf against sand, wind in the reedy grass of the dunes, the far off cry of a gull, no more. A trick of his imagination. After several minutes, and a comforting cigarette, he continued digging.

By eleven forty he was crouched low where the beach met the dunes, physically tired but mentally alert. A distant haze of pale yellow light filtered from the direction of the camp, casting a strange glow over the brow of the dunes. The path from the main compound lay several yards to his right. All he had to do now was wait.

The next minutes seemed like an hour. He smoked another cigarette and felt his heart rate gradually rising in anticipation. His bladder was full but he daren't relieve himself in case Ulrich arrived early. It wouldn't do to be caught with his flies open and his cock out.

By the light of a tiny pocket torch, Schneider checked his watch. Four minutes to midnight. He wondered if Ulrich would show.

Don't be late, you bastard.

As this thought crossed his mind, he suddenly heard the crunch of boots on sand. Not his imagination this time, but the regular tramping of one foot after another. He felt his whole body tighten. His bladder was hurting now, it was so full.

The footsteps continued for a while, then stopped. *He's wondering where I am*, Schneider thought. *He doesn't know which way to go, which part of the beach to head for. Come on, my friend, just a few paces more down the path and you'll soon find out.* He heard a match being struck. It sounded very close, only feet away – the other side of the bank that hid him from view.

The footsteps began again. The dark outline of Ulrich's body appeared round the corner of the dune.

The spade swung through the air in a perfect arc and struck the German cleanly on the forehead. The sound of metal on bone pinged loudly and reverberated for a second. Schneider watched as Ulrich slumped backwards, seemingly in slow motion. He landed flat on his back, arms and legs sticking rigidly up in the air, like an upturned turtle. For a moment Schneider was scared he might have overdone it. His intention was to stun, not to kill. Ulrich groaned, then his body went limp.

Schneider dropped the spade, stepping forward cautiously and peering down at the man on the ground. He was unconscious but breathing, loudly and steadily.

It took several minutes to drag him onto the beach, and slightly longer to bind his legs and arms with twine stolen earlier from a store shed. Then Schneider grasped the German under the arms, lifted the dead weight into a sitting position and pushed him forward with a knee in the back. His legs slid neatly into the hole and Schneider propped him up against the edge so that his head flopped over to one side. He ran back to the dunes for the spade, and started filling in the hole. It took ten minutes, by which time Ulrich was beginning to stir.

When he awoke, the German was buried shoulder deep in the sand, facing the dunes, his arms and legs tied so he could not move a muscle below the neck. As his vision returned and he could focus, he saw Ernst, the Englishman, peering back at him through the gloom. He was confused and his head hurt badly.

"You're on the beach, my friend," said Schneider. "Down by the sea – but of course you can't see it because it's behind you, and turning round is beyond you at the moment."

Ulrich muttered something and spat towards Schneider. "Get me out of here," he hissed.

"Who told you I was English?"

"Go to hell."

"Who told you I was English?"

Ulrich sneered. "Have you done this to try and make me tell you? Fool, I wouldn't tell you in a thousand years." Schneider believed him. Ulrich was not the kind of man to be intimidated into doing anything against his will.

"Is there anything else you would like to ask me?" said Ulrich. "While we're here?"

Schneider looked thoughtful for a few moments then said: "Nothing – I want nothing from you. And I have nothing more to say to you. This was never intended to be the opportunity for a deep and meaningful discussion. Goodnight." He looked down on the curious sight below him, a disembodied head sticking out of the sand, and turned away.

"You can't leave me here!" shouted Ulrich.

"Can't I? Watch me." The ache in Schneider's bladder had been forgotten in all the excitement. Now it was back. He remembered the urine in his bed, and the dog shit in his dinner.

He turned back round and unbuttoned his flies. "But before I go I really must take a piss." He could feel the flow beginning. "Don't worry," he said comfortingly as he stood over Ulrich. "The tide will soon be in to wash you nice and clean. Now, I'd hold your breath if I were you . . ."

Chapter 5

(Sunday 28th April 1940)

Grounded! That word had reverberated in Alison's head all night, and she had barely slept.

She wiped oil from her hands and stared towards Lucas Kelly's caravan. She knew he was in there. A man had arrived about twenty minutes before – a fat man, wearing a suit and a hat, with a sweaty brow – and they had disappeared inside together. She'd seen him arrive as she worked on one of the Tiger Moths, tinkering with its engine. She had been staking out Kelly all morning and on the point of confronting him when the stranger had turned up.

Grounded!

Kelly had aimed straight at her Achilles heel and scored a direct hit. She was neither angry nor bitter. In fact she respected Kelly for having done it, and would probably have done the same in his position.

Accosting Kelly straight after his meeting with the fat man would not be the best of timing. There was an argument going on. Kelly's voice, raised in anger, could be heard even from where she stood, next to the plane. But she was determined to speak with him as soon as possible, to level with him, as he had put it. It might even work to her advantage. If he was still angry from his meeting with the suited stranger, he might appreciate knowing he hadn't lost his star pilot for the next show.

Alison had been shocked by her mistakes. In many ways she was a self-effacing person, but when it came to flying she knew she was good and she took pride in her considerable skills. Silly errors of judgment were not part of that skill set. She knew what was wrong – not man trouble, not period pains, and certainly not a lack of confidence in her own ability. It was nothing so specific, more a feeling that she herself had not been able to pinpoint within. A restlessness; an anxiety; a sense of foreboding. It was the war of course. What the papers had dubbed the 'Bore War' was clearly coming to an end; things were beginning to happen, and it was obvious to her, as too many others, that all hell would soon be breaking loose in Europe. And here she was on the other side of the world, flying planes for fun. It was time to go home.

She'd be sorry to leave . . . very sorry. She loved stunt flying, and back in England there would be few opportunities for such indulgence. Two years ago she had come to Australia to work for a flying taxi service. Barely a month after arriving she had landed on an airfield where she saw that *LUCAS KELLY'S CRAZY FLYERS* were preparing for a show. She'd seen similar shows in England and had always wanted to try her hand at such antics. Why she had sought out Lucas Kelly that day and offered her services she still didn't know, a spur-of-the-moment thing. The timing had been fortuitous; Kelly was short-handed. The previous week one of his pilots had flown into the ground and was strung up in hospital, and the day before an engineer had broken his arm whilst hand-spinning a prop. Kelly admitted later he had taken her on out of desperation, just to help out with the joy rides. But within three months, Alison had turned into his greatest crowd puller. He'd never known anyone learn stunts so fast.

He found her attractive, another reason for employing her. One evening, a few weeks after Alison joined the Flyers, he had tried to kiss her, been sternly rebuked, and told in no uncertain terms that romance was precisely what she had come to Australia to avoid. Kelly accepted rejection with dignity and never tried it on again.

The two years had flown by, literally. She owed Kelly a great deal, more than he would ever know. She had left England to lick her wounds, and to heal after the hurt that only a love betrayed can inflict. She had found a greater love to take its place. Stunt flying.

The caravan door swung open and the fat man in the suit stepped out. A shirt tail was hanging loose at the front, revealing an expanse of pink belly. He was sweating harder than when he had arrived. He drew a hand across his greasy dark hair and forehead and wiped it on the side of his grubby jacket. Kelly followed him down the step, his face ruddy and set grimly. He was clutching a piece of paper in his hand. They spoke to each other. The stranger offered a hand to Kelly who mouthed something with at least one 'f' in it and turned away. So the man waddled across to his car, squeezed into the driver's seat and drove off. Kelly went back into the caravan, leaving the door ajar.

Alison threw down the rag she was holding and sauntered slowly across the field. At the door she hesitated, wondering whether or not to go in. Maybe she should give it some time before confronting him. She took a step backwards.

Kelly's voice rang out: "Come in, Alison, if you're coming. Don't pussyfoot around out there."

She stepped into the gloom of the caravan. It was very hot inside. Kelly sat on a battered Windsor chair, tipped back against the wall, the piece of paper still in his hand. There was a whisky bottle on the table; the seal wasn't broken, but Alison had the distinct impression that it wasn't going to stay that way for long.

"Luke," she said timidly. "You needn't ground me. I can tell you what's wrong now. But perhaps this isn't the right moment to . . ."

"Too bloody well right it isn't," he interrupted.

"Can I just say my piece please and go?"

"Alison, whatever you have to say won't make any difference to anything," said Kelly.

"This is important to me, Luke, so shut up and listen will you? It's the war. I'm worried – scared even. That's what's been on my mind. I'm far from home, and it's time to go back. I've been thinking about it for quite a while now. Here I am, giving joy rides and showing off doing crazy stunts when I ought to be doing something more worthwhile. Look at Europe. Hitler has trampled over half of it – and now Norway and Denmark. No one honestly believes he will stop there. It'll be France next, then . . . then England. I have to leave, Luke. Leave the Flyers." She looked at him closely, trying to monitor his reaction. She saw none. "I'll stay for a few more shows, then I have to go home."

Kelly shrugged, reached for the whisky bottle, broke the seal and poured himself a large one. There was a long pause before he spoke. When he did, he just said: "Okay."

"Okay," repeated Alison. "Okay! So you're happy to lose me?"

Kelly swallowed some whisky. "I didn't say that."

"Then what does okay mean? It sounds as though you couldn't care less whether I stay or go!"

"It means okay you've made up your mind to go and there's nothing I can say to make you change your mind. So what's the point of saying anything more?"

"Well thanks very much!" Alison felt tears welling up. She turned away from him to hide her embarrassment, clenching her fists and rubbing her fingers together with frustration.

Kelly stood up and held out the piece of paper, waving it over her shoulder. "Ally, we're all going home – wherever home might be. Not just you, the whole bloody lot of us. Look."

Alison glanced at the paper; it was a letter, typed with an official-looking header. "What does it mean?"

"If you'd let me speak first you would know. That fat-arsed pen pusher has just closed us down. The Flyers have got one week left . . . then I lose the planes."

"Lose them?"

Kelly nodded. "Commandeered by the government. Needed for the war effort, to train new pilots. It's so fucking infuriating. It's not even our war. It's Europe's."

"Yes Luke, and that's why I have to leave."

"I know, I know." Kelly squeezed her arm. "You have to go back and help kick Hitler in the pants – I understand. I kind of guessed. I'm lucky to have held on to you this long." He waved the piece of paper at her. "To tell the honest truth, I expected this before now. We've all been living on borrowed time since last September."

Alison said, "What will you do?"

"Long term, I haven't a clue. Too old for dog fighting, too stupid to push paper around a desk." A blank expression spread across his face. "Jesus, I haven't a flaming clue. Go back to Byron Bay where I came from I guess. I've got a sister there . . . Alice."

"Try thinking short term then," suggested Alison. "It might be easier."

Kelly grinned and topped up his glass from the bottle. "Easy. I'm gonna get wrecked. Care to join me?"

Alison's first reaction was to shake her head and make for the door. But she checked herself. She was fond of Kelly; he had taught her so much, helped her with her flying more than anyone she had known. She knew just how bitter a blow this must be for him. Soon she would be saying goodbye to him, probably forever.

She sat down opposite him. "You know, I think I will."

Kelly nodded approvingly and reached for another glass.

Chapter 6

(Monday 29th April 1940)

Admiral Wilhelm Canaris, Chief of German Military Intelligence, was seated behind his desk at 76/78 Tirpitzufer in Berlin – a rickety old building, nicknamed 'The Foxhole' by those who frequented its maze of small rooms and pokey corridors. With the vast increase in workload and personnel the war had generated, the secret organisation it housed had long since outgrown the premises. But Canaris refused to move. The cover was perfect; the most unlikely building imaginable for the headquarters of the *Abwehr*.

Canaris stood up and wandered over to the window. His small, some would say claustrophobic, office was four stories up, overlooking the Tiergarten with its perfect rows of chestnut and lime trees. They were late coming into leaf this year after a bitter winter. Canaries noticed such things. His two secretaries wished he was as attentive to the appearance of his office; the old Persian carpet was embarrassingly threadbare and the various chairs did not match. An office wit had once suggested swapping his desk for a crate one morning to see if he noticed.

There was a gentle knock on the door and he turned to see Captain Herbert Wichmann enter. The head of the *Abwehr* post in Hamburg looked weary, his eyes bloodshot, having travelled overnight.

"Sit down, Herbert. There will be coffee in a moment. I am sorry to drag you here at such a time as this. I assume you've heard the news from Norway over the weekend? Our troops have halted at Kvam. They are losing momentum."

"I heard," said Captain Wichmann. "A temporary situation, no doubt. And war has now been declared with them – it has been made official."

"Several weeks after the event." Canaris had advised against invasion, because in his view the plans had been poorly devised and inadequately prepared and resourced. But Hitler had been persuaded about the threat posed by a British blockade of Germany through Norway, and nothing would change his mind.

"Your journey here was necessary because I have something I prefer to discuss in person."

"Naturally I shall help in any way possible."

Canaris believed him; Wichmann was a reliable, conscientious officer. They liked each other and had more in common than a naval background; both were men of learning, well-read, thoughtful and knowledgeable about many things. They spoke freely with each other. Canaris returned to his desk, where a model of the cruiser Dresden sat, a symbol of their mutual pasts. "I think this is something for Ritter – an air espionage job. I have a request for a very specific type of intelligence concerning aircraft production in Great Britain. It would appear the *Luftwaffe* is concerned about the defence capabilities of the Royal Air Force."

Wichmann appeared surprised. "I thought we were attacking the Low Countries, not Britain."

"Indeed we are." Canaris dearly wished otherwise. Another mistake, and another opportunity to bring death and destruction to innocent people. He knew of the atrocities the *Waffen SS* had perpetrated in Poland and had been deeply shocked by them. He feared a repeat performance in Holland and Belgium. Furthermore, he had made his views known, as he had done prior to Operation *Weser* – codename for the invasion of Denmark and Norway.

"So why this sudden concern about the RAF?" asked Wichmann. "They have some squadrons in France, but not many. Just a few Hurricanes. Nothing to worry the *Luftwaffe* unduly."

"I think Göring is looking ahead," replied Canaris sardonically. "I imagine he rather believes Operation *Gelb* will be over in a matter of days. The next targets for the expanding glory of the Third Reich will be France and Great Britain."

"The Führer won't attack Britain, surely. He never wanted war with them in the first place."

"That may be, but he has a war with them whether he wanted it or not. And if the British Expeditionary Force is defeated in Belgium, will they lie down over the sea in Britain and wait to be invaded?"

"I think not," said Wichmann. "Chamberlain may wish to come to terms, to cut his losses. That is his style, and I'm sure the Führer would be prepared to come to such an agreement. There will be no invasion if the British are willing to accept the new situation on mainland Europe."

Admiral Canaris sat with his hands together as if in prayer, pouting behind them and shaking his head slowly.

"Wrong, my friend. The British have no faith left in the assurances of Adolf Hitler." He pushed his head back to indicate the Führer's photograph which hung on the wall behind his desk. Positioned where he could not see it? Wichmann wondered. "They won't believe him. He lied to them at Munich and they won't trust him again. Whether he realises or not, the Führer has gone too far down the road to turn back. If the rest of mainland Europe falls, then Great Britain has to be next, hence Göring's curiosity about their air defences."

"Pardon me for saying," remarked Wichmann, "but this is unusually far-sighted for Göring. Forward planning is not his strength."

"I would wager his generals are behind it. Read this."

Canaris passed over a teletyped message. As Wichmann read, the door opened and a plump, ugly, middle-aged woman entered carrying two coffee cups. He glanced up briefly and smiled to himself. The old man had always been against employing women, but due to the demands that war made on the male population there was little choice. He remembered the memo that had been circulated warning against sexual relations between members of the *Abwehr*. The punishment was instant dismissal. If this specimen was anything to go by, Canaris's personal solution to the problem was to ensure that temptation never entered his mind.

When they were alone again, Captain Wichmann said: "You mention there was concern about the defence capability of the RAF. According to this, the cause for concern is more specific. The Spitfire monoplane worries the Field Marshal."

"Does that suggest anything – or anyone – to you?"

"Kesselring," replied Wichmann without hesitation. "Only he would have such foresight. He is a professional. Göring himself would not accept that anything might compare with his own machines. Kesselring, on the other hand, is a realist."

"And if not Kesselring, then Sperrle."

Wichmann read aloud from Göring's orders: ". . . to arrange without delay for an agent to infiltrate the Spitfire factories at Southampton and Castle Bromwich and to supply accurate intelligence concerning output and possible destruction of these units, either by providing precise information for target bombing, or by sabotage."

Canaris said: "That requires two agents. Two factories, two agents."

"Then he says further on . . . 'and with particular emphasis on Castle Bromwich, which is by far the larger in size and has been purpose-built for manufacturing the Spitfire.'" He looked up. "Beppo Schmid has briefed the Field Marshal thoroughly."

"Beppo Schmid probably wrote it!" Canaris tapped a pile of buff coloured folders on his desk. "I don't agree about Castle Bromwich. I have the files here, and there is nothing to suggest the Supermarine factory near Southampton is not still the main production plant. Admittedly this information is not entirely up-to-date, and Castle Bromwich should not be ignored, so we will do as we are bid. Have you any possible candidates for such a mission? I assume there is no one already in the field who could undertake such a task."

"I doubt it. We barely have a handful of agents over there, as you know . . . plus a few informants. Nothing remotely like a network. I'll talk to Ritter." Wichmann took a sip of black coffee. "There are several men undergoing training, any one of them might suit this mission. One or two speak excellent English – in fact one of them *is* English."

"Picking the most suitable men is important, Herbert. Do you understand what I mean by that?" The admiral stared him directly in the face. "The most suitable?"

The most suitable – *not the best*. It was the admiral's way of saying he had little faith in the plan and the best agents should not be wasted on a fool's errand. "How suitable do you think?"

Canaris sat back in his chair, weighing up the situation in his mind. He hated the thought of squandering precious resources. If Göring wanted accurate information concerning aircraft manufacture in Britain, there were more sensible ways of going about it. Trying to pass agents off as workers was not the way. It might result in some mediocre intelligence and mild sabotage, but the chances were slim, and Canaris had no time for schoolboy heroics. He believed in spying from the top, with well-placed agents in positions of influence. But that took time and much planning. In Britain the opportunity to make such plans had been denied him.

In answer to Wichmann's question, he shrugged and said: "About fifty percent. Use your own judgment." He did not elaborate.

Wichmann knew better than to press further. A glassy look had come over the admiral's face, as if his mind had wandered on to other matters.

"Might I suggest sending the two who are chosen to one of our own aircraft factories for training? They are more likely to succeed in their mission if they have some practical skills with which to sell themselves when they arrive in Britain."

Canaris stood up and turned towards the window again. "Do whatever is necessary, Herbert. You have my authority. But don't delay any longer than necessary. Göring will want to know that arrangements are moving ahead quickly. I suggest we aim to have them in place and active one month from now."

Wichmann frowned. "Not much time – but as you wish."

"What do you think their chances of survival are, let alone achieving anything useful?" He knew that he would receive an honest answer from Herbert Wichmann, if not from any other *Abwehr* officer he could name.

"I would say about fifty percent." Wichmann sensed the flicker of a grin on the admiral's face. "We have excellent paperwork – false identity cards, ration books – courtesy of the Spanish and Japanese Embassies' diplomatic bags. But our knowledge of conditions inside Britain is sketchy to say the least."

"What about the Welshman," said Canaris. "What about Johnny – is he still active and behaving himself?"

"He provides intelligence from time to time," replied Wichmann. "With most of our informants interned on the Isle of Man, he's the best of the bunch." Johnny was their longest-serving agent in Britain, an electrical engineer who had been an apprentice in the RAF and offered his services to the *Abwehr* back in 1937. He had a reputation for being temperamental.

"Would he be able to assist these 'Spitfire spies', as you appear to have christened them?"

"He could provide backup, yes. He is a useful contact for new agents. I would be reluctant to jeopardise him in any way, though. He is too valuable to forfeit for the sake of an operation with little chance of success."

"It seems a less than healthy situation."

"Through no fault of our own. Our hands have been tied for too long."

"I know. We have Görtz to thank for that."

In 1936 an *Abwehr* agent called Hermann Görtz had been caught spying on RAF stations and imprisoned for four years. The trial had been a major embarrassment for the German intelligence service. As a direct result Hitler had forbidden any spying activity in Great Britain, ironically for fear of compromising relations between the two countries. Hitler didn't know about Johnny, or not until later at least. It meant that compared to most other countries Britain was a wasteland intelligence-wise. Deep penetration agents were badly needed; and Canaris had none. Görtz was now back in Germany, having served his sentence, and it was a measure of the *Abwehr*'s desperation that he was soon to be sent back on another mission. Whilst in Maidstone prison, Görtz had made contacts within the Irish Republican Army and plans were almost complete to have him parachuted into Ireland to cash in on their willingness to help the Nazi cause.

"Do what you can, Herbert. Go back to Hamburg and talk it over with Ritter. Select your men and arrange a couple of weeks for them with Messerschmitt, Heinkel or Junkers – no matter which. Make sure they are in England by the end of May, latest. We shall do as we are bid. What else can we do!" He could not hide the despondency in his voice.

"Nothing, Admiral."

"Who knows! None of this may be of any consequence. Our land forces may never reach the English Channel. They have done well with surprise attacks against wholly unprepared targets – perhaps they won't be so fortunate against countries that are expecting them."

"Do you think Belgium and Holland know what is coming their way?"

"Of course. They are not fools," said Canaris emphatically. What Wichmann did not know, nor would he ever know, was that although Canaris himself would never do anything proactive to compromise German military plans, there were those within the Tirpitzufer building who hated the Nazi regime enough to do just that. One such man, Colonel Hans Oster, Chief of Central Section, was at that very moment in the process of making sure his friend, Colonel Sas, the Dutch military attaché in Berlin, was aware of precisely what was coming Holland's way – and the date it was scheduled to happen. Similarly, there were plans to warn the Belgians via the Vatican's Papal Nuncios. Canaris was not a party to it, but he was, nevertheless, very well informed.

The admiral glanced over at the bronze letter press on his desk; a version of the Three Wise Monkeys, specially adapted for intelligence gathering. The first was cupping his ear, the second peering suspiciously around, and the third holding a hand firmly over his mouth.

Canaris pointed at it. "There, Herbert," he said. "That's us. We're just a troop of monkeys playing in the jungle."

Wichmann did not know quite what to say to this, so he said nothing, but lifted up a hand and held it firmly over his mouth.

Chapter 7

(Tuesday 30th April 1940)

Captain Wichmann's headquarters in Hamburg were very different from those of Admiral Canaris in Berlin – a three-storey concrete structure in the quiet residential district of Harvesthude. From there, all spying activities against Great Britain and the United States were masterminded.

It was one of many intelligence premises to be found in Germany's largest port. To the north-east, Major Werner Trautmann ran a powerful radio station from a Renaissance-style merchant's house, monitoring messages from agents and eavesdropping on the radio traffic of other countries – friends and foe alike. Receiving and transmitting antennae were dotted around gardens and meadows for several kilometres. Nearer the centre of the city were various training establishments, a complete spy school divided amongst business premises and offices, most of them quite legitimate. Locations were changed occasionally but always remained in the busiest quarters to make enemy surveillance as difficult as possible.

Wichmann had stayed the night in Berlin after his meeting with Canaris, then caught an early flight back to Hamburg. He was in his office soon after nine o'clock. Ten minutes later a blonde-haired figure sat opposite him; Major Nikolaus Ritter, head of air espionage. From his briefcase Ritter pulled a handful of dossiers and passed them across the desk. He smiled, revealing a glimpse of gold somewhere amongst his teeth.

"Your candidates?" asked Wichmann. Ritter nodded. "As I explained by phone, a special mission sanctioned by Göring himself, no less. Two agents, to infiltrate British aircraft factories, to provide intelligence on manufacturing output, and, if necessary and feasible, to sabotage them. They must be trained and in place in one month from now."

"Do we know which factories precisely?" asked Ritter.

"The Spitfire manufacturing plants at Woolston, near Southampton, and Castle Bromwich which is on the outskirts of Birmingham."

35

"We know little about either, especially Castle Bromwich. All reports indicate the Spitfire is an excellent fighter – as good as the Bf 109, if not better."

"Which explains the concern all of a sudden. The Spitfire could well be a threat to *Luftwaffe* air superiority."

Indicating the dossiers, Ritter said: "Any of these men could undertake such a mission – all are fluent in English. Though to the best of my knowledge none of them has any experience of factory work."

"That will be taken care of." Wichmann picked up the dossiers, six in all, and studied them for a few moments. Fifty percent suitable, Canaris had suggested. Don't waste your best men. He decided to let Ritter advise him.

"I shall be frank with you, Nikolaus. Admiral Canaris does not regard this mission as a high priority. Good agents are not to be squandered when they could be used more beneficially, especially at a later juncture. God knows we have precious few. He wants competent men, but not our best."

"They are all good," said Ritter, rather put out that anyone might think otherwise. "I have supervised their selection and training schedules personally."

"No slight on your work was implied," said Wichmann reassuringly. "The character of the men is where the flaws may lie – not in your training."

"Well," Ritter said eventually after a long pause. "The Englishman, Schneider, is probably the least capable of the group. He has found it difficult to apply himself to training – good at aircraft recognition, but poor at radio and cipher work. And the most likely to set himself alight trying to prime an improvised incendiary device. He is a good man, and I like him. But his heart is not in it."

Wichmann found the relevant file. "Agent Number 3549, Schneider, Erich. Born 29th May 1914, Bromsgrove, England." He flicked through the pages. "Schneider is not an English name."

"His real name is Eric Tomlin. He married a German girl and came to live in Heidelberg several years ago. He adopted his wife's maiden name about nine months before the war, hoping it would give him less grief with the authorities. His mother was German. He is bilingual – no accent whatsoever in either language."

"Why didn't he return to Britain when the war started?"

"Two reasons. Firstly his wife – Renate Schneider – would appear to wear the trouser in their household. She did not want to leave Germany, so either he stayed or they split up."

"And the second reason?"

"Flick forward a little – there is a photograph of her in the file." Wichmann found it and let out a soft whistle. The woman smiling up at him was stunningly beautiful, with perfectly proportioned features and long, straight black hair that stretched down almost to her waist. She wore a black satin evening dress and held a violin under one arm. "Would you want to leave her?"

"No, I would not."

"By all accounts she has a character to equal her looks. A Party member, and a good German. I think she virtually ordered Schneider to offer his services to us, which probably explains his lack of enthusiasm. He is here in Hamburg, and she is in Heidelberg."

"And the violin?"

"She plays professionally. Schneider is also a musician – a trumpeter. That's how they met, playing in an orchestra together."

Wichmann took a final lingering stare at Renate Schneider's image then slammed the dossier shut. "Do you think he will last the course?"

Ritter shrugged his shoulders. "I imagine there is only one way of finding out."

"Very well, Schneider is chosen. Not perfect in many ways, so that makes him perfect for this mission."

"He would be suited to infiltrate the Castle Bromwich factory. He is from that region – the Midlands – so he will have local knowledge."

"And number two?"

Ritter moved another dossier to the top of the pile. "I think this might be our man – agent 3538, von Osten, Otto. Older than Schneider at forty-two – born and bred in Berlin, but he spent many years in England running a chain of garages around the London area. He sold up and returned home last August as soon as the Non-Aggression Pact with Russia was signed. His English is excellent – not perfect but good enough. He has excelled in all aspects of training, both practical and otherwise. A fine radio man, very knowledgeable, and a committed Nazi. Whilst in England he was a member of the National Socialist League and the Anglo-German Fellowship."

"I'm impressed," said Herbert Wichmann. "Surely too good for this assignment?"

"He has a weakness," Ritter added. "We have a devil of a job keeping him out of the bars and brothels on the Reeperbahn. Strong drink and women are his only pastimes."

"Does it impact on his work?"

"To some degree – he wakes up with a thick head most mornings. Having said that, when he does come round he is good. Work hard, play hard."

"Excellent – let's not beat about the bush, he too is chosen. Have them start training together immediately. Get von Osten helping the Englishman with his radio work. From now on, they are a team. Von Osten goes to Southampton."

"Very well."

"Meanwhile I shall arrange for them to learn some aircraft production skills. Messerschmitt at Augsburg is probably the best place. I don't suppose making a Spitfire varies greatly from making a Bf 109."

Nikolaus Ritter gathered up the dossiers and opened his briefcase.

"Leave these two," said Wichmann. "I want to familiarise myself with von Osten and Schneider. You had better think about codenames – something musical for Schneider perhaps?"

"I shall give it some thought." Ritter had almost reached the door when Wichmann spoke again.

"This should not be necessary, you know – all this hurried making do. If the Führer had allowed us to set up networks long ago . . ."

Ritter smiled. "Freedom to do some good honest spying at last."

"You could put it that way. Some good honest spying. I like that."

Ritter closed the door and shook his head. "But too little too late," he muttered to himself.

Chapter 8

(Wednesday 1st May 1940)

Erich Schneider arrived precisely on time for the rendezvous; two thirty, outside the offices of the Müller Shipping Company, where a car would pick him up. His scheduled afternoon of studying cipher systems had been postponed. He was puzzled. The training programme had never been altered before, and to pull him out of cipher work was to take him away from the subject that needed most work. He sensed his tutor's frustration, but no matter how hard he tried it just would not come right. He joked about it. "Sorry, I'm only a simple musician. Anything more sophisticated than blowing down a trumpet is beyond me." The tutor commented that surely musical notation was a cipher – a collection of scribbles which need translating – and it ought to come naturally to him. Schneider confessed that he had always struggled with the written aspect of his profession, spending hours learning and memorising orchestral parts to compensate; and his sight-reading had never been good. He was an instinctive musician. His strengths were in performance.

As a distant church bell struck the half hour an innocuous, somewhat shabby Volkswagen drew up in front of him, the back door opened and he heard a voice ordering him to get in. The voice of Dr Rantzau, the man in charge of his training. They drove in silence, heading north-east out of the city in the direction of Lübeck. Schneider and Rantzau sat in the back. The driver in the front was a tall, slim man in his early forties. Schneider thought the back of his head looked vaguely familiar.

"Where are we going?"

"Oh not far, and nowhere in particular . . . just somewhere quiet for a chat away from everything." Rantzau leaned forward and spoke to the driver. "Anywhere here will do."

They turned off the main road onto a narrow track which cut across a stretch of scrubland and petered out behind a small clump of trees. The car continued until it was completely hidden from the road, and the driver cut the engine.

"Sorry to drag you away from your studies, Erich. I expect you are wondering what this is all about."

"I am. What's going on? Are you throwing me out of spy school – stamping my file 'unsuitable material' and shipping me back home?"

"Is that what you would like?"

"I wouldn't mind."

"Sorry to disappoint you. As I have told you on numerous occasions, we are pleased with you. Your training is going well on the whole – a little smoothing off around the edges and you'll make a good agent. I would go as far as to say that your training is now almost complete."

Schneider turned and faced his mentor. "Are you sure about that? I get the feeling my radio tutor thinks he has a moron on his hands."

"There is room for improvement, that's true. But you have been with us for three months now and in most aspects you have done well. We have given you as much training as is possible within the time available. You see, Erich, we have a mission for you."

"A mission? What kind of a mission?"

In general terms Dr Rantzau explained what they had in mind. He didn't refer to the target specifically, just to an aircraft manufacturing establishment somewhere in England. For security reasons Schneider would not know which factory until he had been dropped safely into England, and even then when absolutely necessary. The less he knew, the less he could reveal if captured and interrogated.

"You will work initially as part of a two-man team," continued Dr Rantzau. "You will be parachuted in and stay together until you have acclimatised back into life in Britain under your new identities. Then you will separate and complete your missions independently of each other."

Schneider seemed amused. "You want me to pass as a worker in an aircraft factory? I don't know a nut from a bolt. Whose crazy idea was this!"

Rantzau explained about the special training at a German aircraft factory. "You can only learn so much in a short a time, I appreciate that. But it will be enough to make you useful to them as a semi-skilled worker. The British, like ourselves, are expanding war production at an alarming rate and will make use of anyone with relevant skills."

"And what do you want me to do exactly, once I've managed to get a job in the factory?"

"Keep your eyes and ears open and report back anything – absolutely anything. Technical information, factory output, production targets, strengths and weaknesses of supply, names of key personnel, names of sub-contractors, even what's on the canteen menu. The smallest detail might be of use in evaluating the enemy's resources. If the works manager farts I want to know how long it lasts and what it smells like."

"How long will the mission last?"

"As long as it takes." Schneider appeared despondent at this. "Don't worry, Erich. If the Führer attacks Britain this summer, it will be over in weeks. The *Wehrmacht* will be marching along Whitehall by September. What we are asking of you will make that happen even quicker. You'll be back with your lovely wife before you know it."

"Leave her out of this!" snapped Schneider. "My private life is my business."

The driver turned his head slightly and glanced in the rear view mirror, as if to remind both men of his presence. Schneider caught a glimpse of the eyes. They too were familiar; but he could not place them.

"I apologise," said Dr Rantzau; there was annoyance in his voice. "I was merely trying to put your situation in some kind of perspective for you. May I remind you that you volunteered your services to us? You are here of your own free will. Perhaps you ought to remind yourself of that fact."

"I'm sorry, Doctor." He thought about saying more, but decided against it.

"This evening you will leave your present accommodation and move into a boarding house – The Klopstock – do you know it?"

"I know where it is. I have walked past it a few times."

"Your partner will also be resident there. As you are aware, we have a policy of training agents individually. But from today you are half of a team. You and your colleague will live and work together – you will spend the rest of this week completing your basic training with him. You are fortunate, he is an excellent radio operator and you will learn much from him. I will soon be able to confirm which factory you are to attend."

"A babysitter to hold my hand."

"You will need him, I can assure you."

"When do I meet this wonder man who will turn me into a radio expert?"

"There is no time like the present." Dr Rantzau tapped the driver on the shoulder. "Otto, I would like you to meet Erich Schneider. Erich, this is Otto von Osten."

The driver turned round, and Schneider saw his face for the first time. A very familiar face – last seen buried to the shoulders in sand and shouting foul obscenities.

"*Ulrich!*" Schneider could not believe what he was seeing.

"Hello Ernst . . . or Erich I should say."

"So you know each other!" Dr Rantzau was as surprised as Schneider.

Otto von Osten nodded. "We met at Camp 4."

"But fraternisation amongst trainees is against the rules . . ."

"I did a job for the camp commander. He thought Ernst here was a bit on the soft side – needed toughening up, so he asked me to do a spot of intimidation on him. And did it work!"

"I am aware that goes on," said Rantzau. I don't appreciate it personally, but it does have its merits I suppose."

Schneider stared at Ulrich, who was now Otto, trying to absorb what was being said. Ulrich, the bastard who had made his life hell. "You mean it was all set up," he said slowly. "All of it?"

"All of it . . . apart from your revenge." Otto burst out laughing. "That was some revenge, my friend!"

For Dr Rantzau's sake, von Osten gave a brief résumé of what had gone on at Camp 4. As Schneider listened, everything fell into place; how Ulrich knew that he was English, the head tutor's indifference, everything. They had been clever – very clever. And when he thought what he had done to Ulrich on the beach, he realised that their ploy had indeed worked.

Von Osten said: "I can assure you, Erich, there are no hard feelings on my part. I did a job that was all." He thrust a hand over the back of the seat. "Here, shake. I think we should forget the past."

Schneider's first reaction when he saw Ulrich again had been to climb out of the car and tell Rantzau to stick his mission where the sun never shines. Less than five minutes later, he was shaking hands with the only man he had ever wanted to kill. He couldn't believe himself.

"Excellent," Dr Rantzau declared, smiling a gold-toothed smile. "Get to know each other well. Soon you will be sharing your lives together – and those lives may depend on each other. Come, Otto, drive us back to town, will you?"

Schneider sat back in his seat too bewildered to speak.

Chapter 9

By late afternoon, Schneider and von Osten had moved their belongings into the Klopstock. Before their evening meal they sat in the bar and talked. In the time it took Schneider to drink a glass of the local Holsten, von Osten had downed two and was on his third.

"I cannot believe I'm sitting here talking with you," said Schneider. "I nearly killed you for what you did. I wanted you dead."

"Think nothing of it, my friend." Von Osten brushed it aside as if ancient history. "People have tried to kill me before – jealous husbands mainly."

"A pointless piece of deception, in my opinion."

"Not at all. Your chances of survival in the field have probably trebled as a result."

"Were you in that hole on the beach for long?"

"They found me the next morning. You'd left by then – I'd have killed you on the spot if you'd still been around. I've never been so bloody cold in my life. Almost drowned when the tide came in."

Von Osten offered a cigarette from a leather case. He inhaled the smoke luxuriously. "I have always found Rantzau a fair man, haven't you? I would even go so far as to say trustworthy, despite what he does for a living."

"You don't have to be a liar and a cheat to be in this game."

"Perhaps not. But I think it helps."

"Are you a liar and a cheat?"

Von Osten thought for a second. "That's rather a difficult question to answer."

"Try yes or no."

"It's not quite that simple. I believe there are degrees of honesty. I have never lied to a colleague, for example."

"So who have you lied to?"

"Women mainly."

"I see." Schneider did not see. "It seems to me that a lie is always a lie, whoever is telling it and whoever is on the receiving end."

"Ha!" Von Osten snorted. "Fine words from someone who is about to betray the country of his birth."

"A country has no feelings. You're talking about deceiving individuals, not countries. People you know and who regard you with affection – as a friend, or a lover. To me that's far worse." Schneider sipped his beer. "But in the end, a lie is always a lie."

"So if you hate the idea of deceiving people, what the hell are you doing here learning to become a spy?"

To please my wife. That was the truth of the matter, though Schneider had no intention of saying so. Renate had wanted him to do something positive for the Fatherland; to demonstrate that his heart now lay there and not in England where he was born. She knew he had no friends in England, and only distant relatives. Both his parents were dead. So why not offer to spy on the country from which he was now emotionally released? It was either that or join the German army.

"I'm here because I wish to help the cause of the Reich, said Schneider." A pompous lie and he glanced anxiously at his new friend to assess the reaction. Von Osten seemed to accept it, no doubt because Schneider had made such a big deal about honesty only moments before. "And you," asked Schneider. "Why are you here?"

Von Osten gave a potted history of his life up to this point in time – a saga of affairs with women, short-lived marriages, drunken escapades in various countries of Europe, peppered with jokes and anecdotes, made mostly at his own expense.

"You should write your autobiography," said Schneider. "It would sell like hot cakes."

"I fully intend to one day. I haven't finished living it yet, though. This is only about the ninth chapter. Now where was I?"

"In Amsterdam, waking up one morning in bed with a woman you'd never seen before."

"Ah yes. She said she was the wife of the German Ambassador and that I'd seduced her at a party the night before. I couldn't remember where in God's name I'd been the night before, so I took her word for it. She said her husband was an incredibly jealous man and if he found out what I had done he would have me drowned in a canal. A second later I was out of bed and pulling on my pants. But she leaned over, grabbed my cock and said, 'Oh well, in for a penny in for a pound.' She then proceeded to do things with it that you couldn't begin to imagine of a diplomat's wife!"

Von Osten continued talking throughout the meal and only dried up when they were back in the bar.

From it all, Schneider slowly gleaned an answer to his initial question, put several hours before. Von Osten was there for a variety of reasons; for the money, for the excitement and because he adored the subterfuge. Above all, and rather surprisingly considering his fickle nature, he was a patriot. In his eyes, Hitler had done wonders for Germany and he loved him for it. He was not particularly enamoured with National Socialism – he didn't care for politics – and he disliked the harassment of the Jews, whom he regarded as no less German than anyone else. But Adolf Hitler was the solid, powerful, passionate leader the Fatherland had so badly needed to restore its self-esteem after the Versaille Treaty had stripped it to the bone. Hitler was good for Germany, so von Osten was his man. If Hitler wanted war, then it was the right thing to do and von Osten was happy to oblige in any way he could. His knowledge of England made him useful to the *Abwehr*.

"Have you met any others like us?" von Osten asked.

"You're the first."

"The same for me. They like to keep us apart. You were the only one I spoke to in the camp – apart from the boss. Individual training, no gossip between agents that way. Good security."

"Yes, I suppose so."

"So, Mr Erich the Englishman," said von Osten. "Now we have been formally introduced. That is all that matters, eh? Let us toast a successful collaboration."

"I'll drink to that."

Von Osten leaned forward. "And here's piss in your eye."

Schneider nearly choked on his beer. They laughed long and loud. Eventually they staggered up to their rooms around one in the morning. As they shook hands in the corridor, von Osten said: "Forgive me, this has been rather a dull evening. We should have gone out onto the Reeperbahn for some serious drinking – and who knows what else!" He made a vulgar gesture with his arm. "Perhaps tomorrow? Good night, my friend."

Schneider staggered along the corridor, opened the door to his room and fell onto the bed, not bothering to undress.

Serious drinking? What the sodding hell had this been!

Chapter 10

For the rest of the week the two men lived their lives as one. They ate, drank, talked and trained together, around a schedule prepared and delivered by Dr Rantzau. With time at a premium, training took on the feel of a refresher course. Concealment techniques, use of invisible inks, spotting and losing shadows and other aspects of tradecraft were recalled and reinforced.

Aircraft recognition became a priority. Long hours were spent studying line drawings and photographs of fighters and bombers currently in service with the Royal Air Force. It was easy enough to distinguish a Hawker Hurricane from a Supermarine Spitfire; the latter's sleek, elliptical wings were very distinctive. Others were harder to commit to memory – Defiants, Blenheims and Battles – although Schneider consistently underestimated his ability in this area. He had an excellent memory and outshone von Osten both in speed and accuracy of recognition.

The same could not be said when it came to operating his *Afu*. An abbreviation of *Agentenfunk*, this was the *Abwehr*'s standard issue transmitter-receiver, a battery operated apparatus that fitted neatly into an ordinary suitcase. It was tuned to a single preset frequency and simple to use. It was not the equipment that baffled Schneider but the telegraphy – control of the hand key, learning Morse code, getting to grips with the cipher systems. He wasn't bad, just very slow to transmit and to code and decode messages; and in enemy territory speed could mean the difference between a long, successful career as an agent and an appointment with a firing squad. As an incentive to work hard and learn, Dr Rantzau reminded them at least once a day that even the fair-playing British had no compunction whatsoever about executing spies in wartime.

Von Osten on the other hand was fast, accurate and experienced with the equipment, have been a radio ham for many years before the war. At Major Trautmann's radio centre on the outskirts of Hamburg, they practised for hours every afternoon, sitting in adjacent rooms and sending mock transmissions to and fro. By the end of the week Schneider's skills had improved considerably, which did wonders for his confidence and enabled Rantzau to sleep easier in his bed at night.

Guided by Trautmann, they also worked out their 'tells' – coded warnings that could be fed innocuously into a message to alert *Hamburg* of any danger, most of all that their cover had been blown, or the message was being monitored, or both. It could be as simple as the inclusion of a particular word or phrase, or the deliberate misspelling of a word.

In a room at the back of an office block close to the docks, they were quizzed on the handling of dynamite. In a deserted quarry, their practical sabotage skills were put to the test. They had been taught how to improvise an incendiary device using raw materials that could easily be bought in a chemist, grocery and hardware store; weed killer, sugar, sulphur and potassium nitrate. As each man took his turn to set fire to an old packing crate, their examiner, a cold, crusty, bald-headed man in his fifties, stood silently making notes on a clipboard.

Von Osten went first and concocted a mixture from the ingredients provided. Schneider watched from a distance as he carefully placed his creation on top of the crate and attached a length of fuse cut for five minutes. He struck a match and lit the end which flashed and crackled. Why doesn't he move away, thought Schneider – he's just standing there! He was checking that everything was in order. It took only a few seconds, but to Schneider it seemed an eternity. Von Osten hurried away and stood next to the examiner, who was peering at a stopwatch.

Eventually, a puff of smoke could be seen mushrooming up from the crate and a feeble flame rose momentarily into the air . . . and died away. The examiner grunted.

"That was a seven-minute fuse – too cautious. You next, Schneider." Schneider stepped forward and went through the same process, mixing his ingredients carefully. He placed the bomb on top of the now charred packing case and attached a fuse. Von Osten's had been too long, so he cut his with this in mind. It looked far too short, but aware of being observed, he could not bring himself to change his mind and cut another. It would have to do. He struck a match and applied it to the end of the fuse which took light immediately. It looked alarmingly near the device, but he knew he must do as Otto had done and pause to check that all was well. There seemed no doubt, so he turned to walk away.

He had only taken a couple of steps when it burst into flames. A wave of heat seared across his back, and he staggered forwards, falling to the ground with hands covering his head instinctively. He was grazed and shocked, but otherwise unhurt. When he stood up, he saw his incendiary device smoking feebly and heard von Osten's raucous laughter.

"A shorter fuse than that," the examiner said dryly, "and you might as well just shove it up your arse and set it alight." He scribbled furiously on his clipboard and strutted away.

Von Osten was still laughing. Schneider could not decide whether to be angry or join in the joke.

"It's not funny," he sneered.

"Yes it is, my friend – it's bloody hilarious!"

Schneider cracked, and a smile dawned on his face. "Well, perhaps slightly amusing." They followed the examiner back to the car, presuming that the test was now over. "Do you think I passed – am I a fully competent saboteur now?"

Von Osten put his arm round Schneider. "Erich, the sooner you get back to blowing down things instead of trying to blow up things, so much the better for all of us!"

Chapter 11

(Friday 3rd May 1940)

On the Friday morning, Ritter reported their progress to Herbert Wichmann, who in turn would report to Admiral Canaris over the weekend. Before he began, Wichmann updated him on the latest news from Berlin.

"Operation *Gelb* has been postponed by a day. Reading between the lines, I'd say the Führer is nervous, and I wouldn't be surprised if there were further delays. The deadline now is the tenth day of May. What of our 'Spitfire spies'?"

"They are doing rather well – certainly getting on together." Ritter decided not to mention what had gone on at Camp 4, primarily because he, Ritter, should have known about it. "They are developing a good rapport. Schneider's telegraphy has improved during joint practice sessions. He is still slow, but better than he was – and more confident. His accuracy has improved too."

"Good," said Wichmann. "I heard his incendiary device assessment was not so good."

Ritter frowned. How the hell did he know about that! "Yes, you could say so. I suspect the first one he puts together in the field will have a fuse half a kilometre long to compensate." He shuffled uncomfortably in his chair. "But at least it worked. I would say they are as well trained now as time permits. By no means perfect, but they have a fair chance working as a team. Once they have split up to travel to their individual targets is a different matter."

"How do you mean?"

"I think the chances of them both surviving long-term in the field are not promising. One will make it, the other probably won't."

"You mean Schneider won't."

Ritter nodded.

"If so, then we shall have obeyed the Admiral's instructions to the letter. "Fifty percent success, just as he wished."

"It seems a waste. Schneider would be useful to us in a different capacity – civilian intelligence perhaps. Based in London he would be effective reporting on morale and what he could glean from social activity. And we need couriers . . . badly. Paying agents has been a problem since the war began. Most of our leg men have been interned."

"I know," said Wichmann. "Mathilde Kraffte was a great loss. She's no use to us in Holloway prison."

Mathilde Kraffte had been one of the *Abwehr*'s chief paymasters. Based in Bournemouth, where she worked as housekeeper to a naval officer, she had regularly couriered money to agents throughout Britain until her internment in October 1939. High amongst her beneficiaries had been Arthur Owens, the *Abwehr*'s agent Johnny.

Wichmann shrugged. "It's too late to rethink." He looked down at the papers on his desk. "Arrangements have been made for them to spend the next fortnight with Messerschmitt at Augsburg. They must report there first thing on Monday morning. The works manager has been told they are journalists preparing a series of articles on conditions inside factories engaged in war work. It's feeble but the best we could come up with at short notice."

Nikolaus Ritter scribbled brief notes as he listened. "What are they going to learn?"

"I have no idea – something basic that applies to the manufacture of aircraft of any nationality. They can arrange that when they arrive."

"And when they return, unless any problems arise in the interim, we should have them in England on schedule by the end of May."

"That will keep the old man happy." Wichmann changed the subject. "What about Hermann Görtz – is he all set?"

"He is being dropped into Ireland on Sunday night, weather permitting," said Ritter, his voice betraying his concern. A convicted spy, with a face familiar to the British Security Service; both men knew it was a calculated risk to use him, but one that might just pay off dividends. If Görtz could contact the Irish Republican Army and take them up on their pre-war offer of help, a great deal of damage and confusion might be created within Britain. But Ritter was pessimistic. Even if he managed to avoid capture there was no great confidence at *Abwehrstelle Hamburg* in the ability of the IRA. The occasional bomb in Oxford Street or Euston Station with no substantial impact seemed to be their limit.

"We must give it a try," sighed Herbert Wichmann. "You never know. He might just be lucky this time."

"Once he has established radio contact with us, we shall send in a backup team – the two South Africans, Tributh and Gaertner. They may well succeed if Görtz fails again."

Wichmann suddenly seemed irritated. "We're just not prepared yet for serious infiltration within Great Britain – or the United Kingdom I suppose I should say. Everything is a compromise, an improvisation. Görtz is old hat as far as I am concerned, and no matter how good the other two, they'll probably end up caught in the same net."

"Let's hope it doesn't happen to our Spitfire spies," said Ritter. "I know it looks a bleak prospect at this precise moment, but give us six months and we will be in a much stronger position."

Wichmann stared pensively into space. "We must try and make the best of a bad job. On the other hand, you never know who might turn out to be a diamond. Look at Johnny. I thought he would be a complete waste of time and effort – too moody and temperamental. And there he is, still in place, still passing useful material four years on."

"Thank heavens for Johnny," Ritter murmured. "If Schneider and von Osten aren't due in Augsburg until Monday, what shall we do with them until then?"

"Give them a break. Let Schneider spend some time with that gorgeous wife of his. Von Osten can do what he likes, and no doubt he will."

"Very well, I shall organise travel permits. If there is no other business?"

Wichmann shook his head. "None that I can think of." When Ritter had gone he managed to concentrate his mind. He wondered how Admiral Canaris would react to latest developments. On paper it looked rather good. The plan was taking shape. So why did it all feel so wrong ....

Chapter 12

That evening Erich Schneider found himself flying to Mannheim in a privately chartered civilian Junkers Ju 52, courtesy of the *Abwehr*. From there it was a short train journey to Heidelberg. He had managed to telephone Renate from Hamburg and she was on the station platform to meet him, her perfect face smiling at him like a beacon. She wore a brown trench coat, a trilby hat, and full-length boots that covered her long, shapely legs.

"You're lucky," she said, kissing him firmly on the lips and taking his arm. "We were supposed to be rehearsing tonight for tomorrow's concert, but it's standard repertoire, so Bruno cancelled. Will you come and hear us play?"

"Mozart and Haydn?" asked Schneider. Renate nodded. "Alright, but only if I can bring a good book to read. Bruno always did lack imagination in his programmes." He didn't like Bruno Rolf, the leader of the quartet in which Renate sometimes played second violin. He thought him fatuous and arrogant.

"Nonsense," scoffed Renate. "It's classic quartet répertoire. Beautiful music – sublime music."

"Beautiful, but you've played the same half a dozen works a hundred times. Why not some Bartok for a change, or at least the Debussy or Ravel quartets. They're sublime too."

"Bruno doesn't like modern stuff, you know that. He says it sounds as though the music is fighting the instruments rather than flowing from them."

"Bruno was born a century too late – two centuries."

"He says modern music is all shit."

"Debussy and Ravel shit? I think not!" Schneider could feel his anger mounting. "Let's not talk about Bruno. How have you been?"

Renate smiled her stunningly beautiful smile. They walked hand in hand until they reached the banks of the Neckar, the river that flowed through the centre of the city.

"It's been weeks since you were last home."

"Make the most of me, my love. You might not be seeing me again for quite some time."

"What do you mean?"

"I'll tell you when we reach home."

"Are you being sent somewhere?"

Schneider smiled and tapped his nose. "Wait until we're home."

Ten minutes later Renate was turning the key in the door. Their second-floor apartment was in a modest block overlooking the river. The view from the living room was magnificent; on the far bank was the old town and university, with the castle perched high on the hillside above.

Schneider threw his bag and coat onto the floor and opened the drinks cabinet. On the wall in front of him hung a large photograph of Adolf Hitler taken at the time he was appointed Chancellor in 1933. He had never liked the picture; those piercing eyes seemed to stare you straight in the face and confront every thought in your head.

"Drink?"

"The usual." The usual was a gin and lime. He mixed two and handed one to Renate.

He hated the picture of Hitler, but Renate loved it. She adored her Führer; not so much for his political views but, like Otto von Osten and millions of Germans, for his strength of personality and for what he had done to bring their country back from the misery of the Weimar days. It puzzled Erich that she idolised powerful men and yet wanted to dominate those in her own life. It was one of numerous ambivalent aspects of her nature he had never quite understood. He watched his wife remove the trilby hat. She pulled out a pin and let her dark hair cascade down her back; she was as beautiful as ever. He remembered how flattered he had felt when she showed an interest in him, at his first orchestral rehearsal, here in Heidelberg. She had sought him out afterwards and all but asked him for a date. Why me, he had asked himself, an ordinary-looking, unassuming man who usually attracted ordinary-looking women.

A viola player who had tried his luck and failed clarified it for him.

"It's your playing," he said. "She loves powerful players. You blow that trumpet with all your guts, and it excites her. You wait until we play some Wagner. She'll be all over you like a rash." Then, somewhat despondently, he added: "That doesn't happen when you play the viola."

He had been right. The Meistersingers Overture was on the programme that first season. Schneider was only third trumpet but he played his heart out. After the concert Renate insisted he walk her home – she lived with her parents – and had clutched his hand tightly all the way. In the dimness of the porch she had kissed him full on the lips and rubbed her body against his provocatively. The passion was unmistakable. She wanted him. And she got him.

53

Less than a year later they were married and Heidelberg became his new home. That was four years ago. Then, they had been Eric and Renate Tomlin. When war clouds became ominous and international tensions impossible to ignore, he added an 'h' to his first name and they both adopted Renate's maiden name – Schneider.

Renate sat opposite him on the sofa, glass in hand. She was still wearing the trench coat.

"So tell me what is happening, Erich," she said. "Where are they sending you . . . is it England?"

Schneider pretended to answer reluctantly. "Well you know, I'm sworn to secrecy. I'm not really supposed to tell anything to anyone, not even you."

"Come on, I'm your wife. You can tell me. You know that I can keep a secret."

"I may be in deep trouble if I do."

Renate dipped a finger in her drink and flicked it across at him. "You'll be in deeper trouble if you don't. Come on, you big tease. Tell me, or else."

"Or else what?"

"Or else I won't take my coat off all evening."

"That would be cruel for both of us. You'd never last out."

"Maybe not – but come on, tell anyway."

"Alright, but I won't tell you everything." He explained the bare bones of the mission; that he would be parachuted into England, something to do with aircraft production and he may be there for some time until the job had been done, however long that may take. He would spend the next couple of weeks undergoing specialist training.

Renate looked puzzled. "How long do you think it will be – weeks, months, years?"

Schneider shrugged. "That depends – as long as the war with Great Britain continues. Chamberlain will probably try and negotiate a peace settlement, especially if France falls quickly."

"So it's true what people are saying. We are to invade."

"I have only heard rumours. But for a long time it has been a matter of 'when' rather than 'if'. I have heard the second week in May."

"When the *Wehrmacht* reach the English Channel, there will be an end to it." Renate spoke emphatically. "The Führer has no quarrel with the British. Your job, whatever it may be, will be over before you know it."

"I am not so sure. I'm one of them, don't forget – the British. We don't give up that easily. They have no faith in Hitler any longer. Not a gentleman. On the other hand, so long as Chamberlain remains Prime Minister there is always the possibility of compromise. Either way, we shall know soon enough."

54

Renate looked at her husband longingly and pursed her lips into a mock kiss. "I've missed you."

"In that case, darling, now I have told you what you want to know, might I suggest you relax a little. Take your coat off for a start."

She lifted herself from the chair, kicked off her boots and moved across to the window. The river, old Heidelberg and the castle were fading rapidly in the twilight and she closed the curtains until there was just a small gap remaining. She turned and faced him. The brown leather belt was undone in seconds and fell loose. The buttons – six in all – were tight and it took longer to undo them. She took her time, starting at the top and working downwards. When she had finished, the leather coat fell open.

Despite the semi-darkness, he could see her body clearly. She was wearing just a black lace bodice and matching cami-knickers. Her long slim legs were naked to the tops of her thighs, her slim waist curved immaculately beneath the bodice. The small breasts that Schneider knew so well were pushed hard upwards to give the appearance of being larger than they were – so much so that it seemed they might burst from their shell any moment.

"You'll catch cold one of these days," said Schneider.

Renate moved forward and straddled him, sitting firmly on his groin. She placed her arms round his neck, leaned towards him and kissed him full on the mouth. As she did so, she felt his arms slide around her back, underneath the coat, and squeeze her just under the rib cage, thumbs massaging the flesh around the tops of her thighs, moulding delicate circles that made her squirm with delight.

Moving his hands down and around, he grasped her firmly by the buttocks and stood up. Renate locked her legs tightly round his back and allowed herself to be carried into the bedroom, still kissing him. She fell backwards onto the bed and wriggled out of her coat, then watched Schneider as he undressed hurriedly – jacket and shirt first, then shoes and socks, and finally trousers. His underpants were bulging.

She knelt forward, eased his pants down and pulled them to the floor. As she did so her hair brushed against his stiff cock and it quivered slightly. She kissed the end, licked it, and then lay backwards with her arms stretched over her head. Schneider stood still for a moment, surveying the gorgeous curved landscape before him.

"Beethoven," she ordered.

He reached across to the gramophone and fumbled along the shelf for the first record of the Eroica Symphony set – Wilhelm Furtwängler conducting the Berlin Philharmonic. He wound the handle, placed the needle at the edge of the record and paused as the music crackled into life with its two great opening E flat chords.

Lifting her legs in the air, he tugged at the cami-knickers and had them over her bottom and along her legs in one fluid movement. With a flick of her toes, Renate sent them spinning across the room. Suddenly she pulled him down on top of her. His hands loosened her bodice to free her breasts. His mouth closed around one of them, sucking and licking the nipple, gently at first then rougher. He switched to the other one, and as he did so he felt Renate's hand grasp his cock and guide it into her. She was very wet. She gasped loudly – a sound of pure ecstasy that almost had Schneider climaxing instantly. He pulled back, then entered her again more slowly until he was comfortably in his stride.

At the end of side one, the record spun for a time, but neither of them was conscious of the monotonous scratching sound which gradually slowed as the clockwork mechanism ran itself down.

*

Schneider woke several hours later. It was pitch black and he could hear the distant sound of a violin.

He swung his feet onto the floor, crossed the bedroom and opened the door. Silhouetted against a soft sheen of moonlight stood Renate, naked, playing her violin with the mute on. Schneider recognised the Paganini Caprice in E major. He stood and listened until she had finished playing.

"Come back to bed," he said quietly.

Renate placed the violin back in its case. "I'm sorry, I just had to."

"I know. Making love makes you want to play . . ."

"And playing makes me want to make love."

They stood together for a while, kissing and caressing. Then they went back to bed. This time Renate took charge which she loved to do. She pushed Schneider down on his back and straddled him with his cock deep inside her, rocking to and fro, back arched, nipples thrust outwards and a quiet hum, almost a moan, permanently in her throat.

"You bastard!" she muttered from time to time. "Oh you bastard!"

Chapter 13

(Saturday 4ᵗʰ May 1940)

It was almost light when they eventually collapsed in a hazy afterglow and sank into a deep sleep. Neither of them woke until almost midday. After a lazy breakfast that also served as lunch, they crossed the river and made their way up to the castle. They leaned over the parapet and peered down at the city below.

"I'm very proud of you, Erich," said Renate as she gazed across the valley. "You've sacrificed a lot – your music, your country. Me."

"This is my country now."

"You have no doubts? What you are about to do would be regarded by some as a betrayal."

"Perhaps, but I don't see it that way. I used to be English and I used to live in England. Now I live in Germany, married to a German woman, and to all intents and purposes I am German."

Renate brushed against him. "It means a great deal to me to hear you say that. I love my country very much."

"And I love you."

They walked along a little and sat down on a bench.

"Mind you," said Schneider, "I had precious few options. If I had not volunteered my services to the *Abwehr* I would either have had to leave Germany or rot in an internment camp somewhere. I doubt the army would have had me. This is the only way I can be sure of staying with you. It's an irony that I have to leave you to stay with you."

"I'll be here waiting when you get back."

"I must make sure I don't get caught then."

"You're too smart to get caught."

"I would not be so sure about that. I am not exactly top of the class at spy school."

"If they had lovemaking on the curriculum you would be – I ache all over! Please take care, Erich. They shoot spies in wartime."

"I don't know who told you that but it's not true."

"No?"

"No. They hang them."

"That's not funny … not funny at all."

"Don't worry, they'll have to catch me first. I have an unbelievably strong motive for avoiding any such eventuality. You." He stood up and tugged at his wife's arm. "Come on, let's go home and get you ready for your concert."

That evening Schneider sat towards the back of the church hall where the Rolf Quartet were playing. He enjoyed the music more than he later admitted to Renate. At least Bruno Rolf achieved fine results within his limited choice of répertoire. The Haydn and Mozart were performed stylishly and with finely chosen tempi throughout. Rolf himself was a superb player; what a pity, thought Schneider, that as a man he was such an arsehole.

In the Green Room afterwards, Bruno Rolf was in loud, ebullient mood.

"Ah!" he said when he saw Schneider. "Our second fiddle's second fiddle." He placed his arm around Renate and squeezed tightly. "I do not understand how you can possibly leave such a divine creature for weeks on end in that lonely apartment. What are you doing with yourself, anyway . . . playing bugle when the *Wehrmacht* advances?"

Schneider smiled politely. "I'm working as a translator actually." An agreed blanket cover story – vague and uninteresting enough to dispel curiosity. It didn't work with Rolf.

"Come on, there's more to it than that," he said in a mountainous whisper. "Renate here says the same thing, but I know when she's lying. It's secret work isn't it?"

Several heads turned. The room was small and every word could be heard by everyone.

"Not anymore, it would seem," said Schneider dryly.

"Come, you can tell me – I'm the most discreet person in the world."

Renate came to the rescue. "We must be going, Bruno. See you for rehearsal on Monday. 'Bye everyone." She grabbed her violin case and they made their way out onto the street. "Sorry about that, Erich. Dear Bruno is not the most tactful person at times. Such a wonderful player though."

He knew that his wife admired Bruno Rolf greatly and he was prepared to suffer his company for her sake, but for her sake only. He also knew they had been lovers once, before he and Renate had met, a piece of knowledge that did nothing to warm him to the man.

On the Sunday they took a longer walk, climbing to the top of the steep valley and wandering along the brow of its wooded slopes. They talked about a hundred different things; the war, Adolf Hitler, music, England, Bruno Wolf and the quartet. The hours passed like minutes.

Back in the apartment, Renate played the violin and Schneider shut himself in the bedroom and took his trumpet from its case. With a practice mute in the bell to deaden the sound, he played some long sustained notes. His lips had lost little of their muscular strength, mainly because he always carried a mouthpiece in his pocket and blew down it whenever the opportunity arose. Soon he was rippling through scales and arpeggios and playing excerpts from orchestral pieces with ease and grace.

Renate stopped playing for a moment and listened at the bedroom door. The sound made her tingle slightly, the way she did when she heard any musician with a gift that rose beyond mere skill and hard work.

That evening they went to bed early and made love just once, slowly and tenderly. It was their physical *Aufwiedersehen*, and neither of them knew how long it might be until they saw each other again. It gave their union an added dimension that neither had experienced before, a bitter-sweet blend of finality and foreverness. Renate wanted to cry afterwards, but no tears would flow.

The journey back to Augsberg involved returning to Mannheim by train and then a flight direct to the Messerschmitt airfield. Schneider lay awake long into the night, determined one minute not to leave on that early train, eager to get it over with the next. When they woke in the morning there was a tension between them that neither of them wanted but neither could shake off.

At the station little was said. Schneider promised to contact her whenever possible, if it was possible at all. He would insist that *Hamburg* pass on news to reassure her that he was safe. Both knew that in reality it would not happen.

Eventually Schneider's train was ready to depart and he kissed Renate gently on the mouth.

"I'll see you again soon," he said. "September at the latest." It sounded a hollow promise, so he said no more. As the train pulled out of the station he waved and mouthed ... *I love you*.

Renate tried to do the same but her lips could not form the words. They seemed frozen; so she waved instead, watched his carriage until it was no longer discernible from the rest of the train, then turned and walked away. Deep inside she was convinced she would never see her husband again. Despite her love for him she felt a change come over her. On the walk back to the apartment, a door closed inside her.

When she got home she took out her violin and practised for hours. She thought about tonight's concert and what she would wear.

Chapter 14

(Monday 6th May 1940)

Schneider's plane landed on the airfield of the Bavarian Aircraft Company in Augsburg shortly after nine. As he walked across the grass he was impressed by the huge hangars, four in all, in which he could see dozens of aircraft. A month ago he wouldn't have known what they were, but his aircraft recognition training had encompassed German as well as British planes and now he knew them instantly – Bf 110s, twin-engine fighters that could also function as light bombers.

Adjacent to the hangars was a large new building that housed administration and design departments, towards which he was escorted, specifically to the office of one of the works officials, a brusque middle-aged man called Gerber. The first thing he saw after stepping through the door was Otto von Osten slumped in a chair, apparently asleep. When the eyes struggled open they were even more bloodshot than usual.

"Greetings, Erich. Ready to learn how to make airplanes?"

"More ready than you, by the looks of it."

Herr Gerber sat stoically at his desk, less than pleased at having to deal with two 'journalists', one of whom was obviously the worse for wear. He had more than enough problems worrying about maintaining manufacturing target levels without having to entertain a couple of timewasters. But he was an efficient administrator and when told to do a job, whether he liked it or not, he did it well and without question.

"So, you wish to learn certain skills," he said, "typical of those used in an aircraft factory."

"That is correct."

"For an article in a magazine."

"A series of articles."

"Do either of you have any technical or engineering experience?"

Von Osten said: "I mended a puncture on my bicycle once."

Gerber was not amused. "I assume then you are both ignorant in this field. Very well, I shall keep the tasks as simple as possible. After all there

60

is not a great deal you can master in two weeks. Come." He took them to a cloakroom and supplied them with overalls.

Schneider looked von Osten up and down as they changed their clothes. "You look dreadful. What the hell have you been up to?"

"To be honest, my friend, I really can't remember much. I know I was in Berlin, and now I am here. In between, as to the detail, it is all a somewhat hazy. How was your weekend?"

"Fine." Schneider had no intention of elaborating.

Gerber explained there were several jobs he could show them. The main one was riveting, an essential part of all metal plane construction. Hundreds, if not thousands, of rivets were required to attach the body panels of an aircraft to its frame. "A fast efficient riveter is worth his weight in gold," he said. He led them across the factory site to a large workshop. Along one side stood a row of half a dozen fuselage frames, devoid of engines, wings and tail planes; skeletal in appearance without coverings. A small army of workers crawled over them like ants, fitting parts, checking alignments and gradually bringing them to life.

"These are Bf 110s," explained Gerber. "We're concentrating on them at present. 109 production has been transferred to Regensberg. But we have some 109 airframes which are being used to test features for the new F model. It should be ready in a few months." At the far end of the workshop he came to a halt. The last frame in the line looked different from the others and was set slightly to one side, resting on some wooden trestles. "This is your own practice frame, gentlemen. We set it up especially." He nodded to a man standing by the frame. "Karl here will be your instructor. He will show you the equipment and explain everything you ever wanted to know about riveting."

Von Osten was having trouble coming to terms with the noise in the workshop and winced at every bang and thud – and they were constant. "I hope this plane is not earmarked to fly ever," he said. "It'll be a deathtrap when we've finished with it."

Gerber grunted. "We would never let a *Luftwaffe* pilot loose in anything knocked together by amateurs. The parts will be stripped and reused."

They set to work. At first Karl was abrupt and short tempered with them. He was used to training new men for the factory, but these two would never become part of the workforce. A waste of his precious time. If they fumbled with the riveting gun he snapped at them and swore if they failed to grasp a point easily. Von Osten, because he had a thick head, was slow to catch on and received the worst of the flack.

At the end of the day von Osten invited Karl for a drink before their instructor went home to his wife and evening meal. He refused initially, but once they were out of the factory and had walked in to town, he allowed himself to be led into the bar of the hotel where the newcomers were staying.

Four hours later Karl staggered through his front door to a tirade of matrimonial abuse and a flying plate of dried up schnitzel and potato. He was late for work the next morning and greeted by a beaming von Osten, who was in fine shape, having paced his drinking after the heavy weekend.

"Karl! Thank you for such a pleasant evening. Most enjoyable. Same again tonight?"

Karl managed a smile. From then onwards he treated his pupils with greater respect and by the end of the week they were the best of friends.

Riveting demanded concentration and a firm, steady hand and both men picked up the skills without difficulty. In a few days they were producing smooth and even lines of rivet heads that had Karl nodding with approval. When he saw them beginning to appear smug at their achievements, he said: "Now try increasing your speed – by half as much." The lines immediately became erratic again. Karl laughed and pointed across the workshop at men who were firing in lines of rivets at high speed. "You'll be as fast as them in a couple of years."

Disheartened, Schneider slumped onto a stool and fished out a trumpet mouthpiece from his pocket. He placed it on his lips and blew for a few seconds. He said: "If I had pneumatic lungs I could triple tongue the buggers in twice as fast with this thing."

Von Osten slid a hand into his pocket and drew out a small hip flask. "I'll drink to that."

Karl snatched it from him. "Don't be a fool! Drinking is strictly forbidden. Start messing about with some of this equipment when you're half pissed and you'll lose your fingers before you have time to say *Prost*." He handed back the flask. "Save it until after work."

Von Osten tucked the flask back in his pocket. "You are quite right, Karl. Stupid of me."

As they turned their attention back to work, three men entered the workshop by the door nearest to them and walked slowly along the centre aisle, pointing occasionally at the line of fuselages.

Karl said: "See the one in the brown suit?" They looked across at a man of about forty with receding hair and finely chiseled features. He was doing most of the talking. "That's Willy Messerschmitt. He designed these machines."

The men moved on and out of sight.

"A very clever man."

"Where would we be without him," mused von Osten. "I admire men who can create. All I've ever done is sell cars and run garages. The only thing I can ever remember building was a long line of bar bills."

Karl stared at him inquisitively. "I thought you were a journalist."

With barely a pause, von Osten covered his mistake. "I am now. But before that I was in the motor trade. I started writing in my spare time, for journals mainly, and decided I liked it more." Karl nodded, accepting the lie he was being told.

Schneider whispered: "Careful, you idiot."

"Sorry, I wasn't thinking."

On the Friday news filtered through in radio broadcasts during the day. German troops had entered Holland, Belgium and Luxembourg and were advancing along a line that stretched from the North Sea to the Swiss border. Operation *Gelb* had begun and the German High Command were already reporting successes against Allied forces. Hitler was reported to have announced as his Order of the Day: *"Soldiers of the Western Front! The battle which is beginning today will decide the fate of the German nation for the next thousand years."* There were cheers from some of the factory workers; others were more subdued. One or two were tearful, either from joy or pity, depending on their point of view.

Gerber told Schneider and von Osten they would not be needed over the weekend and that on the Monday morning they would be assigned to another section of the factory.

"Surely you work weekends?" said von Osten.

"Oh we'll be busy in here, don't you worry," explained Karl. "But you two aren't exactly helping to speed up production. You're just a pain in the arse which the management could do without right now."

With two free days to fill again, Schneider's first thought was to visit Renate, but he decided against it. Their farewell at Heidelberg Station had been painful enough and he didn't want to put her, or himself, through it again. It was best left as it was. Besides, Karl had invited him and von Osten to his home for a meal cooked, and hopefully not thrown, by his formidable wife. It would be impolite to refuse.

So he stayed in Augsburg.

Chapter 15

(Saturday 11th May 1940)

On the Saturday morning they heard that in London Neville Chamberlain had resigned as Prime Minister the day before and Winston Churchill had taken his place.

"That'll make a difference," Schneider murmured to himself. "There'll be no compromises now. Winston won't concede anything. He'll fight Hitler all the way." For him personally it was potentially bad news. His time in England might now be a great deal longer than anyone in the *Abwehr* had anticipated.

Karl's wife, whose name was Else, was a stout, plain woman with a quick temper. From the moment they arrived, von Osten passed her one compliment after another which clearly delighted her. Schneider guessed she hadn't been flirted with for years – if ever – and she visibly melted at his every word. Karl didn't seem to mind, remaining entirely indifferent, if a little curious that anyone should wish to pay his spouse any attention.

True to form, von Osten had brought a bottle of schnapps with him and was liberal in its distribution. After a splendid meal, whilst von Osten was in the kitchen helping Else with the washing up, Karl, already drunk, leaned over and grabbed Schneider's arm. He nodded towards the kitchen.

"We've been married twelve years," he mumbled, then indicated the stairs in the corner of the room. "Up there asleep is our son, Gunther. His twelfth birthday is in a few months from now. Work it out." He held a hand to his head, pointed a forefinger at his temple and pulled an imaginary trigger. "One mistake like that and your life is never your own again. Do you understand what I am saying?" He sniggered. "Your friend Otto, if he fancies my wife he is welcome to her." He belched. "God knows he must be desperate."

"He's like this with all women. He likes to create a reaction in them. It's nothing more than that."

"Thank God," said Karl. "For a moment he was plummeting down in my estimation. He is a good fellow after all."

Schneider found his remarks distasteful. He thought of Renate; he was missing her badly. And here was Karl, with all the time in the world to spend with his own wife, yet full of contempt for her. The irony overwhelmed him and he stood up to seek fresh air, strolling out of the front door and into the street. He lit a cigarette and walked, nowhere in particular.

An hour later he came back. Karl was stretched across the table, unconscious and snoring loudly. He wandered into the kitchen, which was empty. Hearing noises from the back garden, he moved across to the window and peered out. It was dark, but as his eyes became accustomed to it he was able to make out Else. She was leaning over almost at a right angle against the garden wall, the palms of her hands pressed firmly on the brickwork and her head almost touching it. Her skirt was hoiked up over her back, and her drawers were somewhere between her knees and her ankles. Behind her stood von Osten, his trousers at half-mast, taking her vigorously from behind. One hand gripped a buttock for support, the other held a pocket flask from which he took occasional sips. She was squealing – a noise halfway between pleasure and pain.

Schneider watched for a while then turned away. He walked back to the hotel, wishing he had gone home after all. He felt sick at the wasted opportunity.

Chapter 16

(Monday 13ᵗʰ May 1940)

The next week dragged interminably for Schneider. Gerber gave them dirty, complicated jobs, operating lathes and capstans to create washers and screws. He wanted them to leave with an impression of the reality of factory work, and he balked at the idea of their writing articles eulogising the romanticism of man and machine working together in idyllic harmony. He had no idea of their real reason for being there.

Schneider knew this work was not specific to aircraft production; washers and screws could apply to most any type of manufacturing process. But neither he nor von Osten complained. It was a means to an end, and any skills they could learn quickly would improve their chances of finding work in the Spitfire factories. So they operated their machines and got used to the mess of oil and suds that sunk through overalls and stained their clothing beneath.

Von Osten didn't mention his encounter with Else, nor did Schneider. Karl obviously remembered nothing of the evening. Besides, the escalation of the war was in the forefront of everyone's mind. The next day came news that Panzer divisions had crossed the River Meuse at Sedan and were routing the French armies to the south. On Wednesday the Dutch army gave in and capitulated. One success after another for Hitler's troops; one nail after another in the coffin of the British Expeditionary Force as its position was rapidly undermined on all sides.

No clear instructions had been given about when to return to Hamburg, so on the Thursday evening Schneider telephoned Dr Rantzau and was told to stay at the factory until the end of Friday's working day, then they could do as they pleased so long as they were back in Hamburg on Monday morning. He was delighted and this time knew precisely how he would be spending the weekend. He thought of phoning Renate to let her know, but decided against it. He would surprise her.

The following afternoon he was anxious to get away from the factory as soon as he could. But von Osten, having thanked Gerber and his staff

66

for their cooperation and promised them free copies of the magazine articles, insisted on taking them all for a farewell drink. Schneider spent a miserable two hours wishing he could escape. Eventually he succeeded and hurried off to cadge a flight back to Mannheim. It was some time before a plane could be organised. Eventually it took a wire from *Hamburg* before authorisation was given and it was almost dark by the time the Bf 110 – the only plane available – took off. The young pilot clearly begrudged having to perform taxi duties. At Mannheim he barely allowed the plane to come to a halt long enough for Schneider to alight before accelerating off for the return journey.

Just after eleven his train pulled in to Heidelberg Station. Tired and frustrated by so many delays, Schneider set off through the dimly lit streets towards the apartment. He didn't know whether or not Renate had a concert that evening; either way she should be home by now he imagined. He wouldn't ring the bell or knock the door, he would just creep in. If she was already in bed asleep he would slip between the sheets next to her.

The sky was empty of clouds and a brilliant moon bathed the city in a crisp silver light. There were few people about and his footsteps echoed on the pavement. When he turned the corner of his street he could see the apartment block clearly. There were no lights on at any of the windows on the second floor. He entered the main door of the block and climbed the stairs two at a time. He turned the key as quietly as he was able and eased the door open.

It was pitch black inside the hallway and he blinked to get used to the dark. He could hear orchestral music playing quietly, too muffled to recognise. He placed his bag on the floor and fumbled for the living room door. It slid open easily and the music became more distinct.

Beethoven's Third Symphony, the Eroica – a passage near the middle of the first movement.

The curtains in the lounge were not drawn; moonlight poured in, allowing a clear view of the room. On the coffee table were two wine glasses, both empty, and on the floor nearby, two violin cases. One was Renate's, the other he did not recognise. On the far side of the room was the bedroom door – half open. The music was coming from inside.

He walked slowly across the room and crouched down in front of the door. The music was louder now and he could hear nothing else. Schneider had never appreciated before how loud the gramophone played. The walls must be thick otherwise the neighbours would have complained about it.

He knew this recording of the Eroica well, and side one was nearly over. He waited for the familiar sound as the needle spun to the centre and clicked endlessly. Moments later it happened and the clicking began.

Beyond it another sound became apparent. Schneider recognised it instantly – the distinctive guttural moan of pleasure Renate made as she gradually worked her way towards orgasm. He squatted on the floor and moved his head several inches round the edge of the door. With one eye he was able to glimpse a scene that sent a bolt of ice cold shock searing through his body.

On the bed, silhouetted against the moonlight, knelt Renate, her back towards him and her long hair shimmering down almost to the top of her buttocks. Her haunches were gyrating slowly back and forth in an easy rhythm above the man who lay flat on his back beneath her. His hands were raised, each one cupping a breast.

Renate growled: "Bastard. You bastard."

Schneider was frozen to the spot, overwhelmed with disbelief. It was like watching a film of himself with Renate. It was exactly how they made love together, on that bed, to the same music, in their favourite position, with Renate using gutter language to help reach a climax. Only it wasn't Schneider beneath her. Who?

He knew of course. As if responding to a cue, the man spoke.

"You're beautiful, so beautiful. And so exciting. I'd forgotten just how exciting you are."

Schneider clenched his fist, resisting the temptation to charge into the bedroom and pummel the quartet leader's face with his bare knuckles. Bruno Rolf! With an irony that was lost on him entirely he murmured the word Renate had used just moments before. "Bastard."

Rolf was talking again. "It is a long time since we did this."

Renate groaned. "Shush."

But Rolf continued. "I have wanted to many times."

The gramophone clicked on, punctuating their conversation.

"I know you have. But I have been married."

"You still are."

Renate shook her head and looked towards the ceiling. "I don't think I shall ever see Erich again. He has gone on a suicide mission."

"I had no idea translation work was so dangerous," remarked Rolf flippantly.

"You know that is not what he is doing. He will never come back – I'm convinced of it. That's why you're here and I am allowing this to happen."

Rolf groaned as she pressed herself down into his groin. "You sound so certain."

There was no answer for a while and the clicking gramophone filled the silence. Renate's moans ceased and the faint sound of sobbing took their place. Her body was no longer moving.

"I know. I just know."

"Sorry," said Rolf. "Bad timing."

Renate cried for a while, remaining static over Rolf. Then she wiped an arm across her eyes and began to move again.

"Unbelievably bad timing," she sniffed. "Now pay for it." She pressed down on him again, harder this time. "Come on, you've wanted this for a long time – you've tried it on enough times. Now's your chance – do it to me." Her forcefulness stirred Rolf into action and their bodies began rocking in unison. "Harder . . . harder!"

Schneider could take no more. He staggered backwards, reeling across the living room as if from a blow to the stomach. He had to get out, fast. He stumbled towards the hallway, and for some reason grabbed Rolf's violin case en route, then fumbled for his bag. He found the front door latch and all but fell through the door. A few seconds later he was down the stairs and in the street, running blindly. Without knowing how, he found himself in the centre of the great bridge that spanned the Neckar. He peered over the parapet, leaning dangerously out until his feet left the ground. The water below looked dark and inviting, and for a brief moment he considered throwing himself off, to embrace the oblivion that would quickly follow.

The feeling passed. His heart was pounding hard against his ribcage. He felt anger more than despair and, as if to reassure himself of the fact, he picked up Bruno Rolf's violin case and opened it roughly. He knew the instrument inside was a fine one – a Stradivari copy by Arnold Voigt. Rolf had boasted of it frequently. His pride and joy.

In a fit of impotent rage, Schneider took the violin by the neck, raised it high above his head and smashed it against the parapet. It disintegrated in a shower of varnished wood splinters and fragments. What remained hung limp, held together only by the strings. He dropped it back into the case and threw the whole mess into the river.

He lit a cigarette and slumped down on the pavement, drawing the smoke deep into his lungs. How could she do it! As soon as his back was turned, and with that heap of shit Bruno Rolf. For a moment his mind flashed back to von Osten and Karl's wife, pressed up against the garden wall. Twice in a week he had watched a man fucking someone else's wife. This time it was *his* wife. It sickened him.

A wave of nausea rose up in him. He stood up, leaned over the parapet again and vomited, retching painfully. He immediately felt a sense of release, the physical reaction helping to clear his mind. He could think now, and was able to decide what to do next.

His first thought was a simple one – get the hell out of Heidelberg. Leave Renate and the entire sordid situation behind. He slung his bag over his shoulder and trudged towards the station. He looked up at the huge clock on the concourse and was shocked to see the time; five minutes after

69

midnight. He had been in Heidelberg for just an hour. In that short time span his life had been turned upside down. He hurt inside; an agony as bad as any physical pain he had ever known.

The next train wasn't until six in the morning. Sleep was impossible, so he sat in the buffet with a steaming mug of coffee and began an all-night vigil. He eventually boarded the train bleary-eyed and exhausted. As it pulled out of the city, he gazed at the roads and buildings of his adopted home town.

He knew he would never see it again.

Chapter 17

(Monday 20th May 1940)

Schneider travelled all the way back to Hamburg by train, stopping off at various places en route, drinking a lot of beer and staying the Saturday night in a cheap hotel; he didn't really know where. He arrived back at the Klopstock late on Sunday evening, fell into bed, and slept. At breakfast the next morning von Osten was his usual groggy self, but he sensed all was not well with his comrade.

"Is everything alright with you, Erich?"

"Good thank you – and with you?"

"Good." They ate in silence for a while. "Is there something bothering you?"

Schneider swallowed a mouthful of coffee and placed his cup down. "Now you come to mention it, Otto, yes there is."

"Tell me."

"You – asking all these dumb questions. That's bothering me!"

Von Osten did not press any further, and talked about telegraphy instead. But he was aware of the tension in Schneider; there was a hard edge to him that had not been there a few days earlier in Augsburg. In between he had been to Heidelberg to visit his wife. Where the problem lay was obvious.

As the week progressed they heard more of the tremendous speed at which the German High Command was achieving its *Blitzkrieg*. The enemy was crumbling and being pushed right back to the coast. On the Tuesday came news that Panzer Divisions had reached Abbeville, at the mouth of the River Somme, having advanced an incredible three hundred and eighty-six kilometres in just ten days. All they had to do now was strike north towards the coastal ports – Boulogne, Calais, Dunkirk – and the enemy would be virtually surrounded. Trapped by their own English Channel.

71

The following day Dr Rantzau called them to a meeting and told them how much this success emphasised the urgency of their mission. The conquest of Western Europe would soon be complete and if the Führer decided to invade Great Britain, their intelligence about aircraft production would be of paramount importance.

"Their first line of British defence," he explained, "will be the Royal Air Force. The *Luftwaffe* must destroy them ahead of any invasion. Once that is achieved there should be little opposition. The British Army is about to be wiped out it would seem, and reports from inside England suggest the morale of the people is extremely low. Already they are resigned to defeat and many are looking forward to embracing the Third Reich. Churchill's appointment as Prime Minister is unpopular. Britain is a peace loving nation and they are angry at being saddled with a brandy swilling warmonger as their leader."

Von Osten said: "Are you sure you're talking about the right country? I lived there for quite a few years and know the English well. They're stubborn. Frankly I find it hard to believe what you are telling us."

"I agree," said Schneider. "I think your reports are wrong. They probably aren't even aware of the gravity of their position yet. I shouldn't imagine the BBC is revealing the whole truth."

Dr Rantzau shook his head. "I can assure you my sources are reliable. Great Britain is in turmoil."

"I shall believe that when I see it," said von Osten cynically. Schneider agreed. He knew Winston Churchill would be the last person to lie down and allow Nazi jackboots to walk over his beloved country. The man had been warning against Hitler for years, prophetically as it had turned out. "What if Hitler decides against invading Britain, or an armistice is agreed? What about us then?"

"Then your job will be done. If Great Britain sues for peace, we shall have no further need for subversive methods. Now pay attention please." He stretched a large map of the country across the table and pinpointed the distinctive bulge of East Anglia. "You will be parachuted in on Sunday night – four days from now. If the weather is poor, then it will be the first clear night thereafter. This is where I want you to drop – Norfolk, a very rural area with plenty of wide open spaces and not many towns."

"Very flat, Norfolk." said Schneider.

"I beg your pardon?"

"Noël Coward. No matter, please carry on."

"Pay attention please. I have selected this area as the target – an approximate triangle of land, each side of which is roughly twenty miles long." They all peered at the map. Two sides of the triangle were roads that stretched out from Norwich at a right angle, one northwards to

Cromer and the other eastwards towards Great Yarmouth. The third side was the stretch of coastline between the two towns.

Otto von Osten frowned. "I took a holiday in Norfolk once. All I can recall is a maze of rivers and man-made lakes – Broads they call them. Wouldn't it be better to fly further inland where there's less chance of getting wet, or drowning even?"

"Not all of Norfolk consists of lakes," replied Rantzau. "The longer you are flying over British airspace the more chance you have of being intercepted and shot down. This is the plan we have decided upon. I suggest from there you travel together to London and find somewhere to hole up for a while. We have no safe house, so you'll have to find your own accommodation. Take your time – there will have been changes since you were there last. The slightest slip could give you away. When you are ready, you will go your separate ways. The rest is up to you."

Schneider and von Osten looked at each other. Rantzau smiled.

"Simple really."

That evening, in the bar at the Klopstock, von Osten said to Schneider: "Suppose Rantzau is right. Suppose the British are already staring defeat in the face. There could be mass panic over there right now, for all we know."

"Do you honestly believe so? Speaking as an Englishman, I'd say it's not in our nature to crumble when things get tough." His thoughts flashed to Renate momentarily. He wasn't going to crumble over her infidelity. "We'll find out for ourselves soon enough."

Von Osten sensed again the coldness in Schneider's manner. Not a bad thing, he thought, bearing in mind what lay ahead.

Chapter 18

(Wednesday 22nd May 1940)

Later that same evening in Dublin, capital city of the Republic of Ireland, there was fierce banging on the door of a house called 'Konstanz' in Templeogue Road. When the owner, one Ricky O'Brien, eventually opened the door, the huddle of men from G2, the Irish Secret Service, barged past him, ignoring his protests and swept from room to room, emptying drawers, ransacking cupboards and collecting a variety of exhibits.

Since the outbreak of war, G2 had been successful in mopping up the activities of foreign agents and maintaining the Republic's neutrality. But in the house in Templeogue Road they made some discoveries that ensured they were not complacent in their duties; a parachute, a wireless transmitter, some German medals from the Great War and documents in the name of one Lieutenant Krause. In a locked safe they found some American dollars – twenty thousand of them. Proof, if ever there was any, of the presence of an active *Abwehr* spy.

And if G2 had thought to post a man at the back of the house, they would have discovered Lieutenant Krause himself, clambering over the garden wall as fast as his flabby fifty-year-old body could manage and vanishing into the Dublin night.

By the skin of his teeth, though only for the time being, Hermann Görtz had given them the slip.

Chapter 19

Alison Webb stared out of the window as the plane lifted off the runway at Sydney (Kingsford Smith) Airport and floated into the morning sky over the outskirts of the city. Below her, somewhere, was Lucas Kelly. She waved feebly, knowing full well he couldn't see her.

Before she boarded, Kelly had hugged her and kissed her on the cheek and told her that he would miss her. She felt tearful and made a great effort not to cry in front of him. But once inside the plane the tears flowed. That was over and she felt better now the plane was in the air. The tears were partly for Kelly; he had been a great friend and a great teacher, and the poor man had nothing now. Kelly had lost his planes and the Crazy Flyers had been disbanded. He was trying desperately to find a job with a flying school – so far without any success.

She also cried for the flying she had grown to love so much. She knew it would never be the same again. There would be no opportunities for stunt flying in Great Britain in the foreseeable future, if ever for a woman.

She relaxed in her seat and listened instinctively to the hum of the engines. Strange being a passenger. She closed her eyes. It was going to be a long journey. She fell asleep thinking that it might be months, years even, before she flew a plane again.

She slept badly.

Chapter 20

(Saturday 25th May 1940)

All preparations were complete. Von Osten and Schneider were in possession of their *Afu*s – radio transceivers – and had tested them half a dozen times. Dr Rantzau supplied fake identity cards and ration books in the cover names they had been allowed to choose for themselves. Schneider was Henry Mansell, the name of an old school friend from Bromsgrove, although he didn't tell Rantzau as much. Von Osten, with tongue in cheek, had chosen Edward King; a veiled reference to Britain's abdicated monarch.

"I always did admire a man who's prepared to make sacrifices for a woman," he chuckled. "And you can't sacrifice more than your country."

The remark was made in jest, but it hit home hard with Schneider. Wasn't that precisely what he was doing, sacrificing the country of his birth for the sake of a woman? Only in his case a woman who was prepared to leap into bed with another man the minute his back was turned.

They were also formally allocated new codenames. In deference to his musical talents, *Abwehr* Agent No. 3549 Erich Schneider, born Eric Tomlin, alias Ernst, alias Henry Mansell, was to be referred to in all radio traffic as Quaver. Bearing in mind his connections with the motor trade, Agent No. 3538 Otto von Osten, alias Ulrich, alias Edward King, was christened Mechanic.

In addition to the *Afu* radios and codebooks, they were each given fifty pounds in cash, a map of East Anglia, a compass and a small emergency food ration consisting mainly of chocolate removed from its German wrappers. Their last meal at the Klopstock was a sullen affair. The food stuck in their throats and when the dessert had been served but pushed to one side uneaten, Schneider confessed: "I'm scared."

"Me too," said von Osten. "Now everything is ready and in place I just want to get on with it. Pity we're not going tonight."

"Fancy a drink?"

Von Osten laughed out loud. "Do pigs smell of shit?"

"Come on, let's go to the bar."

"I have a better idea. Let's find somewhere a bit livelier. This place is like a mortuary. Besides, I wouldn't mind saying farewell to a Fräulein – or two."

Soon they were marching purposefully along the Reeperbahn. It was still early evening, yet there were people everywhere; soldiers, civilians, tradesmen, criss-crossing each other at a range of speeds depending on their intent. Von Osten knew the area like the back of his hand and soon had Schneider seated in a seedy bar being served by a no longer youthful waitress whose skirt was split right to the waist on one side, revealing almost as much as her very tight blouse.

"Greetings, Otto. Beers for you and your handsome friend?"

"Yes please, Suzie, my angel. Will you marry me?"

Suzie tutted. "I told you the other night – yes! You keep asking me, I keep saying yes, but you never do anything about it."

"Tomorrow, I promise."

"Tomorrow! That's all I ever hear from men."

When the beers arrived, they raised their frothing steins in the air.

"A toast to two British aircraft factories," declared von Osten. "May their future employees be incompetent in the extreme and ensure that every new plane they produce falls to bits on its maiden flight."

"And here's to the British hangman. May our paths never cross."

Von Osten drank fast. For once, as this was something of a celebration, Schneider determined to try and keep up with him. The dryness that had been in his throat all day helped, and by the time they left the bar an hour later they were level on three steins each. Schneider was already drunk, his spirits high as much from the occasion as the beer. The training was over and now the action was about to begin. In just over twenty-four hours they would be in England. The alcohol made him see Renate in a different light. She kept creeping into his mind as if to be judged over and over again by him; to test his reactions to the thought of her. Throughout the week his mood had been changeable – anger, bitterness, disbelief at her fickleness. He thought he knew her so well; clearly he did not. As the beer set to work, he realised he was better off without her. The innate trust that he had always assumed to be the backbone of their relationship was gone, there was no depth to his feeling any longer. His love for her was being washed away. A necessary cleansing process.

Without quite knowing how, Schneider found himself sitting at another table in some sort of club. The tables were arranged in a semi-circle around a small stage. Von Osten was being very familiar with the waitress who brought them beers. She was younger than Suzie. Having served their customers with drinks, some of the waitresses sat down at the tables and chatted intimately with them.

They were on their second round of drinks when a trio of musicians squeezed into a corner of the room next to the stage and sat behind their instruments; piano, saxophone, drums. The drummer played a roll on his snare and the lights around the stage burst into life.

"Cabaret time!" declared von Osten.

To the accompaniment of a doleful jazz number – appallingly played in Schneider's critical opinion – three girls appeared on stage and proceeded to perform a long and provocative striptease which had the men in the audience clapping vigorously as each garment hit the floor. The show was engrossing, so much so that Schneider didn't notice the young waitress take a seat next to him. He felt a hand rest softly on his leg, high up, and warm breath close to his ear.

"I'm Trudi. Do you like the show? All those naughty girls."

"Mosht enjoyable," slurred Schneider.

"Would you like to get to know one of them better – somewhere in private perhaps?"

"Thank you but no."

"How about me then?" She bit his ear gently and her hand slid up and down his leg. "Would you like to spend some time with me?"

"Very kind of you but I'm with my friend here."

"Oh Otto won't mind being left alone, will you Otto?"

Von Osten grinned. "Of course not. Might even join you."

This was all the encouragement the girl needed. "Come. The more the merrier."

Von Osten stood up and indicated that Schneider should follow. The girl took his hand and led them to the back of the room just as the striptease reached its climax in a flurry of interwoven female bodies. On the sidewall was a doorway hidden behind a floor length curtain. She ushered them through then down a narrow corridor that ran the length of the building and up a short flight of steps to the side of the stage. As they reached the wings, the girls were coming off stage, naked apart from high-heeled shoes.

"Hello," said one as she brushed past Schneider. A strong smell of perfume on a warm body filled his nostrils. "Are either of these for me?"

Von Osten replied: "My friend seems to have taken a liking for Trudi, so perhaps you would like to join us, to even up the numbers?"

"Good," said the stripper. "I'll see you in a moment."

The waitress led them into a room directly behind the stage, sparsely furnished apart from a huge bed and a chaise longue. Everything had happened rather too quickly for Schneider and he slumped onto the edge of the bed with a bemused look on his face.

"A moment pleash," he said to von Osten who was counting out banknotes to the girl. "I don't think I want to do thish."

"Of course you do. Don't worry about the money – this is on me."

"Not the money . . ."

"I understand – you've never been unfaithful to your wife and never been with a whore before."

"True – but not my point."

"Let yourself go, Erich, enjoy the moment. Your wife will never know. Anyway, by the time you see her again all this will be ancient history."

The stripper entered the room wearing a toweling robe and flung herself onto the bed. The waitress Trudi had taken off her blouse and skirt and was helping von Osten with the belt on his trousers. Schneider stood up and backed towards the wall. Von Osten was down to his underpants and Trudi was naked. The stripper stood up on the bed and let the robe fall away. She too was naked.

"Come on, Erich, it's only a bit of fun. Are you shy? Would you like to take Trudi into another room?"

Trudi turned towards him and smiled appealingly. Schneider shook his head and held a hand up to make it clear she should leave him alone.

"Not shy. Not interested."

Von Osten shrugged his shoulders. "Well they're both paid for. If you don't want them, I do. Stay and watch if you like – I don't care." He collapsed onto the bed, pulling Trudi on top of him and indicating for the stripper to join them.

This was too much for Schneider. Once again he would be watching others fornicating.

"I . . . I'll wait outshide." He made his way to the door and slammed it shut behind him. His head was swimming and he needed air. He felt disgusted by the whole situation.

The lights had gone off when the cabaret had finished and it was dark back stage. Schneider couldn't remember which way they had come. He stepped forward, feeling along the walls with his hands. All sense of direction had left him. He could see a glimmer of light but it seemed a long way ahead of him, probably coming from the door to the club. With this as a beacon he stepped forward, despite the darkness, heading straight for the small strip of light.

His left foot, stretched out in mid-stride, found nothing but empty space where the floor should have been. He hurtled down the invisible steps and felt a sharp stab of pain as his foot struck the floor and twisted under the weight of his body.

His head cracked hard against the wall. He slumped down in a heap, and the world faded into oblivion.

*

When Schneider awoke he was in the back of a car, slumped unceremoniously between von Osten and Trudi. As he came to, he felt pain in his ankle and groaned.

"Don't talk," said von Osten. "We're on our way back to the Klopstock. I'll have a doctor called to take a look at you. Nasty fall – you've got an impressive lump on your head."

"My ankle," moaned Schneider.

"Quiet, let a doctor sort you out. I don't think it's broken. Trudi here volunteered to come along and give you some tender loving care . . . when I'm done with her of course. We have some unfinished business – no thanks to you."

Between them they manhandled Schneider to his room. The night porter knew a doctor who lived in the next street and von Osten ran round to knock him up.

"You're in luck," the gruff doctor told Schneider as he examined the swollen ankle. "No break, only a sprain. I'll bind it up for you. A week or so without any pressure on it and you'll be fine." He took a cursory glance at Schneider's head. "That's nothing – just a bruise."

"A week without pressure on my foot? That's going to make a parachute jump difficult."

"Impossible," stated the doctor emphatically.

"What will happen now?"

Von Osten lit them both a cigarette. "That's for Dr Rantzau to sort out. I suppose they'll have to postpone the drop. There's nothing else they can do."

Schneider looked crestfallen.

"I don't think he's going to be very pleased with me."

Chapter 21

Alison Webb stepped down from the train, pulled a bulky hold-all out after her and slammed the compartment door firmly shut. The engine slowly pulled away into the darkness of the tunnel at the end of the platform in a shroud of steam and smoke, and she looked around at Sutton Coldfield Station.

Sandbags were stacked against the walls and on the hoardings were huge posters. One pronounced *DIG FOR VICTORY* in large lettering above a photograph of a spade being pushed forcefully into the ground, whilst another, slightly weather worn, announced *FREEDOM IS IN PERIL – DEFEND IT WITH ALL YOUR MIGHT*. But other than these obvious reminders that there was a war on, it was still the same rather ordinary Midland station she had seen a hundred times before; solid, reliable and never changing. A good place to come home to, she thought, and after two years on the other side of the world it felt good to be back.

She made her way up the long sloping walkway to the ticket barrier where her parents were waiting for her, as she knew they would be, craning their necks to catch a first glimpse, waving frantically until she reached the concourse and then swamping her with hugs and kisses.

"Hello Mum, hello Dad – how are you?"

"Oh Ally, it's so wonderful to see you!"

"It's wonderful to be home." She always said this, but had not always meant it in the past. This time the words were spoken with sincerity.

"Two years – it's been two years!"

"I know."

"Look at the colour of you . . . I've never seen such a tan."

"They have a lot of sunshine in Australia, Mum."

They piled into the car and Leonard Webb drove off in the direction of Four Oaks.

"You've lost weight. You haven't been ill and not told us in your letters, have you?"

"Of course not. I'm slim because I'm fit. What about you, Dad – that paunch looks a sight larger than I remember." She leaned over from the back seat and squeezed his side.

He laughed. "Thought I'd better stock up before rationing takes away all my worldly pleasures. Isn't that right, Iris?"

"I'm afraid so. He eats like a horse. Heaven knows where he puts it."

"I think I can see," said Alison. She squeezed him again. "Is rationing bad? I'm out of touch."

"Not bad – but it's going to get a lot worse, mark my words."

They turned off the main road onto a quiet side street and into the drive of a large detached property with a wooden garage to one side and wisteria covering most of the brickwork. Above the porch hung a circular wire basket containing plants that dangled down from every side. Alison wondered if her father would say and do what had made her laugh so as a little girl but gradually annoyed her to the point of distraction when repeated many times over the years. He did not disappoint her. As they approached the front door he bent low and said: "Mind your heads!"

Alison stopped dead. Her mother glanced anxiously between the two, ready to diffuse the situation with a flow of inane chit chat if necessary.

"Sorry, Ally," said her father sheepishly. "It just slipped out – in the excitement, you know. And I did sort of mean it this time, you having been away for such a long time." He hesitated. "I thought you might have forgotten."

Alison remained stone-faced for a moment. Poor old Dad, always saying the wrong thing. So good to see him. She grinned. He grinned back, and then they were laughing and hugging spontaneously.

The joke was that Leonard Webb, at five feet three inches tall, would have needed a step ladder to hit his head on the basket.

"You know, parents," announced Alison, throwing her jacket over the banisters in the hall, "it really is good to be home."

Chapter 22

Alison was twenty-eight years old. Unlike her father she was above medium height and in high-heeled shoes gave the impression of being quite tall. She had a good figure, thick brown hair, which she always wore short, and an oval face with a prominent bone structure. Without makeup she would have been in danger of looking gaunt were it not for two additional features of note; a perfect set of pearl-like teeth and large, clear hazel eyes.

She was not beautiful, but strikingly attractive. Her warmth of personality melted almost anyone she met, male and female alike, and her nature was so easy-going that it sometimes left her open to being taken advantage of by lesser members of the species; especially the males. Invariably she ended up the victim in love affairs. The last – the longest and most hurtful by far – had resulted in her escaping to the other side of the globe, there to experience a gradual recuperation with Lucas Kelly and his Crazy Fliers. A lost cause in love, but when it came to flying airplanes she was an unequivocal success. Kelly and the other pilots had treated her no differently for being a woman, and she had learnt fast out of necessity. She had gone to Australia a talented and keen amateur flyer, and returned to England a seasoned professional with a passion for airplanes welded finitely to her soul. Australia had been a baptism of fire and she had loved every minute. At the same time the scars of the dismal love affair had been purged from her system.

She smiled when she saw her old bedroom. Her parents always kept it exactly as it had been when she first left home to work in London eight years before. Apart from redecoration, they once told her, it would remain that way until she married and had a permanent home of her own. With her past record of romance, she mused, that was a long way off. The bedroom was at the rear of the house and looked out onto the garden, which was tidy and well kept with a neatly-mown lawn leading down to a privet hedge, and a vegetable garden beyond. Nothing had changed there either; apart from a strange mound of earth next to the cucumber frames.

Having unpacked and soaked her travel-weary body in a hot bath, she dressed and went downstairs for tea. It was a warm afternoon and they sat in the back garden under the shade of an apple tree, eating scones and sandwiches, drinking tea and talking as if there were no tomorrow. She told them of her journey home; a series of long commercial flights via Hong Kong, Egypt and Portugal. The last leg had been from Lisbon to Croydon, an aerodrome Alison knew well from pre-war days. The BOAC pilot had fluffed the landing and she cringed as the undercarriage raked into the turf. Kelly would have grounded her for that, she mused. Then a train to Victoria where there had been a great deal of activity. Red Cross units were setting up reception areas on the platforms, and military personnel were everywhere. Someone had told her that troops were trickling back from France and Belgium, but it seemed to her that such measures implied a good deal more than a trickle.

"I read a newspaper on the train," she said. "I didn't realise quite how serious things are. The Germans have gained an enormous amount of ground, haven't they?"

"I'm afraid so," sighed Leonard Webb. "They don't tell us half the story on the news, of course, or in the papers for that matter. He mimicked a newsreader's voice: *'Self-denial in the matter of news is the public's contribution to the outcome of this battle. This is John Snagge not telling you anything.'* But there's heavy fighting going on over there and we're not coming out on top. The Dutch have given in – the Belgians will be next, mark my words. We'll either end up being pushed back to the coast or retreating to the south."

"Surely it's not *that* bad," said Alison.

"I'm afraid it is. The King came on the wireless last night and announced that tomorrow is to be a Day of National Prayer. That means it's bad. We're going to lose Belgium, France and most of the British Expeditionary Force if we're not bloody careful."

Iris Webb frowned. "Excuse your father's language – it hasn't improved while you've been away. The poor French. We'll be next."

"Hitler wouldn't dare," said her husband. "Besides, he's only interested in mainland Europe. He won't cross the Channel, provided that warmonger Churchill doesn't antagonise him too much. I presume you know he's Prime Minister now, Ally. They replaced Chamberlain a couple of weeks ago, the fools. We're told he resigned but I'm convinced he was pushed. The one man who could negotiate a settlement to avoid anymore bloodshed and they get rid of him!"

"Why are you so sure Hitler won't want to invade England? Surely it's the obvious next step."

"Not possible. Nobody really believes we're going to be overrun by Nazis. There are enough sane people in Westminster who will pacify Hitler rather than meddle any further in Europe."

"Even so, your father's signed up with the LDV," said Mrs Webb. "He can't be that confident there won't be an invasion."

84

"It's only a precaution," grunted Leonard Webb.

"What is LDV?" asked Alison.

"Local Defence Volunteers. A couple of days after Churchill took over, they broadcast on the wireless for volunteers to come forward and help keep an eye out for parachutists. So I took the next morning off work and went along to the police station. You've never seen so many people! They were queuing right out into the street and round the block – hundreds of them." He took a quick sip of tea. "Eventually I registered my name and now I'm in a platoon based at the Town Hall. We patrol two nights a week, covering this side of the park and part of the town centre."

"They all take it very seriously," said Iris Webb. "The other day they arrested a postman doing his rounds."

"He shouldn't have been in the park at six o'clock in the morning! He was breaking the law."

"They've got a uniform too. A tin hat, and an armband with 'LDV' written on it. Armed with his old service revolver your father is enough to frighten any Nazi parachutist right out of his boots."

Alison giggled. "Ignore her, Dad. I think it's wonderful. At least you're doing something to help instead of sitting around listening to the news and worrying. I hope I can find something to do as well. I didn't come home to mope about."

Her father nodded. "I didn't think that for a minute. Judging by your letters it sounds as if you were having a ball in Australia, and ten thousand miles is a long way to come just to check on your aged parents."

"I couldn't have stayed any longer, knowing what was going on here. At first the papers said it would be over in a couple of months, by Christmas at the latest, so I didn't worry too much. When that didn't happen I began to get itchy feet. Then when I heard about Norway and Denmark being invaded that was the final straw. I had a few loose ends to tie up first, and here I am."

"I hope none of the loose ends were too upset about that."

"Nothing of a romantic nature, if that's what you mean."

"And what about loose ends you left behind here two years ago?" asked Iris Webb.

"You mean Jan-Arne? Oh I am cured of that unpleasant affliction, thank you. I wouldn't have missed going to Australia for anything – and I'm grateful to him for giving me the incentive. If I ever see him again I must remember to thank him."

Leonard Webb grunted his disapproval; he still had a long way to go before he could joke about the man who had treated his daughter so despicably. He decided a change of conversation was necessary.

"If you've finished your tea, Ally, how about inspecting the Anderson shelter? It's at the bottom of the garden."

"Alright, parent. What's an Anderson shelter?"

"Oh dear, what a lot about this war you have to learn, child. Let me enlighten you."

Beyond the lawn was a neatly trimmed privet hedge with a gap to one side. They stepped through into the vegetable garden – roughly the size of half a tennis court – and past neat rows of potatoes, onions, tomatoes and runner beans. In the far corner was a low, arch-shaped hut made of corrugated iron, with sandbags around the entrance and along the sides. The roof was covered with earth. Alison had never seen anything quite like it; rather like a huge dog kennel. As they got closer she saw that it was sunk into the ground and larger than it had first appeared. She stood at the entrance and peered inside at two wooden beds, a stove, a tiny cupboard and an oil lamp hanging from a hook. It looked grim. They made their way inside.

"Guaranteed bomb-resistant and excellent for dinner parties," declared Leonard Webb proudly. "I think an estate agent would describe it as compact and in need of some modernisation."

"I'd call it pokey and very basic – have you actually spent the night in here yet?"

"Once . . . as a trial run. Hopefully we won't have to use it at all. I'll squeeze another bed in here for you, just in case."

Alison sat on the edge of one of the beds; it was lumpy and very uncomfortable. "Don't trouble yourself on my account."

They talked for a while about the possibility of air raids and various other related topics. Then Alison asked: "Dad, do you know if they are looking for pilots – women pilots, I mean?"

"Who?'

"Anyone."

"I was hoping you wouldn't ask me that question. Your mother and I had our fingers crossed that you would want to settle down a little, now you're back home."

"You mean go back to being a shop assistant? Never in a million years, Dad. I broke away from drudgery when I started to earn a living from flying. I could never go back to it now."

"Not necessarily shop work. There are all sorts of options opening up now with war work."

"Driving a bus ... making gas masks?"

"I was thinking more of clerical jobs – secretarial, administrative. Plenty of opportunities around here, so you wouldn't have to go to London again."

Alison eyed her father knowingly. "You mean nice safe jobs, where if you make a mistake you simply have to retype something rather than tumble perilously from five thousand feet."

"I wouldn't put it quite like that, Ally, but that's the gist of it."

She squeezed his arm. "Sorry to disappoint you, but if I learned anything in Australia it's that flying means more to me than anything in the world. It's not just a way of earning a living for me – it's a passion. It always has been, I suppose, ever since you bought me a flying lesson for my eighteenth birthday. So it's all your fault, Dad. When I got my commercial 'B' licence, it was the proudest day of my life. After Jan-Arne, I clung to flying like someone drowning clings to a raft. Flying was an escape from all that unhappiness."

"That bloody Norwegian has a great deal to answer for."

"Dad, it's all ancient history now. As far as I'm concerned Margery Ashford-Hope is welcome to him. But going back to flying, after two years of performing stunts I'm totally addicted. It really is flying or nothing for me."

Leonard Webb listened with complete understanding. He knew only too well how a passion for something can take hold of you. He had felt the same about medicine as a young man. The more he learnt about the subject the more he knew that only one career would satisfy him. After thirty years as a GP he had never once regretted his choice.

"There's the WAAFs of course."

"Yes, I heard about them. They started up last year I believe. I don't know if that's for me – might still be a nice comfy office job only in uniform. I was hoping for something less formal – civilian even. To be honest I don't know what's available. I'd be fine for a stunt flying group."

Her father moved towards the entrance of the shelter. "Don't go away – I'll be back in a jiffy." He disappeared up the steps but was back within minutes. In his hand was a folder containing a number of clippings from newspapers and magazines. "Here, I think these might interest you. I saved them for you . . . but for goodness sake don't tell your mother. If she finds out, I'll get 'the look'."

Alison took the clippings and started to read the first one. It was from the *Daily Mail* and dated the previous December:

WOMEN TO FERRY R.A.F. 'PLANES
By Daily Mail *Reporter*

Nine women, the first of a team of women pilots who will "ferry" new R.A.F. planes from factory to aerodrome, beginning next January, were selected yesterday. Miss Pauline Gower, 27 years-old daughter of Sir Robert Gower, M.P., and the first woman to hold an "A" and "B" licence, is on the selection committee. She told me: "The women are experienced pilots. I should think that their average flying hours

must be about a thousand. Their average age? Somewhere about 30.
The aim of the scheme is to release men pilots for active service."

The article went on to name the women and gave a brief biography of each. Another, from *The Sketch*, was dated January 17th 1940 and included head and shoulders photographs of all the women, wearing dark uniforms and fore-and-aft caps. There were also some very unflattering shots of a few wearing bulky flying suits and seat parachutes, which hung low like jaded bustles.

WE TAKE OFF OUR HATS TO – THESE PILOTS OF THE AIR TRANSPORT AUXILIARY,

For being the first women ferry pilots for R.A.F. machines.
Women last week made history in the youngest Service, for the first delivery flights of airplanes from factory to storage depot, "somewhere in Great Britain", were carried out by the Women's transport section of the Air Transport Auxiliary. There are ten members of this body, which is managed for the Air Ministry by British Airways. Miss Pauline Gower is the First Officer and has nine Second Officers under her – all women pilots of daring, skill and experience. They receive salary and flight pay, and wear dark blue uniform with special A.T.A. wings. When flying they don Sidcot suits, Sutton harnesses, and seat parachutes.

Alison pointed at the photograph. "Good heavens, I know most of these girls!" she exclaimed. "That's Susan Wharrad . . . and those two are the Northam sisters." She scanned the row of faces. "And look, it's Heather – Heather Norbury! She's an old friend. We used to fly together at Hendon. A splendid pilot."

"As good as you?"

"Hardly!" Not an arrogant remark, Leonard Webb knew, simply a statement of fact. Alison reread the piece, pointing to other faces as she did so. "I know her too. We met at Croydon several times. And her . . . one of the best female pilots in the country." She lifted her head from the article. "This is for me, Dad. I want to join the Air Transport Auxiliary. It's perfect, just what I was hoping would turn up. But I never imagined it would happen so soon."

"Don't count your chickens before they're hatched," said her father. "Who's to say they need more women pilots. Perhaps they won't be recruiting any further."

"Don't be silly. They will want as many good pilots as they can find."

"They might not accept you."

She pulled a face. "Parent, if they took Heather Norbury they will take me. I have well over a thousand flying hours logged. Of course they'll accept me." She couldn't sit still and started pacing up and down. "How do I go about it, I wonder . . . do you think I ought to phone someone, and if so who? The RAF – or British Airways? Perhaps I should telephone and see if I can talk to someone."

"Not on a Saturday afternoon you won't," said Leonard Webb. "Calm yourself down until Monday and start thinking about it then. Meanwhile, relax and spend a bit of time with your old folks. After all, we haven't seen you for two years."

Alison sighed. "Sorry, Dad. Yes, of course."

"And there's your mother to break the news to . . . which is not an inconsiderable hurdle, as you can imagine." He stood up. "Come on, let's see what she's up to. My guess is she's scouring the Sutton News for local secretarial jobs."

Chapter 23

(Sunday 26th May 1940)

"Canaris had no choice," sighed Herbert Wichmann. "He had to inform Göring." Nikolaus Ritter was by his side as they walked along the quayside in the early afternoon sun. The docks were surprisingly busy for a Sunday, mostly citizens of Hamburg out for an after dinner stroll. "He's furious."

"I'm not surprised. Where did you catch up with him?"

"On *Asia*. It's sitting in a siding next to the Führer's carriage on the Belgian border." *Asia* was Göring's own private train and the mobile headquarters for the *Luftwaffe* when the Field Marshal was in residence. "He has ordered that under no circumstances must the operation be delayed and has wired a contingency plan via Canaris. Here, read it for yourself." Wichmann took a teleprinted sheet from his pocket.

Nikolaus Ritter scanned the page, then looked up in disbelief.

"The first part makes sense. Drop von Osten in tonight as planned – that's what I assumed we would do. But as for Schneider . . . it's a ridiculous idea!"

"My reaction initially," agreed Wichmann. "But perhaps not as ridiculous as it first appears. There are tens of thousands of British troops in disarray, retreating towards the English Channel. The British are bound to try and uplift as many as possible before they are finished off on the beaches. Göring is arguing that if we dump Schneider as close as possible to the front, chances are he'll get swept up in the retreat. The Royal Navy will carry him across to England for us. One amongst so many. It could just work."

Ritter was almost speechless. "But surely, the number of men they can evacuate will be infinitesimal compared to the number that are either going to surrender or be killed. And they must surrender, otherwise there will be one hell of a massacre."

"That's true," said Wichmann, "and the chances are slim. But the word is that the Panzer divisions have been halted since Friday. They're exhausted and need time to prepare for any further advance. Göring has promised that it will be the *Luftwaffe*'s role to finish off the British Expeditionary Force. But they too need breathing space – their losses in Holland and Belgium have been significant. The British will take advantage of this lull to save as many men as they can. If we act quickly I think we can get Schneider across. At least we can try. Let's face it, there is no way he can parachute in."

"It's madness. It will never work."

"Do you have a better plan – that doesn't involve waiting weeks until Schneider's ankle has healed?"

"The stupid bloody fool. If he'd stayed in his room none of this would have happened."

Wichmann had no time for such recriminations. "Well he didn't and it *has* happened. Whether Göring's plan is madness or not, that is our order and it's our job to carry it out."

"Göring is suggesting we plant Schneider in the very place that currently tops the *Luftwaffe*'s list of priority bombing targets."

"We must do as we are bid. Arrange to have Schneider transported to the front line as soon as possible – before it's too late."

*

Admiral Canaris kept a cot in his office and had slept in the Tirpitzufer building regularly in recent weeks. When the message had arrived from *Hamburg* that one of the Spitfire agents was injured, he was there to arrange the communication with Göring in person. His reaction to the response had been equally incredulous; the idea was seemingly ridiculous. His main objection was on moral grounds. Sending an immobilised agent to the front was wrong, and his chances of coming through it alive virtually non-existent. Even if they could get Schneider to the Belgian or French coast he was more likely to end up a prisoner of the *Wehrmacht* than to find safe passage back to England. It seemed more like a vindictive punishment.

Canaris glanced at his clock. Six. He would phone Wichmann then go home and spend a well-deserved evening with his family; he suspected he would be seeing even less of them in the coming months. There were *Abwehr* stations to set up across the newly occupied territories, an area that seemed to be expanding by the day, which would mean a great deal of travelling around mainland Europe.

When he heard Wichmann answer, Canaris pressed the scrambler button on his phone and a green bulb lit up to indicate the line was secure. Even so, both knew to keep the dialogue as guarded as possible.

"Herbert, did you get the information you needed?"

"Yes thank you. Everything is fully understood and is being actioned. The first consignment – the undamaged one – has left for transportation as originally planned and will be delivered on time. The special requirements for the second are being looked into."

"Has Johnny been told of the change of plan?"

"Not yet. I'll inform him that the delivery has been reduced to one item. He need not know anything more for the time being – the second might not arrive at all. I am trying not to involve him directly. He failed to make a 'treff' last week. Our friend the doctor went to the trouble of sailing into the middle of the North Sea to meet with him, and he did not show. Until we find out precisely what went wrong I shall remain cautious."

"Don't you trust him?"

"I just want to be reassured."

"Very well. Tell me, do you think our chief's idea will work?"

"I think waiting until the second item is in a better condition to travel would be preferable."

"He won't have it."

"We shall do our best. I think it might work, although this view is not shared by everyone."

"The doctor?"

"The doctor."

"Make the best arrangements you can, Herbert, and keep me informed. In particular try and see that the two consignments are reunited on arrival."

"I shall see to it, sir."

"Any news of our Irish connection?" A reference to Hermann Görtz.

"Not a word since delivery three weeks ago. I think we have to assume the worst."

"Good night, Herbert."

"Good night, sir."

Canaris hastily donned his coat and glanced around the office. Everything else would have to wait until morning. By then there would be one more *Abwehr* agent in place in England. He wondered how long he would last.

Longer than Görtz hopefully.

Chapter 24

The service at Holy Trinity Parish Church that morning was a sombre affair; an extended service incorporated special prayers for the troops across the Channel and long silences for individuals who wished to pray privately for loved ones. It was clear from the ashen expressions on the faces of some of the congregation that they had relatives in danger and feared for their safety. Alison, seated in a pew with mother and father on either side of her, was deeply moved, and she returned for Evensong; the first time she had been to church twice in one day in her life.

That evening she sat with her parents and listened to the news, although there was little to hear under the circumstances.

The newsreader said: *"Everyone in this country is waiting – many are waiting with great personal anxiety – for news of our men in France. So is the enemy; and the giving of news at this moment might cost the lives of men. No one in this country would want to obtain news at the price of a single British or French or Belgian life. We must all wait patiently and confidently until the news can be given to us with safety."*

Chapter 25

(Monday 27ᵗʰ May 1940)

The Heinkel III was painted all black, with no insignia or markings. Inside the fuselage the noise was deafening beyond belief, or so it seemed to Otto von Osten as he sat huddled behind the pilot's position. It was cold too, bitterly cold, despite the thickly padded flying suit he wore over his civilian clothes. Glory be to the man who invented pocket flasks, he reflected, as he took one of many sips from the silver container tucked in his gloved hand.

Despite the discomfort, von Osten felt magnificent. At last he was on his way. The past few months had been a period of preparation; now the action was about to begin. His mind was lucid and alert, his reactions sharp. Not just the effects of excess adrenalin in his system; the *Abwehr* gave agents an injection of Benzedrine before a mission. He was warned that although he would feel on top of the world for twenty-four hours, extreme tiredness would kick in afterwards. He should be in a secure place by then and lie low until his metabolism was back to normal.

Beside him were the radio suitcase and hand grip containing other equipment, his papers and some clothes. They were to be dropped on a separate parachute. If he chose to he could lean slightly forward and see right through the plane's fishbowl-like nose, but he wasn't much interested. There wasn't a great deal to see, mostly blackness.

He shivered violently and peered at the luminous dial of his watch. Almost 3.30am.

It was two hours since they had taken off from Hamburg, and a direct course would have seen them approaching the English Channel by now. But the pilot, Captain Gartenfeld, had explained that the skies over Belgium and Holland weren't the safest place these days, so he would fly over Denmark, approaching East Anglia from the north-east. His brief was to deliver his cargo safely, not to pick a fight with the RAF.

Shortly before takeoff, Dr Rantzau had lied to von Osten, telling him it was now a one-man mission and he was on his own. Before this had sunk in, von Osten found himself in the back of a truck with his belongings, heading towards the aerodrome. Schneider had been moved out of the Klopstock that afternoon and there had been no opportunity for goodbyes. Rantzau's lie was only temporary. Once von Osten was in place, he would be told to expect Schneider after all, if providence allowed. He presumed his friend was now lounging in a hospital somewhere, recuperating in readiness for another mission.

He was nervous at the pre-flight briefing when it came to discussing the precise location of the drop. Without his *Abwehr* controllers to interfere, he had a suggestion to make and was worried that it might be taken as a breach of orders. Never having met the pilot before, he was unable to predict how he might react.

"You see," explained von Osten as they studied a map, "they want you to drop me around here." He stabbed a finger at the area to the north west of Great Yarmouth. "I know the area from before the war – there are lakes and rivers all over the place." His finger moved to the left and down slightly. "Whereas here, in the region around Ely . . . look, there are many kilometres of open countryside, and no water. Far more chance there of a dry landing."

Gartenfeld listened intently. "That would mean flying further inland," he pointed out.

"I appreciate that, but there is another reason. I know the area very well. I used to have friends in Cambridge and we used to cycle all around the Fens at weekends. I will be able to get my bearings much quicker there and so reach the safety of London sooner."

This was enough to convince Gartenfeld. It was obvious to him that this agent knew more about the drop area than his controllers. A few more minutes over England were, to him, neither here nor there. Between them they agreed on a new target reference point; a stretch of open land several miles north of Ely called Burnt Fen, bordered on the left by the A10, the King's Lynn road.

"I cannot promise to hit it exactly," warned Gartenfeld, "however I will have a damned good stab at it. Much depends on the weather . . . but the forecast is promising."

*

The co-pilot held both his gloved hands up with fingers outstretched, indicating they should be reaching the drop point in approximately ten minutes.

Von Osten checked that the suitcase and grip were firmly secured to their parachute and carried them to the hatch. When it was opened, a blast of air roared through the fuselage, rocking the aircraft slightly.

A hand appeared in front of von Osten's face. Five minutes.

As he peered downwards from the plane's belly his eyes adjusted to the gloom and the ground was just visible several thousand feet below. An occasional bank of cloud obscured his view, but mostly the moonlit countryside stretched out like a map etched upon black parchment. The clear visibility was making the navigator's task easier; he was able to plot their position precisely. Captain Gartenfeld had recommended that he bring the Heinkel in over the huge square inlet known as The Wash and fly due south, bypassing King's Lynn to the west and following the A10. When the drop was over they would bank sharply to the east and reach the coast over Lowestoft. All being well, they'd be back in Germany for an early breakfast.

Downham Market floated past beneath.

One finger. A minute to go.

Von Osten braced himself at the edge of the hatch. He could see that Gartenfeld had made a gradual descent and the ground looked closer now. They were following a road that meandered in a series of gentle curves through flat countryside boasting few, if any, distinguishing features. The road veered off to the right, but the Heinkel continued on a straight course, across open fields.

Von Osten felt a hard smack on his back. He crouched forward and launched himself through the hatch. The shock of the slipstream made him catch his breath as he tumbled through the air, rocking backwards and forwards and momentarily losing all sense of direction. He snatched instinctively at his ripcord and felt a violent jolt as the parachute deployed. Out of the corner of his eye he could see the other parachute gliding gently to earth.

His landing was rough but he came through it without serious injury, nothing more than a gash to the side of his forehead. Ten minutes later he was burying both parachutes under a thick gorse hedge and dabbing his head with a handkerchief. Other than that, both he and the equipment appeared unharmed.

He sat down on the grassy bank beneath the hedge, pulled out a packet of cigarettes and lit one contentedly. Captain Gartenfeld had done him proud. He was sitting on the southern edge of Burnt Fen.

An obliging chap, Gartenfeld, thought von Osten, smiling to himself as he inhaled some smoke. Without his cooperation he would not be within striking distance of Cambridge; and in Cambridge there lived an attractive widow called Audrey he had not seen for nearly a year.

"You see, Gartenfeld," he said to himself, addressing a man now halfway across the North Sea, "the thing I object to most about Norfolk is that I don't know any women there."

*

It was almost light when the four men abandoned their vigil. The flat Norfolk countryside was clearly visible as the pinkish orange glow of sunrise lit up the sky from the direction of the coast.

"He won't be coming now."

"Perhaps it was postponed at the last minute."

"They wouldn't cancel a drop on a night like this. Conditions were perfect."

"Then we've been misinformed."

"I don't think so. It's been too precise and accurate all along. First a double drop, then down to one. Why bother with all that nonsense if it was a bluff? Plus, the detailed location information."

"What the bloody hell is going on then?"

"I don't know. I just don't know."

"Come on, let's drive into Norwich and get some breakfast."

The only sound they had heard all night was the faintest hum of an aircraft about an hour before. But it was way to the south and heading out to sea. Probably something to do with Coastal Command.

They tumbled despondently into their car and set off as fast as the thin slit in the headlamp covers and the coming dawn would allow.

Chapter 26

Shortly before noon Alison went into town with her mother where she requested, and after considerable delay received, an identity card from the Town Hall and ration books from the local Food Office. She then registered with various shops for her food rations.

In the afternoon she was on the telephone, but not to British Airways. Heather Norbury was also from the Midlands and Alison had scoured the pages of old diaries for her parents' address in Warwick. Eventually she found it under July 1937 with a scribbled note saying: *Heather crashed, fractured arm and leg, poor dear. Home to recuperate.* She had botched a landing, overshot the airfield, ploughed into a hedge and spent the rest of the summer lounging around at home, bored silly. Alison had meant to visit her, but at that time she was madly in love with Jan-Arne and everything else seemed to have been eclipsed by him. Keeping up with friendships had gone by the wayside.

That was three years ago; the Norburys might have moved away by now for all Alison knew. She dialed the number and crossed her fingers. After several rings a woman answered.

"Is that Mrs Norbury?"

"Speaking."

"This is Alison Webb here. We haven't met, but I'm an old friend of Heather's. We used to fly together."

There was a moment's silence at the other end of the line. "Oh yes, I've heard her mention you. Aren't you the one who ran off to Australia to join the circus?"

"Sort of – it was a flying circus. I was there for two years and arrived home at the weekend. Actually I was wondering how I might get hold of Heather. It's been ages since we saw each other and I'd love catch up."

Mrs Norbury explained about Heather joining the Air Transport Auxiliary and Alison mentioned having seen the newspaper reports. "You must be very proud of her," she said.

"We are, very proud indeed. Well, Alison, you are in luck . . . Heather is coming home tomorrow for forty-eight hours' leave. You can call her here if you like. Where are you now?"

"Staying with my parents in Sutton Coldfield."

"My dear girl, not far at all – why not pop over and see her, I'm sure she would be thrilled. She hasn't got a young man at present, which is presumably why she's coming home for a change!"

"Oh thank you," said Alison. "I'd love to."

"She's based at Hatfield and will probably deliver a plane to Cowley, where she keeps her car, then drive the rest of the way home. She should be here in time for dinner. Why not be here to surprise her – you can stay the night if you wish."

"Well if that's not too much trouble. It's awfully good of you. I'd very much like that."

"Good, that's arranged then. Here's the address . . . ready?"

That evening there was some news on the wireless, and it was depressing. The Germans had captured the port of Boulogne, whilst the British Expeditionary Force was being pushed rapidly back towards the coast. It was beginning to sound as though the very targets of the retreating forces were already in enemy hands.

Leonard Webb consulted his atlas. "They must be heading for Calais or Dunkirk," he surmised. "There's nowhere else left for them to go."

They went to bed with heavy hearts.

Chapter 27

When the plan was outlined to him, Erich Schneider knew immediately that his wellbeing was of no real consequence. As Dr Rantzau was honest enough to admit, not so much an ingenious contingency plan as a punishment for being fool enough to mess up a strategy sanctioned personally by Field Marshal Hermann Göring.

This was the first Schneider knew of how high the authority for the mission went. Dr Rantzau should not have divulged such a thing, he knew. "I am telling you this," he was saying in effect, "because I don't believe you will come out of it alive. So what the hell." Rantzau gave him instructions with as much enthusiasm as he could muster, though it was impossible to hide the hollowness in his tone. Get across the English Channel any way he can; then take a train to London and von Osten will be waiting for him, in the buffet at Victoria Station. He would wait for him at certain times – which Rantzau told Schneider to memorise – for the next few days.

It sounded so easy.

As Schneider was hoisted down from a Junkers Ju 52 hospital plane onto the grass of a tiny airfield after an uncomfortable flight from Hamburg, he didn't believe for one minute that he would make the appointment with von Osten. Soon he would be in the front line of fighting, and from what he gleaned from the flight crew, who seemed very well informed, the fighting was extremely fierce. The Tommies may be in full retreat but they were resisting to the end and causing high casualties amongst German infantry divisions. The hospital planes were at full stretch ferrying the wounded home.

Placing the crutches he had been issued with under his arms, and somehow holding on to his only piece of luggage, the suitcase containing his *Afu* radio, Schneider limped his way to the wooden huts at the edge of the airfield. He presumed he was somewhere in northern France, though he had no idea where. It was late afternoon and a grey blanket of cloud covered the sky. A few spots of rain were falling and it looked as though there was more to come. A young man wearing *Wehrmacht* uniform approached him.

"Schneider? I have been instructed to escort you to a billet for the night. Follow me."

They had to walk through one of the sheds to leave the aerodrome. It was crowded with stretcher cases, waiting to board the Ju 52 for the flight home. Their injuries varied from seemingly mild head wounds to missing limbs. Were they the lucky or the unlucky ones, Schneider wondered?

The car journey was brief, a matter of minutes, and they were soon entering a small village. The roads were crowded with people, a scattering of civilians but mainly soldiers, moving in all directions on motorcycles, in armoured cars and on foot. An occasional ominous deep rumble indicated that tanks were not far away, though Schneider did not see any. A crowd of dust seemed to shroud the town as wheels churned up the earth. The oncoming rain would be a mixed blessing; the dust would settle, but in its place would be mud.

"Where the hell are we?" Schneider asked.

His escort half turned as he drove. "Norrent-Fontes – roughly halfway between Bethune and St Omer." It meant nothing to Schneider. He had heard of St Omer but that was all.

"How far are we from the front line?"

The driver shrugged. "Who knows! We're advancing so quickly it's hard to tell. Some say there is no longer a front – our Panzers are ploughing through leaving the enemy behind for others to mop up. It's the same further north with the Belgians. Sometimes the line can be in several places at once. I'd say the only real front line remaining is around Dunkirk. They are becoming trapped there like rats in a barrel."

"And how far are we from Dunkirk?"

"Seventy kilometres – maybe less."

The driver pulled the car up outside a *pension* and helped Schneider slide out from the back seat. Inside the front door sat an elderly man and woman who struggled to their feet when they saw the driver's uniform. There was fear in their faces and they were clearly bewildered by what was happening to their lives.

"Here is your new guest," barked the soldier. "He will be staying for one night only. Make him as comfortable as possible. As you can see, he is wounded."

The old man cowered slightly, smiled at Schneider and nodded towards the staircase. He offered to support Schneider as he approached the stairs, but instead Schneider handed him the crutches and hopped up a step at a time, grasping the banister with both hands.

"You will be collected tomorrow morning at zero six hundred hours," called the soldier. "They will take care of you until then. I recommend sleeping as much as possible. You are going to need it."

Schneider turned on the stairs to acknowledge the advice, but the soldier was gone.

In his room, Schneider collapsed on the bed. His ankle was throbbing painfully but the mattress was soft and he immediately relaxed into it. Within moments the noise of men and machines in the street were a faint buzz. There had been no Benzedrine shot for him and the anxiety of what lay ahead had drained him.

Sometime later he was woken by the old man who had brought a tray of food; meat broth with half a baguette and a glass of wine. He thanked the man and swallowed the meal hungrily. Soon afterwards he was asleep again.

Chapter 28

(Tuesday 28th May 1940)

Alison borrowed her father's car, an Austin 7, and after lunch set off towards Warwick, using Dr Webb's supplementary petrol ration.

"Take them," said her father, handing over the coupons. "I cycle almost everywhere. Use them up before things get even tighter."

She drove through Sutton Park; it looked beautifully green at this time of year, the grass lush and deep and the trees in full leaf. She reached the far side of the park and drove out through the gates, turning onto the Chester Road. Several miles on she came to a junction, the other side of which she slowed down to a snail's pace and peered to her left. A line of trees partly obscured her view, but between them she could see the familiar buildings of Castle Bromwich aerodrome; the small hangars, the control tower, the Midlands Aero Club hut, and between them the open space of the airfield itself. She knew it well. Whenever she had flown home before the war she would land there, and her parents drove over to meet her. She parked her plane – a Miles Hawk Major – at the flying club. They didn't mind, especially the club secretary, Arthur, who was totally infatuated by this mysterious young woman who came and went but never stayed around for long. Every time he saw her, he asked her out but the answer was always a polite refusal. Typically, Alison would land at the aerodrome, pop her head into the clubroom and say: "Hello Arthur darling, mind if I leave my plane here for a day or so? Oh and thanks but no thanks – got a lot on while I'm here." Arthur adored her no less for it.

As the car crawled along Alison was astounded to see the vast factory complex that had mushroomed on the other side of the road. They hadn't even started building it when she left for Australia. She couldn't believe the enormity of the finished plant. As she drove past the main gates she could see down a long avenue with giant hangar-like buildings on either side, and a covered walkway between the two. She thought about pulling over to see if Arthur was still around at the flying club, then decided against it and drove on. She wanted to be sure of being at the Norburys' before Heather.

As it happened she very nearly didn't make it in time. Every few miles, or so it seemed, she was halted by makeshift roadblocks. Approaching the first one she saw it was manned by elderly civilians. When she drew closer she noticed their armbands inscribed with the letters LDV.

They wanted to see her identity card. Where was she going? Where had she been? Had she seen any suspicious activity anywhere along the way? Was her journey of national importance? The last question annoyed her and each time she told a different story; she was going for a job interview at a factory; she was collecting urgent medical supplies for her father – anything that came into her head. They were suspicious of everyone and everything. Invariably she heard the same words at every stop: "You can't be too careful. There may be fifth columnists anywhere you know."

She began to respect just how seriously the threat of invasion was being taken. Her father's view, that Hitler would never cross the English Channel, appeared to be in the minority. She admired the LDV's vigilance, at least for a while; the first roadblock was praiseworthy, the second tolerable, but the third and fourth were plain annoying.

Eventually she reached the Norburys' house, a detached, Georgian-style building set in about two acres on the edge of the town. Very impressive, she thought. As she pulled up the drive, a smartly dressed, middle-aged lady stepped from the porch to greet her.

"What a journey!" gasped Alison as she followed Mrs Norbury into the house. "I rather feel like the most suspicious, shifty-eyed person in the country."

Mrs Norbury laughed as she took Alison's bag. "Obviously you have encountered the LDV! You need a G and T." From the spacious hallway they entered an even more spacious lounge and Alison sank gratefully into an armchair. She was soon sipping the largest gin and tonic she had ever seen.

"Reginald, my husband, is upstairs changing," said Mrs Norbury, "and Heather is due home in about an hour. She telephoned from Cowley a while ago to say she's on her way, so you've only just beaten her. I haven't said anything about your being here. If you wait until she arrives you can freshen up together."

They chatted about the situation in France and speculated as to what was really going on. If the army were being routed would there really be an invasion? It was too awful to imagine. Mrs Norbury asked about Australia, and how Alison had met Heather. What flying had they done together, where, and whom else did they know in common? Alison got the distinct impression that Heather was not too forthcoming at home about her social life. As far as Alison remembered, it was probably just as well. Heather was not exactly a candidate for a Vestal Virgin.

After a while Mr Norbury joined them, a jovial man of about fifty, tall with a ruddy complexion and almost completely bald. The sound of a car in the driveway had them heading for the front door. Heather ran up to the porch to greet her parents. She was as tall as her father, slim with blonde curly hair, pretty and looking very feminine in a light summer skirt and blouse. Anyone would have been forgiven for not believing she had just piloted an aircraft across the south of England.

"Mummy, Daddy, hello," she cried. "Hope I haven't held up dinner."

"Not at all. We have a surprise for you."

Alison stepped forward from the hallway. Heather's face broke into beams of delight. "Ally – Ally Webb! You're back! Oh good heavens, what on earth are you doing here!"

"Hello Heather darling, I thought I'd spoil your day."

"You must be joking, you've *made* my day! Wonderful to see you." They strolled into the house arm in arm and hurried upstairs to change, chatting incessantly about everything imaginable.

Dinner was a jolly occasion and temporarily blocked out the severity of the situation in France and Belgium. A bottle of wine followed by port and liqueurs helped no end and Mr Norbury – who was a barrister, Alison discovered – was only too happy to replenish glasses as fast as they were emptied. At nine o'clock he switched on the wireless and there was silence as the broadcaster spoke the headlines of the news.

"Belgian capitulation took place at an early hour this morning . . .

The situation which the British Expeditionary Force finds itself in is one of extreme gravity . . . Part of the BEF is being provisioned through Dunkirk."

Reality came flooding back and suddenly no one felt jolly any longer. Later, when Mr and Mrs Norbury had gone to bed, Heather and Alison sat alone together in the lounge, sipping their drinks and mulling over old times, the friends they had known and the fun they had had together. When she felt the moment was right, Alison turned the conversation round to what had been on her mind all evening, the Air Transport Auxiliary. As Heather was telling her all about it, talking rapidly and with passionate enthusiasm about the recruitment, the training, the jobs, the planes, the other girls, Alison couldn't hold back any longer.

"Heather, do you think they would have me? I really have to fly, and it seems just the thing. Are they taking on more people?" She was worried Heather might feel she was taking advantage of their friendship, but as it turned out Heather didn't see it that way at all.

"It's a wonderful idea, Ally. They're taking on people right now and they'd be crazy not to have you. You're one of the best pilots I know. Every bit as good as Amy Johnson."

"I wouldn't quite go that far!"

"Did you know we're based at Hatfield?"

"Yes, your mother told me. Are you anything to do with the de Havilland factory? That's in Hatfield isn't it?"

"That's right. They make Tiger Moths there and we fly them off for storage; usually in the remotest depths of Scotland or Wales. By the way, talking of Amy Johnson, she's one of us now."

"No, really?"

"Joined earlier this month. So did Grace Brown, you know, who flew in the last war. Amy had been doing Army Cooperation work flying out of Cardiff, and Grace was ferrying medical supplies over for the troops in France. Now they're both with the ATA at Hatfield. And you'll never guess what the brass did, Ally – they made them pass an elementary flight test in a Tiger Moth!"

"Damn cheek," said Alison, truly shocked. "That's like asking Einstein to sit a school exam in physics."

"They'll make you do it too." Heather giggled. "Do you think you can handle it?"

"Only if the test includes trick stuff – you know, loops and low flying. I've been doing all that for so long now I'll have real trouble flying in a straight line."

"In that case you'll fail. It's one circuit round the aerodrome to see if you can avoid all the buildings and land the right way up."

"Oh well, it was a nice thought. Better start looking for an office job."

"Seriously, Ally, they'll snap you up. Shall I speak to Pauline Gower on your behalf? She's in charge of the women's ferry pool. You know her don't you?"

"We met a few times, but I don't know her terribly well."

"She'll remember you. She'll certainly know you by reputation as a pilot." Heather's tone changed to one of caution. "Mind you, the work isn't terribly exciting – we're only flying Moths. The men don't trust us with anything else. They really don't. We could have done a huge amount of important work ferrying Hurricanes over to France during the past few weeks, but they won't let us near them. Instead they've been sending men with virtually no experience, bloody awful pilots some of them. Some of the girls have been really frustrated about it, me included."

The warning had no effect on Alison. "I don't care. It's flying – that's all that matters."

"A lot of the ferrying is up to Scotland – Lossiemouth, Kinloss, and Perth – those sorts of places. It means a pretty long train journey back if there are no lifts going. That's no fun at all."

Alison didn't really take this in, she was too excited at the prospect of getting back into the air again. "Heather, I don't care. Will you do it for me – will you speak to Pauline?"

Heather picked up her liqueur glass and raised it to her lips. "As soon as I get back, promise. Now . . . on to more important matters. Have you got a boyfriend?"

"Give me a chance! I've only been back in the country a couple of days. Have you?"

"No, but I'm looking."

"You never stop looking – even when you're madly in love with someone."

"I do have that tendency. Tell me about Australian men. Are they all strong, muscular and tanned? I bet they make wonderful lovers."

"Sorry to disappoint you," sighed Alison. "I never got the chance to find out. I led a very celibate life over there. One man took a fancy to me, but I wasn't interested."

"I can't say the same," murmured Heather. She watched her friend staring thoughtfully into her glass. "Was it because of Jan-Arne Krobol that you went away?"

"Yes. I needed to get far away to sort myself out, and to get him out of my system. And you'll be pleased to know that it worked. I'm back to my old self. But it was hard – I was as low as anything for a long time. I've been off men. I prefer airplanes . . . they let you down gently."

Heather chuckled. "Depends who's at the controls."

"Have you seen Jan-Arne?" asked Alison. Heather didn't reply. "It's alright, I honestly have no feelings about him anymore. You can tell me – I won't get upset."

"Nobody has seen him. I believe he went back home to Norway as soon as war was declared. At least that's what I heard."

"I see."

"Did you know he got married?"

"No." Alison's voice was deadpan. "But I'm not surprised to hear it. Who is the lucky lady?"

"I'll give you one guess."

"Margery Ashford-Hope? Of course, it had to be." There was a hint of bitterness in her words that she could not disguise. "Don't they say that a criminal always returns to the scene of the crime?"

Heather fidgeted awkwardly. "I'm not really the one to answer that question. You see before you someone whose love life consists of one ghastly crime after another. I don't know if it's any consolation, Ally old

107

girl, but he did the dirty on her too. Ditched her. He's a cold-hearted beast. Always was."

"I know that now," said Alison. "I just wish I'd known it at the time. Never mind, it's all water under Sydney Harbour Bridge as far as I'm concerned. Perhaps there are some kind gents in the Air Transport Auxiliary who won't mind taking on a couple of lame ducks."

"My dear," exclaimed Heather, "if you can't find what you're looking for in the ATA, there are plenty of RAF pilots swanning about. Mind you, the Brylcream boys tend to look down on us civvy pilots. They say ATA stands for Ancient and Tattered Airmen – and that everyone in the women's pool has a face like a horse."

Alison looked defiant. "Present company excepted!"

"But of course," agreed Heather, who proceeded to gallop around the room snorting loudly and leaping over chairs.

Chapter 29

Shortly after five, the old man was knocking on Schneider's door.

"*Monsieur, il faut partir.*"

He had with him another tray, this time with bread and coffee, which he placed on a table. He also brought a jug of hot water. Schneider staggered out of bed and hobbled around, eating and drinking as he washed. Dr Rantzau had warned against shaving; no soldier in his condition, wounded and struggling back from days of savage fighting, would be clean shaven.

From a bag Schneider took out a small waterproof pouch, containing his false papers and the few pounds he had been given, and a roll of thick industrial tape. With the tape he strapped the pouch firmly to his chest. Then he discarded the bag under the bed and got dressed. He was still wearing his own clothes.

"What about a British uniform?" he had asked before leaving.

"Pick one up on the way," Rantzau said. "There'll be plenty lying about. Take their papers too – they could be useful."

Schneider was appalled. The thought of stripping a dead soldier of his uniform and then wearing it revolted him, but he said nothing.

Downstairs, in the front room of the *pension*, sat a soldier wearing a camouflaged smock. On his head he wore a black beret with a silver eagle and death's head badge; on the right-hand side of his collar was the distinctive motif of the *Waffen SS*. An empty coffee bowl lay on the table next to a pair of dirty goggles, a dog-eared map and a pair of leather motorcycle gloves.

"*SS Rottenführer* Klaus Wastian," he announced. "Heil Hitler!" Wastian did not salute, nor did he stir from his chair. Instead he thrust his arm forward and shook Schneider firmly by the hand. The grip was like a vice.

"I have instructions to be your chauffeur for the day. You want to get as close to the British as possible, I gather."

"Yes, though not by choice."

Wastian stirred lazily in his chair. "What's it all about? We don't often get orders like this. I'm used to straightforward soldiering, no holds barred, if you understand me."

"I cannot tell you anything you have not been told already. I just need to be dropped somewhere the British can pick me up."

"Don't worry, I'll follow orders and ask no questions." He picked up the map. "My division is in the thick of it, and closing on Dunkirk fast. We could have been there already if some moron in high places hadn't given the order to halt for a couple of days. Crazy! Sitting on our arses while the enemy slips between our fingers. But we're on the move again now. I had to drive back here to pick you up."

"Which division are you?"

"*Liebstandarte Adolf Hitler.*" His hand swept across the map in an arc to a point due south of the port. "I'll take you here. No better place for your needs. The Tommies have obviously been ordered to hold out as long as they can and the fighting is very close – street to street in places. I should be able to hand you over to them in person." He laughed.

Schneider was shocked to realise how near the German troops were to swamping the Allies. "Are you really that close?"

Wastian nodded. "The British will soon be in the sea – there is nowhere else to go."

"Or crossing it."

"Impossible. They would need an armada."

This did nothing for Schneider's confidence. His chances of crossing to England seemed remote; non-existent even. If he wasn't killed he was more likely to end up in a prisoner-of-war camp than back in England. Göring could feel satisfied that his punishment would soon be executed to the full.

"Come," said Wastian assertively, "we must leave. The roads are clogged as it is."

Schneider thanked the *pension* owner for his hospitality, but the old man turned away without any acknowledgment. His face reflected a cocktail of emotions that included anger, hatred and fear. He murmured something under his breath as they left, but Schneider could not make it out. Wastian helped Schneider into the sidecar of a mud-spattered motorcycle combination. It had rained overnight, although the sky was clear again now and mostly blue. He slotted Schneider's suitcase into a pannier at the back of the sidecar then picked up the crutches and started to feed them in next to Schneider's legs.

"Leave them," said Schneider. "They won't lend me much credibility as a wounded British soldier."

"Nor your clothes," added Wastian. "We must find you a uniform." He slammed his foot down hard on the kick starter and the engine fired immediately. They sped away from Norrent-Fontes along a fairly straight but poor quality road, still wet from the rain, and Schneider was soon covered in a thin coat of fine mud. He held a hand over his face to protect his eyes. Wastian saw the problem and pulled a spare pair of goggles from his pocket.

"Here, put these on. Things will improve when we find ourselves a decent road."

The corporal drove fast. Along their route there were pockets of refugees, some still sleeping huddled together under makeshift covers, others already on the move. Sometimes they blocked the road, trudging dejectedly along, pushing hand carts or children's prams, or carrying suitcases and bundles tied with string; whole communities uprooted by the Nazi onslaught. Without exception their faces were haggard, numbed by the shock of their lives being torn apart. They probably had no idea where they were heading, no clear destination in mind; they just wanted to escape the bullets and bombs. Ironically, for the most part, they were following the direction of the fighting, having already been overtaken by the *Blitzkrieg*'s nightmare advance.

After half an hour of slow progress, they came to a main road. Wastian turned on to it and was able to zigzag between vehicles and pedestrians. The refugees were more thinly spread now, allowing military vehicles to pass with ease; trucks full of soldiers and artillery following in the wake of the Panzer divisions. Empty trucks were coming towards them on their way to pick up more men. At the side of the road were the remnants of battle; burnt-out trucks and armoured cars, and the occasional tank – British and French alike, but mostly British – pushed aside and sometimes toppled into fields to keep the roads clear. There was evidence that the fighting had been heavy; fresh shell craters buried deep into the tarmac, and bodies, or parts of bodies, charred and mutilated beyond recognition. Some of the vehicles were still smouldering.

The refugees seemed oblivious to their surroundings. In just two weeks they had become numbed by the traumas of war.

Jesus Christ, what a hell hole, thought Schneider, who had never seen anything like it. As a passenger in the sidecar he had nothing to do but sit and observe and stare. He digested each scene, memorising individual images like stills from a film. In seconds they were branded into his mind, never to be erased.

The drone of aircraft engines became apparent, gradually building in an ominous crescendo as black shapes began to fill the sky. The refugees glanced up, fearful of what they might bring. Schneider sensed that they expected the worst. Then, without further warning, the worst happened.

They had passed a military convoy and reached a relatively clear stretch of road where only civilians were in evidence. Suddenly a lone

Messerschmitt appeared ahead of them, its engine audible just seconds before its machine guns started to fire. The pilot must have been following the line of the road, seen only people and not vehicles and decided to use up some ammunition. The refugees scattered, running for the sides of the road and falling flat on their stomachs, men covering women and children. Some of them never got up again. In amongst the civilians a solitary military motorcycle could not be distinguished by the pilot at such speed, and even if he had caught a glimpse of them, it would have been too late to avoid firing at his own.

SS Rottenführer Wastian neither swerved nor slowed down and made good of the empty road as cannon shells tore past him on either side. His only reaction had been to remove his beret and replace it with a metal helmet.

Schneider's anger burst out of him. "Why did he do that!" he screamed at Wastian. "He's killing innocent people!"

"This is war," yelled back Wastian. "There are no niceties so don't allow yourself to be sentimental. Kill or be killed . . . that's the only way."

"But not women and children. That's inhumane – monstrous!"

Wastian drove on. "Shit happens in war."

Schneider glanced back at the devastation that had befallen innocent people in a few terrifying seconds. He cried unashamedly.

Chapter 30

The columns of refugees began to thin out and eventually disappeared altogether, a sign that the fighting was getting close. They reached a point where the road was completely blocked by debris and bomb craters. Wastian braked sharply and observed the problem for a moment. He steered the motorcycle to one side and careered across a grass field with the throttle fully open. He had no intention of slowing down over the rough terrain and Schneider bounced uncomfortably in his seat, stabs of pain searing through his ankle at every jolt. Shortly after regaining the road they reached a junction, a crossroads, with no signpost to give directions. The corporal stopped and pulled out his map from a slit pocket in his smock. He flicked up his goggles and studied it for a while.

"Only a few kilometres from Watten," he explained. "We should be catching up with the Panzers soon." He set off again, taking the right turn. German infantrymen were in evidence now, marching along the roadside or being moved forward in trucks. There were also numerous motorcycle combinations similar to Wastian's. The sound of gunfire and shells could be heard in the distance, faint but unmistakable over the throbbing of the motorcycle engine. Schneider began to feel very dry in the throat.

They were approaching a small town along the east bank of a canal. The marshy landscape was flat and featureless, with one exception; a mound, arguably a small hill, on top of which stood a ruined castle. Wastian headed straight for it and braked to a halt at the summit minutes later.

"Home sweet home," he grinned, climbing off his saddle and stretching luxuriously. "Welcome to the headquarters of *Liebstandarte Adolf Hitler*."

"What now?"

"I have no idea. Wait here. I'll report your arrival."

He disappeared into the ruins and left Schneider sitting in the sidecar. The view in one direction was down to the canal they had recently driven along and to the marshland beyond; in the other, fields cut across by straight, tree-lined roads. Black smoke billowed from a point beyond the fields and the sound of sporadic gunfire, softened by the distance, hung in the air.

Soldiers came and went; commandeered cars and motorcycles buzzed backwards and forwards. Eventually Wastian returned with an SS officer and pointed to his vehicle. They were talking animatedly, just out of earshot. Their expressions told the story. Wastian wanted direct orders, to know what to do so he could do it. The officer had a thousand more important things to worry about and couldn't care less about this piece of nonsense. He looked exhausted and extremely anxious. Eventually he raised his voice in an emphatic final sentence before disappearing back into the ruins. Schneider half heard, half guessed the words. "He's your problem, not mine – do what the hell you have to, get rid of him, then rejoin your company."

Wastian remounted his cycle. "Looks like I'm stuck with you a while longer."

"Your officer looks a worried man. I thought he'd be brimming with glee, the way the advance is going."

The corporal was fitting his gloves back on. "Casualties are high." He glanced across the fields ahead. "There's one almighty fight going on down there. What's bothering him most is our commanding officer is missing – Sepp Dietrich. He went forward this morning to see the situation for himself and hasn't been heard of since. He isn't confirmed as a casualty and no one knows whether to take control or not. It's all confusion."

Wastian kick-started the engine and pointed vaguely ahead. "Come, we have almost taken a village a few kilometres from here – Wormhout. Let's find you a Tommy uniform. Then I will be looking to part company with you as soon as possible. I want to be back fighting by lunchtime at the latest." He twisted the throttle savagely and sped down the hillock onto the flat road below.

The noise of battle became louder almost immediately. For the first time Schneider saw a Panzer, ploughing its way across a field ahead and to their left; in support, on a road beyond the field, were several motorcyclists and a handful of infantry. The object of their attention seemed to be a farmhouse some distance ahead. Tracer bullets flashed through the air, and the acrid smell of smoke and cordite permeated Schneider's nostrils. As they sped on, he saw the tank manoeuvring into position within close range of the building. He turned away and only heard the explosion as the shell hit its target.

"Watch out for snipers," warned Wastian. He indicated an M28 rifle tucked in the sidecar and pulled a magazine from the pouch slung over his shoulder. "Here, use this if you need to."

Schneider inserted the cartridge and held the rifle across his chest; his hands were shaking and he hoped to God that he would not have to use it.

He'd never shot anyone, or anything, in his life and had no idea how he might feel about it. Nor was he sure any longer who his enemy was!

Another Panzer came into view to their right, closer than the other one, a line of soldiers strung out behind it. Schneider stared at them aghast. British soldiers, clutching rifles and advancing with the German line. Schneider tugged Wastian's arm and pointed at them.

"What's going on over there?"

"We take the uniforms off dead Tommies and wear them in an advance. It makes the enemy think twice before shooting, by which time we have shot *them*. It scares the shit out of them to think they are being attacked by their own. Good idea, huh?"

"Until one of your men mistakes them for the real thing."

"It happens – it's a chance you take. If they've any sense they keep their own uniform on underneath, like I always do. In case a quick change is needed."

As the motorcycle approached the outskirts of the village, a group of *Waffen SS* could be seen crouching behind an upturned lorry. One waved them down and Wastian screeched to a halt. He helped Schneider out of the sidecar and set him down next to the soldiers.

"Klaus, where the fuck have you been? We thought you'd caught a bullet." The man who spoke wore the collar badge of an *SS Untersturmführer*. He offered them both a cigarette and handed his own over as a light. His face was black with dirt and two bloodshot eyes suggested he was behind with his sleep by at least a week.

"I was pulled back for a special duty – to collect our guest here and bring him to the front."

"What for?" asked another soldier.

Wastian ignored the question. "That was the easy part. Now I have to try and get him behind the enemy lines so they can ship him back to England for us."

The soldier with the cigarette eyed Wastian suspiciously. "Now why would they want you to do that?"

"I asked but he won't say. To spy for us is my guess."

"There must be easier ways of getting into England."

"I was supposed to be parachuted in," explained Schneider. "But I sprained my ankle so it was out of the question."

Another soldier said: "Why not drop you off from a U-boat?"

Schneider shrugged and told them his story in brief. The mention of Göring seemed to impress.

"Well," said the cigarette soldier, "if the fat man thinks it's a good idea, it must be." The sarcasm was heavy. He laughed. Then someone else laughed and suddenly they were all laughing.

Wastian broke in. "Where is Paul?"

"Dead."

"And Ulli?"

"Hit in the leg – pretty bad. I think they had to amputate. We've lost many friends today. These British fuckers have got a lot to answer for." Schneider wondered at the irony; they were crouching next to one.

"I have to get Schneider here a Tommy uniform. I'd better get one too. Any suggestions?"

"Easy. If we're not shooting them we're rounding them up by the dozen. Come on, let's see what we can find. Wait here."

The soldiers skirted round the side of the truck and disappeared. Wastian was torn between following his mates and staying with Schneider.

"Go," encouraged Schneider. "I will be fine . . . I'm hardly going to run off anywhere."

The corporal nodded. "I won't be long." He took the M28 rifle, then as an afterthought tossed over his Luger pistol. "Here, don't shoot yourself in your good foot." Then he was gone.

Schneider lit another cigarette. He looked up; dark clouds were gathering and he prayed Wastian would be back before the rain came.

Chapter 31

It was two hours before Wastian returned. During that time Schneider saw several tanks on the move and heard shell and machine gun fire. For a long time a solitary British plane, a Lysander, circled overhead; at first he presumed it must be reporting on German positions, but eventually it headed off east rather than west. He wondered if it had been captured by the Germans and was being used to taunt the enemy, like the wearing of dead men's uniforms.

Wastian looked exhausted. He slumped down wearily.

"Why so long?" demanded Schneider.

"Fighting. There are pockets of British everywhere. Most have surrendered now and the town is clear. But it was tough – some of the men you met earlier are dead."

Schneider didn't know what to say, and all that came out sounded feeble: "I'm sorry."

"Come, I'll take you to the others."

They drove into the village and stopped at the end of a street where they dismounted. Schneider was bundled through a door into the corner building, which turned out to be the village *boulangerie*. Inside, squatting in front of the counter with their hands on their heads and wearing only their underwear, were four men. Their bloodstained faces showed fear, exhaustion and bewilderment. Two German soldiers Schneider recognised from behind the truck earlier had rifles trained on their prisoners. There was no one else in the room. On the floor lay a pile of khaki uniforms and black boots.

"Here," said Wastian, "we've got dozens of the English pigs and we've chosen these four to volunteer their uniforms. Try one on for size." He rummaged through the clothing; Schneider did the same, then stripped down to his underpants and vest and selected a uniform at random. It was far too large, so he tried another which was a better fit. It stank of stale sweat. Soon he was wearing British Army battledress, boots and tin helmet. So too was Wastian who looked decidedly plump with one uniform on top of another.

"There's a couple of rifles here. No ammunition – they ran out." Wastian held a Lee Enfield in his hand, balancing it on his palm. "Not a bad weapon but useless without bullets."

Once fully kitted out they crossed the room to a table in the corner where hunks of bread and some cheese were laid out. There was also a bottle of wine, three-quarters empty.

"Eat," ordered Wastian. "We found this in the back room."

As he chewed gratefully at his first food since breakfast, Schneider surveyed the faces of the prisoners. None of them had spoken a word since he arrived. One had fair hair and a roundish face, the closest physical resemblance to himself out of the four. His build was similar too and Schneider guessed it was his uniform he was now wearing. He fumbled in the pockets of the battledress and pulled out a crumpled envelope containing a handwritten letter, three pages in all. It was addressed to Private Bernard Wakeley, Royal Warwickshire Regiment, and was dated early April.

Schneider glanced through the contents of the letter, enough to realise it was written by the soldier's wife, giving news from home. It was signed – *With love, Marion*. He pointed to the fair-haired man on the floor.

"I would like to speak with this man alone for a moment. He may be able to give me some information about his regiment. It will be useful later on."

Wastian's mouth was full but he managed to splutter his approval. "Good idea."

Schneider hobbled across to the soldier and spoke to him in English.

"Are you Wakeley?" The soldier nodded. "Come with me please – just across the room."

One of the SS soldiers poked his rifle hard into the prisoner's side. Schneider shouted: "That will not be necessary!"

"These bastards killed our comrades."

"And you have no doubt killed some of theirs."

The soldier got to his feet slowly and followed Schneider to the far corner of the room.

"Listen," said Schneider in barely a whisper. "I am English. I am taking your uniform to get back home. The Germans think I am their agent. I'm trying to get back to BEF headquarters with some vital information. I need your dog tags. Give them to me please."

Private Wakeley looked at him with fear in his eyes. There was no resistance; he did as he was told, lifting the leather bootlace containing the pressed fibre green and red identity disks over his head. On them were stamped his surname, initials, service number and religion. He handed them to Schneider.

"You're from the Royal Warwickshire Regiment? I found a letter in your pocket – you'd better have it back." Schneider handed it to him. "I'm a Midlander too . . . from Bromsgrove."

The soldier responded to this. "Coventry me. Yes, I'm in the Royal Warwicks" The voice was barely a croak. The Midland accent was strong.

"Married?"

"Yes."

"Children?"

"Two."

"I expect you miss them. Do you have a photograph?"

Wakeley's left hand came up slowly. Clenched in his fist was a dog-eared photograph; a woman's hair was just visible.

"May I see?"

The soldier snatched it back and shook his head. "It's all I have left."

Schneider put a hand on his shoulder. "Don't worry, I understand. I imagine you will be sent to a prisoner-of-war camp and you'll be able to write to your wife from there. Her name is Marion? That's the name on this letter." Wakeley nodded. "Marion will be hearing from you in no time. Then as soon as the war is over, you'll be back home with her and your children."

The soldier shook his head, denying any comfort the words might have brought.

"It could be years. That's no bloody good."

"At least you're alive – unlike many of your mates."

"You're going back to England?"

"I'm going to try."

"If you make it, will you tell Marion I'm alright? Will you contact her and set her mind at rest? She'll be worried."

Schneider hesitated. The man's eyes had a glimmer of hope in them now, a tenuous link with home amidst the horror of his situation; if Schneider only did this simple thing for him.

"How can I contact her?"

"I'll give you the address."

"Wait." On the counter were a small pile of paper bags and a mug containing pencils. "Here, write on this. I promise I will let her know you are alright and a prisoner."

Wakeley scribbled for a few moments then smiled feebly.

"Thank you, thank you so much." As he moved back to his place on the floor with the others, Wakeley clutched Schneider's shoulder and said: "I was a lousy husband – she's better off without me."

As he spoke, an SS soldier struck him across the cheek and Wakeley fell heavily to the floor. He crawled back into line, holding a hand to his now bleeding jaw. The door opened and the *SS Untersturmführer* who had given Schneider a cigarette earlier strutted in.

"Klaus, take a look. I have something to help you on your way." Wastian stepped outside and saw, parked in front of him, a British motorcycle combination. "This should complete your disguise. It's battered but it works . . . and it's got petrol. You'd better get moving – there's going to be one hell of a downpour soon." The clouds that had been gathering all day were now black and heavy. "Dietrich is still nowhere to be found – not looking good. The bastards may have got him. We are to move the prisoners out now."

As Schneider struggled into the sidecar, slotting the radio suitcase into a luggage space at the back, he saw the four prisoners being manhandled into the street and force-marched up the street. More prisoners were being led in the same direction from another building. Their captors jabbed them with their rifles, kicked them from behind to keep them moving, and spat at them. The procession disappeared out of sight.

Wastian had been talking with the *SS Untersturmführer* who then hurried off to catch up with the others. As the motorcycle cleared the far side of the village, Schneider caught sight of the column of men again, making their way across a field in the direction of a barn.

"Where are they taking them?" he asked. The corporal did not reply in words, but with a gesture. He raised his hand to a point just beneath his left ear and raked it across his throat.

"Oh my God . . . no!" Schneider looked back over his shoulder for a final glimpse of the British soldiers as trudged towards their slaughter. "That's barbaric."

The motorcycle sped on. Before they had gone far, fat globs of rain began to smack against their faces and soon it was pouring down in torrents. They were drenched within seconds.

Schneider hardly noticed. He was thinking of Private Wakeley, the man whose clothes he wore and whose wife he had promised to reassure of his safety. The man who was probably dead now, and whose wife in the space of the last few minutes had become a widow.

Chapter 32

SS Rottenführer Wastian, now wearing a British uniform and riding a British motorcycle, did not realise at first that the road he had taken was still behind the line of the Panzer divisions. A hail of bullets from some *Waffen SS* soldiers soon put him in the picture and he made a rapid detour to his right and away from them across country to try and outstrip the German advance. Once again Schneider had a rough ride, aggravated by the rain, and was relieved when they joined another road.

Wastian was navigating by instinct now, taking any turn he thought might lead them towards the coast and the British line. The shelling overhead was intense, the noise deafening. Small arms fire crackled incessantly whilst figures darted across the fields on either side of the road and between the trees and ditches. Occasionally bullets ricocheted off the sidecar; miraculously none hit either driver or passenger. They were in fairly open country now and to his left Schneider saw several tanks in a line. They were soon left behind as the motorcycle careered ahead. But this brought them in range of the Panzer shells. Great clouds of dust billowed around them when they exploded. A tree, split in two as a shell hit its trunk, crashed down onto the road, forcing Wastian to swerve violently. He almost lost control of the machine as a wheel clipped the edge of the roadside drainage ditch. Kicking the ground with his foot to help him steer, he managed to stay on the road and drove on.

A hamlet came into view at the end of a poplar-lined avenue. A tank and several artillery guns blocked the road. As they approached they realised it was the British stronghold, the latest in a series as they made their retreat.

The rain had been heavy but had not lasted long and the black clouds were already thinning out.

Wastian said: "You do all the talking. I don't know a word of English."

"What shall I say!"

"I'll drop you off. Say we saw a wounded officer a little way back down the road and that I'm going back for him. Then I'm buggering off to where I belong. This is as far as I can take you. Dunkirk can only be a few kilometres from here."

"This will do fine."

British guns were firing over their heads as the motorcycle pulled up in front of the barricade. Two men in khaki ran out and helped Schneider out of the sidecar.

"Come on, mate, you're safe now," said one.

"I'm not badly hurt," said Schneider. "Just a bloody sprain – but I can't walk."

Wastian revved the motorcycle and turned the machine round.

"Oi, where the hell do you think you're going!" called the other British soldier.

"Let him go," said Schneider. "We passed some men in a ditch back there. One of them was an officer – looked pretty badly injured. He's going back to pick him up."

"Jerry's moving up fast. He's a brave bugger to do that."

"Yes he is brave. If he wasn't, I wouldn't be here now."

They watched as Wastian drove away, waving one arm high in the air.

He was almost out of site when Schneider realised the suitcase containing his *Afu* radio was still in the sidecar.

Chapter 33

Propped up in the farmhouse doorway, Lance-Corporal Baldwin knew he was going to die. The shell had landed very close to him and cut his legs to ribbons. He had lost a great deal of blood and he was cut off from the British rearguard. No one even knew he was there.

He had seen the motorcycle pass by, just yards away from him, on the road towards Dunkirk. He waved feebly in the hope he might be seen, but it was travelling fast and neither the driver nor the soldier in the sidecar looked in his direction. Several other vehicles had passed in the hour or so he had lain there. None had seen him. With a supreme effort he thought he might have been able to drag himself the few feet from where he lay to the roadside to improve his chances of being noticed; but the loss of blood had drained all energy from his body. He tried several times, but it was beyond him.

He knew the Germans were advancing along the road and would be here soon. He held a grenade in his hand as a welcoming gift. When he died he would at least take a Kraut or two with him.

Despite his condition, Baldwin could see well enough, and when the same motorcycle returned only minutes later, minus the passenger in the sidecar, he watched with puzzlement. Nothing had come in that direction; no one was daft enough to want to head back towards the enemy. For some reason this motorcyclist was.

As the bike reached the farmhouse the rider slowed down and ground to a halt, just a few yards from where Baldwin lay. His spirits rose; he must have been seen after all and this saviour had come back for him. He tried to call out but managed only a croak. No matter. If the rider had seen him earlier he had not moved an inch.

The motorcycle was ticking over and the rider dismounted. Now he was doing something strange, stripping off his battledress and throwing it onto the ground. Underneath was another uniform, that of a German infantryman. He then swapped his British helmet for a German one and remounted his vehicle.

Baldwin was confused. He couldn't work out in his mind what he had just witnessed. It didn't make sense. What he did know was that this last chance of being saved had vanished for sure, like a lifeline torn from the clutches of a drowning man.

Then it dawned on him. This Kraut had been masquerading as a British soldier. His passenger too probably. A bloody fifth columnist!

Clutching the grenade in one hand he tugged at and released the pin with the other. With the last remaining ounces of strength in his body he flicked his wrist, sending the grenade in a low arc onto the road. He watched it roll until it came to a halt underneath the sidecar. The driver glanced down, distracted only for a second. He fired the engine and revved it high several times before releasing the clutch. Just as the motorcycle started to edge forwards, the grenade exploded, lifting rider and machine off the ground, toppling them sideways towards him in a shower of metal, wood splinters, hot oil and petrol.

Wastian died instantly. His body fell to the ground, landing with a sickening thud in a heap of mangled limbs.

Lance-Corporal Baldwin never saw the fruits of his labours. He lay dead in the doorway, a jagged shard of metal lodged deep in the middle of his forehead . . . his eyes staring blankly ahead into nothingness.

Chapter 34

It was dark by the time Schneider reached Dunkirk. He saw nothing of the journey, having been bundled into the back of a lorry with other wounded soldiers soon after reaching the BEF's rearguard line. No one asked him what regiment he was from, in fact no one spoke to him at all. The others were either in pain, exhausted or barely conscious. A medical orderly shuffled on his knees from one stretcher to another, tending to them as best he could.

The truck's progress was very slow and it seemed like hours before they eventually arrived on the edge of the town, although only a few kilometres away. The wounded soldiers were eased down gently onto the ground and carried into the basement of what was once a building but now mostly rubble. The room below ground was for the most part intact and safe enough to act as a makeshift hospital.

Every building in view, without exception, had been damaged by either bombs or shells to one degree or another; several were on fire or smouldering, the flames illuminating the surroundings and smoke rising in a black plume barely distinguishable in the darkness of the night sky.

When Schneider's turn came to be hoisted down off the lorry, he wrapped his arms round the neck of the orderly and hopped to the ground.

"I feel a bit of a fraud," he said. "I'm not hit, just a sprain. Give me some crutches and I'll waste no more of your time."

The orderly stared at him quizzically. "Crutches? You must be joking. Might be able to find you a plank of wood to lean on. There's enough debris lying around. Then you can join the queue for a ship. We're only a couple of hundred yards from the seafront here."

"I'll take my chances. You've got enough to worry about."

The orderly left him leaning against the derelict wall of the building and disappeared inside. He came back with a section of floorboard about four feet long. The splintered end of a cross-piece jutted out two thirds of the way along giving the improvised crutch something of a handle.

"Will this do?"

"Perfect," said Schneider. He pressed the end under his shoulder and took a step or two. "Which way do I go?"

"To the end of this street, then follow the crowd."

Schneider made his way along the street and found himself in the midst of a column of soldiers, British and French alike, filing their way slowly in the dark. He joined them, letting himself be taken by the flow, seeing nothing of what lay ahead.

The soldiers in the column were silent, but above them the noise of aircraft and anti-aircraft guns being fired from somewhere nearby was intense. The drone of bombers was punctuated by the piercing whistle and muffled crump as their deadly load exploded. Flares lit up the sky for long periods and more buildings were on fire. Many of the bombs were incendiaries.

The men moved slowly forward. The buildings started to thin out and a soft breeze brought the smell of the sea to Schneider's nostrils. The column was spreading out to the right along a road which seemed to run parallel with the beach. Someone ahead was shouting orders.

Most of the soldiers seemed to be part of small groups, either self-made or the remnants of platoons. Nobody was concerned about a lone straggler. A flare lit up the sky ahead and as it died away Schneider saw sand dunes beyond the road. He limped across the tarmac and onto the sand. His improvised crutch sank in and he almost lost his balance, but managed half a dozen steps before stumbling again, this time falling flat on his face on the edge of an incline.

"Watch where you're stepping, mate," came a voice from the darkness. "There's people trying to kip 'ere."

"Sorry," replied Schneider, unable to see where the voice came from.

"Just arrived?"

"Yes."

"Best lie down and take it easy for a while. You must be knackered if you're anything like us."

Schneider's eyes gradually became accustomed to his surroundings. He could make out a line of men lying along the shore side of a natural hollow that had been made bigger by digging. Most of the men were motionless, either asleep or trying to sleep. He settled down next to them.

"What are you doing here?" he asked the nearest soldier.

"Waiting for a boat to Blighty, what d'yer think? There's a hell of a queue. It's the bloody rush hour."

"How long have you been here?"

"Since yesterday."

"Are there no boats?"

"Oh there are boats alright," said the voice, "just not enough. And the bloody Looftwaffer has a tendency to sink 'em. If they miss them the Yoo-boats get 'em. I reckon this is the safest place to be, in these sand dunes. So we're in no hurry, are we boys?" There were grunts of agreement from along the line.

126

Schneider winced as he jarred his ankle trying to make himself comfortable in the sand.

"Wounded?"

"Only a sprain. Makes walking difficult."

"Don't worry mate, you stick with us. We'll help you out of 'ere. You'll have to do your own swimming if we get sunk, mind."

"Thanks. What regiment are you?"

"Royal Essex – what's left of 'em. Have you heard the latest?"

"I haven't heard anything for days."

"The Belgians have packed up – couldn't take it no more so they surrendered. The Frenchies are still fighting but have pretty much given up the ghost. A right bleedin' shambles."

The voice trailed off and shortly the sound of soft snoring took its place. Schneider also succumbed to sleep, a remarkably deep sleep considering his surroundings.

Chapter 35

In Berlin, SS Headquarters at Prinz Albrechtrasse were quiet. It was late and few office lights still shone. But for Reinhard Heydrich, Chief of Reich Security, there was no formal beginning or end to the day's duties. His cold, reptilian eyes never tired, and meetings were often scheduled by him for times when most of his colleagues were either at home with their families, enjoying a supper with friends, or making love to their mistresses. Heydrich did all these things; only he spent less time about them.

Picking up a file, he eased his wide hips squarely into a chair and motioned for the two men to sit. On the left, Heinrich Müller, Chief of the Gestapo; on the right, Walther Schellenberg, Chief of the SD Foreign Branch. For a long time Heydrich said nothing, a deliberate ploy to gain a psychological advantage, a trick he had learnt from the Führer himself. By the time he eventually spoke, both Müller and Schellenberg were feeling uneasy. What he said made them downright nervous.

"There is no longer any doubt. We have traitors in high places, gentlemen. As you know, I have suspected for some time. Now I have proof." He opened a file and spoke as if he addressed the papers inside. "Earlier this month we intercepted cipher messages sent from the Vatican City to the Belgian and Dutch governments. They contained precise details of our attack in the West, including the date and exact hour that Operation *Gelb* would commence. All this two days before it took place." Heydrich looked up, staring firstly Müller full in the face, then Schellenberg. "I have never seen the Führer so angry! He has ordered the traitors to be tracked down at all costs. He wants us to make an official enquiry – and he wants Canaris to do the same."

"But surely . . ." began Heinrich Müller.

"Precisely. How can Canaris be trusted to do so when the leak in all probability came from within the *Abwehr* . . . specifically, from your namesake, Dr Josef Müller and his friends in Munich? It will be interesting to hear the *Abwehr*'s findings. Fortunately for us, we have already begun our enquiry. Any progress, Müller?"

"Not yet – not enough to come to any firm conclusions."

"Schellenberg?"

"We know that Joseph Müller has access to the highest circles in the Vatican – and that he was recruited into the *Abwehr* by the Portuguese consul in Munich, a man called Wilhelm Schmidhuber, whose anti-Nazi tendencies we have been aware of for some time. That in itself generates cause for suspicion."

"I know the name. Have all these *Abwehr* people watched. Dig into their backgrounds and see what you can glean. I am convinced there is a connection and that the peace overtures emanate from there."

Müller said: "Do you think it reaches the top – do you believe Canaris is involved?"

"I don't know." Heydrich's eyes half closed in thought. "The *Abwehr* seems to be remarkably unsuccessful when it comes to achieving results in the West. Their agents are either incompetent or non-existent in areas where it really matters. I wouldn't be at all surprised if we didn't sniff out complicity there somewhere. For all we know he might be feeding intelligence to the enemy through intermediaries. But there are other more likely candidates at the Tirpitzufer. Oster for one – Chief of Central Section. He hates National Socialists, always has done. What is more, he is friendly with the Dutch military attaché here in Berlin. As for Canaris – we must dig deeper. We must talk with him." Heydrich turned his gaze towards Schellenberg. "You can help us there, I think. I believe you go riding together some mornings."

"We do," replied Schellenberg. *You damn well know we do*, he added to himself. *It's in the file you keep on me.* "I shall speak with him."

Heydrich clasped his hands together, his Nordic-looking features thinning into an icy smile. "It's going to be interesting. Reich Security and the *Abwehr* investigating the same leak, with the *Abwehr* as the prime suspect. We can hardly be expected to reach the same conclusions."

Müller and Schellenberg glanced at each other uncomfortably.

"Incidentally," said the Chief of Reich Security, "I have renamed the dossier on Canaris and his cronies. I have called it 'The Black Chapel' . . . rather appropriate, I thought, considering their newfound religious connections."

Chapter 36

(Wednesday 29th May 1940)

When Schneider awoke it was light. His body ached and he was cold. The men lying next to him were already stirring. To Schneider, seeing them properly for the first time, they looked like young men grown old before their time; unshaven, dirty, with the haunted expressions of those who have experienced things that no man ever should.

The soldier he had spoken with the night before had disappeared. "Where's this chap gone?" he asked no one in particular.

"Reg?" replied someone. "Said something about rustling up some breakfast. He'll be back soon."

"Where are we exactly? I'm a bit confused."

"Poke yer head up and take a butcher's," suggested the same soldier.

Schneider propped himself up on his knees and peered over the edge of the sand dune. To his right he saw a vast expanse of beach, covered in men as far as the eye could see. Some were lying or sitting towards the back of the beach, seeking shelter in and around the dunes, others were forming queues down to the water's edge and even into the sea itself. A mass of boats dotted the shore line, smaller ones close in ferrying men to larger ones in deeper water. Thousands of soldiers, an entire army waiting for salvation.

Some distance away to the left was a long narrow jetty, reaching far out into the sea. Alongside was a tightly packed row of boats, with others waiting to take their place as soon as one pulled away. The jetty was solid with men, the queue stretching way back inland and out of sight from where Schneider knelt. An enormous pall of black smoke hung in the air beyond, over the main harbour of Dunkirk, which was now blocked and useless.

"Take yer pick," said the Royal Essex soldier. "There's the East Mole over there or the beach over 'ere. Personally I reckon we're better off over 'ere. Jerry will be awake soon and these dunes are the best place to be.

The sand absorbs the shells, so provided one don't land too close, you'll be alright."

Presently Reg returned. In his arms he held something wrapped in cloth and the pockets of his battledress were bulging.

"Breakfast is served!" he declared. "Nothing but the best for me and me mates." The cloth fell away to reveal a bottle of champagne; he had the foil off and the cork out in seconds and the bottle was passed around, much to the delight of the men. "Sorry it ain't chilled – no ice to be found round 'ere."

"Where the hell did you get that from?" asked one.

"There's a bloke back there with a lorry full. Says a Frenchie gave them to him rather than let Jerry have any. And there's more . . ." Reg began to empty his pockets, scattering packets of cigarettes around. "Don't ask where they came from coz I ain't tellin'."

"Any food Reg?"

Reg clicked his fingers. "Bugger, I knew there was something I forgot."

"Looks like biscuits again then." Dry biscuits were handed round from a tin and Schneider took several gratefully. He hadn't eaten since the bread and cheese at Wormhout.

"Well lads," said Reg when the champagne bottle was empty and several cigarettes had been smoked, "don't life seem rosier with a bit of booze inside?" He stood up and surveyed the scene in front of him. "Time we was getting in the queue. I like these beach holidays but all good things come to an end. Come on, or we'll never get home."

They scrambled to their feet, light-headed from the alcohol, collected their meagre belongings, and followed Reg onto the beach. A man was marshalling troops in various directions and he indicated they should join a line ahead of them and to the right. It was three-men wide and zigzagged to the water's edge some distance away. The tide was coming in and the men at the front were up to their knees in the water. They watched as boat after boat filled with men and ferried them to larger vessels off shore; a Royal Navy cruiser and a coaster were absorbing an incredible number and did not leave until their decks were buried under a sea of heads. The line gradually moved forwards.

Schneider became aware of a dreadful stench. He put his hand to his mouth and nose to try and stop himself from retching.

"It's the 'orses," said Reg. "Half the French cavalry's dead and rotting on this beach. Been there for days, I'll be bound. I used to work in a knacker's yard – recognise that smell anywhere."

The drone of aircraft engines could be heard faintly in the distance. Soon it turned into the wailing sirens of Stukas that had everyone throwing themselves to the sand and covering their heads. Bombs landed at random, hurling clouds of sand into the air, and with it the bodies of those unlucky to have been in the wrong place at the wrong time. Then Messerschmitts were strafing them with cannon fire from all directions, whilst heavier bombers concentrated on the ships. The sight of quantities of German aircraft and not a single British fighter brought shouts of derision from the soldiers on the beach.

"No RAF again, lads. They're like bloody coppers – never around when you need them."

Despite the deathly interruptions, the work of lifting men off the beach never faltered and the lines continued to move lethargically forwards. It took Schneider five hours to reach the sea. He guessed it was around midday when he eventually got his feet wet. He was very thirsty but there was nothing to drink. He was hobbling on his one good leg but was in much better shape than many around him. Most had barely slept for a week and eaten virtually nothing for longer. Nearly all had retreated through Belgium or France on foot, fighting as they went and under constant aerial bombardment.

Supported by Reg, Schneider waded slowly into the sea which was now at high tide; it was as calm as a millpond, though numbingly cold. The makeshift crutch was abandoned, allowed to float aimlessly away along with a mass of discarded detritus. By the time they reached the front of the queue they were waist deep. A small dinghy approached and Schneider was hoisted aboard by the two-man crew, then Reg and eight other men. Dangerously low in the water and the outboard motor straining against the load, the boat made its way out to a larger vessel, bearing the name Kilkenny. It was medium-sized and painted in Royal Navy grey, though clearly not a fighting vessel. When on board they discovered it was a personnel ship.

The final obstacle was a rope ladder slung over the side, almost too much for some of the men who were on the verge of collapse. Only goading from their mates and helping hands from the crew enabled them to make the climb. Schneider's ascent was painful as it meant bearing down on his sprained ankle. He compensated by using his upper body strength as much as possible and struggled to the top. Eventually he slumped to the deck with a feeling of intense relief. Some men were laughing, others were crying; some were asleep the moment they reached the deck. Schneider was herded into a corner by a crew member to make room for more men.

When the ship was eventually full, and every foot of deck was taken by soldiers plucked from the water, the anchor was raised and the Kilkenny edged away from the beach and out to sea. Schneider watched as the shore line faded away until smoke was all that was visible. Aircraft flew overhead and plumes of water gushed skywards as shells rained down. But no one on board minded a soaking if it meant a near miss.

Schneider wept as he looked around him. His experiences were nothing compared to the hardship of these men, and they were the lucky ones; the survivors. Thousands lay dead behind them. He thought of Private Wakeley and tried to imagine his death, probably mown down by machine gun fire in that barn. And all for what purpose! One lunatic's desire to dominate Europe. He knew now that he could no longer do anything more to further the cause of Adolf Hitler. Renate had been his motivation, and that emotional tie was now severed. Göring's sadistic little punishment had been the final nail in the coffin. Any sense of loyalty towards Germany faded away with the crossing of the English Channel.

The *Abwehr* had lost an agent; not in body but in mind. A far more permanent break.

Chapter 37

The Kilkenny weaved its way amongst the strange armada of vessels that swamped the waters around the coast off Dunkirk. To avoid shoals and the risk of running aground in shallow water, she steered due west for a time along the coast, bringing her temporarily in range of German artillery batteries. As soon as it was practical to do so she altered course out to sea and the shells fell short. Mercifully not a single one struck the ship, but it brought home to those on board just how close the enemy were to the BEF's final stronghold.

Royal Navy ships were by no means the only vessels to be seen. Ferries, yachts, fishing trawlers, cabin cruisers, even pleasure steamers were taking their turn to rescue men from the beaches. The Stukas were spoilt for choice. Schneider saw several direct hits. The one that stuck in his mind most of all occurred soon after he had climbed on board. An empty ferry, almost within reach of the harbour having crossed from England, and barely two hundred yards from the Kilkenny, took the full force of a shell that exploded amidships. She started sinking immediately and he saw crew members leap into the water from both sides. In less than three minutes, there was nothing left of her.

"Thank God it weren't full," said someone.

"Thank God it weren't us," said Reg.

The farther away from the coast they travelled the lighter the shelling became, only to be replaced by bombs as Heinkels and Dorniers took advantage of the sitting targets in mid-channel. Poor weather had prevented them from taking off for most of the previous day; now they were making up for lost time. Even before dawn several destroyers and numerous auxiliary and merchant ships, most of them packed with soldiers, had been sunk by either the *Luftwaffe* or U-boats. The RAF's visible presence by comparison was minimal, an impression that brought more bitterness from the men. Only once did they see a bomber formation broken up by a squadron of Hurricanes.

"Blimey lads, it's the RAF! Thought they'd retired for the duration."

"So that's what a British fighter looks like – I'd forgotten, it's so long since I saw one."

Despite the lack of air cover, and by sheer good fortune, the Kilkenny managed the crossing without mishap, reaching the English coast unscathed. She passed a stream of vessels travelling in the opposite direction and many more were waiting to offload soldiers at Dover. The boats then refuelled and set off back across the Channel.

Dover was a blur. Schneider glimpsed the white cliffs as they approached the coast, then the scrum of boats around the harbour entrance, but nervous exhaustion was setting in and despite having slept during the crossing his mind had slumped into a trough of weariness. He was helped down a gangplank onto the quayside and without knowing how found himself on a station platform. Then he was on a train, still with Reg and the men from the Royal Essex Regiment. The compartment seats felt luxurious after the ship's hard deck and most of the soldiers fell asleep again. The train pulled away in a haze of smoke and escaping steam, gradually picking up speed as it left the port behind and entered open countryside.

"Anyone know where we're heading?" asked Schneider wearily.

"London I suppose. I heard someone talking about a reception camp. I suppose they've got to regroup us – what's left of us."

"They can bloody well give us passes first," announced Reg. "I want to see my missus. She don't even know if I'm dead or alive."

The carriage became silent. The train pulled into a station; the sign read 'Headcorn'. On the platform was a small army of volunteers, mainly women, manning tea urns and trestle tables covered in sandwiches, meat pies and rolls, passing food and drink through the windows to eager hands.

"Grub up lads!" called Reg as a box entered the carriage and was passed around. The food was gone in seconds, sandwiches filling mouths and slices of pie devoured in just a few bites. Tin cans of tea followed to wash it down.

"Welcome home, boys," called a female voice from the platform. "You've done a good job."

"A good job?" came the reply. "We've been shoved into the sea by Jerry. I'd like to know what a bad job is then."

The unexpected refreshment stop was like a mirage and had a rejuvenating effect upon the soldiers in the train. Exhausted, dirty, thoroughly demoralised and beaten, they had nothing to feel bright about. Yet this small but hugely precious gesture brought smiles to faces and words of thanks from parched lips. Some men tried to pay, but their money was refused. Some French soldiers in the next compartment threw francs in the air and called out: "Please take – no good anymore."

Reg had stepped out onto the platform and was chatting to a porter. When he got back in he said: "We're off any moment – they've got to get

135

us fed and watered in under ten minutes and away before the next lot. He says they're taking the station signs down when they have time, so Jerry won't know where he is if he invades."

As the train was about to depart there was a shout of "Sling them out!" and a hail of tin cans hit the platform, to be collected, washed and filled in readiness for the next arrival minutes later.

The sprawling landscape and neat towns and villages of Kent gradually faded as they approached the suburbs of London. To Schneider's relief it became apparent they were heading for the centre, and when they passed the huge chimneys of Battersea Power Station and crossed the Thames at a snail's pace, he recognised the approach to Victoria Station. The train crawled into the platform. As soon as it came to a halt, doors swung open and the shouting began. Soldiers were juggled into a rough semblance of order and marched off to awaiting trucks and on to camps, or to other stations.

Reg helped Schneider out of the carriage. They were the last onto the platform was a heaving mass of people; rush hour, only without bowler hats or pinstriped suits.

"Reg, it's no good, I'm going to have to go to the gents," said Schneider. "Any chance of heading in that direction?"

"Alright, mate, wouldn't mind a jimmy meself."

They made their way along the platform edge, between the crowds and the side of the train.

"If we get separated in this, Reg, I want you to know just how grateful I am for your help."

"That's alright – someone 'ad to do it. I'll keep my eye on yer. We'll probably end up at the same camp if we stick together."

They reached the main concourse. It was an undulating mass of human beings; railway officials, military police, Red Cross personnel, and anxious relatives searching for loved ones. The two men fought their way towards the buffet. The glass was steamy and it was difficult to see inside.

"This way," said Reg who led him down a long flight of stairs into a large marble cloakroom. An end urinal was free. Schneider propped himself against the wall and fumbled with his trouser buttons.

"Thanks Reg, I'll be fine now," said Schneider.

"Just as well – the next part you can do yer ruddy self." Reg moved along to another free urinal, peed profusely, then retreated to the back of the room and lit a cigarette.

Schneider peed too, but took his time. He had to part company with Reg and needed time to work out how. He stood at the urinal as long as he dared, long after the flow had finished. When he felt he couldn't drag it out any further, he did up his flies, still with no plan in his head. A man came and stood at the urinal next to him. Schneider paid him no attention.

A familiar voice whispered: "Don't look at me, just listen. Go outside then send your friend back down here."

Schneider couldn't help but glance in his direction, albeit briefly. Staring at the wall next to him stood Otto von Osten.

"Mission accomplished?" called Reg. "Come on mate, we'd better get back to the others." They climbed up the stairs to the concourse. At the top Schneider stopped, hesitated and patted the pockets in his trousers, trying to look puzzled as if he had lost something.

"My wife's picture, it's gone. I had it in the train not five minutes ago. Now I can't find it."

"Maybe it fell out in the carriage."

"No, I know I had it when we got out. I think I might have dropped it down there." Schneider pointed down the stairs leading to the gents.

"I'll go and see, shall I?"

"Would you mind, Reg? I never showed it to you, did I? She's a beauty. I'd hate to lose it."

"You wait here. I'll take a look." Reg disappeared down the steps and searched around the urinals for several minutes. There were a few empty cigarette cartons lying about, but no sign of a photograph. When he felt sure he'd looked everywhere, he again climbed the stairs onto the concourse. He looked around. Schneider was nowhere to be seen. He glanced in every direction. He scratched his head in bewilderment and wondered back to his mates.

"Any of you seen wotsisname with the limp?" No one had. "I lost 'im in the crowd when we came out of the bogs. Funniest thing – he was there one minute and gorn the next."

"What was his name?"

"Blowed if I know," said Reg. "He never said."

Before long the men from the Royal Essex regiment were on the back of a lorry, their nameless companion forgotten.

Chapter 38

Alison spent most of the following day with Heather pottering around the Norburys' garden, reliving old memories and recalling mutual friends. It was late afternoon before she was able to drag herself away. She reminded Heather of her promise to speak to Pauline Gower about joining the ATA.

"Leave it to me, old girl." Heather gave her a huge hug. "I'll speak to her as soon as I get back to Hatfield. Then I'll phone you."

"Do make it soon. I can't wait."

"Promise."

Alison drove off, waving madly with one hand and steering perfectly with the other; she was as excellent a driver as she was a pilot. She felt very happy.

At six o'clock that evening, the Webbs crowded anxiously around the wireless set. *"The British Expeditionary Force is intact,"* they heard, *"and has withdrawn some miles towards the coast; a desperate battle is going on. The whereabouts of the BEF cannot be stated at the moment, but Dunkirk is not in immediate danger and Calais is still in Allied hands."*

On the nine o'clock news the following evening came the first official confirmation of what was by then the inevitable. *"A number of troops have been successfully evacuated with the assistance of the Royal Navy and the Royal Air Force. They are now back in England."* The British public was at last being told about an evacuation that had been going on all week.

The next day, a Friday, Alison sat at home waiting patiently for the phone to ring. If Heather had returned to Hatfield the previous day she must surely have had a chance to speak to Pauline Gower by now. Why hadn't she phoned last night? Whatever the reason, if she was flying today she wouldn't have a chance again until the evening. Alison knew this but nevertheless stayed within earshot of the phone all day. By dinner time she was anxious. She didn't eat much and sat uncomfortably on the sofa, trying to read *Picture Post*, but not taking in any of it.

The news that evening reflected a more accurate picture of what was happening across the English Channel: *"The men of the BEF are coming home day and night; all services are helping in the re-embarkation."*

"There must be a lot of loved ones sighing with relief tonight," commented Iris Webb.

The news came to an end on a lighter note with an announcement that *Band Wagon* would be back on the air for one show, featuring Arthur Askey and Richard Murdoch. Leonard Webb switched off the receiver. It seemed appropriate to sit quietly for a moment. The unthinkable was happening . . . the British Army was being pushed into the sea. Not even after four years had it come to that in the last war.

Alison's thoughts were of a very different kind. She was thinking that Heather Norbury was the most unpleasant, most untrustworthy person she had ever known. It was obvious now there would be no phone call and that Alison had been forgotten the minute her car had pulled away from the Norburys' house. Little things from the past began to come back to her; how Heather had stood her up at the pictures; how she had deliberately flirted with a man she knew Alison was keen on; how she stared her up and down sometimes as if in disbelief that anyone could wear such dreadful clothes. And now she had back-tracked on a solemn vow to help an old friend. She really was a dreadful woman.

The telephone rang.

Leonard and Iris Webb looked across at their daughter.

"I think you'd better answer it, Ally – it's probably for you."

Alison jumped up and rushed over to the telephone table. She picked up the receiver.

"Hello, Ally, is that you? It's Heather."

"Oh hello," said Alison timidly, embarrassed suddenly to be talking to the person she had been mentally flaying alive moments before. "I was just thinking about you."

"Are you alright, darling? You sound down."

"I'm fine – sorry, it's the news. We've just been listening to the wireless. Very worrying."

"Such an awful mess. But listen, darling, it's not all bad news for you today. I've spoken to Pauline. She wants you to come down and see her as soon as you possibly can."

"That's wonderful. Have I got an appointment? When, what time?"

"You don't need one – just come to Hatfield as soon as you can make it and she'll see you. Ally, her face was a picture when I told her you were back and wanted to join the ATA. You're just the ticket."

"I'll be there as soon as I can. Monday morning, first thing."

"No you won't!" boomed Heather. "You've just heard the news – the Germans are coming! Hop on a train tomorrow and be here by early afternoon at the latest. You can stay with me, I'm renting a flat. I won't be here until the evening so I'll leave the key with the lady in the flat opposite – Mrs Elliott. Here's the address. Have you got a pencil?"

139

There was a pad and pencil on the telephone table. "Fire away."

Alison could hardly contain her excitement as she told her parents. They shared their delight for her as best they could, only voicing their concerns to each other when Alison had gone to bed. Home for less than a week and now she was off again. Leonard Webb was more anxious than he allowed his wife to know. Whatever the outcome of the Dunkirk evacuation, the fact remained that British ground forces had taken a savage mauling. Whether Hitler now chose to invade Britain or not (and Leonard Webb still believed he would not), it was obvious that the next major battle would be in the skies; either as a prelude to invasion or as an act of consolidation on the part of the Germans.

If he was right, then an ATA girl delivering planes to front line airfields would find herself too close to the fighting for comfort. Airfields would be prime enemy bombing targets. And Leonard Webb would be responsible for putting his daughter in the firing line.

As he lay in bed, unable to sleep, he wished he'd never kept those bloody newspaper clippings.

Chapter 39

"Was I glad to see you!" said Schneider as he sat next to von Osten in his car. They were driving away from Victoria Station along the Kings Road, heading for Putney Bridge.

"The feeling was mutual," said von Osten. "Those fuckers did not tell me what they were planning on doing to you. Only when I made radio contact two days ago did they instruct me to watch for you here."

"I was very lucky to be on a train direct to Victoria . . . otherwise I would have taken longer and we may have missed each other. Had you been waiting long?"

"Since yesterday."

"Sorry to keep you hanging about."

"It's a miracle you made it at all . . . I never expected you to, and frankly I don't think *Hamburg* did either. How in God's name did you manage it? I assume you got across from Dunkirk – what was it like?"

"I'll tell you all about it as soon as I've eaten. All I've had today is some sandwiches and a mug of tea. I haven't had a proper meal for days. Where are we going?"

"Somewhere safe – but we must take our time and an indirect route. Here, these might keep you going for a while." He indicated the back seat. "More sandwiches I'm afraid but better than nothing. And a bottle of beer."

They crossed over Putney Bridge and turned right along the side of the Thames, passing through Barnes and Mortlake towards Richmond. From there they kept with the river and at Ham turned into a tiny lane that brought them to a clearing surrounded by trees at the water's edge.

The two men sat and talked. Between mouthfuls of sandwich Schneider told his story and von Osten listened, taking swigs from a bottle of light ale. By the end Schneider felt depressed; the horror of it all seemed worse in the telling, yet words alone could not express the sounds and the smells of war. Perhaps it was just as well. Experiences such as those were best kept locked inside and away from the second-hand imaginings of others.

He told everything, apart from his conversation with Private Wakeley, the man whose uniform he was still wearing, and the promise he made to contact his wife . . . his widow. Wakeley he regarded as an entirely personal business between him and the dead soldier.

In response, von Osten told of the flight in the Heinkel and how he had persuaded the pilot to alter the drop point. "I buried my chute and flying suit, then I smartened myself up as best I could and headed off for Ely, which was about a five mile walk. They pumped me full of Benzedrine before the drop and I felt on top of the world. From there I caught the first train to Cambridge and was knocking on the door of a lady friend of mine by eight o'clock. Audrey Parsons. She was delighted to see me, so much so that she was an hour late for work. I tell you, Benzedrine does wonders for your love life! Audrey's a librarian at one of the university colleges, don't ask me which one. I stayed there until the following morning – told her I was doing secret work for the government. She seemed to accept that without question. Nothing much is out of the ordinary in Cambridge."

Von Osten drank more beer. "That evening I thought I'd better check in with *Hamburg*, so I waited until Audrey was asleep and set up the *Afu* in her spare room. Reception was poor but I managed to get through. They told me to get to London as soon as possible and to hang around the buffet at Victoria Station – said you were coming over by boat courtesy of the British military. I couldn't believe it! So I said my goodbyes a little sooner than I had hoped, and caught a train. Apart from picking up the car and checking on the house I've been waiting for you ever since. The Benzedrine wore off ages ago and I'm struggling to stay awake."

"Is this car yours?" asked Schneider.

"Indeed it is. I had it in storage in Acton, in one of the garages I used to own. A Wolsey – nice little motor. I had to settle the storage fee which was huge. Drained away much of the cash *Hamburg* gave me. Have you brought any?"

"Almost nothing . . . a few pounds. The fifty I was supposed to have were confiscated. Wasted on a lost cause obviously."

"Well we must pester *Hamburg* for more now that we are both here. And soon."

"What about the house – is that yours too?"

Von Osten nodded. "I'm not telling *Hamburg* about it and I'd be obliged if you would keep it to yourself. I told them I've rented a place in Brentford, which isn't far away, just over the river from Kew. A bit of security of our own isn't a bad thing. It makes no difference to them, so long as we do what they want."

The beer bottles were in plentiful supply; von Osten had a whole crate in the boot. By the time it was dark both men were drunk, and as soon as the Wolsey started to move Schneider's stomach churned. With no proper meal in days, and in a state of nervous tension, the alcohol was too much

142

for him. Minutes into their journey he ordered von Osten to pull over, pushed open his door and vomited. The last time he had done that had been on the bridge in Heidelberg. The recollection was shrouded in mist inside his head and only half discernible. By the time the car was moving again he was drifting off into sleep.

Von Osten's house was a short distance away in Richmond. He drove past the station, turned right then left into Larkfield Road, and pulled up outside a row of narrow three-storey houses that backed onto the railway line. He opened the door of number forty-five, checked to make sure no one was in sight, then dragged Schneider's limp body out of the car and half carried him into the house.

"My friend," he said as he dumped Schneider onto a couch in the front parlour and stripped him down to his underwear, "you stink." Von Osten saw the waterproof pouch containing his papers taped to his chest, pulled it off unceremoniously, then covered him with a blanket and went to bed.

Both slept until late the next morning. Schneider bathed and shaved while von Osten went out to buy what he could for breakfast. He came back with milk, bread, butter, sausages, bacon and tomatoes, and a ration book stamped up for the next week. He'd had a quiet word with the butcher and managed to extract more than he was due, at three times the normal price. Eating well was going to be an expensive business. It was a bright, warm day and they sat at a table next to open French windows looking out onto the tiny high-walled garden. Schneider ate ravenously.

"You must stay indoors," warned von Osten. "For the time being no one must know you are here. This is my own house so the neighbours will not be suspicious of me, although they won't have seen me around for a while. They don't know I'm German. I bought this place under an assumed name which I use from time to time – Charles Mortimer. Very English, don't you think?"

"Very," agreed Schneider. "What about Otto von Osten, does he still have a house in England?"

"Oh no, that gentleman sold up everything when he left England forever last August. He realised as soon as Germany signed the Non-Aggression Pact with Russia that it was time to return home – and fast. He sold his garage business and attractive detached house in Purley Oaks in under a week. Got a miserable price for both."

"So why did you buy this house under a different name?"

Von Osten shrugged. "There were times when it suited me not to be Otto von Osten, a German and a known Nazi sympathiser at that, living and working in England. Especially after Munich. You see I was a fully paid up member of several right wing organisations. The National Socialist League for example – have you heard of them?"

Schneider shook his head.

"Founded by William Joyce. He's in Germany now and broadcasts to Britain every night . . . the British call him Lord Haw Haw. Anyway, the NSL was overtly pro-Hitler and consequently came in for a good deal of scrutiny. So I invented Charles Mortimer as a sort of escape. I used to come here and pretend to be him for the weekend. I even managed to get a passport in his name. It was an enjoyable game to play." Von Osten's tone softened. "It was also a convenient place to bring women whose husbands were of a suspicious nature. Charles Mortimer was a difficult man to track down because he didn't exist."

"So why didn't you sell this place when you left England? You must have anticipated never coming back, surely?"

"I simply ran out of time. There were complications about selling a house in an assumed name. So I just left it."

"Why have you lied to *Hamburg* about it? Why have you told them we are somewhere else? I don't see the point."

"I told you," said von Osten. "A piece of personal security."

"Security against what? Nobody knows we're here apart from *Hamburg*."

"Perhaps I have a suspicious nature. I learnt many years ago not to trust anyone in this life. Somebody once told me that it's a good thing always to stand with your back against a wall so it is not exposed."

Schneider didn't really understand, so he let it drop. He decided instead to present an idea that had been growing in his mind. "I have been thinking about a little personal security of my own," he said tentatively.

"Is it something you would like to share with me?"

"Well, you say you think *Hamburg* did not expect me to make it to England. I agree. Dr Rantzau virtually told me so. I fouled up their plans for this mission and being dumped into the front line was my punishment. If I don't report my arrival in England they will expect you to fulfil the mission single-handed."

"That's a fair appraisal," agreed von Osten, "only quite how they expect me to infiltrate two aircraft factories at the same time, I haven't got a fucking clue!"

"Quite. But here I am, alive and well. *Hamburg* will not have anticipated my being here." Schneider saw his colleague's eyebrows begin to rise and his face adopt an expression of understanding. "Do they really have to know? Suppose Quaver didn't make it. Suppose he never appeared at Victoria Station. Suppose he was killed on the beach at Dunkirk, or drowned crossing over from France . . ."

"Very plausible," said von Osten. "But to what end?"

"Then as far as the *Abwehr* is concerned I don't exist any longer. And if I don't exist I won't be missed."

"Missed? How do you mean?" Von Osten's voice was tinged now with suspicion.

Schneider sensed this but had gone too far to pull back and so decided to tell everything. He found it all flooding out without restraint. He talked about Renate and how he had witnessed her screwing Bruno Rolf. He talked of the nightmarish scenes he had witnessed on his journey to Dunkirk. His feelings had changed and he no longer believed in what they were trying to achieve. At the peroration of his speech he said: "I don't want to do this anymore. They dumped me in France and expected me to be killed – and now I have survived they expect me to work for them. They must think I'm stupid."

There was silence in the room. Schneider wondered what reaction there might be from von Osten, who sat still, mulling over everything he had heard. When he eventually spoke his tone was calm and controlled, but with a sinister edge.

"I'm not quite sure what you have in mind, my friend, however failing to tell *Hamburg* the whole truth is one thing . . . betraying them is another entirely. No matter how your feelings may have altered, we are here to do a job. I would strongly advise you not to suggest treachery against the Fatherland again. Put the idea behind you. Tonight I shall report your arrival." He stood and stretched. "Now, I think it is time we made a bonfire and got rid of that disgusting British Army uniform of yours, don't you agree?"

Schneider sat rigidly, staring through the French windows into space. He realised he had made a mistake by speaking his mind. He suddenly felt vulnerable and very lonely.

Late that evening, von Osten set up his *Afu* wireless in the tiny attic room of the house and prepared to transmit. Reception was better here than it had been in Cambridge and when he tapped out his call sign the response from *Hamburg* was clear. He transmitted his prepared message.

Quaver arrived safely against all odds but needs rest. Money and Afu lost. Send replacements.

An acknowledgment crackled through his headphones. Von Osten lit a cigarette and waited for the full reply. It was not long in coming. He scribbled down the letters and referred to a decoding pad to translate.

Congratulate Quaver. Will organise equipment. Money may take longer. Mechanic to go active in seven days. Target details will follow shortly.

He read through the message twice and muttered: "Tight-fisted sods." Then he fired off a staccato burst from the Morse key and closed the suitcase before *Hamburg* had a chance to respond.

Will go active on receipt of both equipment and money. Not before.

Leaning back in his chair, smoking a cigarette, he thought about his fellow agent. He was a good man and he liked him. But he could foresee problems looming ahead with him, and if that was the case he would have to act ruthlessly if it became necessary.

He hoped he would not have to kill Schneider.

Chapter 40

"I dropped in to see Canaris this morning," said Walther Schellenberg as he stood in the Chief of Reich Security's office. He did not sit down as he did not wish to stay. A few minutes in the company of this odious man was enough for him. He had never forgotten the time when Heydrich had accused him of having an affair with his wife, Lina. He had gone crazy just because the two of them had gone out boating together on one of the Berlin lakes. A dangerous, volatile man.

"And what news?" asked Reinhard Heydrich.

"He broached the subject first – asked me if you had told me of this 'unbelievable affair' concerning the date and time of the Western offensive being revealed. He then proceeded to give me his version of events."

"Tell me – in brief."

"According to Admiral Canaris, a German diplomat visited the Dutch Embassy in Brussels the day before the launch of Operation *Gelb*. He reported that the ambassador's wife was hysterical about something. She clearly knew what was about to happen. Then, when we took Brussels, a note warning of the attack was found in the embassy there. It was from the Dutch Ambassador in Berlin. Canaris claims he doesn't know how the leak occurred, but he has ordered one of his men, Colonel Rohleder, to investigate."

"No mention of Rome?"

"None."

"The Vatican?"

"No."

"Intercepted messages to the Belgian and Dutch Ambassadors?"

"Nothing."

"Do you believe him?"

"I think credibility is a little thin on the ground."

"I would go further," said Heydrich. "I think it's a pack of lies. And what Rohleder finds out during his investigation is entirely predictable. He will find nothing."

Schellenberg was anxious to leave. "Would you like me to look into this further?"

"Oh yes. I want to know everything that Canaris gets up to . . . every single detail. Whom he talks to, where he goes, what he does and what he says. It's about time we put pressure on the Chief of the *Abwehr*. I don't trust him at all."

"I'll brief Müller. This is a domestic job."

"Do so, but it is not entirely domestic. I want your Foreign Branch to find out as much as possible about *Abwehr* agents abroad – the Low Countries, France, and Great Britain. If the treachery is as deep-rooted as I suspect, they could well be his mouthpiece to the Allies. Oh and let's not forget the neutrals – Portugal and Spain. I seem to remember Canaris being rather well in with Franco."

Schellenberg acknowledged the orders. It was a mighty task. As if anxious to get started, he saluted hurriedly and left. He knew Heydrich was relishing every minute of the operation. This was personal. It was common knowledge in Berlin that back in 1931 the Chief of Reich Security, then in his mid-twenties, had been drummed out of the German Navy by an Honour Court for dishonourable conduct towards a young woman. Nine year later it seemed he was bent on revenge for that shattering blow to his reputation.

The Honour Court had been presided over by Admiral Wilhelm Canaris.

Chapter 41

(Friday 31ˢᵗ May 1940)

By a coincidence of sorts, the Air Transport Auxiliary came into being on the same day that Neville Chamberlain announced to the British population they were at war with Germany. Gerald d'Erlanger, a director of British Airways whose brainchild it was, received official approval from the Air Ministry that he could go ahead with the scheme on Sunday, 3rd September 1939.

The ATA's function was simple. To supply a reserve of civilian pilots for non-combat duties: carrying dispatches and medical supplies; transporting civilian personnel; air ambulance duties; and most importantly of all, ferrying new and repaired aircraft from factories to storage units or operational airfields. All of these tasks would normally be carried out by RAF pilots. Relieving them of this burden allowed them to concentrate on their prime function; fighting the enemy. Although a civilian organisation, the ATA was under direct RAF control.

When Pauline Gower was invited to set up a women's pool within the ATA, ferrying Tiger Moths from where they were built at the de Havilland factory in Hatfield was the ideal soft option to start them off. Moths were classified as 'small light aircraft', easy to handle and used by the RAF as trainers. The obvious location for their headquarters was near the factory itself, and she established an office there in December 1939.

She had soon selected thirteen candidates, all known to her, for flight testing with the understanding that only nine would be chosen. A week before Christmas, she travelled down to Whitchurch, near Bristol, to witness the tests which were carried out by a British Airways instructor. She took them all out to lunch before their ordeal, then in the afternoon watched as they took turns to perform a few simple manoeuvres around the airfield. As it turned out, the unlucky four were rejected due to family or other commitments rather than inadequate flying skills. Heather Norbury had screamed with delight when she received her letter of acceptance a few days later. That evening she went out with friends to celebrate and got delightfully drunk.

Shortly afterwards, in a blaze of unwelcome publicity, they started work, and as Heather had warned Alison, working conditions were nothing like the glamorous picture the press did their best to paint. That winter was severe, one of the worst in living memory, with snow, ice and bitterly cold winds making flying even more hazardous than usual at that time of year. Tiger Moths had open cockpits and the journeys were long – to airfields in Scotland, North Wales and the north of England. The only way they survived was by cocooning themselves in layers of warm clothes underneath their flying suits, and sitting on fur cushions. Once a delivery had been made there was no guarantee of a return flight which often meant a long and arduous train journey home.

At first the women were ordered to fly in gaggles, a frustrating demand for experienced pilots used to cross-country flying. The official reason was that it made them more recognisable to the Observer Corps, but most members of the women in the pool suspected it had more to do with a male lack of faith in their ability as pilots and navigators.

"After all," complained one of the girls whimsically, "who's going to mistake a bright yellow biplane pottering along at sixty miles an hour for a bloody Messerschmitt!"

Gradually the order was relaxed, due mainly to the fact that they failed to live up to the expectations of cynics and consistently managed to deliver planes in one piece, on time, and to the right location. It also became apparent that if half the pool had been sent to the north of Scotland and the other to Yorkshire without return transport, further deliveries had to be suspended for days at a time while they found their way home. The only advantage the pilots could see to gaggle flying was that it meant there was company on the train journeys back to Hatfield.

The freezing weather conditions persisted into early April, by which time it was generally accepted that the women's pool was extremely useful and there to stay; they had proved themselves equal to the task. With the German invasion of the Low Countries the following month, and the breathtaking speed of the advance across France, pressure was mounting on the RAF. Hurricane squadrons were suffering heavy losses in France, and if they continued at that rate, able-bodied reserves would soon be needed for combat duty. The ATA would be forced to release as many pilots as possible. Pauline Gower was given official sanction to double the size of the women's pool. The taking on of Amy Johnson and Grace Brown increased their total number to eleven. At least twenty were needed. So at the end of May, with the Dunkirk evacuation in full flow, Heather Norbury could not have chosen a better moment to mention an ideal recruit. Pauline Gower knew of Alison Webb, by reputation as much as personal contact, and was only too keen to speak to her as soon as possible.

Alison arrived at the de Havilland factory shortly after lunch by taxi from Hatfield Station. She was very nervous and on the train down from the Midlands had failed miserably to tackle a meat paste sandwich her mother had prepared for her. Her stomach churned into knots as she made her way to the offices of the women's ferry pool, smartly dressed and carrying an overnight bag. Apart from two Tiger Moths outside a hangar, the airfield appeared deserted. She presumed the pilots were out doing what was expected of them; delivering planes.

Five minutes after meeting Pauline Gower, all her nervousness had vanished. To her utter astonishment it transpired they were both veterans of flying circuses; Pauline too had spent several years performing crazy flying and giving joy-rides. She wanted to know all about Australia, what type of aircraft Alison had flown, what tricks she had learnt, how many hours she had logged and so on. They talked about the 'falling leaf' stunt, bottle shooting, and all the other things that no ordinary pilots ever did. After an hour it seemed as though they had known each other intimately for years.

Before she knew it Alison was changing out of her dress and into a flying suit. Pauline was not one to let an opportunity pass her by and she was determined to see if her prospective new recruit was as disciplined a flyer as she ought to be, bearing in mind the split second timing necessary to perform stunt work . . . and survive. Was she highly skilled, or a cat using up her nine lives?

They climbed into the dual cockpits of one of the Tiger Moths and taxied across the grass, picking up speed for takeoff, with Alison at the controls. Although she was in the pupil's seat, she knew there would be no interference from behind. She had flown Tiger Moths so many times that it felt the most natural thing in the world, and Pauline would sense that.

The takeoff was smooth and well judged. There was little wind and just a few fluffy clouds in an otherwise clear blue sky. Once she had gained some altitude, Alison banked gradually and circled the airfield as Pauline had instructed. She was well aware this was a test and that whatever tricks they had discussed on the ground, this must be a demonstration of straightforward, disciplined flying. It was a thrill to be airborne again, her first flight since leaving Australia a month before, to feel the rush of wind in her face and to see the countryside flowing past below with its ant-like people and model buildings. This was when she felt most alive, surrounded by vast expanses of air and totally in control. The sense of freedom was almost overpowering. As they circled the aerodrome, she savoured every moment.

She brought the Tiger Moth down with a faultless landing and taxied to a halt outside the hangar within inches of their starting point. As they climbed down she knew from the smile on Pauline's face that she had passed the test. Back in the office Pauline explained that if she had her way Alison could join them immediately. There was plenty of work ferrying Tiger Moths and she was keen to move some of the women up a grade to help clear Oxfords from the de Havilland factory too. At present this was not possible without additional training at the RAF Central Flying School. Taking on more pilots to ferry Tiger Moths would free up others to undergo the training. But there were formalities to be observed, not least of all an official flying test and an approach to the Air Ministry before a contract could be offered. Under normal circumstances this might take weeks to organise, but these were anything if not extraordinary circumstance and Pauline said she would try and push it through much faster. With invasion imminent, everything was time critical.

As if to justify the haste Pauline indicated a copy of the *Daily Express* on her desk. The headline read:

TENS OF THOUSANDS SAFELY HOME ALREADY.
THROUGH AN INFERNO OF BOMBS AND SHELLS THE B.E.F.
IS CROSSING THE CHANNEL FROM DUNKIRK
IN HISTORY'S STRANGEST ARMADA

Beneath was a map of the Belgian / French coastline and a diagram indicating precisely where the Allied troops were pinned down. It was in the shape of a square, with the coast forming the base, French and British outposts on both sides, and the French rearguard forming the top. All three land sides had menacing arrows pointing directly towards them, indicating the threateningly close proximity of German troops.

A smaller headline below caught Alison's eye. It appeared almost banal compared with the main news item:

SIGNPOSTS TO BE REMOVED
Sir John Reith, Minister of Transport, announced last night that Highway Authorities have been instructed to remove signposts and direction indications which would be of value to the enemy in the case of invasion. The work was put in hand on Wednesday.

She suddenly had a vivid mental image of a car full of German stormtroopers careering around the English countryside, brandishing a Michelin map and desperately trying to find their way. She smothered the impulse to giggle; a sure sign of nervous excitement.

A telephone conversation confirmed for Pauline Gower that she could take on Alison for a trial period. They shook hands and spent the rest of the afternoon together, with Pauline explaining precisely the nature of ATA duties. On a wall in her office hung a large map of Great Britain with all the airfields and factories marked in red. As Heather had warned, most of the delivery points were in Scotland and the north of England, but Pauline explained that was already beginning to change. With training programmes expanding rapidly, there were far more opportunities for ferrying planes back down south on return runs than had been the case a few months earlier, and ferrying jobs to destinations closer to home were becoming available throughout England and across into Wales. Additionally, the women's pool would soon have access to a taxi plane, an Avro Anson – possibly two – on loan from ATA headquarters at White Waltham. Pilots would be able to reach home most evenings.

After a brief explanation of the paperwork – consisting mainly of what to do with the triplicate copies of a pilot's ferry chits – they went for a tour of the airfield and factory. As they talked, Alison's respect for her new commanding officer began to grow. She was obviously the right person for the job; her knowledge of flying was second to none, she was intelligent and perceptive, got things done and, most importantly, had a resilience that enable her to survive in a male-dominated environment.

Alison was beginning to feel at home already.

Chapter 42

Alison left the airfield at around six with instructions to report back first thing the next morning. The flat Heather Norbury had rented was close to Hatfield town centre, on the first floor of a purpose-built block, overlooking a pleasant street. Alison retrieved the front door key from Mrs Elliott, the elderly lady who lived in the adjoining flat.

"Charming young lady, Heather," chattered Mrs Elliott as she fumbled in a drawer for the key. Alison wasn't very good at guessing ages but thought she might be around eighty. "Always got time for a chat. Brave too, flying those contraptions here there and everywhere. I'm surprised she hasn't settled down with a nice gentleman by now. Ought to be settled at her age."

"Oh I'm sure she will in time," said Alison, who was two years older than Heather.

"Not that she's short of callers, mind. Like wasps round a jam pot."

"She's an attractive girl."

"So are you, my dear. Alison, that's your name isn't it?"

"Yes that's right."

"Well, Alison, you're quite a charmer yourself." Mrs Elliott chuckled. "Care for a cup of tea?"

"That's very kind," replied Alison. "Perhaps another time? I've had rather a long day and would like to freshen up now, if it's all the same."

The old lady handed over the key. "As you wish, but do feel free to pop in any time. I'm on my own – have been for many years. My husband was killed in South Africa during the Boer War. And my son fell in the Great War, at Wipers. It's happening all over again. You'd think they'd have learnt by now."

Alison thanked her for the key and let herself into Heather's flat. There were two bedrooms – one littered with clothes and shoes (clearly Heather's) and the other empty – a moderately large living room, bathroom and toilet. It was comfortable, though in need of redecoration. She threw her overnight bag onto the bed in the empty bedroom then ran a hot bath. In the kitchen was a scribbled note: *Welcome to the palace! I'm sorry Her Majesty is not at home to greet you, she had to nip out and*

*deliver a plane. Estimated time of return, sometime this evening. Make
yourself comfy. H*

Having discovered a well-stocked drinks cabinet, she returned to the
bathroom with a large gin and tonic, stripped off her clothes and slid
gently into the water, which was ever so slightly too hot. She lay
motionless for several minutes, acclimatising to the heat and watching her
tanned body undulate slowly under the surface of the water. Gradually her
muscles started to relax and the tension of the day's events eased away,
leaving her feeling limp and drowsy. She sipped her drink leisurely,
resting the glass on her sternum, and dipping her finger into the liquid
occasionally and licking her fingers.

Her thoughts turned to Jan-Arne Krobol. They had often done this
together, lying in the huge cast iron tub at his parents' flat in Kensington.
His father was a diplomat at the Norwegian Embassy and he and his wife
were often called upon to attend official engagements. With the place to
themselves, Jan-Arne would make love to her, usually on the floor of the
lounge or across the settee; then they would race each other to the
bathroom, naked, fighting a mock battle to get there first and avoid the tap
end. She nearly always won, and Jan-Arne would sulk off to make the G
and Ts. Then they would wallow together in the deep water, talking,
giggling and teasing each other. Jan-Arne would sometimes contrive to
spill some of his gin over her breasts, then lean across and lick it off. His
mouth would alternate from one breast to the other, sucking and gently
biting her nipples until she could bear it no longer. Soon they would be
making love again, either precariously in the bath, or leaning over the
side, water dripping off them onto towels on the floor. By the time his
parents came home they would be sitting demurely playing chess, reading,
or listening to the gramophone.

Alison gazed along the contours of her body. No man had seen or
touched her for more than two years; she had forgotten how it felt. There
had been offers of course in Australia, from Lucas Kelly and others, but
she had been unable to give herself; to put her trust in any man. Nor had
she met anyone who had stirred her enough to want to try.

Those halcyon days with Jan-Arne were the happiest times she could
remember, though not entirely due to their relationship. By then she was a
qualified flying instructor, held both a class 'A' (private) and 'B'
(commercial) pilot's licence and had given up the drudgery of a shop
assistant's life and was making a living in the air.

At twenty-four she had become a professional flying instructor at
Hendon Aerodrome. One of her first pupils had been Jan-Arne Krobol.
The combination of the two had made her blissfully happy.

Chapter 43

(Tuesday 4th June 1940)

When the news was over, Otto von Osten switched off the wireless and whistled to himself.

"You weren't exactly alone on the beach then. More than three hundred thousand men lifted from Dunkirk! That makes you being here a little easier to understand. I bet the Führer will be kicking someone's arse for allowing so many to get away."

Schneider shook his head. "I can't believe it. We were sitting ducks on that beach. How so many came through safely I don't understand."

"To hear Churchill speak you'd think the British had just won a huge victory. Goebbels could not have turned things round more eloquently. You British are so stubborn. *We shall fight them on the beaches . . . in the fields and in the streets.* What with? Your soldiers may have escaped but they must surely have left all their equipment behind. I think Churchill will be less bombastic when the *Wehrmacht* comes knocking on his door in Downing Street in a couple of weeks from now."

These comments annoyed Schneider, but he said nothing. They had spoken little since he had suggested keeping his presence a secret from the *Abwehr*, and there was now a distinct barrier between them. Schneider knew von Osten had told *Hamburg* of his arrival; he had almost gloated about it. After every subsequent transmission, Schneider asked what had been said, but the responses gave little away and he knew von Osten was not telling him everything. He asked if there were instructions yet about their targets, with as much enthusiasm as he could manage. None, he was told. He thought about asking to borrow von Osten's *Afu* and codebook to transmit a message himself, but he was in no great hurry to make contact; quite the opposite.

Schneider was now seriously considering the idea of escape; getting away from the house and von Osten. His ankle was much improved, far more so than he allowed his fellow agent to realise.

156

The excerpts from Winston Churchill's speech to the House of Commons quoted on the wireless had moved Schneider deeply. It appealed to a sense of patriotism within him that he barely knew existed. *We shall never surrender!* Churchill meant what he said. Schneider felt an innate disgust with everything to do with the Nazi regime, Hitler, and all the pain and suffering the madman had unleashed on the world, some of which he had witnessed with his own eyes. He knew now where his allegiance lay. He would give himself up and report von Osten to the authorities as soon as an opportunity presented itself.

The previous evening von Osten had received instructions from *Abwehrstelle Hamburg* to travel to Winchester. They had given him the address of a hotel and he was to ask for the assistant manager. He would have an envelope addressed to a Mr Turnbull which he would part with in exchange for five pounds. Inside the envelope would be a ticket for the left luggage office at Southampton Station. With it he could reclaim two items; a suitcase and a holdall. The suitcase would contain a replacement *Afu* transceiver for Schneider, and the holdall a variety of spying requisites including codebooks.

"Bloody quick work. They only knew I got here last Thursday."

"I asked about that," said von Osten. "Apparently the stuff's been here since January. A spare set deposited for emergencies. Hope it still works."

"The batteries will be dead."

"Batteries can be replaced. Otherwise you'll have to resort to sending messages using invisible ink."

Von Osten made the journey the following day. This was Schneider's opportunity. He lay awake most of the night preparing in his mind what to do. His plan was simply to walk into the nearest police station and give himself up. He would be safe there – safe from von Osten if there was a foul up and they failed to apprehend him.

As if he had read Schneider's mind, von Osten gave him a warning before setting off.

"My friend, I hope you don't have any fanciful ideas about not being here when I return. Don't forget they hang spies in wartime, even in England. With the threat of a Nazi invasion any moment you won't have a hope in hell of leniency. They'll just string you up . . . or shoot you even, whatever they do here. And where can you go" – he waved the pouch containing Schneider's papers in front of his face – "without these or money? I'm holding on to them."

When von Osten had gone, Schneider wondered around the house, testing his ankle, exercising it gently, deep in thought. The bastard was right; giving himself up as a German agent was tantamount to committing suicide the way things were. Perhaps it would be wise to hold on a while

157

longer. His ankle would soon be back to normal and he would be fully mobile.

Von Osten did not return that night. When he didn't show the next evening either, Schneider started to worry. Maybe he had been caught, or had abandoned him, just as Schneider had considered abandoning *him*. Von Osten's own wireless suitcase was still in the house, but he would have the one from Southampton by now. He had no reason to return. He may even have tipped off the authorities. Schneider decided to wait until noon the next day; then he would leave, papers or no papers. Besides, the small amount of food in the house would be gone by then.

Von Osten reappeared the next morning. He looked exhausted and slumped into a chair with the suitcase and bag on his lap.

"I got them, but only just. They were waiting for me."

"Waiting for you – but how?"

"I don't know. They must have had the left luggage office in Southampton under surveillance, waiting for someone to come and claim this." He tapped the suitcase. "Luckily for me they weren't paying enough attention. I made the pickup and was outside the station before anyone stopped me. Even then it was only a young copper, nervous as hell. I kicked his shins as hard as I could and ran. He tried to blow his whistle but it came out like a high-pitched fart. That slowed him down long enough for me to get to the car and away. I was certain I was being followed so didn't come straight back. I booked in at a hotel in the New Forest, then another near Guildford last night."

"But how did they know about the *Afu* suitcase?" asked Schneider. "Someone must have tipped them off."

"Not necessarily. It's been there since January. It could have been discovered by chance and monitored ever since."

"That's a long time to monitor a suitcase."

"Who knows! I am only guessing."

Von Osten was telling the truth about the incident at Southampton Station, but the rest was lies. Three nights earlier *Abwehrstelle Hamburg* had disclosed to him his target; it was the Supermarine works, the main Spitfire production factory, at Woolston . . . coincidentally an area of Southampton! He realised he could kill two birds with one stone and took a preparatory look at the place. *Hamburg* had given the precise location of the factory and even recommended a pub frequented by Supermarine employees. Clearly this path had been trodden before. He played it low key, drove past the gates in Hazel Road a few times, then parked nearby and strolled around the area. That first evening he spent an hour or so in the pub, listening in on conversations and trying to pick out factory workers, but with no great success. On the second night he spent longer in there. He spoke to no one, just sat and drank beer and pretended to read a newspaper. Watching. Observing people. He slept in the car parked in a remote country lane, not wanting to risk a hotel room.

On several occasions he was stopped by the LDV at roadblocks and questioned. His papers were accepted – good forgeries, so it seemed – but the questions were more difficult to counter. Back in London he would try and get hold of some sort of pass that would allow him to move around without challenge. He had a friend in the East End from his pre-war garage owning days who might be able to help, if he wasn't in prison for passing forged banknotes – his speciality.

Back in Richmond, von Osten's broadcast that evening read:

Target reconnoitred. No foreseeable problems. Quaver's equipment retrieved but its presence known and nearly caught. Source of leak unknown. Intend move to target area without delay but money situation desperate. Will jeopardise entire mission.

Abwehrstelle Hamburg replied:

Leak of grave concern. Enquiries a priority. Do not leave until Quaver fit and in radio contact and completed reconnaissance trip. Money will arrive soon. Give details for postal delivery.

For a brief moment von Osten panicked. He couldn't give an address; as far as *Hamburg* were concerned they were in a house in Brentford. After some thought he transmitted:

Postal delivery not secure. Make other arrangements by tomorrow evening without fail. Recommend a drop.

Hamburg must have pulled out all the stops. The next evening they had alternative arrangements in place but warned that the cash would be less as a result; an intermediary would have to be paid. They promised a larger amount in a week's time.

Von Osten considered transmitting: *I'll believe it when I see it you tight fuckers.* But he decided against . . . then sent it anyway.

Chapter 44

(Monday 10ᵗʰ June 1940)

Otto von Osten took the train to Waterloo, arriving as close to twelve noon as possible. It was a hot and humid day. He travelled by Underground to Kings Cross, then boarded a bus to Oxford Street. Throughout the journey he carried a folded copy of the *Daily Express* resting on his lap. He did not know what was going to happen, or when, but if no contact had been made by the time he reached Oxford Circus, he was instructed to make his way back to Kings Cross and make the same journey again. He was to repeat this four times. If no contact was made he was to return home and follow exactly the same routine the next day at the same time.

He sat patiently on the double-decker – upstairs towards the middle as instructed – and had almost reached Oxford Circus for the second time when the bus came to a halt and a number of people stood up to alight. As they did so, a short, scruffy-looking man with whisky breath stumbled as he passed von Osten's seat and stretched out a hand to steady himself. Von Osten felt the newspaper move on his lap.

"I beg your pardon," said the man. Von Osten recognised the gentle lilt of a Welsh accent. "Please excuse me," he added then made his way down the stairs. Von Osten glanced down. There was a different newspaper on his lap, rolled rather than folded with the ends tucked inwards to make a crude package. Two stops further on he got off the bus. He didn't notice the Welshman sitting on the lower deck, his face buried in a copy of the *Daily Express*. Nor did he see him hop off the bus behind him just as it started to move away. Von Osten walked the length of Oxford Street until he reached Marble Arch. There he went into the public conveniences, locked himself in a cubicle and unfolded the newspaper. Inside were eight five pound notes. Forty pounds! Split between two that wouldn't last long. He felt anger welling up inside him, then after a while he decided it was better than nothing and divided the money between his trouser and jacket pockets. He tossed the newspaper into a waste bin.

From Marble Arch he retraced his steps along Oxford Street, checking once to see if he was being followed by stepping into the doorway of a shop and monitoring those who walked past. No one seemed to falter or look his way. It was still early afternoon and the pavements were busy with shoppers and late lunchers. The scene was one of normality. No hint of the panic and disarray predicted by Dr Rantzau. He stood for a moment at Oxford Circus and glanced down Regent Street, trying to imagine Nazi banners and flags hanging from the facades of the buildings on either side, blood red streamers billowing swastikas in the breeze. He envisaged crowds of Londoners pressed against barricades as a motorcade wound its way up from Piccadilly Circus. The Führer would be standing in the back seat of his official Mercedes, saluting to left and right, surveying the latest of his many conquests; the newest and most prized addition to the ever expanding empire of the Third Reich.

It might only be weeks away – just a few short weeks.

Von Osten meandered his way through a maze of side streets towards Soho, an area he knew well, and crossed Oxford Street. He was hot and perspiring freely. Ahead of him he saw a pub, The Wheatsheaf, not one of his old haunts and so little chance of bumping into anyone from his past. He entered the saloon bar and sat down with a pint of bitter and a large whisky chaser.

England, and all of Britain, was within Hitler's reach, and von Osten was convinced he would grasp the opportunity eagerly. It was a week since the last troops had been evacuated from Dunkirk. Hitler was probably standing on the French coast at this very moment, gazing avariciously across the English Channel. And when he thought of the speed at which the Low Countries had been crushed, von Osten was convinced that the German *Blitzkrieg* would be equally devastating here when it came. And it would come soon, he was certain. The *Luftwaffe* would start to pave the way any day now.

In this wider context, his contribution seemed insignificant. Was it needed at all? No matter how successfully he infiltrated the Spitfire factory at Woolton his information would hardly make a difference when the *Luftwaffe* was bound to annihilate the RAF come what may. One plane was hardly going to make or break the situation. Besides, it would take time before he was able to pass on useful information, or sabotage production. It would all be over by then.

He was a good German, and he would see the mission through. Despite having lived in England for more than ten years, he felt no loyalty towards the country or its people. As for Schneider, he knew what to do about him. *Hamburg* had not disclosed details of Schneider's target.

161

Perhaps the Hawker Hurricane factory, wherever that was. It made sense, one spy in each of the two main fighter factories. As soon as he reached Southampton he would report his concerns about Schneider's loyalty to Dr Rantzau. Once they had gone their separate ways and Schneider had no idea of his whereabouts, *Hamburg* could deal with the problem.

The rush hour had begun by the time von Osten made his way back to Waterloo Station. The Underground was crowded with sweating office workers, grubbing their way home. The journey was unpleasant and he was glad to step onto the open concourse at Waterloo. He had almost reached the ticket barrier when a voice to his side said: "Excuse me, sir."

He turned and saw a policeman standing against the fencing.

"May I see your papers, please?"

"Certainly." Von Osten fumbled in his jacket pocket and pulled out his identity card and ration book. He handed them to the policeman and watched as they were scrutinised. Stay calm, he told himself.

"Name?"

"It's on the card."

"I'm asking you to make sure you are in possession of the correct papers, sir," said the policeman with an edge of irritation to his voice.

"Why wouldn't I be?" Von Osten immediately regretted saying this. To provoke any unnecessary attention was foolish. Before the policeman could respond, he added: "I'm sorry, you're doing your job, I understand. These are dangerous times. The heat is too much for me I'm afraid. My name is Edward King."

The policeman continued looking at his papers, in more detail now. Were they good forgeries after all? Good enough to fool the LDV several times, but this was different and he was rapidly convincing himself otherwise as he stood waiting for the verdict. Beads of sweat were appearing at his temples.

"On your way home, sir?"

"Yes that's right."

After a long pause, the policeman handed back the papers. "Thank you. Sorry to have troubled you." He turned and addressed a man in a pinstriped suit. "May I see your papers, please?"

Von Osten sighed with relief. With shaking hands, he lit a cigarette and inhaled deeply. At the barrier he showed the return stub of his ticket.

He was told: "Richmond, platform three, ten minutes."

The man in the crowd immediately behind von Osten overheard.

"Well there's a coincidence," he said to himself. He too had a return ticket to Richmond. He boarded the same train, a copy of the *Daily Express* still clutched under his arm.

Chapter 45

Lieutenant-Colonel Ballard Ruskin sat anxiously in his prison cell waiting for the phone to ring; waiting for news of agent Snow and the man he had gone to meet – the man they should have bagged when he first landed. The fact that they had missed him had been a source of great frustration and concern. This was a crucial second bite at the cherry.

The cell was the strangest office Ruskin had ever known. In theory he could not have asked for a more secure place to work; but the reality had turned out to be quite different. The door had to be jammed open because there were no inside handles, and accidental closure meant either much shouting and thumping on the door or an embarrassing phone call asking to be let out. The irony of turning Wormwood Scrubs into MI5's temporary wartime home never ceased to amuse Ruskin, Head of B1A Section and prime operative in the struggle to keep tabs on German agents in Britain. "Best place for a bunch of crooks," it had been said by wags in the Security Service, partly in jest and partly in self-derision as they went about their spurious activities.

Ruskin saw both the good and the bad. Good in that it was a marked improvement on the cramped Horseferry Road premises that had previously housed B Division; bad in that the novelty of setting up shop in a prison had done little to maintain tight-lipped, need-to-know security. Had someone really heard the conductor on the 72 bus outside the Scrubs call out "All change for MI5"? He doubted it, but the anecdote was symptomatic of the problem.

As he waited for the phone to ring, he wandered how the new man in charge would fare. Churchill had recently sacked Major-General Vernon Kell, Director-General of the Security Service for over thirty years, giving him twenty-four hours to clear his desk. Pretty harsh on the old man; but these were desperate times and Kell was the victim of desperate remedies. New blood was needed, someone with a fresh approach who could guarantee results. In his place Churchill had appointed Brigadier A.W.A. Harker, commonly known as 'Jasper', to oversee MI5.

Although new to the job, Harker was a familiar face to Ruskin, having directed B Division for some years, and he was proving receptive to an idea that had been germinating in Ruskin's mind since before the war, so much so that in principle he had been given the green light. It was now Ruskin's job to make it happen by setting up a special section; its function, to manage exclusively the day-to-day running of German agents who had been successfully 'turned' by MI5 and who were now passing false information back to the *Abwehr*. As contact with Germany was made mostly using captured *Afu* transmitters, the section had been christened 'Wireless Branch'.

There were few *Abwehr* agents active at that time in Britain. Many potential fifth columnists – as all those suspected of disloyalty or treachery were labelled – now languished in internment camps, mostly on the Isle of Man. Ruskin knew there would soon be more on their way, as the vanguard of Hitler's mighty invasion. They were beginning to trickle in already. In anticipation of increased numbers, a new interrogation centre was almost ready, a project initiated with foresight by Kell but incomplete when he fell foul of Churchill's new broom policy.

Merely running a few double agents was not what Ruskin had in mind. His plan was far more ambitious – *he intended turning every German agent ever sent to Great Britain*. To run their network, feeding back a controlled mixture of false and factual information.

It was not as gargantuan a task as it might have appeared. It only took one agent to start a chain reaction – a man or woman in whom the *Abwehr* had complete trust but MI5 were controlling. Establish them as the linchpin of your network, the one new agents contacted initially on arrival, and you soon had them all in your pocket. Persuade the *Abwehr* to tell him in advance where drops were to be made and you could catch each agent as they landed, still attached to their parachute. The plan could work. Ruskin knew this, because it had already begun. He had his linchpin. Snow had been B1A's double agent since the start of the war, and had been known to them longer. He had helped to mop up the German operatives that internment had missed and established additional double agents with whom the *Abwehr* were now in direct contact. He had even travelled abroad on occasions for personal meetings with his *Abwehr* controllers.

Such was his credibility in the eyes of Dr Rantzau and his colleagues in Hamburg that Snow was forewarned about every new agent sent into Britain, just as Ruskin had hoped. Snow was turning his dream into reality. The object of Wireless Branch was to exploit this reality to the full. The down side was that Snow could be moody and unpredictable; and he was obsessed with money. Everything had a price.

But the system was only workable provided every *Abwehr* agent could be swept into the net; fail to capture just one and he could report back intelligence contradicting that of a double agent. If that happened, the *Abwehr*'s suspicions might be aroused and the deception would crumble.

There was a danger of it happening right now, and Ruskin prayed that when his phone rang the news would be good. Snow was potentially in contact with the agent they had missed at the drop site. But he was a prickly character who liked to play the game his way. He had insisted on making contact alone; no shadows, no babysitters, and no surveillance. All Ruskin could do was wait and hope.

When the phone eventually rang, the bell echoed harshly against the stone walls of the prison cell. Ruskin had the handset off its cradle in a second.

"Yes?"

"I have news, sir." No names required; Ruskin recognised the voice. There was traffic noise in the background. Atkins was using a public telephone box.

"News from our wintery friend. He's made contact with the new boy."

Thank the Lord! Ruskin clenched a fist triumphantly. "Any details?"

"Few as yet. He has an address but he's holding out on us."

"For money?"

"What else with him!"

"Have you suggested he might enjoy a trip to the Isle of Man?"

"That one is wearing a bit thin I'm afraid, sir. He told me to piss off."

"How much does he want?"

"Fifty pounds."

"Offer him twenty and settle on no more than thirty – absolute tops."

"And if he refuses?"

"Bring him in and we'll persuade it out of him if necessary. We must have that address. Full report in writing – as soon as you can."

"Will do, sir."

"Get on with it then. And thank you." The receiver clicked back onto the cradle.

Snow! Ruskin loved and hated the man. As a person he was obnoxious, but as a double agent he was the goose that laid golden eggs. Thirty pounds was a cheap price to pay for having a rogue agent in the bag, and for securing the double agent network in the making. It was the thought of his getting away with it that riled Ruskin. Snow knew damn well they wouldn't intern him; they needed him too much. For the time being at least.

"Snow, your turn will come," he muttered. "Mercenary bastard."

Chapter 46

(Wednesday 19ᵗʰ June 1940)

Schneider sat reading the newspaper. It was late morning and both he and von Osten had slept until nearly ten, having spent much of the previous night with the new transceiver, complete with a fresh set of batteries. It was Schneider's first communication with *Hamburg* since arriving in England. His key technique had been erratic, but all in all it had gone quite well, if rather slowly. Von Osten's offer to help with coding and decoding of messages had been flatly refused.

Abwehrstelle Hamburg had given no instructions and asked no questions. They congratulated Schneider on arriving safely and told him to keep in touch. Very casual and something of an anti-climax.

They had missed the news on the wireless the evening before with its details of Winston Churchill's latest speech to the House of Commons earlier that day.

"Listen to this," said Schneider, quoting from his newspaper. "*What General Weygand has called the Battle of France is over. I expect that the Battle of Britain is about to begin.*"

"I don't understand why it hasn't started already," said von Osten. "The Führer should have followed through immediately instead of trying to sew up the French."

Schneider continued reading aloud. "*The whole fury and might of the enemy must very soon be turned upon us. Hitler knows that he will have to break us in this island or lose the war.*"

"Lose the war? Pah! The British just took the beating of their lives. We should be taking advantage of the situation."

Von Osten was feeling very frustrated on two counts. Firstly, he couldn't understand why there was no sign of an invasion yet. He appreciated that a brief respite might be needed after such rapid success in Belgium, Holland and France, but the pause had turned into a complete halt. His biggest worry was that Hitler had decided not to invade at all. Secondly, *Abwehrstelle Hamburg* were stalling. He had repeatedly asked that he be allowed to leave Schneider and get on with his part of the mission. Each time the reply had been the same; he should wait until Schneider had reconnoitered his target. Yet they had still not disclosed what his target was. Instead they asked questions about morale, weather conditions and road blocks. The urgency seemed to have disappeared.

"Let us therefore brace ourselves to our duties, and so bear ourselves, that if the British Empire and its Commonwealth last for a thousand years, men will still say, 'This was their finest hour.'"

Schneider rested the newspaper on his lap. "Churchill certainly knows how to stir up patriotism when it's needed."

"No more than the Führer," countered von Osten. Schneider was annoying him. It was obvious he wanted nothing more to do with the mission. He was a risk, a liability, and the sooner he was rid of him the better. The week before von Osten had visited his friend in the East End who had supplied him with two new forged permits, in the names of Edward King and Henry Mansell, entitling them to travel unchallenged on public transport and in private vehicles. They were typed on War Office writing paper and signed with a bogus name. The cost had been high and he was now short of cash again; yet another grievance that put him in fighting mood with *Hamburg*.

That evening he transmitted alone, and wasted no time on pleasantries, tapping out his message with venom:

Insist on Quaver target details and money immediately, repeat immediately. Four hundred pounds each. If no response by tomorrow you can find new agents. Quaver perfectly fit now. Has been for a week. Act now or lose us both.

Hamburg acknowledged and von Osten awaited their reply. When it came it was another stall.

Quaver target shortly. Give postal address for cash delivery.

Von Osten clenched his fists. We're going round in circles, he said to himself, tapping out a response.

Disclosing address unsafe. Make other arrangements as before. Money and Quaver target tomorrow or stick your radio up your arse.

He didn't expect any further response, but minutes later the Morse code was buzzing in his ear again. The message was short. Von Osten decoded and gazed at the words:

Why are you in Richmond when you tell us you are in Brentford.

He slumped backwards, momentarily stunned. How the hell did they know that! His brain began to race, going over the implications of this revelation, trying to work out how they knew. It could only be Schneider; he must have made a transmission on his own somehow and told them. But when? He had hardly left him alone for a moment since he arrived back from Southampton; once, when he had nipped across to the local

167

pub, the Orange Tree, for a few drinks, that was all. There wasn't enough time to set up the *Afu* and transmit – not at Schneider's speed – then decode and pack away. Nor could Schneider have transmitted while he was away in Southampton. Von Osten had left his *Afu* in the house but taken the batteries with him.

Why were they stalling for time . . . doubts about their loyalty, or worries that they had been captured, or turned even? Von Osten thought for a long time, and came to the conclusion that honesty was the best policy to try and restore their faith in him. He drafted a short explanation regarding his house in Richmond and his concerns about their security. At the end he apologised; then he asked how they knew. *Hamburg* acknowledged receipt and the transmission ended. He never really expected a reply.

Von Osten said nothing to Schneider, other than that he had asked again for money and instructions. He watched Schneider all the time now, observing every expression and gesture. He slept with his Luger under the pillow.

The following night they transmitted together, using their *Afus* alternately. To von Osten's surprise, and relief, *Hamburg* gave Schneider the details of his target and ordered him to make a reconnaissance trip there as soon as possible. But Schneider refused to decode the details in von Osten's presence and waited until he was in his own room. It was the Spitfire factory at Castle Bromwich near Birmingham. A 'shadow factory' the British called it.

Von Osten had not shared his target details with Schneider and in return Schneider refused to disclose his. The mutual distrust was consolidated by *Hamburg* who ended both messages by making it clear that once Quaver had returned and reported back from his reconnaissance trip, they were to go their separate ways and there would be no further contact between them.

Von Osten felt unsettled by this. Did it mean that *Hamburg* had accepted his explanation about the house and were pressing on with the mission to plan, or were they eager to separate their two agents as soon as possible because in their eye one or other, or both, were no longer to be trusted? Perhaps Schneider had planted seeds of doubt with them by reporting the lie about their location; perhaps it was von Osten they no longer trusted, when in fact he was the loyal one.

That evening von Osten drank heavily from a whisky bottle in his room until his brain could no longer juggle the facts. Despite the alcohol he slept restlessly, fully clothed on his bed, his gun by his side.

Chapter 47

(Friday 21ˢᵗ June 1940)

The next morning, with a bag over his shoulder, Schneider set off for Birmingham. As he walked away from the house in Larkfield Road towards Richmond Station, he felt an enormous release of tension. He had no intention of spying for the *Abwehr*, but until he had a concrete idea of how to break away he would go through the motions. It felt wonderful to be rid of von Osten, albeit for a few days. The German had been drinking even more than usual and picking fights at the slightest opportunity. He claimed in sober moments it was because he hadn't had a woman for so long.

Schneider had never been to Castle Bromwich, which was on the opposite side of Birmingham from Bromsgrove where he was born and bred. He was excited at the thought of being close to home. He thought of his grandmother, the demure old lady who had brought him up after his mother had died of influenza when he was four years old. The last war had just ended and an epidemic ravaged the country. Ironically, the daughter had died and the mother survived. Much later he had learned that his mother had been pregnant. His father had died on the first day of the Battle of the Somme two years earlier and she had not remarried. One of Schneider's earliest memories was of his grandmother weeping at what she was convinced to be the Lord's retribution for her daughter's sin. With his grandmother's death in 1935 he lost his only family tie. That summer he auditioned successfully for the orchestra in Heidelberg, met Renate and she became his new family; and Germany his new country. Or so he had imagined for the past five years. When the train pulled into New Street Station after a pleasurable journey through lush English countryside in full midsummer bloom, he fully understood the nature of his self-deception. The sense of wellbeing brought about by knowing he was once again on home ground almost overwhelmed him. Bromsgrove was just a half hour train ride away. Birmingham Town Hall was a short walk from where he stood; he had heard the City of Birmingham Symphony

Orchestra perform there many times in his youth and it was there he had fallen in love with classical music. This was home.

Schneider lunched at the Lyons Corner House in Corporation Street, then sought out a tiny side alley where, years before, there had been a bicycle shop. It was still there, and he purchased a second-hand bike for ten shillings. He wheeled it back to New Street and bought a return ticket to Chester Road Station; not the nearest to his destination . . . Dr Rantzau had advised against always taking the direct route. From the station he cycled along the Chester Road southwards towards Castle Bromwich.

After about twenty minutes, he saw the factory coming into view on his right from a distance. You couldn't miss it; it was huge. The buildings were next to the main road and towered imposingly above it. He wheeled his cycle past the main entrance and stared down the long avenue between two seemingly endless camouflaged blocks. From the front it was impossible to tell how much ground they covered, but it was clearly a massive complex, far bigger than Schneider had anticipated. The Messerschmitt works at Augsburg seemed tiny by comparison.

Bloody hell, he thought; if all this was devoted to making Spitfires they must be churning them out by the hundreds.

From across the road came the distant sound of an aircraft engine revving for takeoff. The airfield was not visible from the road at that point. Schneider cycled on until he could see down a road that ran alongside a wide expanse of grassland. As he stood there the distinctive shape of a Spitfire soared into the air directly towards him and banked away to his right. Apart from a couple of biplanes on the field it was the only aircraft in sight.

The plane made a circuit of the airfield, watched by a small group of men in suits and overalls. The pilot was going through a routine, banking gently to left and right to test control response, then flying dead straight whilst trimming the aircraft.

Schneider watched in awe. It was his first sight of a Spitfire and he had never seen anything quite like it. He knew nothing about aircraft beyond his training in Germany, but you didn't need to know anything to appreciate the sheer style and elegance of this machine. It resembled a bird with its beautifully-shaped wings, and seemed to fly like one. It even sounded beautiful.

The plane came into land and taxied over to the onlookers. The pilot climbed out of the cockpit and under his supervision several adjustments were made. He was young with a long face, striking features and dark curly hair, parted severely to one side. Then he was off again, circuiting once more before disappearing through wispy cloud in a full throttle climb. The plane was soon back, buzzing in from another direction and sweeping low across the airfield, the start of a short display of aerobatics that left Schneider open mouthed. Loops, spins, rolls – most at nerve shatteringly low altitude. The climax came with the pilot bringing the Spitfire in from the far side of the field in a long shallow dive, targeted right at the group of men. Halfway across, the plane flipped over into an inverted position and continued its approach.

He's too low, thought Schneider; he's misjudged his height. Too low and too fast! He glanced anxiously at the spectators. Some were ducking down instinctively as the Spitfire hurtled towards them, still upside down. Suddenly it was rolling back into the upright position, banking and turning with absolute precision over the buildings to Schneider's left. At its lowest point, the wing tip could not have been more than head height above the grass.

Schneider sighed with relief. The pilot was either a genius or a lunatic, he decided. As the plane came into land, he turned away. Crossing the main road, he approached the main entrance where two men in uniform stood at a barrier next to a gatehouse.

"Excuse me," he said, "could you tell me who I should see about a job here, please?"

"What kind o' job, mate?" replied one, in a soft Midland drawl.

"Anything on the production line. I'm a riveter."

The man pointed towards an administration block. "You'll be alright then. They need 'undreds on 'em."

In a spacious office Schneider explained to a desk-bound man wearing a poorly fitting suit that he was enquiring after work. The man took down some details and asked about previous work experience. Schneider told of a series of jobs with garages and construction companies, concocted with the help of Dr Rantzau back in Germany.

"Where was you working most recently?"

"London docks," explained Schneider. "Working on merchant ships. But I want to do something more directly involved with the war effort. Seems to me it's aircraft the country needs right now, and I want to help make them. I heard Lord Beaverbrook's appeal on the wireless the other week for the fullest output from aircraft factories. I've got family up here and they told me about this factory."

"We need people with experience," said the man. "Not much we can do today, time's getting on. Can you come back in the morning? We'll get you down to a workshop – see what you can do."

"Tomorrow will be difficult – I have to sort out a few things. How about Monday?'

"The sooner you come back the sooner we can help you."

'Monday first thing then, thank you."

This was going to be a piece of cake, thought Schneider. What a shame the *Abwehr* would never benefit from it.

"One question." The man stood up behind the desk. "You're a fit and healthy young man. Why haven't you been called up?"

Schneider reached into his pocket and drew out a sheet of folded paper. "Medical exemption – I'm asthmatic."

"Does that affect your ability to work?"

"No. It's only the army who says I'm not fit enough to kill Jerries. I'm fit enough to do heavy manual work, though."

Schneider wheeled his bike out of the factory gates, deep in thought. Something was troubling him and he couldn't quite put his finger on it. Nothing important; but enough to nag away at the back of his mind. He still hadn't nailed it by the time he'd cycled half a mile back up the Chester Road and pulled up outside a pub called The Bagot Arms. It was nearly opening time and the thought of a pint was very appealing. He leant his bike against a wall, lit a cigarette and sat on the pavement in the warmth of the late afternoon sun, waiting for the doors to open.

*

Several tired-looking men were leaning against the bar. It was obvious from their conversation they worked in the factory and were having a regular Friday after-work drink.

"Excuse me," said Schneider, addressing no one in particular. "I've just applied for work down the road there. What's it like – is it a good place to work?"

After an initial silence a middle-aged man with dark hair slicked back replied gruffly: "Depends."

"Depends on what?"

"If yow're a sodding masochist."

"Hard work, eh?"

"Arr, yow can say that again. Thay're pulling out all the stops right now."

Schneider recognised the distinctive accent; more Black Country than Brummie. "What about wages?"

"Mustn't grumble."

One of the others piped up. "C'mon, Charlie, you know the wages are good. Long shifts, but they pay alright."

Schneider nodded his approval, then said: "Can I buy a round? I hope to start next week so sounds as if I can afford it."

The middle-aged man hurriedly downed the rest of his pint. "Mine's a light ale, ta very much. What's yer name, pal?"

"Henry Mansell."

"Charlie Rix – Parts Inspector."

"Charlie the Checker," said another. "That's what we call 'im."

172

When the drinks had been bought, Schneider mentioned the test flight he had witnessed earlier.

"Arr," said Charlie. "That'd be the whiz-kid just up from Supermarine – Henshaw his name is. We mekk 'em, he tries to crash 'em."

Schneider smiled. "Unlikely he'll be doing that judging by what I saw. He really knows how to fly."

"Some says he pushes 'em too far. Kill himself one of these days, mark my words."

"You're wrong there, Charlie. I bet he'll outlive us all."

"I expect you keep him busy, churning out new planes," said Schneider.

Charlie seemed to take offence at this remark. "Are you tekkin the piss or what!"

"I'm sorry?" Schneider looked bemused.

"Listen, we get enough stick with bloody Beaverbrook giving the works manager ulcers without your sarky comments. Poor Dunbar, he's working his bollocks off. We all are."

"I didn't mean to be rude," apologised Schneider, not quite sure what he had said wrong.

"We're motor industry folk trying to mekk airplanes. It's not the same. Now we've got Supermarine people up here from Southampton tellin' us what to do – showing us what we're doin' wrong. Mekks us feel like fools, but it ain't our fault."

"Southampton?"

"That's where the main Spitfire factory is – the Supermarine works."

Southampton! Schneider's mind began to race. Von Osten had gone there when he went to pick up the *Afu*. Perhaps that was why he had been away so long; perhaps he had known his target all along and spent some time taking a look around. He wouldn't put it past him to lie. So, two Spitfire production plants, two agents. Christ, the Germans must really see the Spitfire as a threat to go to such lengths. Now he had seen one in flight he began to understand why.

One of Charlie's mates said: "At least things are moving now, since Supermarine took charge. You must give 'em their due."

"So output's improving then?" suggested Schneider.

Charlie had almost finished his second pint. "No doubt about it," he said. "In fact, production this month will be ten times what it were last month. We've promised Beaverbrook."

There were a few chuckles of laughter. Schneider took the bait.

"So what was production last month?"

"Nil."

"Nil?"

"Nil – fuck all. But this month it'll be ten. Ten in June, we've promised."

A while later Schneider said 'cheerio' and promised to meet up with them again the following week. He pedalled his way back towards the station. None in May, and ten in June; what was Germany worrying about! Ten Spitfires out of a factory the size of at least a dozen football pitches, which had been up and running for how long . . . a year? He hoped the Southampton factory was doing better. If not, God help the RAF. As he waited for the train into Birmingham, he noticed a poster on a billboard on the far platform. In a comic illustration, two women were sitting on a bus gossiping. Behind them sat Hitler and Göring in full military uniform. The caption read: *You never know who's listening!* Then in bold underneath: *CARELESS TALK COSTS LIVES.*

Tell that to Charlie the Checker, thought Schneider.

Something was still bothering him; he still hadn't placed it. Then, halfway back to New Street it came to him. The man behind the desk at the factory had asked him his age. "Twenty-five," he had replied. He thought back to the end of May – to the twenty-ninth. Where had he been? Eventually he worked it out. The day had started on the beach at Dunkirk, swigging champagne from a bottle, and had ended with him sitting in von Osten's car by the Thames, drunk on a crate of ale and throwing up.

That day had been his birthday. He was now twenty-six.

Chapter 48

It was almost dark. As the last glimmer of natural light faded from the sky, the full effect of the blackout became evident; no street lamps, no chinks of light oozing from behind poorly closed curtains. In a matter of minutes, semi-darkness turned to pitch black.

Schneider stood on the corner of the street and peered again at the address on the piece of paper. He couldn't see the writing any longer, but he'd memorised it long before. He wheeled his bicycle slowly down the pavement, along the line of terraced houses, edging forward with his eyes on the curb which had been painted white as a guide. He paused outside the house – 29 Spencer Street.

He propped the bicycle against the wall and fumbled his way down the short path to the door. His first knock was feeble and elicited no response. He rapped harder; a door opened somewhere inside and he hear footsteps padding down the hallway.

"Who is it? Who's there?" A young woman's voice; a naive sounding voice, like an adult imitating a girl. There was a faint lisp on some letters that strengthened that impression. No anxiety in the voice, just curiosity.

"Mrs Wakeley?"

"Who wants to know?"

"My name is Henry Mansell – I'm a friend of your husband's."

After a pause he heard a bolt being slid back and the door opened slightly, until a chain stopped it. He could just see the vague outline of a woman's head.

"A friend of Bernard's?"

"Yes, I was with him in France. Can I have a word with you?"

"Hang on." The sound of the chain being removed followed and the door opened further. Schneider could not see the woman's face; it was darker inside the house than out. He felt a hand take his arm.

"Come in." She tugged gently until he was inside, then closed and bolted the door. She flicked a switch and a dim light came on. She led him down the hallway into the back room. The light was stronger there and Schneider saw the woman clearly for the first time. She was short, with a mop of fair, curly hair; younger than him, he guessed, although the housecoat she wore made her appear older; slim, with a full chest that pressed the housecoat tight. There was a warmth about her that he liked immediately.

"Sorry about that," she said. "This blackout's a blessed nuisance. Can I offer you a cup of tea?"

"Thank you, that would be very nice." The room was small but comfortable. A large Welsh dresser covered one wall, neatly decorated with plates and copper saucepans. There was a gate-legged dining table at one end and two easy chairs at the other, one either side of the fireplace. On the mantelpiece was a wedding photograph and several ornaments. Everything was neat and tidy, and immaculately clean. The only thing out of place was a scattering of toys in one corner; a doll, a wooden tommy gun and some bricks. Mrs Wakeley had disappeared into the kitchen to put the kettle on. When she returned she hurriedly picked up the toys and threw them into a cupboard.

"Please excuse the mess," she said. "The children have only just gone to bed. I let them stay up a bit later than usual of a Friday."

"That's quite alright, Mrs Wakeley. Please don't bother on my account."

"You can call me Marion. It doesn't seem right calling me misses." Schneider tried to place the accent. Newcastle perhaps? He couldn't be certain. Up north somewhere.

There was an awkward silence. He wanted to sit down but thought he should stay standing. He had something extremely difficult to say and it somehow felt correct that he should stand.

"Are you from Bernard's regiment? You're not in uniform. Is it bad news?"

"No – yes. I mean, no I'm not from his regiment, I'm from the Royal Essex. We were with the Warwicks in France." The words were sticking in his throat. Lying was not coming easy to him. "We got to know each other quite well." He had concocted a story sitting in a pub round the corner, keeping as close to the truth as he was able. He was about to continue when the kettle started to whistle and Marion Wakeley wandered into the kitchen to make the tea. She returned with a tray and set it down on the table. As she poured from a teapot beneath a knitted tea cosy, Schneider opened his mouth to say something, but she beat him to it.

"Are you going to tell me Bernard is dead?"

Schneider was taken aback by the simplicity of the question. A simple reply seemed appropriate.

"Yes I am."

"I thought so."

"At least I'm fairly certain." Schneider desperately wanted to soften the blow. In his mind he pictured the prisoners being force marched across

176

a field towards a barn, and Wastian's finger gesture across his throat. How much more certain could he be!

Marion handed him a cup of tea and sat down, indicating that he should do the same.

"What do you mean – fairly certain? Is he dead or isn't he?" She seemed devoid of any emotion; her voice was deadpan. "I though they usually sent a telegram."

"This is not an official visit, Mrs . . . er Marion. I wanted to explain to you as a personal favour to Bernard. Officially he is missing. But I was there and I saw him captured. And . . . and I also saw ...."

"Please," interrupted Marion. "No details. It won't make any difference to anything."

What should he say now? Schneider's mind had gone blank. He sipped his tea and waited for inspiration, but none came.

"I've known it for a while," said Marion softly. She looked across at the stranger. He was nervous, and sympathetic; she felt herself warming to him in his awkwardness. "When all the troops came back from Dunkirk and I didn't hear anything, I knew then. I'm not stupid. I can't imagine Bernard as a prisoner – he isn't the type. Wasn't I mean. I'll have to get used to thinking about him as gone now."

Still no words came to Schneider. He needed a cigarette and pulled a packet from out of his pocket. He couldn't even say, "Do you mind if I smoke?" His expression said it for him.

"Go ahead. I don't, but Bernard did. He smoked forty a day. He was a right chimney."

Schneider lit a cigarette and inhaled deeply. The nicotine didn't help at all. He glanced at the woman sitting opposite him. No sign of sorrow or grief, not even a teardrop in her eyes. Why didn't she collapse in hysterics and uncontrollable weeping? He could handle that more easily. Instead she appeared calm, sitting drinking her tea and talking as if her husband had died years ago. Maybe she was relieved at the news. A blessing, perhaps, that an unhappy marriage was over. He remembered Bernard Wakeley's final words to him: *"I was a lousy husband to her – she's better off without me."* For all Schneider knew she was thinking the same. Whatever her feelings, there were things he didn't know and didn't understand. It wasn't any of his business and he had no intention of prying.

"I've thought about how to tell the children," said Marion. "They haven't seen their dad since March when he came home on leave for a few days, so they're used to not having him around. I'll tell them he's had to go away for a long time and leave it at that. Simon's only four and Annette's not even two yet – far too young to understand. I'll give them the truth when the time is right."

Schneider watched her as she spoke. She was pretty, and her mouth fell naturally into a half smile that made her face very appealing. Her eyes were blue, her complexion slightly florid, and her lips full.

Marion finished her tea. "Well, Mr Mansell."

"Please call me Henry."

"Henry. This must have been a very difficult job for you, coming here like this when you needn't. I appreciate it very much, and I'm sure Bernard would thank you for it too." Schneider though this was an indication that he should leave and started to get up from his seat. Then she said: "I don't drink as a rule, but this is exceptional circumstances. I don't know about you but I fancy a glass of brandy. What do you say?"

Schneider was taken aback and sat down again. He was in need of something stronger than tea. "If you're sure."

Marion opened a cupboard and took out a bottle and two glasses; she poured a small measure for herself and a larger one for her guest. As the liquid burned its way down his throat Schneider relaxed at last.

"I promised Bernard I would come. It was what he wanted."

"Thank you." Her tone suggested to Schneider that she didn't want him to talk about it anymore. Conversation was coming back to him. He changed the subject.

"Where are you from, Marion? Not from around here."

"Sunderland born and bred."

"So how did you find your way to Coventry?"

Marion sipped from her glass, wincing a little as she swallowed, and told her story. Her father was a docker and she was the eldest of nine children. He was a kind, gentle man when sober, but after a night in the pub – which was often – he turned into a brute, swearing and lashing out at anyone or anything. Her mother forever had bruises on one part of her body or another. He hit the children too, which made them cry; then he hit them for crying. So her childhood had been a bittersweet blend of happiness and dread. As she developed from childhood into adolescence, the balance tipped firmly towards dread, and she became desperate to leave home.

She had a friend, her best friend since infant school – Nancy – a wild girl who was always in trouble, and who ran away from a similarly unhappy home life at sixteen. Marion envied her but never had the courage to do the same. They wrote to each other, Nancy travelling around the country getting into all kinds of scrapes, Marion fantasising about being in her place, reading her letters over and over. One day, Nancy wrote to say she had met someone and was getting married. Her fiancé lived in Coventry. Her parents had completely disowned her and refused to attend the wedding. Nancy pleaded with Marion to be there for her, so she borrowed some money from her mother and travelled down to be the one and only bridesmaid.

Nancy's husband-to-be had a friend, Bernard, who was his best man. Bernard took Marion under his wing and looked after her, before and after the brief ceremony. At the reception, held in a function room above a pub, they danced together for most of the evening. He walked Marion back to the cheap boarding house where she was staying the night, and they kissed. It was her first ever kiss, and it felt wonderful. A year later, in Sunderland, a week after her eighteenth birthday, they were married.

"The funny thing is," said Marion, with a little giggle, "Nancy was responsible for me and Bernard meeting, yet by the time we got married she'd cleared off and left her husband. It was embarrassing because Bernard had asked him to be *his* best man and he insisted on going through with it. That meant I couldn't invite her to the wedding – not without a fight starting." Schneider nodded understandingly. "And here I am, five years later, with two kids and a house – and now a widow."

"What happened to Nancy?"

"She's in London, living with husband number two. We still write to each other." What about you, Henry? Tell me about yourself."

So he did. From his childhood and upbringing in Bromsgrove to his marriage to Renate, he told the truth. Then he started to lie. He told Marion that he and his wife had argued when war was declared; he wanted to return to England and she insisted on staying in Germany. So they had gone their separate ways. Schneider came home, signed up and was sent to France with the British Expeditionary Force.

"Do you miss her?" asked Marion.

"In all honesty, no. I did at first, but not anymore."

Marion looked at the clock on the dresser. "My word, look at the time! It's very late. With all this talking I lost track of time. You'd better be on your way."

"Yes, I suppose so."

"Have you got far to go?"

"London."

"London! Good heavens, I thought you must be staying somewhere local. Did you come all this way to tell me about Bernard?"

"Not entirely," said Schneider. "I had another matter to attend to."

Marion looked concerned. "You'll be lucky to catch a train at this time of night."

"Not to worry. I'll hang around at the station and catch the milk train." He moved towards the door. "Thanks for the drink and the conversation, Marion. It's been a pleasure meeting you. I'm just sorry I had to be the bearer of bad news."

Marion stayed in the middle of the room, not following him towards the door. She muttered something but Schneider didn't quite catch what she said.

"I beg your pardon?"

Marion spoke louder this time.

"You can stay if you like. I can make you up a bed in the front room."

Schneider really did not want to leave. He smiled, but again words escaped him.

"We don't have a spare bedroom I'm afraid, with the kids, but at least it would be better than spending the night in a draughty waiting room."

Schneider cleared his throat. "That's very kind of you, but I've imposed upon you too much already. I imagine you would prefer to be alone now."

"No, not really. I appreciate you coming. The least I can do is repay you with a roof over your head for the night. If Bernard was here he would insist. I'm sure he would."

Schneider smiled nervously. "To be perfectly honest, Marion, I don't really fancy stumbling about in the blackout. If you're sure it's not too much trouble. I'll be gone first thing."

"Good, that's settled," said Marion. She led him into the front room and together they pushed the furniture to the sides. Then they manhandled an old mattress from a cupboard underneath the staircase and lay it on the floor. Marion fetched a sheet and some blankets from upstairs and Schneider watched as she tucked them neatly around the mattress and then laid a cushion from the settee at one end. When everything was done, she stood upright with her hands on her waist.

"There, that should be nice and comfy. Goodnight, Henry. Don't forget to turn out the light before you fall asleep."

"I won't. Goodnight, Marion."

She half turned towards the door, then hesitated. On an impulse she turned back towards him, leaned forwards and kissed him on the cheek. "Thank you," she said softly, then left the room and closed the door behind her.

Schneider undressed and climbed into the makeshift bed. But he couldn't sleep. He thought about Marion Wakeley. He was attracted to her, and glad of the opportunity to see her again the next morning. Perhaps she might invite him to stay a while longer. He hoped so. It would be infinitely nicer than returning to Richmond and Otto von Osten.

He lay on his back. It was very quiet, the silence broken only by the sound of a vehicle passing by slowly in the street outside his window. Just as he was resigning himself to a sleepless night and considering the possibility of sitting up for a smoke, he thought he heard something. A creak on the stairs. He lay still, listening. There it was again. A definite creak. He heard the door handle turn. His eyes were fully accustomed to the dark and he could see the door as it slowly opened. A weak circle of orange light panned across the wall; a torch, Schneider guessed, with batteries close to dying.

"Henry, are you awake?" Marion whispered, hesitating in the doorway, the torchlight flickering across her face.

"Yes," replied Schneider. "I can't sleep."

"Me neither." She entered the room, closed the door and tip-toed across to where Schneider lay. The torchlight revealed she was wearing only a thin cotton nightdress. Marion lay down next to him and slid beneath the blanket, nestling gently against his side. As if the most natural thing in the world, he put his arm around her shoulder and they lay still together. Not a word was spoken for five minutes. Then Schneider heard a whimpering sound, and her body started to shake. She was sobbing, almost imperceptibly at first, but gradually increasing in intensity. Soon the sobs turned into full-throated cries, her whole body shuddering as a torrent of pent up emotions poured out of her. When it was over, Schneider's chest was wet from her tears. Still lying on her side, Marion squeezed her legs around his and let an arm fall across his stomach. He could feel her heavy breasts pressing against him.

"Hold me," she whispered. "Please hold me."

For a while they both slept, lying together in a cocoon of mutual need. There was nothing sexual about it; neither of them was aroused. It was comfort they wanted from each other.

And it felt wonderful.

Chapter 49

(Sunday 23rd June 1940)

"About bloody time!" snarled Otto von Osten when Schneider arrived back at the Richmond house on Sunday evening. "Where the hell have you been for the past two days?" He was drunk. In the living room a pile of empty beer bottles overflowed from a crate onto the floor, and a half empty whisky bottle lay on the table.

"Where do you think?" came the sullen reply.

"You were only supposed to take a look at the place. Why did it take so long – was your target in fucking Scotland?" There was malice in every phrase.

They sat at opposite ends of the table, the whisky bottle between them. Schneider wanted to ignore von Osten, but he repeated his questions, demanding answers.

"I did a lot more than look," said Schneider. "I discovered a lot of information about my target, including some aircraft production figures. I even got halfway to securing a job there. All I have to do is turn up again with proof of previous work experience and I'm in." He stared von Osten in the face. "That's what I've been doing."

He omitted to say that all this had taken place on Friday and the rest of the weekend had been spent with Marion Wakeley. She had asked him to stay for dinner, then tea, then breakfast and Sunday lunch. They talked incessantly about a hundred different things. He met her children, Simon and Annette, who were delightful, and took them to play in a local park while Marion got on with some household chores. She showed no sign of emotion about the death of her husband, in fact she didn't mention it. On the Saturday night Schneider had again slept in the front room, only this time without a nocturnal visitor. At least he assumed so; he fell into a deep and contented sleep the moment his head touched the cushion. When the time had come to leave, he felt depressed and would have happily stayed in that cosy little Coventry terraced house forever. It seemed like an oasis of joy compared with the desert of his existence in Richmond. He had promised Marion faithfully he would come and see her again, as soon as he could. And he meant it. As he stood in her hallway about to leave, she pulled him into the front room and kissed him passionately, pressing her body against his. This time there was everything sexual about it. Please come back, the kiss said. I want you.

Von Osten resented the fact that Schneider's trip had gone well, in particular his success on the job front.

"You'll blow your cover if you move too fast," he warned. "Too hasty altogether." Schneider said nothing, which annoyed him even more. "Thank the Lord I'll be rid of you before you get us both hanged. I'm clearing off tomorrow, whether *Hamburg* like it or not."

"Where are you going?"

"None of your damned business."

"It's Southampton, isn't it? The Supermarine factory."

Von Osten glared at him. "How did you know that – who told you?"

"No one. I worked it out for myself."

"Liar! *Hamburg* told you. You've been in contact with Rantzau, haven't you?"

"Of course not. How could I when both *Afu*s were here with you? Nobody told me – I guessed. It's the main Spitfire production plant. It's not my target so it makes sense that it has to be yours. Anyway what does it matter?"

"*I guessed*," mimicked von Osten. "You liar, somebody told you. And so where is your target, if it doesn't matter?"

Schneider remained silent. He had no intention of saying.

"Come on, out with it. If I'm on Spitfires, maybe you're on Hurricanes. I've discovered there's a Hawker factory in Kingston, not far from here. Or a big new place out at Langley, near Slough. I've been doing some research. Which is it?"

"Neither."

Von Osten suddenly stood up, tottering slightly, and slammed a fist down onto the table. His face was red and his eyes open wide with rage.

"Answer me! Who told you about my target? And where have you been for the past two days! There's something going on and I demand to know! TELL ME!"

Schneider recoiled, stumbling as his chair toppled over behind him. Von Osten looked as if he would lunge at him any moment. His fists were clenched tight, the knuckles white. Schneider backed up against the wall, von Osten rounded the table towards him. They stared at each other for a brief moment, then von Osten charged forwards, grabbing Schneider's shoulder with one hand. He was by far the stronger and Schneider could do nothing. Von Osten's other hand drew back ready to launch a close range punch into Schneider's face.

The punch never happened. Both men froze at the sound of a loud knocking, coming from the front door. They looked at each other, all animosity between them on hold. The effect of the alcohol seemed to drain out of von Osten in an instant, anger turning to apprehension.

"Who's that?" whispered Schneider.

"How should I know?"

"Blackout – are we showing a light?"

"No I'm sure not. I checked earlier."

Another knock. Louder this time.

Schneider said: "There's only one way to find out. You go, it's your house. I'll be listening from here."

Von Osten moved into the hallway and called out: "Who is it? What do you want?"

"Mr King?"

"Who wants him?"

"I've come from your doctor. I have the urgent prescription you requested." It was the voice of a Welshman.

"Which doctor?" called von Osten.

"Is that Mr King? Edward King?"

"Which doctor? Tell me."

"Doctor R. The Mr King I am looking for is a *mechanic* I believe. Let me in please."

Schneider whispered: "A courier from *Hamburg*."

Von Osten slid the bolts at the top and bottom of the front door and turned the latch. A short figure barged his way in and slammed the door behind him.

"Hurry up for Christ's sake will you!" he snapped. "I haven't got all bloody night." It was dark in the hallway and the Welshman barked: "Switch the bloody light on."

Von Osten did so. "Who are you?" he said.

"Which one of you is King?"

"I am," replied von Osten. The Welshman peered at him.

"Mechanic, eh? So you must be Quaver." Schneider nodded. "Any chance of a drink? I'm parched."

They went into the living room and Otto von Osten poured three large whiskies. "Who are you?" he asked again.

"Never mind who I am – I've something for you. When you realise what it is perhaps you'll be a bit more courteous." From an inside pocket he drew out an oblong package tied with twine and placed it on the table. "There, with the compliments of the Third Reich. Six hundred quid."

Von Osten undid the package to reveal tightly folded wads of banknotes. He set about counting them, laying them down in two equal piles.

"That will keep you in scotch for a while," said the Welsh stranger. He turned to Schneider. "What happened to you? First I was told there'd be two of you, then one because of an injury, then two again. You didn't parachute in, I know that, so how did you get here?"

"By boat," said Schneider without elaborating. It would sound too fantastic – chauffeured across France by the *Waffen SS*, then ferried over from Dunkirk courtesy of the Royal Navy.

Von Osten finished counting and said to the Welshman: "Who are you? Some kind of a courier?"

"Only when I have to be – and if it doesn't take me too far out of my way. As it happens I only live up the road. Quite a coincidence. I'm here doing what you're here to do, only I've been at it much longer. Whereas you're amateurs playing at being secret agents, I'm a professional. I don't normally do deliveries, but they told me you were desperate for cash." He downed his whisky and helped himself to a refill.

"How did you know the address?"

"*Hamburg.*"

"How did they know?"

The stranger shrugged. "Didn't you tell them?"

"No."

"Well now, that just goes to show. There's no such thing as a secret nowadays."

Von Osten watched him as he spoke. "Haven't I seen you somewhere before?"

"Perhaps we bumped into each other once, on a bus or some such place. How about you – parachuted in, I assume?"

"That's right."

"Why didn't you use the prearranged drop location?"

Von Osten hesitated. "I did."

"No you didn't. I had people looking out for you. They drove all the way to bloody Norfolk and you didn't show. Waste of time that was."

"You seem to know a hell of a lot. So where did I drop then?"

"That I don't know. If I did we would have met before now. I was supposed to help you out."

"*Hamburg* never said anything about it."

"It wasn't necessary for you to know. So what is your brief now, gentlemen?"

"You tell us," said Schneider sarcastically.

"*Hamburg* haven't let me in on everything. They only disclose on a need-to-know basis."

"Well you don't need to know our brief," said von Osten.

"Only making conversation," said the Welshman. "It's just that you may need me again one of these days. I'm a useful person to be able to contact." He picked up a five pound note and waved it in front of them. "There's plenty more where these came from."

Schneider said: "I agree we should not tell you anything unnecessarily. But I can tell you we are leaving here tomorrow. How do we get in touch, should we need your help again?"

The Welshman sat pensively, weighing up whether or not to offer his services to the men. With an air of condescension, he took out a large brown wallet and threw a business card on the table. "Memorise the details on that card. Only use it if absolutely necessary, and speak only to the man whose name is printed on it. Speak only to him. Tell him you want to discuss some electrical supplies for a house in Richmond. Then I'll know it is you." He waited until they had scrutinised the card, then replaced it in his wallet. He stood up.

"Time I was off. May I wish you luck, gentlemen? I think you are going to need it."

"What's that supposed to mean?" said von Osten.

"Nothing in particular. Only now France has fallen I reckon things are going to liven up around here. They'll be expecting Hitler to knock on the door any day now and everyone's getting fifth column fever. That's if Hitler decides to come at all."

"Don't you think he will?" said Schneider.

The Welshman shrugged. "Some say he thinks of Great Britain as a brother nation – that he'll try and negotiate a settlement rather than invade. Others believe he's gone too far down the road to turn back. Who knows what he's thinking."

"If there is no invasion, we're wasting our time here," said von Osten.

"Now that remark is very revealing," said the Welshman. "Your brief must be connected with the invasion in some way then. Intelligence gathering, or sabotage perhaps? Or both. Spying on the Royal Air Force maybe. They're in the front line now – aircraft establishments would be a prime target for a couple of would-be saboteurs."

Otto von Osten did not like that at all.

"Mind your own business and get out!" he shouted. "You nosey Welsh midget."

"Shut up," hissed Schneider. "He's just fishing."

The Welshman was clearly stung by the reference to his height. In return he gave von Osten a look of intense venom.

"Midget! I've just brought you a small fortune, and all I get in return is insults. Forget that card you just memorised, I won't be available when you phone. But it hardly matters. I don't believe you will last ten minutes more before being picked up by British Intelligence. That's not a prediction, that's a guarantee. Anyone who allows themselves to be

186

followed around London and straight back to their base is a non-starter in this game."

"Who followed me?" exclaimed von Osten.

"I did, you fool. I virtually told you just now if you had brains to work it out. *Hamburg* didn't have to tell me your address here, you told me yourself. You led me here. It was so easy." He stepped into the hallway and turned to Schneider. "My advice to you, Mansell – or Quaver if you prefer – is to get away from this oaf as soon as you can."

At the front door the Welshman's final words were spoken quietly. "Next time you transmit to *Hamburg*, put a good word in for me. Tell them Johnny made the delivery."

The diminutive figure melted into the darkness.

Chapter 50

In Berlin, it was Heinrich Müller's turn to report to Reinhardt Heydrich. As usual the summons came late at night and the Chief of Gestapo had to suppress his annoyance at being inconvenienced by the Chief of Reich Security. He was relieved to see Schellenberg there for moral support.

Heydrich began. "So, we all know the outcome of Canaris's investigation into the leaking of Operation *Weser*. Despite being very thorough, his Security Chief, Rohleder, has drawn a blank. The Black Chapel have covered themselves very well. Hardly surprising under the circumstances, eh, Müller?"

"If our suspicions are correct, then yes, I agree."

"I am told that Rohleder was almost too thorough, Schellenberg."

"It would appear so." Schellenberg spoke with a fluidity that suggested this was not the first time he had related the facts. "Canaris did not expect Rohleder to go so far as to send a man to Rome to investigate from the Vatican end. Canaris had also sent Dr Joseph Müller there, to muddy the waters. All the evidence indicated to Rohleder that Müller was the source of the treason, which he reported initially. Then Canaris came up with some nonsense about such allegations being old hat and told Rohleder to forget about it, claiming it was a deliberate attempt to undermine Müller's connections with the Vatican. Rohleder had no choice but to accept what his chief was telling him."

Heydrich looked at Heinrich Müller. "Your namesake was almost certainly responsible then, with Canaris the overseer. But no proof."

"There is no evidence to implicate Canaris," Müller proffered. "Plenty of rumours and talk, but then there is gossip about anyone you care to mention, if you listen out for it." *Including about you*, thought Müller. The possibility of Heydrich's parents being Jewish had long kept tongues wagging behind closed doors. "He's a busy man at present. The *Abwehr* suddenly have a lot more territory in which to operate, and Canaris is on the move, establishing new offices. He's in Paris now, as will be the Führer in a few days' time."

Heydrich tapped his fingers impatiently. "I need to know what he's really up to. Schellenberg, can you shed any light on this? What about *Abwehr* foreign agents – are any stepping out of line to your knowledge?"

"So far as we can ascertain, no. There are strong networks in most countries – all seem to be functioning well enough. It is impossible to know the activity of every agent."

"Any weak links?"

Schellenberg shook his head thoughtfully. "We know virtually nothing of what goes on in Great Britain. As you know, the Führer forbade any activity until six months ago."

"That's not necessarily going to stop a good intelligence man, is it?" mused Heydrich. "England, I would imagine, is the prime country a traitor to the Reich would seek as an ally. How many agents are there operating there at present?"

"No more than a handful."

"Any recent additions?"

"Two were sent in under Göring's instructions a few weeks ago. He wants intelligence on aircraft production."

"Are they being productive?"

"Not yet."

"Well I wonder what they are up to – making unofficial peace overtures, perhaps?"

Schellenberg shook his head. "Unlikely. They are low level operatives."

"But not impossible!" snapped Heydrich suddenly. "As such they would go unnoticed. That's precisely the kind of shrewd move Canaris would make – to play a double game with agents you would least suspect. Look at the Black Chapel! The Vatican is hardly a direct route to Belgium and Holland!"

Müller sat forward in his chair and said: "What are you suggesting – that Canaris is feeding information to the British through his agents?"

"Possibly."

"But how could we ever be sure? How can we check? We're having enough trouble finding evidence against Canaris here. Intelligence wise, Britain is a closed book to us."

Heydrich glanced across at Schellenberg for a moment. "Not entirely a closed book."

"I'm sorry," said Müller. "I do not follow."

Heydrich's mouth spread into the beginnings of a smile that lasted only a second. "You wouldn't . . . eh, Schellenberg?"

"Indeed not."

The ice cold eyes of the Security Chief seemed to freeze over even more than usual. "We have a trump card to play. Someone we can call upon to do that checking. But not yet. Not yet. That is all I will say on the matter. Goodnight, gentlemen. Keep me informed."

Chapter 51

A door slammed shut somewhere in the house. Schneider woke with a start. He sat up in bed and glanced at the dial of his luminous watch. A few minutes before four.

Footsteps on the stairs. His mind flashed back for a second to the night Marion had come to him in the night; his first awareness had been the sound of footsteps like this. But these were the loud, clumsy steps of von Osten stumbling his way upstairs from the living room where Schneider had left him after the Welshman had gone. He heard him reach the landing. A loud, sickly belch ripped through the otherwise silent air; then nothing. No sound of a bedroom door opening, no thud of shoes being thrown to the ground, no click of a light switch, no creak of a bed under the weight of a drunken man. Only silence.

A minute passed. Still nothing. He must be standing on the landing, Schneider thought. Just standing there. He couldn't have collapsed; there would have been a thud as he hit the floor. What was he up to? Listening for something? There seemed no sense to it, and that worried Schneider.

He eased himself out of bed and tiptoed across the room. He was wearing only underpants. At the door he placed an ear to the wood and listened intently. Nothing.

No, wait. He could just hear faint breathing; muffled, laboured breathing, coming from the other side of the door. He heard a click. Crisp, staccato, distinctive; the sound of a pistol being primed. Von Osten was getting ready to kill him. That was the only explanation. Schneider had no gun, but he needed a weapon, fast. He hurried back to the bed and fumbled underneath. His fingers found a solid metal rod and closed around the poker he had hidden there days before, when things started going wrong between them. He was half way back across the room when the door burst open.

Von Osten staggered in, Luger in one hand, torch in the other. In the half-light from the landing light beyond, the Luger looked obscenely long, with a fat silencer protruding from the muzzle. Schneider crouched instinctively, diving forwards into a roll. As he did so he whipped the poker round fast in a scythe-like motion, hoping it would hit home around waist height, where the Luger was. But it was too low. Instead the poker raked across von Osten's shins.

Von Osten was taken aback by the semi-naked figure caught briefly in his torch beam. His brain could not register the significance fast enough in his drunken state, and for a brief moment he stood in the centre of the room, his torch trained on the empty bed. The next thing he knew, he was slumped on the floor, pain flooding through his lower legs. He fell on his back with the Luger and torch still in each hand, and through a mist of alcohol and pain he saw Schneider rushing towards the door. He fired without aiming. The bullet missed its target by several feet and the 'phut' of the bullet was followed by the sound of wall plaster shattering.

Schneider charged out of the bedroom. The sound of the gun gave him agility he didn't imagine possible. Still clutching the poker, he rushed down the stairs, taking them two at a time, not daring to look back to see if he was being followed. Halfway down was a tiny square landing where the staircase turned to the left. He struck the side with a combination of chest, shoulder and arm before ricocheting onto the lower stairs. The poker went flying. The hallway light below was off and beneath him lay a void of darkness. Plunging forward, he immediately lost his footing and reached out for the banister, but he was moving too fast to keep a grip. He thrust both arms out in front in a defensive gesture, and with a sickening thud his body hit the hallway floor. Every ounce of air was crushed from his lungs, and he lay as though pinned to the linoleum, gasping for breath.

He lay still, his chest hurting badly. From behind him he heard a series of thumping noises. He half turned and looked up the stairs. A pair of feet appeared at the edge of the small landing from the upper stairs. Von Osten was sliding down on his backside. His shoes were shiny with blood, as were his trousers as they came into view. When von Osten's face became visible, it was ashen with pain. He was shaking from a mixture of shock and exertion. He shuffled himself round awkwardly until he was slumped against the wall, staring down into the hallway. Gradually he was able to make out the shape of Schneider spread-eagled on the floor below. The Luger was clenched firmly in his right hand. He raised it slowly. Even with a shaking hand it was an easy shot to make.

Schneider could not move; he seemed rooted to the spot. The fact that von Osten was pointing a gun at him and intent on firing made no difference. His body was a dead weight. A voice in his head was saying: "This is it. This is the end."

Von Osten's finger squeezed the trigger, trying to control the shot despite his shaking hand. It didn't matter if he missed first time. Schneider wasn't going anywhere and he had plenty of bullets.

"Traitor," growled von Osten. "Fucking traitor!"

Crack!

Schneider felt nothing. Strange, the shot sounded as though it had come from above his head. Not a shot in fact, more like the sound of wood splintering. Von Osten was staring past him, a blank look on his face. Schneider managed to twist his head round, just as the sound was repeated. Crack!

The front door collapsed inwards, its hinges shattered by two mighty sledgehammer blows. The top edge missed Schneider's head by inches, and a gust of air sent grit and dust into his eyes. He blinked painfully and did not see the powerful beam of light pinpoint von Osten, Luger in hand, on the stairs. But he heard the retort of a rifle, and von Osten's scream as he slumped sideways, his right arm shattered.

There was a great deal of shouting as heavy footsteps thundered past Schneider. Some charged past von Osten and up the stairs, others could be heard in the kitchen and other downstairs rooms.

"Upstairs clear!" he heard. "Downstairs clear!"

Someone was kneeling next to him, and he felt a blast of stale breath as the person leaned forward to scrutinise his face.

"This must be Quaver. The one on the stairs will be Mechanic." The voice was that of a well-spoken Englishman.

"Looks like they was fighting, sir." A different voice, with a London accent.

"Right. Get someone to look at that man's arm, will you?"

"His legs are bleeding as well."

The well-spoken voice said: "Are you alright? Anywhere hurting?"

Schneider shook his head slightly. "I think I'm alright. A few bruised limbs, nothing serious. Dirt in my eyes is the worst." His breathing was almost back to normal, but he too was shaking now. The man helped him into a sitting position against the wall.

"What's going on?" asked Schneider. "Who are you?"

The reply was chillingly simple. "You are being detained on suspicion of being an enemy agent."

Schneider felt an enormous wave of relief on hearing these words. He looked up at the man who spoke them. He couldn't make out his features, so he smiled in the general direction of the face and gasped: "Thank God. Oh thank God!"

PART TWO

Chapter 52

(Monday 8ᵗʰ July 1940)

It was several hours after dawn by the time the two Tiger Moths eventually rose into the sky over Catterick and headed due north. Alison Webb would have preferred to set off at first light, but circumstances had determined otherwise, and the delay had made her irritable.

Firstly, the airfield had to be cleared of the debris that was scattered every night to prevent enemy planes from landing, as it was at Hatfield. Invasion fever was rife. German troops were reported to be massing along the northern coast of France and landing barges were moored in the Channel ports. Hitler's troops would soon be on their way, and anything that could possibly hamper them must be done. Then Heather had complained of a headache and clambered out of bed with remarkable lethargy, the result of too many gins in the RAF mess the night before. Finally, to top it all, she had insisted on leaving a note for the charming young squadron leader she had flirted with all evening, which involved rushing around trying to find a pencil, paper and an envelope; not an easy task at six thirty in the morning.

Despite all the delays, the sun still hung low on the horizon as they took off; the sky was deep blue with not a cloud visible, even from several hundred feet above the ground where the horizon stretched further. The forecast was good. The people of Great Britain would enjoy a warm and sunny July day.

Heather was leading and they were flying low, a standard procedure which Pauline Gower insisted upon for various reasons: it was warmer close to the ground, it helped the Observer Corps recognise them as friend rather than foe, and it was easier to keep out of the way of other aircraft. Alison followed, a hundred yards behind and slightly to starboard. Her irritation gradually faded to be replaced by a deep sense of pleasure at being airborne.

A month had passed since her interview. She had successfully completed her circuit of the airfield at Whitchurch in a Tiger Moth to the satisfaction of the British Airways instructor and was now a fully-fledged member of the Air Transport Auxiliary. He had passed her, but equally reprimanded her for performing a loop followed by a roll just before coming in to land, which, he claimed, had damn near made him change his mind. He told her bluntly to cut out the clever stuff; the ATA had been created to deliver aircraft safely, not mow them into the ground. Soon afterwards she had been fitted for and received delivery of her official ATA uniform, consisting of fore-and-aft cap, dark blue tunic and skirt, blue WAAF shirt, black tie, wings and stripes in gold, black silk stockings and shoes. Flying in a skirt was draughty, so most of the women wore slacks instead. The shoes were abandoned for fur-lined flying boots. It could be bitterly cold in the cockpit of a Tiger Moth, even in summer, and over their uniforms went thick Sidcot suits. Additional clothing consisted of thick leather gloves, several pairs of socks, woolen knickers and a well-padded cushion. Alison had to harden herself to the cold, having become used to the baking Australian climate. Heather showed little sympathy and assured her that compared to the appalling conditions they had suffered earlier in the year, this was the height of luxury. Flying Moths the winter before had consisted mainly of struggling to maintain control of an aircraft with totally numb hands and feet.

They were to deliver their aircraft to Kinloss, an RAF repair and storage unit on the Scottish coast, north-east of Inverness. Alison had already made several trips there, also to Lossiemouth, a similar base further along the coast. With good weather and favourable winds it was possible to make the outward journey in a day, but the morning before Heather had been held up getting back from South Wales and all the other ferry pilots had left on assignments shortly after breakfast. Forbidden by regulations to make such a long flight alone, Alison had no choice but to wait. They hadn't left Hatfield until early afternoon.

It was usual to fly north-west to Oxford and bypass Birmingham to the south-west to avoid the mass of barrage balloons protecting its many factories and manufacturing plants. Then north through Shropshire to a corridor of air space between the balloons at Liverpool and Widnes, past Blackpool, over the Lake District and so across the border into Scotland. It was the safe route, keeping them well away from the exposed eastern coast and any possible enemy activity.

As they were late setting off, Heather suggested an experiment; a more direct route, flying due north towards Lincolnshire, staying to the east of the Pennines, heading for York, then Newcastle, keeping the Northumberland coast well to starboard and entering Scotland across the Firth of Forth. Alison agreed and they set off feeling rather like pioneers, mapping new territory. So long as they stayed clear of the coast itself and any anti-aircraft batteries there, all should be well. She just hoped Pauline Gower would approve if she found out and not tear them off a strip.

As was often the case on ATA flights, the decision to land was made through necessity. With light fading rapidly, Catterick was in the right place at the right time. As they approached to land they saw a line of Spitfires to the left of the airfield, the late sun glistening off the canopies and adding an orange glow to the camouflaged wings. It was a magnificent sight from above.

The duty officer found them beds in a WAAFS' hut, and the majority of the evening was spent in the officers' mess. Heather flirted outrageously with all and sundry, Alison smiling tight-lipped by her side, making polite conversation as she sipped a tomato juice. This was their first trip together alone, and Alison was not finding it easy. She thought Heather's behaviour embarrassing. When they were alone at the flat in Hatfield they got on splendidly, and if there were other girls around. But when surrounded by handsome pilots, most of them younger than her, Heather was like a bitch on heat.

Alison was sorely tempted to leave her to it, and would have done had it not been for the flight lieutenant. She had barely noticed him at first, sitting at a corner table, seemingly oblivious to the presence of the two women. Then he glanced in her direction for a moment, and their eyes met; he smiled, she half-smiled back and turned away. And that, so it appeared, was that.

There was something about his face – a nice, warm, inviting face. She found herself stealing glances across at him whenever she could. He appeared engrossed in conversation and not once did she catch him looking her way again. Each time she glanced at him she absorbed a little more until she had a clear mental image of his appearance. Light brown hair, slim, roundish in the face, about her age. Definitely, most definitely, attractive.

Then all of a sudden he was gone, and another man was sitting in his seat. Alison glanced around, trying to see if he was still in the mess. But he seemed to have disappeared, probably back to his quarters, she surmised. How disappointing. Such a lovely face, the kind of face you could gaze at for hours and never tire of it. His mouth was perfect, the kind of mouth she would be happy to kiss. Alison surprised herself as she daydreamed. She hadn't had thoughts like that for a long time, and about a complete stranger! He might be married for all she knew, or engaged. She turned her attention back to Heather and a silly conversation full of innuendos and suggestiveness.

Then a voice at her side said: "Hello, I hope these wolves aren't pestering you too much."

A crop of hills forced Heather to gain altitude, and Alison followed. They took it in turns to navigate, and although Heather was as fine a navigator as anyone in the women's ferry pool, Alison kept an eye on her map through force of habit. The richness of the Yorkshire Dales gradually changed into the more barren landscape of Northumbria. A map and compass was all they had to rely on. On a day such as this it was easy; but in fog or low cloud it could be a nightmare.

By mid-morning, fuel was getting low and Alison scrutinised her map for a place to fill up. She drew level with Heather and pointed towards the ground. Heather nodded and allowed Alison to take the lead. Shortly afterwards they landed on the small grass airstrip of a private flying club and taxied over to the wooden shed that acted as a clubhouse. The young man who came out to greet them was visibly stunned to see two women climbing out of the aircraft and when Heather kissed him on the cheek he blushed profusely. Three quarters of an hour later they were back in the air with full tanks and hot coffee inside them. They were several miles due west of Alnwick, and right on course. Soon Berwick-upon-Tweed floated past below their starboard side, and shortly before noon they flew out across the Firth of Forth for the most dangerous stretch of the journey because of the concentration of anti-aircraft positions along the coastline. There was always the chance of coming across a trigger happy unit that fired first and consulted aircraft recognition charts later. Alison took the lead for a while as she knew Heather hated crossing water. She took the Tiger Moth as low as she dared, steering clear of the numerous ships in the vast estuary, and soon reached land on the far side. Then a short hop across Fife to St Andrews Bay and the Firth of Tay, and inland again to refuel at the RAF storage unit at Edzell.

The final hundred miles or so were the most spectacular, with the peaks of the Cairngorms visible to the west as they flew over the Grampian region, gaining height to maintain a steady flight path. The Scottish landscape stretched out like a three-dimensional map before them. As they eventually descended towards Kinloss weather conditions were still as perfect as they had been on leaving Catterick. Alison was tired and cold, but blissfully content.

Before they even landed it was obvious all was not well at Kinloss. They could see people scurrying around like ants and the anti-aircraft guns were manned and ready to fire. As soon as the Tiger Moths were down, Alison saw airmen waving frantically at them to clear the runway. She taxied into a corner of the aerodrome, Heather close behind. As they stretched their cold and aching limbs, a young NCO ran up and shepherded them into a slit trench on the edge of the runway.

"Sorry about this, ladies," he said, breathlessly. "There's a flap on. Bandits in the area, though we're not quite sure where exactly."

"Well!" declared Heather indignantly, "I didn't think this sort of thing went on up here. Aren't we supposed to bring these kites all this way to keep them safe from the Germans?"

"I know," said the NCO. "Most unusual . . . and in broad daylight. Don't know what they're playing at. Probably lost." He handed over two tin helmets. "Here, better put these on."

Alison took one and placed it firmly on her head.

Heather ignored the offer. "No thanks, can't bear the beastly things. Simply ruin the hair."

"You've been wearing a flying helmet all morning," said Alison.

Heather winked. She took a mirror from her handbag and sat on the floor in the slit trench to apply some lipstick.

Alison turned to the NCO. "Have you dispersed any of the aircraft?"

He shook his head. "We don't have any orders to. They're supposed to be dispersed enough up here. Anyway, this is only a precaution. If there are enemy planes about, the boys at Wick will deal with them. They've got a squadron of Hurricanes."

"We can put a couple in the air for you," offered Alison. "At least they won't be sitting targets on the ground."

"I'll inform the duty officer," said the NCO, with a somewhat condescending smile. "I'm sure it won't be necessary."

It wasn't. Forty minutes later the all-clear sounded and news filtered through that Wick itself had been the target. There were casualties, both men and machines, and Kinloss was to expect several Hurricanes for urgent repair within the next few hours. For Alison and Heather this meant it would be wise to leave as soon as possible. Normally they would ask the commanding officer or his adjutant to telephone around to see if they could beg a lift on a plane back south, but a tentative enquiry was met with little hope.

"Awfully sorry," the adjutant said. "You know we help whenever we can, but we're stretched at the moment. The best I can offer you is a lift into Inverness. I've a driver leaving in about half an hour."

Heather groaned. "On no, not the bloody train!"

"That's all I can do." The adjutant looked genuinely sympathetic. "Unless you'd like to wait until tomorrow. Things may have eased up a bit by then."

Heather and Alison both knew what that meant; an uncomfortable night in a draughty Nissen hut, and no guarantee of a flight the next day.

"We'll take the lift into Inverness," said Alison. "Thanks all the same."

"Jolly good. Get yourselves something to eat and I'll have the driver pick you up from the mess."

It was early evening when they were dropped off outside Inverness Station. The overnight did not leave for two hours, so they settled in a hotel bar with pink gins for company. They wore slacks; their skirts were packed away in overnight bags, together with their Sidcot suits. A few heads turned, and a disapproving "tut-tut" floated their way, such attire regarded by some as rather *infra dig*. The two ferry pilots neither noticed nor cared. Heather talked about her squadron leader.

"He's so wonderfully handsome. Didn't you think so, Ally?"

"Very." Alison was thinking about the flight lieutenant.

"His family are very well off."

"Always a bonus." Alison knew nothing of the flight lieutenant's background. Her mind floated back to that moment the night before when she suddenly found him standing next to her, saying he hoped the wolves weren't pestering her. He was even better-looking close up.

"I thought you were supposed to be eagles, not wolves," Alison had responded.

The flight lieutenant laughed, a little too loudly. He was nervous! "Only when they're in their kites. On the ground they resort to wolf-like behaviour."

"Oh dear, I'd better be on my guard." Neither of them spoke for a few moments. Alison could sense he was looking at her and she felt herself blushing.

"Forgive me for staring at you like that," he said. "Very rude I know, but I'm sure I've seen you somewhere before. I just can't think where."

How disappointing, Alison thought. Such an ordinary line from someone who had all the promise of being rather extraordinary.

In the Inverness hotel bar, Heather chattered on. Her squadron leader's names was Stuart Innes.

"He's commanding officer of 188 'Midas' squadron – they fly the Spits we saw when we landed. Stuart's simply aching to get at the enemy, but they haven't had much of a chance yet."

"They will."

Heather lowered her voice. "I know I only met him for the first time last night, Ally, but I just had to let him kiss me, when he escorted me back to the WAAFS' hut." Then as an afterthought she added: "Only a kiss."

"How very restrained of you, Heather. It's not like you to be so coy."

Heather looked hurt. "You make me sound like a ten-bob tart!"

"Well you are!" Alison chuckled. "Only teasing. But let's face it, you do have a bit of a reputation for getting your man. And you have been known to disregard the rule book."

"I know. And as far as Squadron Leader Stuart Innes is concerned, the rule book goes out of the window in future – if there is a future."

Alison had not been kissed by the flight lieutenant, whose name was Daniel Rodigan. Nor had he even tried.

"I've got it!" he had cried. "Hendon! You used to teach flying there."

"Well, yes I did – for a while."

"That's right, I remember now. It must have been – now let me think – thirty-seven. The year I learnt to fly . . . at Hendon."

"I'm awfully sorry," said Alison. "Your memory is better than mine. I don't remember you."

"Oh that's understandable," said Rodigan. "You didn't teach me, and I don't think we ever spoke. But I remember seeing you around." He thought for a moment. "As I seem to recall, you were nearly always in the company of an infuriatingly good-looking fellow. A Scandinavian, I seem to remember."

"Norwegian. He was my fiancé."

"Ah," said Rodigan, with a slight flatness in his tone. "Presumably your husband now?"

"It never came to that. Not quite."

"I'm sorry," said Rodigan, who wasn't sorry at all.

"It's quite alright. I'm rather flattered you should remember me."

"There aren't many female flying instructors around. You'd be pretty hard to forget. And you're quite a pilot, I remember watching you. Impressive stuff."

The more they chatted, the more Alison warmed to him. The crowded room seemed to fade into the background as they became absorbed in each other's company. Shortly after ten o'clock, Alison said she ought to be leaving, and he offered to walk her back to the WAAFS' hut. Heather, rather drunk by this time, opted to stay longer as the squadron leader was gaining her attention against stiff competition.

Flight Lieutenant Rodigan had taken her arm to guide her through the darkness. As they stood at the hut door, a small shaft of soft light from a poorly closed blackout curtain illuminated their faces.

"It's been a pleasure meeting you, Alison. I hope I see you again."

"I hope so too. Perhaps the next time we run out of daylight near Catterick."

Rodigan looked disappointed. "I suppose that could be tomorrow, next week, or never."

"We make the trip fairly often," Alison said encouragingly. "The weather is our guide as much as anything. Probably won't be more than a week or so."

"I doubt we'll be here then."

"Oh?"

"We're moving south soon. Our squadron's earmarked to reinforce Eleven Sector. Losses are high down there."

"Hush." Alison touched her lips with a finger. "Haven't you heard about idle talk costing lives?"

"Goodness, you're right, I shouldn't be telling you such things! You'll keep that to yourself I hope, or I could be for it. But somehow I think you're someone I can trust."

"Mr Chamberlain was saying that about Adolf Hitler not so long ago."

"Well you don't look like a fifth columnist."

"What *do* they look like?"

"I have to admit, I haven't the foggiest!" His face spread into a wide grin. He took Alison's hand and shook it firmly. "Goodnight. It really has been a pleasure."

"Goodnight."

No, Alison had not been kissed by the flight lieutenant; he had shaken her hand. She finished her third pink gin and looked at her watch. "Come on, Heather, we don't want to miss that train after all. Stop daydreaming about Squadron Leader Innes and finish your drink."

"I'm absolutely dreading this journey," said Heather. "It's not so bad the first couple of times, but the novelty wears off rather quickly. I'm used to cadging lifts home."

To their utter dismay the train was very crowded and there were no seats to be found. Soldiers and civilians with their bags and suitcases monopolised every compartment, and people were standing in the corridors.

"I don't believe it!" gasped Alison. "Where are they all going?"

A young soldier with a broad Scottish accent overheard. "They're panicking," he said. "A couple of bombs land nearby and suddenly everyone is overdue to stay with their relatives in the glens. As for us, we're heading doon sooth to finish off Hitler coz you English canna."

The train pulled off and gradually picked up speed. Heather slumped on to the floor in the corridor. "I can't bear this! It'll drive me potty."

"Don't worry," said Alison. "We'll get a seat as soon as some of these people get off."

"Knowing my luck they're all going to London. How about trying to find a lift along the way? We're bound to stop somewhere near an RAF base. We could telephone from a station when we stop."

Alison nodded her approval. "It's an idea. Any suggestions where?"

"Catterick if I have my way."

"Alright, Catterick it is."

"Ally, I was only joking!" Heather looked at her friend quizzically. "You did realise?"

"I'm not, I think it's an excellent idea. We travel part of the way by train then pick up a lift for the remainder of the journey. I'm sure Pauline will be impressed by our initiative."

"Well, if you think so." Heather sounded dubious. "I really was only larking about. It doesn't have to be Catterick."

"Don't you want the chance to see your squadron leader again?"

"Of course I do."

"And so you shall. Now shut up and let's try and get some sleep. Those pink gins have made me feel dopey. It doesn't look as though anyone's going to give up their seats for a couple of worn out ferry pilots."

Heather stood up and pulled her bag onto her shoulder. "They don't need to," she said. "Come on, follow me. This calls for desperate measures. I'll show you a little trick I learnt on one of these blessed trips a while ago." She pushed her way along the corridor, glancing through the glass doors into each compartment, until she stopped outside one. "This will do."

Alison peered inside. "It's full."

Heather pointed upwards. "The luggage racks aren't. Come on Ally, I've found us a couple of hammocks."

Alison watched in amazement as Heather slid open the compartment door and approached a soldier sitting in one of the seats.

"I say, would you mind giving me a leg up?" A moment later Heather was stretched out on the netting of the luggage rack. "Could you do the same for my friend there?" With the soldier's help, Alison clambered up onto the rack opposite. People in the compartment smiled and one or two laughed.

"Bloody good idea, ladies," grinned the soldier. "Any room for anymore up there?"

"Certainly not!" called Heather with mock indignation. "Would someone be kind enough to wake us when we're back in England?"

An elderly lady said: "I will. Don't you worry, my dears."

"Thanks," said Heather. "Tea and toast at the border, Ally?"

There was no reply. Alison was fast asleep.

Chapter 53

(Tuesday 9ᵗʰ July 1940)

"Hello, could I speak to Squadron Leader Innes, please? This is Second Officer Heather Norbury – Air Transport Auxiliary."

Heather and Alison were squeezed in a telephone box at Darlington Station. They had slept surprisingly well in their makeshift hammocks and the old lady had done as she had promised and woken them, albeit well past the border as they were approaching Newcastle. Close scrutiny of a map showed that Darlington was the nearest stop to Catterick. They arrived there at seven thirty; tea and a sandwich in the buffet had revived them and it was now almost eight.

"No this is not a personal call, could you connect me as quickly as possible?" Heather placed a hand over the telephone. "They're trying to locate him. If they don't have any luck I'll talk to the C.O."

Alison was having second thoughts. "I'm not so sure this was a good idea after all. Can't we hop on the next train?"

Heather looked horrified. "What! Too late to change our minds now, old girl. Anyway, it was your idea in the . . . Hello, Stuart? It's Heather, from the ATA. I bet you didn't expect to hear from me so soon! We have a bit of a problem – we're stranded at Darlington on our way back from delivering those Tiger Moths. Yes, quite a coincidence. Anyway, we were wondering if there was any chance of cadging a lift from Catterick. There must be transports or something going our way." Heather listened for a moment. "Splendid, I knew you'd be able to help us out." She put her hand over the phone again and whispered: "He's going to fix it with the station commander." Then into the phone: "Haven't a clue about getting to Catterick. Oh I say, do you think he'd mind? We'll wait outside the station for him. About three quarters of an hour? Wonderful. Yes, Alison, the one who was with me the other night. Really? Well that is news. Bye for now."

Before the hand piece was back on its cradle, Alison said: "What was that last bit about, the bit about me?"

Heather brushed past her and out of the box. "Oh, nothing."

"Don't be silly, of course it was something. Please tell me."

Heather turned and faced her friend. "You sly old goat. Now I know why you agreed to stop off at Catterick."

"What do you mean?"

"According to Stuart, there's a certain flight lieutenant in his squadron who will be rather delighted to see you again."

"I don't know what you're talking about," huffed Alison. "Which flight lieutenant – I talked to several."

"Does the name Rodigan ring any bells?"

Alison looked sheepish all of a sudden. "Yes it does actually. Sorry, Heather, I've been a bit of a fraud. I was rather hoping to bump into him again. He's very nice."

"Goodness me, this is a turn up for the books. Ally with a crush on someone."

"Oh do shut up!" Alison walked away and sat down on a bench underneath the station awning. There weren't many people around and yesterday's fine weather had been replaced by a grey blanket of mist.

Heather sat down next to her. "He must be something special. I won't tease you again, Ally. Promise."

"Thanks. Who's coming to pick us up?"

"Stuart is sending his batman."

"I don't know if this flight lieutenant is special or not yet. How can you tell? I do know that I really enjoyed being with him – and that I keep thinking about him. It seems sensible to try and see him again, since the opportunity has arisen."

"Absolutely," agreed Heather as she took out her mirror and lipstick. "That's just how I feel about Stuart. I know exactly what you mean."

Do you? wondered Alison. Somehow she doubted it.

Chapter 54

Erich Schneider sat on the edge of the crude wooden bed, his fingers running nervously through trumpet scales on his knee. He stared around the spartan cell that was now his home. He hated it. He felt lonely and isolated; the world was going about its business, and he wasn't a part of it.

It was more than two weeks since he and von Osten had been captured in what MI5's B1A operatives later dubbed 'The Richmond Raid'. Everyone involved had been pleased with the outcome; two enemy agents in the bag, plus the welcome confirmation that agent Snow was still proving his worth. The only discordant element emanated from one of the Special Branch team who helped to coordinate the operation and was heard to remark it would have been better to wait five more minutes before going in 'to give the bastard Krauts time to top each other.' Naturally enough Lieutenant-Colonel Ballard Ruskin did not agree. The more alive they were the better; raw material to mould and adapt for his own very specific requirements, and to reinforce the position of the German agents he already controlled. Things were looking decidedly rosy for Wireless Branch.

He had not been ill-treated, quite the reverse. With the exception of one NCO, his captors had been respectful and reasonable. The interrogations were over now, and they had been conducted without any physical abuse, which had surprised him. But there was no need; he could not have been more cooperative. Every question had been answered fully and honestly, and there had been no need to coax information out of this particular enemy agent.

After his capture, Schneider had been taken to an MI5 reception centre near St Albans. After an initial interrogation, which had taken more the form of a friendly chat, he had been transferred to MI5's new detention centre at Latchmere House just off Ham Common in Surrey. So new in fact that he was one of the first to be incarcerated at Camp 020, as it had been designated. He was transported in a van with blacked windows and had no idea where he was being taken. If he had, the irony would have amused him; Ham Common was less than three miles down the road from von Osten's house in Richmond.

He spent much of his time thinking about Marion Wakeley. His feelings for her had escalated since his capture. He badly wanted to see her again and to spend time together. To make love to her. She was the one beacon of light in his otherwise grim existence. There was something about her; a simplicity, a straightforwardness, a naturalness. She was uncomplicated. Very different from Renate. Perhaps that was the attraction. He wanted to send a message to her, but that was impossible. His captors didn't even know she existed.

There was guilt too, for feeling this way. He was a married man with a wife in Germany; an unfaithful wife, but a wife nevertheless. As he had left Heidelberg the night he witnessed Renate in bed with Bruno Rolf, he remembered a strong feeling that a chapter in his life had come to an end, that there would be no going back. Hardly surprising under the circumstances. Later, on the deck of the Kilkenny, sailing away from Dunkirk, he had felt a similar sense of leaving everything behind him forever; more intense this time. Everything in Germany that had been part of his life and meant anything to him, both physically and emotionally, was gone. Yet still there remained some guilt about being attracted to another woman. He did not understand his own feelings.

Naively, Schneider had half believed that once he had told his story in full he might be allowed to go about his business. After all, the whole thing had been a terrible mistake. He should never have let Renate persuade him to imagine for one moment that he was cut out to be a spy. He had realised the error of his ways and could assure the authorities he was indeed a loyal British citizen. Surely the story of Renate's infidelity in itself would convince them that he wanted nothing more to do with Germany, the *Abwehr,* or his fickle wife. As for the way he had been shunted through France to Dunkirk, risking life and limb, that was the decider.

It soon became apparent during the interrogations that these men knew a great deal about German intelligence operations and personnel.

"How is Dr Rantzau?" asked the stocky, monocled colonel who put most of the questions. "I presume he was your mentor."

"That's right, he was," confirmed Schneider.

"Of course that's not his real name. Now what was it – I always struggle to remember."

"I'm afraid I don't know."

The colonel answered his own question: "Ritter – Nikolaus Ritter. Blondish hair, medium build, gold tooth. Lived in the United States for a while before the war. Excellent English, if a little Americanised as I seem to recall."

"That's him," said Schneider, taken aback by the accuracy of the description. "I didn't know his real name."

"How about you, Erich, what do you prefer to be known as – Schneider or Mansell?

"My real name is Tomlin."

"Eric Tomlin it is then. Tell me, why did the *Abwehr* choose Quaver as your codename? Are you musical?"

"I play the trumpet."

"Aha, classical or the other?"

"Both. I've worked in dance bands and played some jazz, but mostly I've played in orchestras. I don't have a preference."

"We didn't expect you, you know. Of course we knew you were supposed to arrive with your mechanic friend, Otto von Osten. But we were rather led to believe that Dr Rantzau had changed his mind and was only sending one agent on this mission."

The depth of their knowledge staggered Schneider. "How the hell do you know all this?" he asked. There was no answer. He picked up on this cue and told how he had hurt his ankle during training and been flown into France, driven by motorcycle to near Dunkirk and evacuated from the beach. There was silence around the table as he told his tale, and for a few moments when he had finished. He knew they believed him; it was too preposterous a story to be made up.

"Great Scott!" exclaimed the colonel. "No wonder we couldn't keep tabs on you. It's remarkable you're here at all."

It continued throughout the rest of the day and every day. Gentle conversation, a gradual easing out of all that Schneider knew until every drop of information had been gleaned, and noted down. He told them everything they wanted to know; how he was recruited, details of his training, names and descriptions of the tutors, locations of premises, layout of the Messerschmitt factory at Augsburg, equipment issued to agents, codes and ciphers, sabotage techniques, his target, the reconnaissance trip to Castle Bromwich. He spent an entire afternoon alone explaining everything about his *Afu* radio, most of which they knew already. He left out only one aspect. He told them nothing about his conversation with Bernard Wakeley at Wormhout, or his visit to Marion in Coventry.

Lt.-Col. Ballard Ruskin sat inconspicuously throughout these sessions. He listened more than he spoke, but his occasional questions were significant when they came.

"Did Dr Rantzau give you background information about the factory at Castle Bromwich? Was he able to tell you much that might help you in your attempts to infiltrate the plant?"

"Weren't told the identity of our targets until we were here in England. They were keen for us not to know in advance in case we were captured . . . so no, we were told nothing. Nor did they want us to know each other's targets."

"Surely they would have shared information with you – if it might benefit your mission."

"I suppose so."

"Then I think we can assume they had none." Ruskin spoke this last sentence quietly, as though thinking aloud. He jotted down a few notes as the monocled colonel continued with more questions. He was thinking that it also meant the *Abwehr* had no other agents active in the area. He was confident there weren't, but it was gratifying to have it confirmed.

Schneider thought back over those long hours of questioning as he sat alone in his cell. It had been such an easy process, and it made him feel good to 'get it all off his chest', as the colonel had put it early on. But now, for the first time, he felt uneasy. He sensed something was in the air; something was about to change. He wondered if it was because he had told them all he knew. What would become of him now? Everyone had treated him decently, apart from the NCO who brought food to his cell and led him to and from the interview room; a master of the innuendo and half-muttered remark. It was chiefly the sinister turn these had taken over the last day or so that was at the core of Schneider's anxiety. "Cell next door's empty now. Hanged the bugger yesterday." Then that very morning: "You'll be next. Now they've pumped you dry, you're excess to requirements."

Surely they wouldn't kill him, not after being so cooperative. But he could not be sure, and his options had been made perfectly clear to him during one of the recent sessions when the colonel had sensed he was holding back and had put him straight on his possible fate. "They always try and save something for their pension," observed Ruskin later.

"Listen," the colonel had said, "I'll be frank with you because I think you're being frank with us. When this debriefing is over, you have two options available to you. You can either work with us and help us to keep tabs on precisely what goes on over there in German Military Intelligence, or you can choose not to, in which case we shall have no alternative but to have you tried as a spy. In wartime I'm afraid that will almost certainly mean you will be hanged." He paused for a moment for effect and then added, ". . . or shot."

Schneider knew this was no bluff. It was a stark choice. He assured them that he would cooperate in full. But it shattered his naive hopes of being able to walk away from all this; and that was the colonel's intention. It had been the right moment to make it clear there was no escape from his role as a spy for the duration, only now he would be working for Britain and not Germany.

The same evening, he was asked to transmit a message back to *Abwehrstelle Hamburg*.

"Dr Rantzau will be concerned about you," Lt.-Col. Ruskin explained. "He needs to know you are well and safely ensconced somewhere near to your target."

The message was sent from a room in Camp 020, under Ruskin's strict supervision. A wireless expert, known as a Voluntary Interceptor, or VI, was present to monitor every move Schneider made, and to familiarise himself with, and memorise, the agent's key technique in order to emulate it, should the need arise. Every agent transmitted with their own individual characteristics which to the trained recipient were as distinctive as a fingerprint or written signature. Crucially, the VI was also looking out for any attempt to include coded warnings – 'tells' – in the message. Schneider, however, had no intention of alerting the *Abwehr* to his capture. The agreed message was short and non-committal, and had been prepared by Ruskin:

Arrived Birmingham three days ago. Have found lodgings close to target and attempting to find work there. Nothing more to report.

Hamburg acknowledged:

Good to hear from you. Please continue with all speed. Information concerning Spitfire production required urgently. What news of Mechanic.

Ruskin and the VI huddled in discussion and drafted a quick response:

No contact with Mechanic. Was having radio problems prior to parting company. Will transmit again soon.

Despite his seemingly cosy relationship with MI5, Schneider was still niggled by the NCO's remarks. Perhaps there was something they weren't telling him. Had *Hamburg* found out about his capture, and were they stringing him along? Perhaps the Welshman had told them. If so, then Schneider was no longer any use to MI5. And what of von Osten? No one had said a word about him. Schneider had asked if he was alive early on and been told that he was; that was all.

There was something in the air, and Schneider was beginning to feel a strong sense of foreboding. This was the first day he had not been taken for interrogation. Why?

It was early afternoon when he was eventually escorted along the corridor of the cell block and into Latchmere House. He entered the usual interrogation room to be confronted by the monocled colonel, the man who had supervised sending the message to *Abwehrstelle Hamburg*, and a civilian he had never seen before. In front of the table stood the usual chair. Without being asked, he sat down, his mouth dry, his tongue feeling like a piece of old leather.

"Eric, your days with us are over," said the colonel, shuffling papers around as if he was about to leave already. "We have no further need of you here."

Schneider could barely utter a response. "Wh . . . what do you mean?"

"I mean that you are leaving, within the hour."

"Where am I going?"

"Birmingham."

"Birmingham! What for?"

"You said you'd like to help us and we believe you. We would like you to continue sending messages back to the *Abwehr,* from the place where they currently believe you to be – Castle Bromwich. We want Nikolaus Ritter and his boys in Hamburg to think that you're seeing your mission through."

"You're not serious!"

"Absolutely serious."

"Send them back false information? They'll never fall for that."

"We think they will – if it's done convincingly, and with your full cooperation naturally."

Schneider felt a heady mixture of emotions, chief amongst them relief. He had managed to convince himself they were going to send him for trial as an enemy agent. This came as a total surprise, and a vastly more attractive proposition.

"How long do you think you could keep up the pretence?"

"For as long as it takes."

That could be a week or a year, thought Schneider. But what alternative did he have!

"Of course I will help. But I'm not convinced it will work, they're not fools you know. Dr Rantzau is a pretty shrewd fellow."

The colonel nodded in agreement. "I take your point, Eric. However, when it comes to shrewdness we know a thing or two. If we didn't, we wouldn't be sitting here now. Leave those concerns to us. Just do as you're instructed and all shall be well."

Before being led away, Schneider asked a final question.

"May I ask what has happened to Otto? I know he's alive, but can you tell me if he's alright?"

The colonel glanced towards Ruskin who, after a moment's thought, nodded almost imperceptibly.

"His physical condition is fair," said the colonel. Unfortunately he has lost an arm due to the damage caused by a bullet, but he's mending well. As for his state of mind . . . not so good."

"Let us say he is not being as cooperative as you, Eric," added Ruskin. "I think we shall leave it at that." He stood up.

The session was at an end.

Chapter 55

After the Richmond Raid, Otto von Osten had been taken directly to a secure hospital, where a military surgeon examined the remnants of his right arm and decided to operate immediately. The bone around the elbow had almost completely disintegrated and was beyond repair. There was no choice but to amputate just below the shoulder.

A mixture of anaesthetic, painkillers and shock had kept him subdued for several days. He lay in bed under twenty-four-hour guard, barely moving except to be fed and to accommodate bodily functions. MI5 left him alone for almost a week before transferring him to Latchmere House. Schneider was occupying Ruskin and the monocled colonel for most of that time, keen as they were to reap the benefit of his willingness to cooperate in case it dried up. When the time came and von Osten found himself sitting before them, the colonel came straight to the point.

"We've been expecting you of course. In fact we should have been introduced sooner, if Captain Gartenfeld had dropped you out of his Heinkel at the agreed location. Just out of curiosity, where did you land?"

Von Osten remained poker-faced but inside he was shocked. *So they knew the location of the drop – and the name of the pilot who dropped him . . . how the hell!* He sensed the game that was being played and did not answer for a while.

"Auf Deutsch oder Englisch?"

"How about English, so we can all understand."

"Alright English. Stuff your stupid questions up your arse and climb in after them."

"Come now, Mr King – or do you prefer Herr von Osten?"

"Call me what you fucking well like."

And so the trend was set, the colonel, aided occasionally by Ruskin, attempting a softly-softly approach, von Osten responding with abuse or silence, seemingly at random. In front of the panel he mostly refused to speak at all, sitting gazing into space as if deep in personal thought. After days of getting nowhere, it was decided to change tactics. On the same day that Schneider was moved to Birmingham – the two agents had been in the same detention block only yards apart from each other – the cell door opened very early. An NCO entered and ordered von Osten to strip.

Initially he ignored the order but complied when the NCO said bluntly, and very menacingly, that he would do it for him if necessary. They took his clothes away. Two hours later he was still sitting naked, shivering in the cold concrete room, unaware that outside a warm July morning had begun. Then the NCO returned, carrying a new set of clothes.

"Put them on – quick! Waste of good clean clobber though. You're for the rope, mate. Just like him next door – swung yesterday."

Von Osten did not react at all.

"Took a bloody long time to die, so I heard. The hangman is very professional but he has a tendency to botch the job when dropping traitors. Nasty way to go."

In the interrogation room, the atmosphere was hostile. The colonel took centre stage and did most of the talking.

"Herr von Osten, I think it is time to stress to you that our patience is not infinite. You have been caught as an enemy spy – there is no doubt about that. We have your *Afu* transmitter, code books, false papers and a range of other evidence. We know all about Dr Rantzau, *Abwehrstelle Hamburg*, and your mission to infiltrate aircraft manufacturing units and possibly to sabotage them. What we did not know prior to your arrival in Britain, your colleague Quaver has told us. We even know your target."

The colonel took the monocle from his eye and cleaned it with a handkerchief. "In front of a military court this evidence would be overwhelming, and you will be executed without a doubt. There is only one way to avoid such an outcome, and that is to cooperate with us. The game playing is over. This is your final opportunity. If you do not answer our questions today, you will have chosen your own fate.

Von Osten sat very still, his head down, staring at the carpet as if he had not heard a word. His left hand rested on his lap, the empty sleeve of his right arm was rolled up and tucked in beneath the stump. He looked a pathetic figure.

The colonel waited a full two minutes before speaking again.

"Come now, we have played this charade for long enough. The time has arrived for you to lay your cards on the table and speak frankly. I'm sorry to have to say this but I must emphasise – *this is your last chance!* We either achieve results today, or the matter is taken out of our hands. I can assure you that in wartime the judiciary has the facility to process spying cases remarkably quickly. This time next week you will be dead."

Von Osten said nothing.

When the colonel spoke again, his tone was suddenly very different. His voice had lost its assertive, aggressive edge. He spoke quietly, rubbing his ear as if it was bothering him.

"Has it occurred to you how we tracked you down? I'm sure it must."
Silence.

"I imagine you believe Schneider betrayed your position to us. Or the Welshman, Johnny – that's the *Abwehr*'s codename for him. Let's face it, you did allow him to follow you from Central London to Richmond. Rather lapse of you, I must say."

Silence.

"We've known about Johnny for a long time. Perhaps you think he betrayed you?" The colonel softened his voice even more. "Well you'd be wrong. It was your own *Abwehr*."

Von Osten's head shook very slightly. *This was a bluff. They were trying to undermine him, and cover their own double agent.*

"Not Schneider. Poor Schneider – he's as much a victim of all this as you. Nor Johnny – at least not knowingly. Oh he followed you to Richmond, but we knew where you were all along. Your real betrayers are in Hamburg. The truth of the matter is that there are those inside the *Abwehr* who do not have faith in this war. They are not, in their own eyes, traitors to the Fatherland, rather disbelievers in the infallibility of Adolf Hitler. They believe their Führer is leading them down a path that may seem initially to be paved with success, but will ultimately lead Germany to self-destruction."

It's a bluff. These bastards will try anything. Ignore them. Think about something entirely different. Think about the girls on the Reeperbahn.

"They wish to shorten this war by any means possible, and their *modus operandi* is to pass on to us here as much intelligence as they possibly can."

Block it out. Think about something completely irrelevant. Not the Reeperbahn . . . think about Audrey in Cambridge. A good fuck.

"In their eyes, the sooner the war is over, the sooner Hitler can be replaced and sanity restored. He is mad of course – you must realise that."

The Benzedrine had given him an erection like concrete. The poor woman must have ached for days afterwards.

"*Hamburg* betrayed you. But they were not alone. Someone else also betrayed you."

She was a panter, especially when approaching an orgasm. Like a dog when it's pleased to see you. And when the moment came, she squealed uncontrollably.

"We were most grateful to hear from a lady in Cambridge. A friend of yours by the name of Parsons – Audrey Parsons."

Von Osten snapped out of his reverie. It was as if they were reading his mind. They knew about Audrey!

"What about her!" he exclaimed, too startled not to respond.

The colonel remained poker-faced. Inside he was excited; he'd happened on a tender spot as he hoped he might.

"She was good enough to report to her local police station after you visited her. She told them you were a German national whom she believed had left the country some time ago – said you had turned up out of the blue. When we heard about this we put two and two together and guessed it was you. We managed to pick up your trail when your Cambridge train arrived in London. We've had you under surveillance ever since."

"She wouldn't," muttered von Osten. "Audrey would not do that to me. Never."

"I'm afraid she did. I must say we are very grateful to her."

"You're lying. I told Schneider about her, and he told you. You're trying to protect your Welshman. He's the traitor."

"I'm sorry, Otto." The colonel's voice hinted at genuine sympathy for a moment. "I can assure you I am telling the truth. We discussed this with Schneider, whose information has so far proved to be extremely accurate, and he confirmed that you told him about a woman in Cambridge. But you never mentioned her name. He is quite clear on that. How then did we know, if not from her directly? Your sexual prowess may be admirable, however you shouldn't underestimate the power of patriotism, certainly not amongst the British people at this particular moment in history."

"Mind what you're saying, you pompous English bastard," hissed von Osten.

The colonel sat back in his chair and folded his arms. "Pompous Scottish bastard, actually."

Von Osten stared downwards, as if mesmerised by the pattern of the carpet. Audrey bothered him more than the claim that the *Abwehr* was seething with traitors. He was inordinately proud of his sexual power over women. It had been a mistake to react to this; now the British could play on it. He wasn't thinking straight. The *Abwehr* nonsense was pure speculation, there wasn't a scrap of evidence. The Audrey information must have come from Schneider. Had he mentioned her name? He couldn't remember, but he must have done. The colonel was talking again.

"We've done a bit of checking on Audrey Parsons. Quite a lady by all accounts. A librarian. They say the quiet ones are the worst – or should I say the best?"

"How would you know – you wouldn't know one end of a woman from the other."

"Come now, let's keep to the point, shall we?"

"And what is the point?"

"That there is no turning back for you. Every bridge you have crossed has been burnt behind you. It's only a matter of time before the *Abwehr* openly revolts against Hitler. Come over to us before it's too late."

"You're insane. Revolt against the Führer when he has succeeded in conquering most of Europe and just driven your entire army out of France into the English Channel? I don't think so."

"But it's not sustainable, Otto! It's all based on tyranny and oppression – and that never lasts. You only have to read the history books to appreciate the fact. We'll be back in mainland Europe before very long. Let's face it, they sent you on a fool's errand, surely you can see that. We've had you monitored from the start. Even your girlfriends won't protect you. There really is no alternative but to cooperate, and the sooner you accept that and stop wasting time, so much the better for everyone." The colonel paused. "Which brings me back to my opening remark – that today is the decisive day. Either we make some headway or we give up and hand you over to the courts to do their worst."

With no response forthcoming from von Osten, the colonel said: "Alright, I think we're wasting our time. We have other fish to fry." Ballard Ruskin nodded in agreement. He stood up, ready to leave.

"Wait." Von Osten raised his head slowly and looked from one to the other in a gradual pan from left to right.

"Give me another day. I must think over what you have said."

The colonel spoke firmly in reply. "Today or not at all."

"No!" shouted von Osten. "You have made many statements today, many claims. My head is spinning. Give me until tomorrow."

The colonel and Ruskin exchanged glances and Ruskin nodded, again almost imperceptibly.

"Alright," said the colonel. "You may have twenty-four hours to compose your thoughts. But if you do not come into this room tomorrow prepared to talk, there will be no more leeway."

Von Osten nodded. When he had been led away, Ruskin said to the colonel: "I think it was a good decision."

"I don't like it. He'll see that as a concession and try to build on it."

"Oh I don't know. Here's a man whose penis rules his life more than his brain, it appears. The poor fellow had quite a shock to learn that his ability in bed failed to fog the lady's brain entirely. We shook his world."

"Hmm." The colonel picked up his briefcase and made for the door. "He'd be furious if he knew it wasn't true, and that we got it from Schneider after all."

"A bluff that paid dividends. Lucky for us von Osten couldn't remember if he'd mentioned her name. A librarian in Cambridge called Audrey Parsons – didn't take long to track her down."

"And she was very complimentary about him in fact. Quite a stallion our Otto, so the report suggests."

"Indeed. Hey-ho for the Aryan race."

Chapter 56

When Heather and Alison arrived at RAF Catterick, Squadron Leader Innes and Flight Lieutenant Rodigan were there to meet them and immediately whisked them off to the officers' mess for tea. Alison recognised the squadron leader from the group that had surrounded Heather the night before last; he had very distinctive gingerish hair and a bushy moustache.

"This is a surprise," said Rodigan as he sat next to Alison, his mouth spread wide in an enormous grin.

"A pleasant one, I hope."

"Rather. Couldn't believe it when Stuart told me you were on your way. How come you were stranded in Darlington?"

"We missed the connecting train. There wasn't another for hours."

"Strange, I thought it was straight through to London." Alison looked blank and said nothing. "Oh well, your bad luck's our good fortune."

"I hope we're not interrupting the war effort."

"Not at all. Nothing much happening this morning – we're not even on standby. There are two Spitfire squadrons stationed here. We are 188, that's Midas Squadron, and then there's 41. We've got a squadron of Blenheims too, so a bit crowded at present. 41's turn to scramble today. Bit of excitement yesterday. After you left, Jerry had a crack at Hull in broad daylight. Couple of the chaps bagged a Heinkel each. I'm damned certain I scored too – but unconfirmed, worst luck."

"They hit Scotland as well," said Alison. "They attacked Wick, but we didn't go that far so missed out on the excitement."

"Glad to hear it! You wouldn't last ten seconds in those Moths."

"Do you think this might be the start of something, Daniel?"

"Please, call me Dan. How do you mean, the start of something?"

"Well, Hitler has left us pretty well alone since Dunkirk. The occasional air raid, but that's all. I wonder if this might be the beginning of the real invasion push."

Rodigan rubbed his chin pensively. "Possibly. Most of the boys in the squadron think it's going to kick off any day now – can't really understand why it hasn't already. The *Luftwaffe* is bound to start trying to soften us up. That's when we move south, hopefully. The boys in Eleven

Sector will be getting all the action and I want to be with them. Should be soon, with any luck."

"I know," said Alison. "Once you are, though, you'll probably wish you were back up here."

"I doubt it. We've been kicking our heels too long already – very frustrating at times. We've had a few scraps. Yesterday was the first main one, but mostly it's been the odd lone wolf over the coast, and they're few and far between. I expect you've seen more action than we have."

Alison shook her head. "None. We don't go anywhere near the danger spots. Our job is to deliver planes safely and avoid trouble. I've yet to see a German plane over England."

"You will. I don't suppose you have any armour if you're delivering kites straight from the factory."

"Hardly," laughed Alison. "We don't even have a radio in the Moths. I hope that will change soon. A few girls have gone for training on small twin-engine aircraft, then they'll be able to fly Oxfords and Dominoes. We also have an Anson that collects us and drops us off – but it doesn't come this far north. At the moment no one in the women's pool is allowed to fly it. A bit silly really."

"Would you like to do that – fly the bigger planes?"

"Of course. I'm booked to do the training later this month. The great thing about that is we're then qualified to fly advanced single-engine fighters. We're all dying to have a go in a Spitfire."

Rodigan chuckled. "Ha, you must be joking. They won't let women near Spits, or Hurricanes for that matter."

"Why not?" asked Alison indignantly.

"Women couldn't handle them. Too powerful – fast reaction times needed. It's a man's plane."

"Nonsense! You've seen me flying at Hendon. Wouldn't you say I could fly a Spitfire?"

"Well, you perhaps," said Rodigan, sensing he was skating on thin ice. "But not many others."

"I wouldn't be so sure," warned Alison. "Our time will come."

Heather was sitting close by, chatting to her squadron leader. "Ally," she called. "Stuart says we're alright for a lift, but it won't be until mid-afternoon. There's a transport due out at three. Suits me if it suits you."

"We don't appear to have any choice," sighed Alison in mock disappointment.

When they had finished their tea, all four walked across to the Squadron Pilots' room, a wooden hut at the edge of the grass airfield. Several pilots were seated outside on deckchairs, reading or playing cards, their yellow Mae West life jackets lying on the ground next to them.

Squadron Leader Innes stood at the doorway and called: "What's the latest, Dowsett?"

A sturdily built young man poked his head out of the window.

"Nothing, sir – not a dicky bird from Sector Ops. The weather's against Jerry today, and it doesn't look as if it's going to lift."

"Sounds as though it would have been a pretty dull day without you around," said Rodigan as they strolled away.

Alison looked him in the eyes. "Is that meant to be a compliment?"

"If you'd like to take it as such."

"I think I would."

Heather and the squadron leader had walked ahead. They stopped near a line of parked cars and waited for them to catch up.

"I say," said Innes, "I've offered to show Heather something of the countryside around here. You don't mind do you, Dan?" He smiled at Alison. "I'm sure you'd prefer to entertain this lovely lady without us hanging around."

"That sounds splendid," agreed Rodigan. "If Alison doesn't mind."

"Not in the least," said Alison. "Provided we're both back here and ready by two thirty. We mustn't miss that transport."

"Don't worry," said Heather. "I shall be."

Alison and the flight lieutenant watched as the couple climbed into a Triumph Gloria sports car and pulled away, Heather waving happily as they disappeared out of sight.

"And what would you like to do" – Rodigan glanced at his wrist watch – "for the next four and a half hours?"

Alison pretended to think for a moment, then she said: "There is only one thing, but you'll say it's impossible."

"I'm sure I won't. Do say."

"Alright, I did warn you though."

"I'm unshockable."

"I'd like to fly a Spitfire."

The unshockable Rodigan looked visibly shocked.

"You *are* joking, Alison! That's impossible."

"Why?"

"The C.O. would never allow it."

Alison took his arm and they started to walk. "He need never know."

"He'd have me over a barrel if he heard I'd been giving joy rides in a Spit."

"Hardly a joy ride, Dan. I'm a more experienced pilot than you."

"Not in Spits you're not."

"Well it's about time I learnt, don't you think?"

Rodigan was at a loss for words. It was a crazy idea. Alison decided to help him see her point of view a little clearer. They were approaching a

218

row of Nissen huts. She pulled him into an alleyway between a brick building and the first hut, and pressed tight against him.

"Come on, Dan, we might all be dead this time next week. I've made up my mind – I want to fly a Spitfire. And I know how to make it happen. Have you got a car?"

"Yes," croaked Rodigan, his throat suddenly very dry. "Nothing as grand as Stuart's – just an Austin 7." He tried to pull away so Alison wouldn't feel the beginnings of an erection.

"Good. Now, you must know the countryside around here like the back of your hand. This is what I want you to do . . ."

*

Flight Lieutenant Rodigan approached the duty officer at his desk and saluted smartly.

"Yes, Daniel my boy, what is it?" The duty officer appeared to be writing a report of some kind.

"I'd like to take my kite up, sir. It was losing power at full throttle yesterday and I need to try and pinpoint the problem."

"Can't the engineers do that on the ground? That's what bloody erks are for."

"They've tried, sir, but I need to be more specific about the symptoms. It might be nothing. Shouldn't take long – and there's nothing happening. Looks like the weather's keeping Jerry at bay, not that he comes up here much."

"He did yesterday," said the duty officer. "Alright, see what you can do to get it sorted."

"Thank you, sir." Rodigan turned to leave.

"Oh Dan."

"Sir?"

"No aerobatics, please, especially over the base."

"No sir."

"And Dan."

"Sir?"

"Don't take long about it."

"No sir."

"And Dan."

"Sir?"

"Where's that ATA girl I saw you with earlier?"

"Gone into town, sir. Shopping."

The duty officer half-smiled. "Alright, off you go."

Fifteen minutes later, Rodigan was seated in the cockpit of his Spitfire wearing his parachute, though not the Irvin jacket and trousers he normally wore on a sortie. He nodded to the ground crew manning the external battery charger, pressed the contact starter and felt the Merlin engine explode into life. He taxied out of the sandbagged revetment onto the airfield and felt the aircraft bounce gently across the grass. Turning into the wind, he opened the throttle and the Spitfire accelerated across the airfield, picking up speed rapidly until Rodigan pulled gently on the control column and the plane rose gracefully into the air. He banked round until the gyrocompass indicated he was heading due south.

For the benefit of anyone watching from the base, he released the wheel lock and pumped the undercarriage lever with his right hand as he held the control column with his left. From below the wheels would be seen retracting into the wings. As soon as he was out of sight of the base, he lowered them again.

*

Eight miles away, Alison found the place she had been looking for; Dan's directions had been perfect. His Austin 7 was just like her father's and she drove it confidently, easily finding the turning off the main road that led on to a winding country lane, through an open gateway and onto a field of flat, hard grassland that stretched as far as the eye could see. An ideal natural airfield if ever there was one.

She parked next to the thick hedgerow and walked out onto the grass, strapping on her parachute as she went. The faint humming of an aircraft engine was already discernible in the distance. As she gazed skywards the Spitfire appeared from the north and banked gently round to make its approach. Rodigan landed smoothly and in what seemed to Alison a remarkably short distance. He taxied over to the corner of the field and manoeuvred the plane so it was pointing directly down the middle of the field. With the engine still running he released the side access door and let it flap down, wriggled out of the cockpit and motioned for Alison to climb up onto the port wing.

"Against my better judgement, here I am," shouted Rodigan, "Get in and I'll run through the controls with you. I'll only explain the essentials – we don't have time for a full lecture."

Alison slid into the pilot's seat and adjusted the Sutton shoulder straps and harness until tight against her body. The cockpit felt snug and secure after the openness of the Tiger Moth. Her feet fell naturally onto the rudder pedals and she placed her right hand on the control column and her left on the throttle lever. There was an easiness about the plane that she sensed immediately. Several ATA men who had flown Spitfires had all made the same remark: *It's a pilot's aircraft*. She was already beginning to understand what they meant.

Rodigan pointed out the various controls, focusing on the ones Alison needed to know about and ignoring the rest. Most of the instruments were self-explanatory to an experienced pilot, and it was a case of familiarising their position around the cockpit and on the control panel. He told her not to bother raising the undercarriage for the sake of a few minutes in the air. It involved swapping hands on the control column which was fiddly.

"Right," said Rodigan, when he had run through everything. "Flaps switch is up, release the brake lever and take her away in your own time. Only a couple of circuits, please, and *don't* go out of sight. Be very sparing with the throttle, especially on takeoff. You've got over a thousand horse-power ticking away in front of you, so don't get carried away. The controls are light and responsive – no need for sudden jerks." He bent close to her ear. "And for heaven's sake bring her back in one piece, or I'll be roasted alive. So will you."

"You worry too much," shouted Alison.

Rodigan closed the access door and jumped down from the wing. He watched as the Spitfire taxied away from him. Behind his back, two pairs of fingers were firmly crossed.

In the cockpit, Alison could see nothing ahead of her; the Spitfire's long nose restricted her view almost entirely. But she knew the field was long and straight and Rodigan had explained that as soon as the tail began to lift the nose would drop and visibility would be excellent. She eased open the throttle and felt a surge of power as the Merlin engine thrust her forward. The speed of acceleration took her breath away. At 40 mph the tail lifted as predicted, and at just over 80 mph the plane lifted gently and naturally into the air.

She soared across the end of the field, the wings dipping in both directions slightly as she got used to controlling the ailerons. The sense of power was exhilarating, like nothing she had ever known. She had left the canopy open and the wind buffeted her face, adding to the sheer physical thrill. Once airborne, visibility in flight was indeed excellent. She banked cautiously to starboard and brought the plane round in a wide circle, a manoeuvre that was so smooth she repeated it several times, each time at a steeper angle. The response was beautiful, the controls perfectly balanced.

She flew out in a gradual climb until she thought it prudent to turn in order to keep in sight of the field. On the return she dropped the nose into a shallow dive and was again stunned at the acceleration. The ailerons became stiffer, the engine noise increased, and the ground approached at an alarming rate. Yet with the slightest adjustment to the controls, she was able to level out smoothly, bypassing the field and over Rodigan who was waving energetically.

She toyed with the idea of doing a roll, but decided against it. He would probably kill her!

By the time she approached the field to land, Alison felt supremely confident in this heavenly flying machine; and she was in love. She loved the plane, and the man on the ground a little for his courage in allowing her to fly it. In the space of ten minutes she had learnt a great deal, and she knew the landing would be a piece of cake. With the flaps switch down, she eased the stick forward and the plane gradually lowered closer and closer to the field. It seemed like an eternity before the wheels touched the ground. The far hedge where the Austin 7 was parked was fast approaching, and for a panicky moment she thought she might overshoot. But as soon as the wheels were on grass she pulled on the stick to get the tail wheel down, throttled back and slowed almost to a halt, turning in an arc to face back down the field. There had been just yards to spare between the port wing tip and the hedge. Alison was shaking with excitement.

Then Rodigan was up on the wing and calling out: "She can float a long way, I should have warned you. She's so aerodynamically smooth there's hardly any drag. You need bags of room to land – until you're familiar with her."

"Tell me sooner next time," gasped Alison.

"You know now," laughed Rodigan. "There's only one first time in a Spit."

As she pulled herself out of the cockpit, Alison circled his head with her hands and found his mouth with hers. As they kissed, her whole body tingled, her excitement level intense. It was instinctive. For a blind moment she associated the man with the plane, and she was kissing both at once. Rodigan put an arm round her back and drew her firmly towards him. Alison responded by clinging even tighter to him. She stiffened, squirming against his body.

"I say, steady on. Getting a bit carried away here, don't you think?"

She pulled away from him. "Sorry, I don't know what came over me. I hope you didn't mind my kissing you like that – not very lady-like."

"My dear lady, I'd like nothing more than to be kissed by you for hours on end. It's just a little awkward standing on the wing of an aircraft, that's all. But I'd be delighted if you promise to continue elsewhere some other time."

"I promise."

"Splendid. Now I think you should hop into that old Austin and find your way back to base. I need to get this Spit back before anyone begins to suspect foul play – and before we start kissing again." Then as an afterthought: "And if you bump into the duty officer when you get back, you've been shopping, not flying my Spitfire. Alright?"

Alison nodded, kissed him again, then jumped down from the plane and watched as Rodigan climbed in and taxied away across the field. Soon he was airborne and heading north towards Catterick. She watched until the Spitfire had disappeared from view, then slumped into the driver's seat of the car. She suddenly felt drained, and her mind dazed.

There was something special about that man – or was it the plane – or a combination of both? She had felt sexually aroused as they kissed on the wing and could feel the wetness inside her knickers. How much the Spitfire had to do with it she wasn't sure. Nor did she care. For some time she sat there pleasantly lost in her own thoughts.

Then she broke out of her reverie, started the Austin 7 and drove towards the gate of the field.

*

Rodigan's short flight back to Catterick was not uneventful.

As he flew low across the countryside he peered down from his cockpit at the fields, hedgerows, farmhouses and lanes below. On the edge of a copse he caught a fleeting glimpse of a car. It looked familiar.

He banked round in a wide arc to port, peering down, trying to pinpoint the spot. There it was . . . Stuart's Triumph. Unmistakable. He could see the copse clearly now, a clump of trees at the end of a dirt track. The Triumph was empty. He circled round again, this time noticing that two hedges joined together in front of the copse. In the shade of a large oak tree, a tartan rug was spread out on the ground. Two semi-naked bodies were entwined upon it. He didn't recognise the pale pink bottom pointing skywards, but the shock of ginger hair on the man's head could only belong to one person. All he could glimpse of the figure beneath him was a shapely leg and an expanse of naked thigh.

Showing Heather the countryside, eh?

He brought the Spitfire round a third time and approached the field where the couple lay, putting the Spitfire into as steep a dive as he dared, and throttling back sharply right above their heads. Out of the corner of his eye he caught a brief glimpse of Innes folding the rug protectively over himself and Heather. Two fingers were pointing upwards in a gesture reminiscent of one that Winston Churchill would soon adopt with an entirely different meaning.

Rodigan flew round once more, spun the Spitfire in a perfectly executed victory roll, and was gone. He wondered what his squadron leader would have to say when the girls had left.

It promised to be a lively evening in the mess.

223

Chapter 57

The sky was orange over Harvesthude as the sun disappeared at the end of a beautiful July evening. Sophienstrasse was deserted apart from Wichmann and Ritter who were talking themselves round in circles.

"There just aren't enough facts. It's pure guesswork without more intelligence."

"I agree, Nikolaus, but we're in the business of making calculated guesses as well as analysing facts."

"If that's the case, my calculated guess is that they're blown – both of them. But I'm not prepared to believe it until we know more."

"I understand," said Wichmann, "and I feel the same way. However, my guess is the opposite. I think they're still with us. Quaver's in place and ready to go – the facts show nothing to the contrary. The only cause for concern is loss of radio contact with Mechanic, and we have information from Quaver that it may be due to equipment failure. Let's not be paranoid."

"I'm not," said Ritter. "What about the silence from Quaver? It doesn't take two weeks to travel from Richmond to Birmingham. That's ample time to be intercepted and turned by the British."

"A fortnight of silence is not out of the ordinary for an agent in the field. They were lucky to be able to transmit almost daily for a while. They are under instructions only to transmit when they have something to report. Your instructions, I might add."

"I know. I just have a feeling about it. A bad feeling."

"So much for the facts!" Wichmann leaned forward from behind his desk. "At least Göring's keeping off our backs. We must be thankful for small mercies."

"Only because he's the blue-eyed boy at the moment. Come to that, the entire High Command can't put a foot wrong after the successes of the last few months. Rumour now has it that the Führer will definitely not invade Britain. If so, then it won't make a great deal of difference whether our Spitfire spies are blown or not." Ritter's words had a hint of disgust about them.

"The whole mission has been precautionary, Nikolaus, you know that as well as anyone. As for invading Britain, it may still go ahead. I have heard rumours that contradict yours. It's immaterial one way or the other as far as Göring is concerned. He'll want to show off his beloved *Luftwaffe* against the Royal Air Force come what may. And if it doesn't go according to plan, we will be his scapegoat – if we allow him the chance. He'll blame it on poor intelligence. Canaris will shield us, but we owe it to him to make this mission work. I believe it will." He picked up a folder and opened it. "This is a general directive from Göring on the conduct of an air war against the United Kingdom. Here, read this part."

Ritter took the folder and read out the sentence indicated: *"By means of reconnaissance and combat against small formations it should be possible to draw out smaller enemy formations and ascertain the strength of grouping of enemy forces."*

Wichmann laughed out loud. "You see! He'll do just that, then if the RAF shoot down more of our planes than we do theirs, he'll say it was the only tactic available because the *Abwehr* couldn't supply him with accurate figures for enemy resources and capability."

Ritter was beginning to feel utterly depressed. Wichmann grabbed his arm and pushed him towards the door.

"Which is why we must have faith in our Spitfire spies. Which is why they are not blown but behaving cautiously or have radio problems. Which is why you should go home and enjoy a stiff relaxing drink." He turned off the light and closed the door behind him.

"Which is precisely what I intend to do."

Chapter 58

Otto von Osten could not sleep. He lay on his hard bed and stared into the semi-darkness, the stark reality of his situation weighing down upon him like a huge boulder.

He still didn't believe them about Audrey. Schneider must have told them about her, and he was certain he had mentioned her to him by name. The *Abwehr* story was preposterous, a total bluff. What was certain was the colonel's assurance that time had run out for him. No more stalling, no more belligerence; he had to give them what they wanted or be hanged.

There was, it occurred to him, a third alternative. Suicide had crossed his mind, and not an unreasonable option under present circumstances. A permanent solution to all his troubles. But how? No laces in his shoes, no sharp implements. The only way he could think of was to stand on the bed and leap head first at the floor, hoping the crack on his skull would do the job. He'd probably just end up with a massive headache, or concussion at worst. He decided against it. If he opted for death then he might as well let them hang him and have it done properly. To live was the greater challenge, to carry on under any circumstances, because tomorrow the tables might turn. The invasion might come, and British Intelligence might have an SS division knocking on its door any day. Keep alive for as long as possible.

There was yet another option. Escape. Then he could set about finding who had really betrayed him, and deal with them. He could also warn *Hamburg* before more damage was done. All this would be ten times more difficult with only one arm, but it deserved serious consideration. From this cell it was impossible. He would have to try and get them to move him somewhere else, somewhere less secure, which would only be possible if they thought they could trust him – if he cooperated with them. Or was at least *seen* to be cooperating.

So cooperate he would.

Let them believe he'd had enough. The *Abwehr* were traitors to the Fatherland and had betrayed him. So had Audrey Parsons. He had bought the entire story; his disillusionment was complete. He lay awake the entire night, planning his strategy and working out what to say the next morning. He had to be very careful. By now Schneider would have told them

226

everything he knew, of that there was no doubt. He must not stray far from the facts they had already been given.

He had to blend his lies with the truth very cautiously indeed.

*

The next morning von Osten answered every question put to him. His manner was subdued and resentful, and he seemed to hold back at times, if he felt himself being too forthcoming. Nevertheless Lt.-Col. Ballard Ruskin felt confident the German had been broken, and he was delighted at the prospect of a new recruit to his small but promising network of double agents. Hanging him would have been such a waste. It was obvious he was holding back at times on key information; that was to be expected. Meanwhile it was important to cross-refer every detail with Schneider's story, to identify any discrepancies and hopefully determine which version was the truth.

Von Osten later transmitted his first message in almost three weeks to *Abwehrstelle Hamburg*. Using his left hand, he tapped away at the keys, accurately but slower than before. He told them he had been involved in a car accident – they were common enough in the blackout – and his right arm had been fractured. (Not amputated, advised Ruskin; that would imply too much hospital treatment and generate awkward questions.) His *Afu* transmitter had been damaged too and needed repair, which he had been able to do via his motor trade contacts. It had taken time. He was now in rented rooms in Southampton and ready to proceed.

The VI (Voluntary Interceptor) watched like a hawk as von Osten transmitted. Afterwards he told Ruskin that he was almost certain there had been no 'tells' in the transmission . . . no deliberate attempts to warn *Hamburg*.

Hamburg acknowledged the message sympathetically and said they were delighted to hear from him again.

Agent Mechanic was back in business.

*

At precisely the same time von Often was transmitting to *Hamburg*, the Minister of Information, Sir Edward Grigg, was standing up in the House of Commons in London describing the day's events. In the afternoon there had taken place what he described as 'one of the greatest air battles of the war.' Around midday, German reconnaissance aircraft had sighted a large British convoy leaving the Thames Estuary. The planes were intercepted by Fighter Command but managed to escape despite receiving considerable damage. Soon afterwards, more than seventy *Luftwaffe* planes were airborne and heading towards the English coast – twenty-seven Dornier 17 bombers escorted by twenty Bf 109s and thirty Bf 110s.

As the convoy passed the cliffs of Dover, six Hurricanes from Biggin Hill came across the German formation and attacked immediately. Air Chief Marshal Dowding ordered twenty-four more Hurricanes to scramble as reinforcements. A massive dogfight ensued, a hundred planes diving, turning and weaving in a desperate attempt to shoot their opposite numbers out of the sky.

Further west, sixty Junkers Ju 88s attacked Falmouth and Swansea, bombing railways, ships and a munitions factory; and fifty German aircraft, mainly Bf 110s, were intercepted off Portland before they were able to attack another convoy. Later in the afternoon, another dogfight took place over Dover in which eleven Hurricanes attacked a force of Junkers Ju 87s (Stukas) and Bf 109s.

Three Hurricanes and four Bf 109s were lost that day, and a seven hundred ton sloop from the convoy was sunk.

Although Winston Churchill had referred to the 'Battle of Britain' several weeks earlier in a speech, the phrase had not yet taken on any great significance, certainly not with the pilots of Fighter Command. But the events of 10th July left them with no doubt as to the forthcoming struggle.

The battle *for* Britain had begun.

Chapter 59

(Thursday 11th July 1940)

The meeting broke up shortly before noon. As Major Schmid made his way towards the front entrance of Carinhall he thought back several months to the time when Göring had taken him aside in the gardens after a similar conference and talked about the Spitfire. How things had changed since then.

Could the field marshal, even in his wildest exaggerations, have imagined that Operation *Gelb* would have been so spectacularly successful? Give him his due, he had predicted it would last only weeks, and he had been right. His confidence now knew no bounds. The *Luftwaffe*'s heavy losses and its failure to prevent the Dunkirk evacuation were of little significance. His beloved air force was beyond challenge from any other in Europe, let alone anything the RAF could muster. The Spitfire spies were forgotten, no longer of any consequence. Redundant.

His words still rang in Schmid's ears. *"The defence of southern England will last four days – the Royal Air Force will last four weeks."* Three months ago Göring had said something similar about Operation *Gelb*; but he had made wild predictions on many occasions. The difference was that now it was possible to believe him.

As he approached the line of cars waiting to take the *Luftwaffe* generals back to Berlin, Schmid heard his name being called. It was Kesselring.

"Major Schmid, let me give you a lift, I would like to talk."

"Yes, General."

The cars sped along the wooded roads. Neither man spoke for a few minutes. Then, gazing through the window as if deep in thought, Kesselring said: "Well, Schmid, what do you think?"

"About the meeting, sir?"

"About the meeting."

"I think there is much work to be done. A full scale attack on England needs to be executed with great thoroughness. Field Marshal Göring has reason to feel satisfied that we – by which I mean the entire *Luftwaffe* – can achieve his objectives. However, there are certain practicalities that cannot be ignored."

"Such as?"

Schmid fidgeted in his seat, hesitating not because he was reluctant to speak his mind but because he did not know where to begin.

"Come now, don't be coy with me, Beppo Schmid."

"It's not that, General. Firstly, there are the heavy losses we incurred over Holland and Belgium. We lost more planes than anyone cares to acknowledge – and pilots also. It was a great victory but one that was gained at a price. Such losses take time to recoup."

"Agreed," said Kesselring afirmatively. "Victory seems to have wiped Göring's memory clean of the cost involved. He has convinced himself that *Gelb* was achieved by the *Luftwaffe* alone, with perhaps some backup from the army. Nevertheless, Schmid, our factories are more than capable of maintaining a steady supply of new aircraft. Even if they were not, numerically the Royal Air Force is way behind us, as you know very well from your intelligence reports."

"That would appear so. But sources are sketchy. We still have no precise figures."

"In which case you must remedy the situation. Göring has given you the weekend to do so."

"I know. I am to report by the sixteenth – next Tuesday."

"Can you do it?"

"I shall try my best."

"You must, Schmid, for all our sakes. It is no secret that I have long had concerns about the abilities of our commander-in-chief, nor am I alone. He is no great military strategist. We are riding the crest of a wave and I truly believe the momentum will ensure victory against Churchill's little island. On the other hand, like you, I am a pragmatist. Effective intelligence is vital, and if not to ensure victory then to reduce losses. You said 'firstly' a moment ago. What is your 'secondly'?"

"I have already mentioned it – lack of intelligence about the air defence capability in England. We were forbidden for too long to use agents inside Great Britain and it has been a considerable handicap. There has been some activity nevertheless, but it is a huge task to make up for lost ground."

"You can hardly be blamed for that."

"I'm not making excuses, General. I merely state the position. I also have a third point to offer."

"Go ahead."

"Göring's general directive on how the air war against Britain is to be carried out. I have it here." Schmid opened the briefcase on his lap and pulled out some papers. He selected a page that had a paragraph ringed heavily in pencil. "The section regarding Fighter Command reads: *By means of reconnaissance and combat against small formations it should be possible to draw out smaller enemy formations and ascertain the strength of grouping of enemy forces.*"

"Yes I have read the directive," said Kesselring. "What about it."

"I do not think it will work."

"Nor I."

"How can we possibly know what percentage of British fighters are being put into the air at any one time? It would be pure guess work. No matter how many fighters we shoot down, we don't know at what rate they can be replaced."

"That is quite correct," agreed Kesselring. "But that is *our* problem, we the *Lutfwaffe* commanders, not yours. You have done an excellent job in compiling information on bombing targets, considering your limited resources. Keep it flowing, and we in the *Lutflotten* will see to the British fighters. As you just heard at the meeting, Sperrle, Stumpff and I also have reports to submit. In ten days we must have our final plans worked out for the air assault on Britain – *Adlerangriff*, our Eagle Attack as it has been designated. We shall do our best to ensure it is carried out with shrewd military precision. If it means going against Göring's wishes, then I for one am prepared to say so. Meanwhile, Schmid, I suggest you prepare your report as best you can, with all the intelligence at your disposal."

"I will, General."

Kesselring leaned forward to make his final point. "Make it positive. Nothing you write will make any difference. The invasion will take place whatever. Give the fat man what he wants – an accurate, encouraging appreciation of the enemy's weaknesses. We're on the crest of a wave remember. Let's make the most of it."

"Thank you, General, I shall do as you say."

Schmid felt uplifted by the words of the commander he admired most within the *Luftwaffe*. That afternoon he set about structuring his report. So confident was he that he felt almost inclined not to bother pressurising the *Abwehr* for news of their Spitfire agents. They had so far produced nothing; frankly, Schmid didn't believe they ever would, nor did it seem to matter anymore, certainly not to the man who had sanctioned the operation. Nevertheless, his professional sense of thoroughness would not allow him to ignore the possibility of something useful coming from them. He picked up the phone.

"Get me Admiral Canaris." Then after a pause: "Well find out where he is and connect me!"

*

Tracking down the Chief of the *Abwehr* proved difficult. He was rushing around Western Europe like a madman, setting up intelligence stations in Amsterdam, Brussels, Paris and strategic points in between, trying to keep up with the demands of the rapidly expanding borders of the Third Reich. When Schmid finally managed to speak to him, the admiral sounded weary and his tone was uncharacteristically abrupt.

Shortly afterwards, Captain Wichmann in Hamburg received a telephone call from Canaris. When asked about the Spitfire spies Wichmann was relieved to be able to offer some news.

"Things are progressing. Agent Mechanic is back in contact after radio problems and is close to the Supermarine works near Southampton, attempting to infiltrate the factory. He assures us it is only a matter of time – they are taking on extra staff. Quaver is further ahead and started work at the Castle Bromwich factory several days ago. We received a transmission from him yesterday giving details of its general layout . . . useful background material. More will follow, there is no doubt."

"Now listen, Wichmann," said Canaris, "send your agents a message. As a matter of supreme urgency, they must supply us with accurate production figures for both factories. This information is of paramount importance and is to be transmitted by Monday evening at the latest – that's the fifteenth – to be with the *Luftwaffe* Fifth Branch first thing on Tuesday morning. Do you understand? It must be on Schmid's desk by Tuesday morning."

"I understand, Admiral – but that is a great deal to ask."

"It must be done."

"If we push them too hard they might blow their cover."

"Do you think they are not blown already?"

Wichmann was speechless for a moment. "No, I do not. That had not occurred to me."

"Well get on with it then – make use of your resources. These two hardly seem reckless by nature, so I doubt they will take great risks. Without pressure they might spend the rest of the war helping to build Spitfires for the British and never give us anything."

Wichmann decided not to argue the point. "Yes, Admiral."

"I have spoken with Fifth Branch. Any further dialogue concerning the Spitfire spies should be between yourself and Schmid directly. I no longer have the time to deal personally with such matters. Goodbye."

Only later did Wichmann appreciate the reasons behind the curtness of the phone call, when he discovered the pressure Canaris had been under during those weeks after the fall of France. He thought he knew the admiral quite well; he was certainly aware of his underlying anxieties

232

about war with Great Britain. He wondered if the Chief of the *Abwehr* was having difficulty coming to terms with the idea – whether he liked it or not – of soon having to fly across the English Channel to set up *Abwehrstelle London*.

And even worse, the prospect that Adolf Hitler might have been right all along.

Chapter 60

(Saturday 13th July 1940)

When Schneider's Voluntary Interceptor forwarded on the *Abwehr*'s message, Ballard Ruskin instantly appreciated its significance. Soon afterwards he received a word-for-word duplicate from von Osten's VI. An urgent request such as this meant that decisions were being made in Germany and they needed every piece of available intelligence. He understood the potential risk involved for the agents, asking too many questions, being caught in areas of the factory that were out of bounds to them, listening too keenly to other people's conversations. All things that could bring then under suspicion.

He took the messages straight to the Director of B Division, Guy Liddell. Within the hour they were both sitting in the Director-General's office in St James's Street. Brigadier Harker talked with them for forty minutes. Then he placed the two slips of paper containing the identical messages into his briefcase and told them to come back first thing on Monday morning. By then he would have instructions for them on how to proceed.

Ruskin drove back to Latchmere House to sit in on the latest session with von Osten, who had been cooperating for a week by then. The lie about Audrey Parsons had worked better than they had hoped; von Osten seemed patently more upset by her betrayal than the prospect of the *Abwehr*'s duplicity. He hadn't given them any nuggets of gold as yet, but what he had told them tallied with Schneider's version of events. There was always the possibility he was stringing them along, playing for time in the hope of invasion. But Ruskin was optimistic. He had managed to avoid any major foul-ups during his seven years with MI5, unlike others. He prayed that having faith in von Osten would not be his first.

Although cooperating, von Osten was not exactly gushing information. He talked, but only in response to direct questions, then he would lapse into silence until the next one. Ruskin sat and listened as

234

others gently probed the German's mind, trying to extract an occasional gem from amongst the detritus.

The interrogation continued the next day. Ruskin stayed the night in his office inside Wormwood Scrubs, deciding against the drive to his large and rather empty house in New Malden. The next morning he went to a church near Shepherds Bush Green and sat listening to the vicar beseeching the Lord for their country's deliverance. In the afternoon he heard von Osten contributing to the solution of how this might practically be done.

Ruskin's mind was elsewhere, imagining the route through the corridors of power that the request for information about aircraft production might be taking. He wondered how high they would have to go to sanction the release of such sensitive intelligence, albeit false and intended to mislead. Someone (or a group more likely) was probably cooking up some figures at this very moment. Which way would the lie go – up or down? An overestimation would go some way towards cautioning Göring and his *Luftwaffe* as to the wisdom of taking on the RAF, and possibly delay Germany's invasion plans, thus giving precious time to strengthen defences. On the other hand, that might also allow time for the *Luftwaffe* to increase its own strength and Hitler to plan more thoroughly an invasion which might otherwise be a messy, improvised affair. In contrast, underestimating the figures might encourage Göring to strike soon in earnest; to fuel his over inflated ego and launch a full-on attack which might be easier to repel now than in six months or a year's time.

The more he thought about it, the more Ruskin was convinced that underestimation was the better option. He believed that an invasion was inevitable, come what may; no grossly over estimated claims about armament levels would dissuade Hitler now. Better to get it over with sooner rather than later.

Besides, if the air battle a few days ago was anything to go by, it had already started.

*

Shortly after nine o'clock on Monday morning, Ruskin followed Guy Liddell anxiously into the Director-General's office. Brigadier Harker came immediately to the business in hand. He held up a sealed buff envelope and passed it across the desk to Liddell.

"Here is the information you require, gentlemen. The envelope contains replies to both *Abwehr* requests – one for your chummy Mechanic, the other for Quaver. Amongst other things, it includes recent figures for Spitfire production at Southampton and Birmingham. We have drafted a precise wording and I would ask that it is adhered to as strictly as possible. Naturally you may need to adapt slightly to suit your agents' styles, but please make the alterations minimal."

We, wondered Ruskin; *who the hell is we?*

Guy Liddell said: "May we know how accurate the figures are? It might be necessary when dealing with follow-up questions from *Hamburg*."

"No you may not. Believe me I had a great deal of difficulty in gaining permission to release any information at all. Its accuracy, or otherwise, must remain beyond top secret." Harker sighed wistfully. "There are certain factions that have no faith in the notion of passing intelligence knowingly to the enemy, and the benefits it might bring. There is no vision how to use this situation creatively. Not yet, at any rate. Too risky. I'm sorry but I can only give you this information, I cannot comment further on the content."

"If this works," said Ruskin, "it could be the start of many similar deceptions, sir. It could be hugely beneficial. With respect, it's important that we as the operatives are fully conversant with the intelligence being fed through our double agents."

"I couldn't agree more," said Harker. "Let's see if it works first, shall we? Meanwhile the 'need-to-know' rule applies, and that is my brief to you. I can assure you, this comes from the top – the *very* top. Please be satisfied with this for the time being. You have what you need."

Liddell and Ruskin accepted reluctantly.

Harker wanted to tell them about his weekend; his meeting at Downing Street with Winston and the Minister of Air Production, Lord Beaverbrook; his trip to the Air Ministry; a discussion with the Commander-in-Chief of Fighter Command, Air Chief Marshal Dowding, in his office at Bentley Priory; and finally a return visit to Downing Street. Surprisingly the Prime Minister had been the least willing to cooperate. Beaverbrook supplied the correct figures and was allowed a hint of what they had in mind from Churchill. The newspaper mogul barked his approval – the hard-headed pragmatist acknowledging a creative initiative – before leaving to get on with badgering and bullying factory managers. His contacts in the Air Ministry were anxious to agree with anything that might lighten their burden and gave their wholehearted support. So too did Dowding, who saw the strategic benefits in the broader context of the battle that was now under way. "Should have been in intelligence," Harker said to himself as he set off from Bentley Priory back to London. "The Brylcream Boys don't deserve him." Winston eventually conceded and insisted on wording the messages that were now in the envelope in Liddell's hand. Harker could hardly prevent him from doing so, but to his relief they were brief and simply constructed with no hint of chiasmus or other Churchillian literary trickery.

236

"Gentlemen," said Harker as he rose to see Liddell and Ruskin out, "let's hope this works. If this is the start of something long and fruitful, then we must talk about setting up a committee to manage it and monitor exactly what we disclose to Germany – and how. It could become a highly complex business." He shook hands with both men. "That all remains to be seen of course. Good luck."

When the door closed behind them, Harker thought for a moment about the messages he had just handed over. It amused him to think that *Abwehr* radio operators in Hamburg would soon be receiving reports from two of their agents that had been written personally by Winston Churchill.

Chapter 61

(Monday 15th July 1940)

Erich Schneider was only too delighted to transmit and receive messages for MI5. Each occasion meant a welcome relief from the boredom of being cooped up in the austere Victorian house that had been his home since being moved to the Midlands. Situated barely two miles from the Castle Bromwich factory and close to a busy crossroads, it was only minutes away from the station where Schneider had alighted with his bicycle during his reconnaissance trip. The War Office had commandeered the house on behalf of the Security Service and handed it over for the duration. The owner had been compensated and told never to go near the place again. It was sparsely furnished, damp even in mid-summer, and depressing.

Schneider had already read the half-dozen novels he found scattered across an otherwise empty bookcase and was bored playing cards with the two minders MI5 had provided for him. He had given them nicknames, Laurel and Hardy, and for obvious reasons – one was fat and the other thin. He still had his trumpet mouthpiece and passed time blowing long notes into it, or arpeggios up and down the harmonic scale. He could feel the muscles in his lips regaining some strength and felt the urge to play again. He would one day pluck up the courage to ask for an instrument. They could hardly deny him that simple pleasure.

An hour never went by without his thoughts turning to Marion Wakeley, just twenty miles away in her cosy Coventry terrace. He desperately wanted to see her again.

That night they took him into the back bedroom from where transmissions were made. Downstairs, he saw the quieter one from the interrogation panel, now his case officer, and christened Uncle Mac by Schneider, after the avuncular presenter of *Children's Hour* on the wireless. It was Uncle Mac who handed the message, already coded, for him to transmit. Schneider guessed the content – Spitfire production figures – and wondered what lies were being told. Ironically he knew the

238

truth; Charlie the Checker had told him in the pub. He wondered if Castle Bromwich had managed to produce their ten Spitfires in June. *Hamburg* were probably being told it was a hundred; two hundred if their intention was to scare off Göring.

Schneider tapped out his identification code. On the third attempt there was a response. He proceeded to transmit the prepared message, stumbling from time to time and having to repeat an occasional word. When it was done he sat back and Uncle Mac offered him a cigarette.

"Is everything alright here for you, Eric? I know it's rather basic here, but it's the best we can do under the circumstances."

"I'll get by, thanks. A bit more tea wouldn't go amiss."

"It's just been rationed I'm afraid." Ballard Ruskin inhaled some smoke. "I'll make sure you get your share. Is there anything else I can do for you? I know how tedious it must be for you, stuck indoors all day long with nothing to do."

"There is something . . . if you can manage it."

"Tell me."

"I wouldn't mind a trumpet."

"A trumpet!"

"A trumpet. With a practice mute to keep the noise down. It would be good to be able to do some playing again. Of course if they've just been rationed . . ."

Ruskin laughed. "Not that I know of. Any particular kind of trumpet?"

"An ordinary B flat would do nicely. A Vincent Bach if you can manage it – that's what I played mostly as a professional. But anything will do . . . under the circumstances."

The Voluntary Interceptor who had been monitoring the headset interrupted.

"Excuse me, sir. We've just had an acknowledgment, and that's it for tonight. *Hamburg* have gone off the air."

"Right, thank you. Let's go shall we?"

As Ruskin was leaving, he said to Schneider: "Leave the trumpet request with me. I can't promise anything but I'll see what I can do."

His car pulled away. Where to Schneider had no idea.

"That's the last I'll hear of that," he thought.

Chapter 62

(Tuesday 16ᵗʰ July 1940)

Major 'Beppo' Schmid was delighted with the wire from *Abwehrstelle Hamburg*, the first piece of concrete intelligence he had received from inside Britain in months. And in time, just, to incorporate into his report for Göring.

All morning he hammered away at his typewriter, retyping sections where adjustments were needed, and a whole page on one occasion. He had not forgotten Kesselring's advice: *Make it positive. Nothing you write will make any appreciable difference to anything.* On reflection, however, Schmid was less inclined to agree. Since his chat with Göring in the gardens at Carinhall, he still had some faith in his commander-in-chief's ability to be influenced by intelligence reports, more so than Göring made apparent. His report was sound and informative; and it was positive.

By midday he was making his way along the corridors of the Air Ministry. Göring had so far spent most of July on holiday with his family at Bad Gastein, or sightseeing in Paris, returning to Berlin only when meetings demanded. Schmid knew that the field marshal had disappeared again straight after the Carinhall conference last Thursday.

As chance would have it, Hitler had recalled him personally, which meant that the report would not sit pending on his desk for too long. The reason for the summons was not known, though speculation within the Ministry was rife.

Schmid handed the report to a stocky, bespectacled secretary whose half-smile revealed bad teeth and whose blouse revealed nothing at all. He returned to his office feeling pleased with himself for a job well done. Sections of the report were fresh in his mind and he could recall some from memory: *RAF fighter squadrons are rigidly attached to their home bases . . . The fact that Hurricanes and Spitfires are not yet equipped with cannon guns, 20 mm calibre, makes them inferior to the Bf 109E, and even more so to the new Bf 109F . . . Total British fighter aircraft production during the prospective period of Operation* Adlerangriff *is*

240

estimated to be as low as 150 and can never exceed 200 machines per month ...

To give balance to this rosy appraisal, he made just one minor concession: *It cannot be denied that the Bf 110 is to a large extent inferior to a skilfully-handled Spitfire.*

This was common knowledge, particularly to those *Luftwaffe* pilots who had to fly the twin-engine fighter. Its slow acceleration and wide turning circle made it easy prey.

Schmid was confident that Göring would find the report welcome reading.

*

The next day, the reason for Göring's presence in Berlin became apparent, as did that of Kesselring, Sperrle, Stumpff and six other of Hitler's generals. In appreciation of their magnificent achievements and unprecedented military successes, all nine were promoted to the rank of field marshal. For Göring, Hitler had devised a unique rank that would maintain the necessary differential for his most significant and powerful ally. Göring was created *Reichsmarshall.*

The war was largely forgotten as the German High Command enjoyed a period of self-congratulation. At a meeting at Carinhall, Göring was in splendidly confident mood. Yet promotions and positive predictions were daily being complemented by reports of continual opposition over the English coast from Fighter Command. *Luftwaffe* losses, especially bombers, were consistently high. A day later, back at the Air Ministry in Berlin, Göring was ready to deride his three new field marshals.

"Our fighters must wake up!" he shouted. "We are losing too many bombers. The 109s should be clearing enemy fighters from the skies before our bombers arrive."

All through the meeting Schmid watched Göring with fascination. The *Reichsmarshall* had swallowed at least five pills in less than two hours. Success was doing nothing to quell his addiction. Schmid was aware, however, that personal reasons might be contributing to Göring's mood. Word had spread that his nephew, Hans-Joachim Göring, had been killed in action a few days earlier, piloting a Bf 110 on a raid over the English coast.

Ironically he had been shot down by Hurricanes, not Spitfires.

Chapter 63

(Friday 19th July 1940)

The taxi Anson bumped to a halt on the edge of the hangar apron. Before jumping out, Alison made her way to the flight deck and pressed a hand firmly on the pilot's shoulder.

"Thanks, Howard. Do the same for you one day."

The pilot turned his head and said blandly: "I haven't seen you, I haven't landed at Biggin Hill today, and if anyone says otherwise, they're a damned liar. You be here at eight in the morning sharp – not a second later – or we're both for it!"

Alison nodded. "We'll be here. Thanks again." She stepped down onto the grass and hurried to catch up with Heather. They watched as the Anson picked up speed, rose into the air and banked round until it was flying due west, heading towards White Waltham.

"Very obliging chap, our Howie," observed Heather.

"Let's hope he's as discreet as he is obliging."

"Don't worry, he's discreet" Heather winked knowingly.

"Do you mean to say he's done this for you before?"

"More than once. He'd do anything for the girl he adores."

"Even fly her into the arms of another man? Sounds like foolishness, not adoration." They walked briskly out through the aerodrome gates and headed for a bus stop.

"You would think that, but the fact is, Howie is so stuck on me he'll do anything I say. He knows he hasn't a chance, so he just likes to do me favours to make me happy."

"Sounds like a raw deal to me."

"He doesn't seem to think so."

"If you say so, Heather."

The bus arrived after a wait of about twenty minutes. It took them through Westerham and along the A25 to Sevenoaks. There they got on another bus that took them several miles on to the tiny village of Crowbourne. The girls stepped down onto a triangular green. Along one side was the road, along another a bank of low rushes beyond which was a still, lichen-covered pond. The third side was a gravel path leading to a half-timbered pub, The Bush, with a fenced-off garden that extended to the edge of the green.

"Just as Stewart described it," said Heather proudly. "Come on, let's see what our rooms are like." She marched ahead with her night bag slung over her shoulder. Alison followed hesitantly.

"I'm nervous, Heather. Suddenly all this doesn't seem quite right."

"Nonsense, it's fun."

"I've never done this before – you know, sneaked away for, well, you know . . ."

"For a wicked night of passion? Come along, Ally, you must have done. Surely with Jan-Arne?"

As they approached the pub entrance, Alison grabbed Heather's arm.

"No, we never did this. It was always at his parents' house, or at my flat. Never like this." She paused. "To be honest, I'm not sure I want to go through with it. Not now anyway. Not here and now with Dan."

"Of course you do. He's a wonderful fellow. He thinks the world of you."

"But is there a future in it, I keep asking myself, with the war and everything? Is there any point in committing to anything during a war? He might be killed tomorrow. So might I for that matter."

Heather hugged her tightly. "You've got it all wrong, darling. Now look, Dan is someone rather special, yes? There's no doubt about that?" Alison nodded. "Well suppose you were to meet him here tonight just for drinks. Suppose that's all, and you didn't allow him to make love to you."

"What point are you making?"

"Well, suppose that, and then suppose Dan was shot down tomorrow, or the next day, and killed . . . and you never saw him again. Wouldn't you regret not having known what it was like to be with him? Now, more than ever, you shouldn't let opportunities slip away. You may not have a second chance."

Alison's eyes filled with tears. Heather was right, Dan was important to her, too important not to take advantage of some precious moments together. She pulled out a handkerchief and wiped her eyes.

"I'm sorry. You're right. It's been a long time since – you know. I think I'm nervous about that as much as anything."

"Oh my Lord!" cried Heather. "Come on, let's register, have a hot bath and I'll give you the benefit of my vast and more recent experience to remind you. I know it's a cliché but it's like riding a bike, my dear . . . you never forget how to do it. It just makes your muscles ache until you're back in training, especially in the saddle department!"

243

They had made a reservation by phone; two adjoining single rooms, which turned out to be at the rear of the building, overlooking a yard surrounded by a shoulder-high brick wall. Heather investigated the stairs down to the back door and tested the lock. There was a key on the inside which looked as though it had never been removed. She reported her findings.

"Looks promising. Should be able to smuggle them up without too much trouble. Come on, bath time. The boys'll be over from West Malling soon."

By seven thirty they had bathed, chatted and dressed with the connecting door between their rooms wide open. When they entered the lounge they wore light cotton skirts and blouses with cardigans across their shoulders. They felt happy and light-hearted, and they were ready to forget the war for the evening. Stuart Innes and Dan Rodigan were there to greet them, but it was apparent from their faces that all was not well. They looked exhausted, with a glaze in their eyes that Alison recognised immediately. Shock. She had seen it on the faces of people at Hendon when a trainer had lost control and plunged into the crowd at an air display, killing several people.

Innes ordered two pints and two pink gins, and they settled themselves in a corner of the front garden, overlooking the green. It was a warm and balmy evening. Gradually they told the girls about the past forty-eight hours. Rodigan spoke first.

"We've lost a third of the squadron since yesterday. Four Spits gone – two chums dead, two missing over the sea – and we only arrived from Catterick a week ago. The first few days were terrific and we had some wonderful scraps, bagged lots of Jerries – Ju 88s, Heinkels, MEs – you name it. Didn't lose a single plane. We'd done our homework, you see, worked out proper combat tactics, and rehearsed them. Thought things through, not like some of the clowns up there, firing out of range, not covering each other. Death or glory boys. We're not like that in Midas Squadron – the boys with the golden touch. Until yesterday." He paused and drank some beer. "Mike Arnold went first – Blue Section leader. We scrambled mid-morning to intercept some Dorniers escorted by Messerschmitts. We were outnumbered, as usual, but we're used to that. The more of the bastards to aim at the better – sorry, excuse my language. Mike shot down a Dornier, then followed it straight off with a 110. But then another two latched on to him and stuck to him like glue. I saw it all. They weren't going to let him off the hook. I tried to intercept, but wasn't in time. One caught him in the engine – blew the cowling right off. He went into a steep dive and I saw his kite smash into a field. He never bailed out."

There was total silence for a while. Innes took over.

"Yellow Two went next. Brian West – really decent chap. I saw him chasing a 109, he got in really close and fired a two-second burst. That was all it took. Jerry caught fire, rolled over out of control and exploded. It was over in a flash. I heard Brian on the radio say 'Got you, you b . . .' – what Dan just said. He banked round and I think was watching the wreckage falling to earth. Didn't even see the one that got him. It was on his tail in a flash. Brian's Spit blew up as well. Just disintegrated! He wouldn't have known a thing about it."

Rodigan had been sipping more beer.

"That was yesterday. Now we have two more missing. They came early today – Dorniers again, probably doing reconnaissance. A scrap developed with the escort over the sea – 109s, but fewer this time, so fairly even in numbers. They realised this and went into a defensive formation, a circle, each following the other's tail. Bloody difficult to break up. Stu here ordered us to leave them alone and concentrate on the bombers. But Vince Bowman wasn't having any of it. He attacked from the flank, zoomed straight in, long burst as he went, and managed to cripple one. As he did, another broke out of the circle behind him and caught Vince. He bailed out into the sea. Seemed okay. There were quite a few boats around so hopefully he'll be picked up."

"Vince is Red Three," said Innes. "We lost Green Leader as well. Roy Nicholson. No one seems to know what happened to him. He was seen parachuting into the drink, but what got him no one knows. Someone reported him appearing limp on his parachute. There was no news before we left, but it's not looking good."

Alison took Rodigan's hand and held it tightly. She had no idea what to say and so remained quiet, as did Heather. Their thoughts were almost identical; Dan or Stuart could be next. Tomorrow, the day after, next week, it was only a matter of time.

"Four planes gone, two men, possibly three killed, and a fourth missing," said Rodigan. "Pretty dreadful, and yet, compared to 141 Squadron we've got off lightly. There's hardly anything left of them."

"They're based at West Malling too," explained Innes. "Flying Defiants. Good planes in their own right, well-armed with a turret gun behind the cockpit . . . but too slow in a dog fight. They went up shortly after us and were bounced by some 109s south of Folkestone. Jerry sussed out their weak point pretty quickly and attacked from below where the turret gunner can't get at them. Six were shot down in a matter of minutes, one limped home, two got away – but only when some Hurricanes showed up. Absolute bloody massacre."

"How awful," said Heather. "How absolutely awful."

"They'd never been in combat before," continued Rodigan. "It was their first contact with the enemy – and their last for most of them. Such a waste, an absolute bloody waste! Sometimes I think the men with egg on their caps don't give a damn. We're not human beings in those kites, with names and personalities, and feelings. We're just numbers, units, and statistics to be hurled at Jerry." He stopped abruptly, perhaps conscious of having said too much.

Alison said quietly: "Mr Churchill was right the other night when he said this is a war of the unknown warrior. He could have been referring to those boys."

When they had finished their drinks, they ambled towards the pond on the far side of the green. Alison slipped her arm through Rodigan's and they walked together, slightly behind the others. Thoughts of dinner had gone; appetites vanished. Occasionally a few words passed between them, but mostly they walked in silence. From the pond they headed down a narrow lane that meandered between hop fields. The cane rods stood proudly in long rows with the rapidly maturing vines hugging close to them. In the distance, the twin white cowls of an oast house turned gently in the evening breeze. Puffy clouds were moving away to the east and the deep orange sun was low in the sky. It was a calm, peaceful scene, a world away from the tales of violent death the girls had glimpsed momentarily.

They walked for a long time, until the sun had disappeared behind the horizon and darkness enveloped the landscape. The lanes they took skirted the village and eventually emerged at the green again. Heather and her squadron leader kissed – tentatively at first, then with more passion. Alison looked up at the man for whom her heart ached so deeply. She wanted to feel his anguish for him, to steal the pain from him. Most of all she wanted to know that he would live.

"The war of the unknown warrior," murmured Rodigan. "That's about right. Winston sums things up perfectly."

"I know, it struck me as being just right. I cut out some of that speech from the newspaper. I keep it in my bag. He went on to say . . . *But let us all strive without failing in faith or in duty, and the dark curse of Hitler will be lifted from our age.* That's what this is all about. It's important to remember, I think."

Rodigan digested this for a while, then he gently pulled her to him and put both arms round her shoulders. "Alison, thank you."

"Thank you for what?"

"For taking my mind away from reality for a few precious moments."

"I haven't really done anything."

"You didn't need to. You've simply been there. But it's more than that. I sense that you really understand – maybe because you're a flyer."

"I don't think you have to fly to understand how you're feeling. It's about loss, and the shock of sudden loss."

"Well you do understand, whatever the reasoning." He kissed her gently on the lips, then pulled away. "I'm sorry, perhaps this isn't the right time for this."

"Don't be – I understand that too. If our plans for tonight don't feel right, so be it. If you want to say goodnight here and now, that's alright. Please don't imagine I'll be upset, or offended." She leaned forward and kissed him on the cheek.

Rodigan pulled her to him. "No, it's the opposite. I want to be with you tonight, not alone in a lumpy cot in a drafty hut, thinking of what tomorrow will bring. I want to enjoy every minute with you. I want you."

Alison rubbed her cheek gently against his. "I never realised, I didn't think . . ."

Rodigan clasped her hand. They walked across to the shadowy couple locked together nearby. The girls were soon standing in the pub doorway, waving goodbye to their airmen as they walked away. Then they went inside, said a hearty goodnight to the landlord and a couple of locals propping up the bar, and hurried to their rooms.

Ten minutes later, Alison was in her night dress, sitting on the edge of her bed. She heard Heather tiptoe along the corridor and down the stairs to unlock the back door. Her window was open and she heard the scrape of shoes against brickwork, muffled whispering, and then footsteps in the corridor. There was the gentlest of tapping on her door. She opened it and let Rodigan in. Immediately his lips were on hers and they kissed, long and deep. She pulled away and got into the single bed. It was dark and she could only see a silhouette as he undressed. He squeezed in beside her and they slipped naturally into a tender embrace. The feel of his naked flesh sent a quiver down her. A hand encircled her waist and slid across the back of her cotton night dress. She hadn't known whether to wear anything, but modesty had prevailed. His hand moved round to her breasts and squeezed them gently. She shuddered as a warm pang flowed through her. She could feel his erection pressing against her side.

He lifted the nightdress up and over her head, and threw it onto the floor. Then he was on top of her, not difficult in such a narrow bed. She could tell he was nervous and so guided him towards the wetness between her legs. When he entered her a shock of pleasure engulfed her. He was gentle enough, but rushing, so she slowed him down by pushing her hands against his thighs.

"Take your time, flight lieutenant," she whispered affectionately. "None of your two-second bursts here."

Chapter 64

(Sunday 21st July 1940)

Four weeks to the day since he was captured by MI5, Schneider decided he could stand no more of British Security Service hospitality. One evening, after much thought and preparation, and following a long session of cards, cigarettes and whisky with the minders, he took his leave.

In the dead of night, as Laurel and Hardy slept, he crept downstairs, unlocked the front door – the key was in the lock for which the minders later received an almighty bollocking – and out into the side alley. He emerged with the bicycle used for fetching supplies, switched on the dynamo and set off gingerly along the Chester Road towards Castle Bromwich. On his back he had a pack containing a few clothes and a razor. Speed was out of the question in the blackout, and the dynamo never generated more than a pitiful glow from the slit in the masking tape over the front lamp. So progress was slow.

He had thought long and hard about his escape route. The railway station was close by and very tempting. But he had no idea how long he might have to wait for a train, possibly until morning. Too dangerous. He settled for the bicycle. In his pocket he had rough directions sketched on a piece of paper, copied from a map he had found in the safe house.

Would there be LDV patrols throughout the night? Possibly, and if not there was the risk of army road checks and barricades. But he had the correct paperwork for a factory shift worker, and if he stayed off the main roads whenever possible, it would minimise the risk.

He decided against cycling past the main gates of the Spitfire factory where there was a very good chance of a road block. Instead he turned left at the junction just before the works and headed towards Minworth and the Hams Hall power station. It was a long way round, adding a good five miles on to the journey; but a necessary precaution. There was no moon. He pedalled slowly, peering ahead into the darkness, following the white-painted curb of the road when there was one. There were no signposts and he occasionally stopped to consult the sketch map and a small pocket compass which he had stolen earlier in the day from Hardy. Its luminous needle helped him stay roughly on a south-easterly course, although avoiding main roads involved much zigzagging and occasional backtracking.

He didn't pass anyone for more than an hour. Then he was cycling through a small village when a figure staggered towards him down the main street, singing tunelessly to himself. The drunk barely noticed the figure on the bike, and even if he had he wouldn't remember much about it the next morning.

Forty minutes later, on a long stretch of straight road, he came to a road block; a tree trunk resting on two trestles. Schneider almost cycled into it.

The two men who questioned him by the pinpoint beam of a torch were drowsy, as if he had woken them up, which he probably had. They were elderly, although their faces weren't clear enough in the dark to be sure just *how* old. They scrutinised his papers and asked where he was going. He explained that he had been working on a night shift and received a message to say his mother was ill. It was a long way to cycle but there was no public transport at this time of night, and he simply had to reach her. One of them asked which factory he worked at. Schneider refused to tell them, indignant that they should want to know such a thing. Didn't they know that idle talk cost lives?

It worked. With considerable effort they started dragging the tree trunk to one side, but Schneider told them not to bother and squeezed around the side. Cheekily he asked them to confirm he was on the right road for Coventry, which they did. A quarter of a mile further on he dropped the cycle and lit a much needed cigarette. He could feel his heart pounding and the veins at his temples throbbing. The nicotine helped. Ten minutes later he was cycling again, pedalling as fast as his limited vision would allow.

Some time later – more than an hour, and nearer two – the vague silhouette of hedgerows and trees began to show as dawn approached. It was almost indiscernible at first, but soon he was able to see the road ahead, and his speed increased. He had started to feel dog tired, but that lifted as it became lighter.

Another road block; less of an ordeal this time. He saw it from a distance and prepared himself for the brief interrogation. Then another on the outskirts of Coventry, a mere glance at his papers this time as there was a queue of people, all wanting to get to their place of work.

At ten minutes past seven, tired, unshaven and in need of a wash, Schneider pushed his bike into the front garden of 29 Spencer Road. If all was well, he would put it in the back garden later, out of sight. When he knocked on the door, he saw an upstairs curtain flicker for a second, then heard footsteps on the stairs. The door opened just enough for him to edge inside.

"Henry!" cried Marion Wakeley as she flung her arms around his neck. "So good to see you. Where have you been – why haven't you been in touch? It's very early. I was still in bed." She was wearing only a nightgown and Schneider could feel the warmth and softness of her body.

"I know, I'm sorry, it's a fine time to be turning up on your doorstep, but I cycled all the way from Birmingham to see you. I can explain."

"Birmingham! My poor thing." She stroked his cheek with the back of her hand. Tears were welling up in her eyes. "You must be exhausted. I'm so glad you came – I was thinking I'd never see you again."

"I always intended coming back."

"I've missed you."

"I've missed you too." He hugged her gently. "I'm so tired. Could I please use your front room again – just to get my head down for a couple of hours? Then I'll tell you everything."

Marion tugged off his jacket and hung it on the coat rack. Without saying a word, she clutched his hand, led him upstairs and into the front bedroom. A large double bed took up most of the floor space. The covers were drawn back on one side where Marion had been sleeping.

"Why sleep down there when there's plenty of room up here . . ."

"But what about the children? It's hardly right – I couldn't."

Marion flicked off her slippers and got into bed, her ample breasts swinging freely, entirely visible through the gaping neck of her nightgown. "They're not here. I sent them to stay in the country, when they said the bombing might start any day. A lot of kids were evacuated at the start of the war, but I wouldn't let mine go. This time I felt I should try it and see how it goes – for their own sake. They're staying with a family in Evesham. So I'm alone, Henry. Come and sleep with me. Please?"

Schneider stripped and piled his clothes onto a chair. "I need a bath – or a wash at least."

"I don't care, just come and hold me."

He climbed into bed and lay on his back. Marion stretched across and wrapped herself around him, burying herself into his tired body. The feel of her gave him an immediate erection, despite his tiredness. Fingers touched his member, then a whole hand, stroking it rhythmically.

"Oh God, Marion, that's really good. But I don't think I can . . ."

"Hush, you need sleep. So sleep."

"It seems unfair."

"Hush. Just sleep."

Schneider could feel himself drifting off, as instructed. Despite being sexually aroused, he could not keep his eyes open. In his semi-conscious state, an incongruous image flashed into his head; he was sitting in an orchestra, trumpet in hand, and there was Renate in front of him leading the violins, looking radiant, smiling across at him. He felt restless, anxious. This was wrong. He wanted to resist. Then suddenly the image was gone, replaced by a delightful sensation of sliding effortlessly downwards, as if in free fall. Nothing mattered any longer; everything was fine. The last thing he remembered was a vague pulsating feeling in his groin as sleep engulfed him.

*

Marion was sitting on the edge of the bed when Schneider awoke, fully clothed and smiling at him as he gradually focused. She had on the same housecoat she had been wearing when he first came to see her a month ago. It seemed like a year.

"Goodness you were tired," she said. "Fancy sleeping through that!"

"You told me to."

"Yes but I didn't think you would!"

"What time is it?"

"Almost midday. Would you like something to eat? Bit late for breakfast, but I can get you something."

Schneider stretched luxuriously. "That would be wonderful. Is there any chance of a bath?"

"Of course, I'll boil some hot water for you." She leaned forward and kissed him. "And after the bath?"

"Well," mused Schneider. "If you haven't anything better to do, why not come back to bed. I'd like to find out what I missed first time round."

"Try and stop me!" Marion lay next to him and rested her head on his chest. "It's not a case of having anything better to do – I don't have *anything* to do. Not without Annette and Simon. I never thought I'd miss them so much. They get on my nerves when they're here, but as soon as they've gone I want them back. You know what it's like." Schneider didn't, but he nodded. "Still, they're safe where they are. Evesham is lovely, in the Cotswolds. I've been down once already to see them."

"Yes they are safer there," said Schneider. "A lot of heavy industry around Coventry. It could well be bombed."

"You're probably right. We're surrounded by factories here. They're all tooled up for war work – making bits of guns, and planes and things. We've had a few raids, but nothing major so far."

Schneider patted her on the backside. "What about this bath then."

She stood up and saluted. "Anything you wish, sir. Then you can tell me what you've been up to and why I haven't heard from you – and how you ended up cycling from Birmingham through the night to see me."

She hovered by the door. "How long have I got you for this time – are you on a forty-eight-hour pass?"

"I'll explain when I'm clean and fed. You may have me indefinitely." He stood up and stretched lazily. "Now about this bath."

Marion stared at his naked body. She moved closer and ran a fingertip lightly over the inside of his thigh. "Follow me, my lover. Bath, food, and then bed until you're exhausted again. We've got lots of catching up to do, you and me."

Washed and dressed, Schneider sat in the back room and ate sausages and bubble and squeak, the best meal he had eaten since Karl's wife Else had cooked for him and Otto in Augsburg. Otto had enjoyed more than her cooking, he recalled, and wondered where he was now. Probably under lock and key in a safe house near Southampton. This business of taking them to the location of their targets had puzzled him. They could as easily transmit false information from London, surely. *Abwehrstelle Hamburg* wouldn't know the difference. He asked his Voluntary Interceptor about it one evening, who assured him it made all the difference. *Hamburg* would be able to tell fairly precisely where a transmission was coming from. He talked about triangulation of radio waves, but Schneider didn't understand a word.

As he ate, he told Marion a story that fitted in with his circumstances as best he could.

"I've deserted. Gone AWOL. I'm not a coward – I proved that in France. It's just that, well, I had a bust up with an NCO last night. We'd both had a few, and he started mouthing off, saying things that were best left unsaid. Talking about dying rather than be captured, and claiming that the lads should have stood their ground at Dunkirk instead of clearing off and letting Jerry humiliate them like that. Ignorant oaf. Of course it turned out he was over here the whole time, so he hadn't a clue what he was talking about. Eventually it got to me and I punched him, a few times in fact. He'll be alright, just a black eye and a few loose teeth. But it would mean a court-martial for me. I decided the best thing was to clear off. So I went back to barracks, changed into some civvies, borrowed a bike and here I am."

Marion looked worried. "That's bad, Henry. You'll have to give yourself up."

"I know. But not for a while. I need time to think this through properly before I do."

"It's wrong to run away from situations. Don't leave it too long."

"Well thanks for your support," said Schneider, his voice heavy with sarcasm.

"You can stay as long as you like, Henry. I won't throw you out. I want you here. All I'm saying is you'll have to go back at some stage – otherwise one day they'll come and take you back."

"You're right, of course. I'm sorry, it sounded as if you were telling me to clear off, and I've only just got here."

"Does anyone know about me – have you told anyone?"

"Nobody." Schneider finished his meal and sipped a cup of tea. He decided to change the subject. "I haven't heard the news recently. What's Adolf up to?"

"Well might you ask. He's made a peace offer, according to the wireless. Calls it 'a last appeal to reason' . . . wants Britain to capitulate. There's fat chance of that happening, I could tell him. Things are slowly hotting up in the skies apparently, mostly down south. The calm before the storm, so they reckon."

"They're probably right." Schneider looked across at Marion; her cheeks were flushed, her hair slightly awry. She amazed him – immensely practical, a good cook, and an adventurous lover. A treasure hidden away in an ordinary street in an ordinary Midland town.

This time he led her upstairs. It was a warm afternoon, so they made love on top of the bed. Sexually, Marion could be gentle one minute and rough the next. She liked to take control, encouraging Schneider to push harder and harder inside her, to bring her to one orgasm after another. When she came she was wild for a few boundless moments, and left scratch marks on his shoulders and buttocks. Eventually they lay wearily in each other's arms, and as the day began to cool they slipped in between the sheets. Schneider lay in a post-coital haze, thinking about the woman in his arms. There was an inner warmth about Marion that transcended anything he had ever felt for his wife, who, despite her beauty, had had a coldness in her that he now recognised.

His thoughts turned to Bernard Wakeley, the man in whose bed he now lay; Marion's husband, lying murdered in a field in northern France. A stab of guilt seared through him. He was stepping into a dead man's shoes. Bad feelings welled up inside him. He felt the need to challenge Marion, and the words came before he could stop them.

"Why are you doing this – making love to the man who came to tell you your husband was dead?"

The question took Marion aback. She turned her head on the pillow and looked at him askance.

"Do you think I'm heartless – that I don't care?"

"I just want to understand."

"It's simple really." She turned her back to him, revealing an expanse of bare flesh from her hips to her shoulder blades, like a virgin canvas awaiting an artist's brush. "I didn't love Bernard."

'Never?"

"At first . . . but I lost it. Or it lost me."

"Did something happen to change the way you felt, or was it gradual?"

"Something happened." She spoke the words firmly and with finality, as if there was nothing more to be said. Schneider realised it would be wrong to pursue the matter.

"I'm sorry. It's none of my business." He wriggled across the bed and pressed himself lightly against her, moulding his body around hers.

"He started hitting me."

"Oh . . ." He hadn't expected that.

"Soon after Simon was born." The voice was so soft it was almost inaudible. He had to listen hard to hear her. "One evening he came home from the pub very drunk, and slapped me across the face – right out of the blue. I couldn't believe it! He'd never laid a finger on me before. He used to go down the pub often enough, and come back drunk often enough. But he never touched me – never. Until then. She shivered and pulled the sheet up over her shoulders. "The next morning he didn't remember a thing. I let it pass. Only a stinger, nothing more. I thought he must have been angry about something and took it out on me." She paused for a moment, as if choosing her words carefully. "Then it happened again, about a week later . . . only this time it hurt. He went to slap me. I saw it coming so ducked a bit and his hand caught me right in the eye. The next morning I had a shiner even a blind man would have noticed. Then again a few days later, and again a few days after that. It was just like mum and dad all over again. Suddenly all my love for him just died."

"Did he say what was wrong?"

"He told me eventually. Turned out he was having it off with the barmaid at the local. She was giving him what he wanted and suddenly he was feeling tied down by a wife and child. Simon was only a few months old. I was breast feeding and permanently tired from lack of sleep – too tired for what he wanted all the time. I think it started when I was pregnant. I knew she flirted with him, but then she did that with all the locals. Anything in trousers. I'd been down there with Bernard and seen her in action, the slut. I never imagined it would lead to anything. Anyway, he was missing his freedom, drinking too much, and taking it out on me."

Schneider listened with furrowed brow. He didn't know how it felt to be physically abused, but he was familiar with the pain of finding out about a partner's infidelity. He knew how deep the hurt penetrated.

"This must have been a few years ago," he said. "Have you been putting up with that ever since?"

254

"Until the war came, yes, although once he told me about *her* it happened less often. It seemed to ease his frustration in some way. But he kept on seeing her. Pretended he didn't, but I knew better. He was a bloody awful liar. Our marriage was a joke from then on. We lived together here, in this house, shared meals, even had another kid and brought them up like a normal family. But Bernard and me, we were more like brother and sister than husband and wife. Annette was a mistake, after a drunken Saturday night fumble. The only thing we ever did as a couple was to go down the Rex every once in a while to see a film. I think he must have got tired of the slut after a while, though he never said anything. But life here was as bad for him as it was for me, and when war came he packed in his job at Dunlop and was down at the recruiting office before you could say Jack Robinson. I've only seen him twice since, when he came home on leave, and even then he was at the pub most of the time. Annette and Simon didn't see much of their dad either, but then he never did pay them any attention."

Bernard Wakeley's words flashed into Schneider's head: *I was a lousy husband to her – she's better off without me.* Now he believed it. He thought back to their meeting. Something was puzzling him. "When we were in France, I saw a letter that you wrote to your husband. It was signed – *With love, Marion.*"

"Writing something and meaning it are two different things." Suddenly Marion spun round and kissed him full on the mouth. "Henry, you must go back and give yourself up. I'm scared that if you don't I might lose you. They're bound to find you eventually, and when they do who knows what will happen. For all I know they might shoot deserters in wartime. Please God, don't let me lose you."

Schneider knew she was right, he had to go back. Not to the army, as Marion thought, but to MI5 and that drab house in Castle Bromwich. Back to Laurel and Hardy, card games and endless boredom. Would they punish him? There was only way to find out.

"I know I have to go back . . . but not yet. Let me stay a while."

"It's Monday. Stay until the end of the week." She closed her mouth around his ear and breathed out warm air until Schneider could stand it no more and pushed her away, giggling. He leaned forward and brushed his head against her breasts, nestling his face between them. Marion purred.

"When you arrived you said you've missed me," she said.

"So I have."

"Show me how much." Their bodies closed together and they made love again before falling into a sleep of warm contentment.

Chapter 65

(Friday 26th July 1940)

Schneider returned to Castle Bromwich late on Friday afternoon.

His time with Marion had been blissfully happy. They had walked, talked, shared their thoughts and feelings, and made love several times every day, on each occasion with a greater intensity than the time before. They visited the cathedral – St Michael's – and Marion showed Schneider the effigy and tomb of the first Bishop of Coventry, pointing out the now incongruous swastikas adorning his mitre. "That should protect the cathedral from Nazi bombs," she joked.

When Friday came, Marion walked with him to Coventry Station. She smiled the whole way because she was happy, and relieved in the knowledge that to part then would increase the chances of his returning soon. Schneider's mood was more somber. On the platform they hugged each other.

"I love you, Henry."

It was exactly what he wanted, and needed, to hear. "I love you too," he replied. "I want to be with you."

"So you shall."

Schneider knew then that the spectre of Renate had left him. The guilt had evaporated.

The train pulled away. As she turned round to walk home, Marion decided on the spur of the moment to travel down to the Cotswolds to see her children. Her heart ached for them and their faces filled her mind, blotting out thoughts of the man she knew as Henry Mansell. Within the hour she was back at the station carrying a small suitcase.

*

At Chester Road Station, Schneider wheeled his bike out of the guard's van and cycled the few hundred yards to the safe house. To his surprise there was no answer when he knocked on the front door. He tried half a dozen times, banging louder each time. He walked down the side alley and into the back garden. The kitchen door was locked and the dining room curtains were shut. He sat down on the edge of the rockery and smoked a cigarette. Should he wait until someone returned? They may have abandoned the place; perhaps as no longer secure. They had no idea where their rogue agent had gone or whom he might have contacted.

Click! The unmistakable sound of a hand gun being cocked was loud, because it was less than an inch from Schneider's ear. A second later the barrel was pressed firmly against the side of his head, the metal cool and hard on his skin.

"Stand up, you bastard . . . and very slowly." Schneider recognised the voice instantly. Hardy. "Now move towards the back door." He did exactly as he was told. He hadn't heard a sound, not even a rustle of grass. Hardy must have come from the garden; maybe from the Anderson shelter.

"Have you missed me?" said Schneider, his voice shaking. "I only nipped out for some fags. I got lost."

"Shut up!" The tone was venomous. "You've caused us a lot of trouble, so just keep your mouth shut." Hardy leaned forward and unlocked the kitchen door. Once they were inside he shut and locked it.

"Home sweet home," said Schneider.

"I told you to shut it!" A fist slammed into Schneider's back – a savage kidney punch. He yowled and fell forward onto the ground, clutching his side in a vain attempt to comfort the searing pain. "You've led us a right old game, so don't push your luck." The big man grabbed him by the collar and twisted it tight into a garroting hold. "Now listen, I'm not going to hit you again, nor will anyone else. And if you say I hit you at all, I'll deny it. Your word against mine. Who do you think they'll believe? It was a bloody stupid thing to do, clearing off like that. If you do that again and we catch you, you can be damn sure the hangman will be receiving a phone call. Understand?"

There was a groan of assent from the floor. Hardy backed away.

Several hours later, as the nine o'clock news ended its detailing of further German attacks on convoys in the English Channel, this time by Stukas and MTBs, Lt.-Col. Ballard Ruskin arrived from London with two men Schneider had not seen before. It was the beginning of a long and arduous night that ended well after dawn with hoarse voices, red eyes and agent Quaver sucked dry of information, or so Ballard imagined. He had been to see an old girlfriend from schooldays; he felt lonely and isolated cooped up in the safe house and she provided him with the comfort he had craved. He promised them on his life he had told her nothing about his being an agent. As far as she was concerned he'd gone AWOL from the army, having been with the British Expeditionary Force and evacuated from Dunkirk – which was true to a point.

"I had every intention of returning," he assured Ruskin. "I just needed some time to myself, to have some freedom for a bit, that's all."

Ruskin threw his arms in the air. "Why didn't you say! We could have arranged a woman for you."

"You mean a tart? That's not what I wanted. I needed to feel part of the real world again, for a while. And I did. Then I came back – as I always intended." He looked Ruskin straight in the eye. "I *did* come back."

"Tell us the woman's name."

"No."

"Where does she live?"

"Birmingham."

"The address?"

He did not reply. He had lied about how he knew the woman, but everything else about his time away was true; he even described the house, her children and her circumstances. He stressed time and again that he had not told her, or anyone else, about his real identity and what he was doing. He had deserted from the army. When the interrogators finally adjourned, Ruskin took them aside.

"Overall I believe him. He's not telling us who he was with and where, but the rest rings true. I think we all know when someone is telling us a pack of lies. But there's something not quite right. There is no good reason why he should protect this woman. She could corroborate his story and we would have no further interest in her. Surely he sees that. Unless there is something about her he is keeping from us. But what?"

"We must find out, sir," said one of the other men, a sallow-faced major. "We have to know if he's still one hundred percent secure."

"I know, Atkins. Either he's being foolishly chivalrous, or she's mixed up in this somehow. For all we know the *Abwehr* might have debriefed him through this woman and sent him back to us. I don't believe so, but it's not out of the question."

"We must know one way or the other," insisted Atkins. "If not, our turned network will be in jeopardy. Can we lean on him? He's no hero, this one."

"Absolutely not – no violence. Somebody has obviously hit him already, before we arrived, and there will be no repeat. If he is merely protecting her then we need to give him reassurance that we're not interested in her beyond confirming his story. If we work along those lines, and his story is true, then we might get somewhere. Let's rest him until noon, then give him the soft treatment."

At midday, Schneider was interrogated again. Ruskin's gentle tactics worked like a charm, and in less than an hour he had everything; the chance meeting with Bernard Wakeley in Wormhout on the road to Dunkirk, how he had visited Marion on his reconnoitre trip, even her address in Coventry. Schneider wept, his resistance sapped dry by subtle means that he had been powerless to combat. He had crumbled so easily in the one area he had been determined to keep private. He was mentally and emotionally drained. He felt he had betrayed Marion.

"Listen," said Ruskin. "I promise you we will only spend as much time with this lady as it takes to verify what you have told us. If what she says tallies with your story, we will leave her alone. Alright?"

Schneider nodded broodily. "Can I see her?"

"That depends. If she's genuine, then that might be possible. But remember, you have run away from us, lied to us and caused us all manner of aggravation. We need to regain our trust in you. Favours must be earned. The first thing you need to do along that road is to get back on the airwaves to *Hamburg*."

Schneider nodded and wiped his eyes with the back of his hand.

"Having said that . . ." Ruskin opened a cupboard in the corner of the room and pulled out a black oblong case. "Here's a favour in advance." He opened the lid of the case to reveal a tarnished trumpet with an ugly dent in the side of the bell. "I had it sent up the other day. Government property – on loan, so take care of it. Not a Vincent Bach I'm afraid, but I'm reliably informed it's a B flat instrument as requested."

Schneider took the trumpet and balanced it expertly in his left hand, flicking down the valves with the fingers of his right. They were sticky. "Thank you, Uncle Mac," he said. He pointed to the dent. "I will take care of it better than its previous owner." From his pocket he pulled out his mouthpiece and tapped it into the end. He flexed his lips and started to play some scales and arpeggios, wincing from the ache in his side.

As he left the house, Ruskin said to the minders: "Take care of him properly this time. I doubt he'll be the slightest trouble, but you can never be sure."

"We'll take care of him, don't you worry," said Hardy.

"No violence," warned Ruskin. "Absolutely no violence, understand?"

"Sir," said the two men in unison.

259

Chapter 66

(Saturday 27th July 1940)

The Coventry house was empty when Major Atkins, accompanied by two men from Special Branch, knocked on the door. The letters *S/O* were chalked on the front gate.

"Sleeping out," called a neighbour who was leaning on a fence two houses along, a plumpish woman with a cigarette jammed in the corner of her mouth like a permanent fixture. "Probably gone to see her kids. Evacuated."

"Any idea when she'll be back?"

"Dunno. After the weekend maybe. What's up?"

"Just want a word."

"Is it about her husband – caught it has he?" The cigarette shifted from one corner of her mouth to the other. "No great loss if he has. Nasty bleeder."

"I'll come back then," said Atkins as he walked away. "Thanks."

And back he came, having arranged for the house to be monitored over the weekend. Marion was observed arriving home at lunchtime on the Monday. An hour later there was a stout knock on her front door.

"Mrs Wakeley? My name is Jones and these are police officers. I wonder if I might speak to you for a moment."

Chapter 67

(Wednesday 31ˢᵗ July 1940)

Otto von Osten, like Schneider, was holed up in a safe house. From the moment he arrived in Southampton, he was looking for an opportunity to escape. It didn't materialise for several weeks. Meanwhile he had been busy putting his minders to sleep with exemplary behaviour.

He transmitted regular messages to *Abwehrstelle Hamburg*, not knowing the pre-coded content or being allowed access to the replies. He was only consulted if some specific knowledge was required that only he could give. *Hamburg*'s interaction was wary to say the least, and reflected suspicions about their agent's credibility. An agent previously fluent in telegraphy claiming he had damaged his hand, thus affecting his transmission style, was cause for concern, if not out and out suspicion. MI5's Wireless Branch were very aware of this. They managed to maintain credibility on two counts. Firstly, their messages were full of the idiosyncrasies they had gleaned from von Osten himself; the disrespectful language, frequent sexual innuendoes and continuous badgering for money despite the small fortune delivered by agent Johnny. Secondly, the intelligence in the messages appeared good, sometimes excellent.

Von Osten soon found that the more cooperative he was, the more trusting, and the more lax, his captors became. Like Schneider he had two full-time minders; Windrow and Nicholson. Windrow doubled as his Voluntary Interceptor. No Christian names were ever used. Von Osten liked them and they struck up a good relationship with each other. Nevertheless, he had no intention of allowing sentiment to interfere with his plans, and if escaping meant killing one or both of them in the process, so be it.

His opportunity came late one evening. Von Osten had managed to persuade MI5 to bring him a woman occasionally. The request was submitted to Ruskin and initially turned down flat. Then von Osten bluntly reminded him that as well as two double agents, the British authorities had also acquired a large quantity of banknotes during the

261

Richmond Raid, courtesy of the Third Reich. Surely a few of them could be put to good use in keeping his libido at bay. Against his better judgment Ruskin relented, anxious as he was to maintain the status quo with his fledgling network of double agents. He handed twenty pounds to Windrow and said: "Here, this should keep him satisfied for . . . well, whatever the going rate is for a prostitute divided by twenty. I leave you to make the arrangements."

"Shall I tell her she's involved in essential war work, sir?" asked Windrow with a grin.

"You'll tell her nothing of the sort. And make sure you blindfold her before coming anywhere near the safe house."

Nicholson was assigned the task of picking up women from streets around the docks and persuading them to be driven blindfold across the city to satisfy the lust of a one-armed man who appeared to be some kind of prisoner. The first woman, a heavily made-up brunette in her forties, agreed but only for three pounds – way about her normal rate. There were plenty to choose from, Nicholson found, which was just as well as von Osten wanted a different woman every time. The minder got the impression, as he drove them back afterwards, that none was eager to make a return trip. As one of them put it: "There's easier men to please than him. The money's good, dear, but bloody hell, he wants to put his old man everywhere you can imagine – *and* a few places you can't!"

It was a Wednesday night. Von Osten had chatted often about sex with Windrow and Nicholson; it became apparent that neither had much experience with women and his tales of fornication in cities across Europe had them enthralled. Eventually, on that evening, he put a suggestion to them; if they were paying a whore over the odds for him, why not make her earn her money and service all of them! Take it in turns. Windrow was keen from the start, aroused by the thought of a sexual adventure. Nicholson was more reserved, but von Osten could tell he was interested. He suggested that this time Nicholson should find a girl that *he* found attractive. Or why not make it two? Now that, he assured him, was an experience not to be missed.

Nicholson came back with just one, a good-looking blonde in her early twenties, petite and quietly spoken. Von Osten nodded his approval and disappeared upstairs with her.

"She wouldn't come for less than five pounds," complained Nicholson to Windrow. "Outrageous."

Half an hour later von Osten was back down wearing only trousers and a vest, and carrying his shirt and jacket. He slumped heavily into a chair, a look of lurid contentment on his face.

"I admire your taste," he said to Nicholson. "She's a lively one. Who's next?"

"I'll go," said Windrow. He was halfway to the door when Nicholson cut in firmly.

"No! I found her, so I'll go next."

Windrow didn't argue the point. He sat down again and dealt cards absentmindedly onto the table for a hand of Patience. When Nicholson had left, von Osten leaned over and slapped Windrow playfully on the shoulder.

"Don't worry, my friend. He'll only be a couple of minutes, mark my words." He winked and Windrow smirked. As he struggled to put his shirt on, von Osten made another remark about Nicholson's anticipated inability to stay the distance. They both sniggered. Then another, and another. Before long Windrow was choking to suppress laughter as the mental picture of sexual incompetence built up. He pulled out a handkerchief to wipe the tears from his eyes.

Von Osten was laughing so much he had to stand up and walk about. "Shush," he said in a mock whisper. "We don't want to upset Valentino's rhythm, do we?"

Windrow shook his head and buried his head in his handkerchief. "You're funny, mate," he gasped. "You should be on the stage."

Von Osten was pacing up and down, giggling and making vulgar comments. He circuited the room several times.

The house brick came down on the back of Windrow's head without his knowing a thing about it, with all the force that a one-armed man could muster. Moments before it had been lying where von Osten had hidden it that afternoon, in a gap between a corner cupboard and the wall. The sickening thud was followed by a stifled moan. The chair toppled sideways and von Osten took the weight of the man and lowered him noiselessly to the floor. Blood was seeping from a deep wound, forming a dark crimson pool. He was unconscious. He'll live, thought von Osten as he felt under Windrow's jacket and pulled out a Browning revolver. He opened the chamber. It was full.

He crept over to the door and eased it towards him until a slit appeared wide enough to peer through. The hallway light was switched on. He made his way to the foot of the stairs and craned his neck to hear better. Nothing. Halfway up to the first floor landing he could just make out voices. At the top, only feet away from the bedroom door, Nicholson's nervous tone was distinguishable from the lighter, rather bored voice of the girl. Von Osten knelt down and put one eye to the keyhole. He could see Nicholson sitting on the edge of the bed, wearing just underpants and socks. The girl was not in view. Von Osten guessed she must be lying on the bed.

"Come on," he heard her say. "Do you want to do it or not?"

Nicholson tugged at a sock. "I'm sorry, I'm not used to this sort of thing. Please don't rush me."

"Just relax, dear. Get your clothes off – then relax. That's all you need to do. Leave the rest to me."

My god he hasn't even got his cock out yet, thought von Osten. If it had been him he'd be washing it clean in the basin by now. His plan was to strike when Nicholson was at his most vulnerable, but at this rate he'd be here all night. Should he go in now, or wait? He decided to wait.

"The laughing has stopped down there," commented Nicholson as the other sock came off. "Lord knows what they're finding so funny." He stood up, still wearing his pants, and turned to face the bed. His erection jutted out in front of him, clearly visible through the keyhole. Von Osten stifled a giggle. Somewhere the drone of a siren penetrated the air, its pitch undulating in an ominous wail; the kind of sound a machine might make if it could feel grief.

"Oh no, an air raid!" said Nicholson. "What do we do now?"

"Just carry on. When we've finished we can go downstairs."

"But suppose . . ."

"My love, can you think of a better way to go?" Her voice rose above blandness for a moment and offered genuine encouragement. "Here, let me take those off for you. There. Well you're a big fellow and no mistake!" Nicholson disappeared from view and the bed creaked as he and the girl lay down on the mattress. "Now put your hands on these. Gently, not too rough. You're new to all this, aren't you? That's better – hmm that's nice."

Von Osten heard rustlings and whispers as Nicholson explored her body. The girl said: "Now see how this feels." The ensuing gasp from Nicholson could mean only one thing; she had guided him inside her. *He won't last more than thirty seconds*, von Osten predicted. *Too nervous, too inexperienced.* He placed the handle of the revolver in his mouth and bit down firmly. With his one hand he gripped the door handle. He listened again. The siren had stopped and the sound of distant aircraft engines could be heard, the slow, dull throbbing of bombers approaching.

Nicholson was groaning loudly. "Oh that's good. Oh Jesus!"

"Harder," said the girl mechanically. "Come on, do it harder. That's it. You're wonderful."

"Oh god, oh my god . . . I think I'm going to . . ."

Von Osten twisted the handle and burst into the room. As the door swung open he took the revolver from his mouth and gripped it vice-like in his fist. Nicholson glanced round over his shoulder, his body rigid on top of the girl, his face registering pleasure and shock in equal measures. The gun swung down and cracked against his temple, the force spinning him sideways and off the girl, who screamed. Nicholson lay back on the side of the bed, his arms waving protectively in the air, his eyes wide with fear. Before he could move further, von Osten dived across the girl and hit him again, much harder than before. The minder slumped backwards and lay still.

The girl was still screaming.

"Shut up!" yelled von Osten, "or you'll get the same."

She regained her composure with almost practiced ease. "What's going on – why did you do that?"

"Because I'm getting out of here, and he wouldn't like it. Get your clothes on before he wakes up. You're coming with me."

"What for? Where to?"

"Don't worry, not far. I need a driver." He indicated the space where his right arm used to be. "I can't handle a car like this. Do as you're told and I won't harm you. Now get dressed, quickly."

She stood up and hurriedly put on her clothes. Von Osten waited by the door. As they left the room, she looked back at the man on the bed.

"You could have waited until he'd finished," she said.

Von Osten laughed. "Come on, move!"

They hurried downstairs.

"You should have warned me about this earlier," the girl said.

"Why?"

"Because it would have saved you a lot of trouble for nothing."

"What do you mean?"

She patted her hair nonchalantly. "I can't drive."

Von Osten grabbed her arm to hurry her along. "You're about to have your first lesson."

Chapter 68

Nicholson's car was parked in the drive at the front of the safe house. Stopping only to pick up the *Afu* suitcase and stuff code books and other papers into his pockets, von Osten shepherded the girl out of the front door. The bombing was getting louder. Bright flashes of orange and yellow lit up the sky to the south, punctuated by steady bursts of flame from anti-aircraft guns.

"The docks are getting it," said the girl. "Not much trade about on a night like this. Your friend picked me up in the nick of time. Where's the other one, by the way?"

"Asleep in the front room." Von Osten placed the suitcase in the boot of the car, then opened the passenger door. "Get in. I'll drive, but you'll have to change gear for me."

"I don't know how to . . ."

Von Osten climbed in next to her. "It's easy. You just move this lever around when I tell you, in this sequence." He went through the gears with his foot firmly on the clutch. When she seemed to have got the hang of it, he twisted the ignition key and started the engine.

"Right – first gear." The girl fumbled about and the gear stick eventually slotted into place. "Good. Now leave it there until I say 'second'." He released the clutch and the car eased slowly down the drive. He turned right, away from the direction of the bombing.

"Where are we going?"

"I don't know yet. Just away from here . . . somewhere quiet."

The girl suddenly felt a pang of anxiety. "Not far, please. You'll let me go when we're a safe distance away, won't you?"

"Of course. Second!" There was a painful grating sound as gear stick and clutch failed to coordinate. With a jerk, the car moved forward at a slightly faster speed. "Concentrate next time. Do it exactly when I say, not a moment later." Von Osten had decided to take the quickest route out of town and into open countryside. The streets were dark and deserted, but the fireworks and the glow from behind illuminated the way enough to maintain a reasonable speed.

"Third!" The girl reacted quicker this time and the change was smoother. "That's better. What's your name?"

"Viv."

"You're doing well, Viv."

The girl took advantage of this moment of praise to ask a question.

"Who *are* you? What's this all about?"

"Never you mind, you just do as you're told. Call me Ted."

"No, I want to know. If I'm going to help you I want to know what's going on."

"Shut up! You've got your money for a night's work and it's payment to keep quiet as well as take your clothes off."

They made slow progress, but eventually the houses began to thin out as they reached the outskirts of Southampton and they were driving along country lanes. They passed a roadblock but it was unmanned, with the barrier pushed to one side.

"What's this . . . the LDV deserted their post?"

"They're probably taking cover, like all sensible people," said Viv. "Anyway, we're to call them the Home Guard now, according to Mr Churchill on the wireless the other night. Everyone's saying it."

In between struggling with the gear stick when told to, Viv tried to work out for herself what was going on. Criminals probably, from rival gangs. She saw some of that down by the docks. The suitcase in the boot probably contained stolen goods . . . swag! Or money perhaps. At a T-junction they turned left and then immediately right onto a single-track lane that meandered up a gentle hill. On the brow of the hill the lane widened into a clearing and von Osten drove the car round in a half-circle before pulling to halt, dousing the lights and cutting the engine.

"Now what?" asked Viv.

"We wait here until the raid is over." He took out a packet of cigarettes and handed them across. "Light two, will you?" They sat smoking and staring through the windscreen. The night sky flashed and flickered several miles away, the sound of the explosions reaching them seconds later. With the car engine silent, the bombs seemed louder, so too did the background drone of invisible aircraft.

"You can hear the bombers are higher pitched when their loads have gone," said von Osten. "Much lighter, so less strain on the engines. The journey home will be faster for them."

"Home?" said Viv curiously as she breathed out smoke. "Home for them maybe. You sound like a Jerry. Actually you really do – you have a bit of an accent."

"I'm Dutch. I meant the return journey."

"Talking of home, Ted, can't I go now? You're safe, up here."

"When the raid is over I'll drop you back in Southampton. I can always drive in one gear then – shouldn't be too difficult in the middle of the night." He was lying. He had no intention of letting her go. "Have you any idea where we are?"

"Not really. Twyford direction at a guess, getting on towards Winchester maybe, but it's so dark I couldn't be sure."

"That's good. If I can reach Winchester I can get a train."

"Where to?"

"I'll decide when I get there."

Viv took a final puff of her cigarette and threw the stub out of the window. "Those Jerries don't sound like they'll be finished for a while."

'We'll just have to wait."

"How long?"

"Who knows . . . an hour, maybe more," said von Osten. His hand moved across onto Viv's knee, then slid under her dress and up the inside of her leg, squeezing the top of her fleshy thigh. "Long enough for you to finish earning that fiver."

"Oh alright then," she replied, with total indifference. "Back seat or over the bonnet?"

*

Viv was buttoning her blouse and patting down her skirt when the distant drone of the 'all-clear' could be heard. Von Osten was drumming his fingers on the steering wheel.

"That was a challenge," he said. "It's awkward enough in a car, but even harder with only one arm."

"You didn't do so badly. Can I go now?"

"Not yet."

"But you promised – when the raid was over."

"I know, but I have to do something first. You wait here, I shouldn't be more than twenty minutes. Then we'll go."

Viv was becoming angry. "What could you possibly want to do up here? There's nothing for miles!"

"That's none of your business." He opened the door and eased himself out. "Just sit there, don't move, and I'll be back shortly. Here, smoke these." He tossed the packet of cigarettes and a box of matches on to the seat next to her.

"Twenty minutes, but no longer." Viv heard the boot being opened and closed, then footsteps as von Osten walked across the clearing. She lit another cigarette and rolled it casually between her fingers. She felt an urge flowing through her, an urge she knew well, and one that had caused trouble throughout her relatively short life so far. Curiosity; the insatiable kind. A man walking away in the darkness, presumably with that suitcase from the boot, and she had no idea what he was up to. She had to know.

Perhaps he was going to bury the contents, or hide it at least, if it was really swag. She simply had to find out.

As quietly as possible, she opened the car door and stepped out. With her shoes in her hand, she hurried across the clearing in the direction he had taken, keeping to the grass verge for both silence and comfort. Two hundred yards or so further on she stopped and listened. The crunch of shoes on gravel was not far ahead of her. She crouched low, aware that although it was pitch black in front, the orange glow from Southampton behind would illuminate her in silhouette if he looked back. Suddenly the footsteps were no longer audible; instead she could hear a rustling sound, like branches of a tree being parted, then a thud and Ted's voice saying "Fuck!" loudly. Viv advanced cautiously for another fifty yards. There was a thick hedgerow on her side of the lane and she stayed as close to it as she could. She stopped again. No footsteps. In fact no sound at all.

No sound, but a momentary flash of light. It came from behind the hedgerow about twenty yards further on. There it was again, the thin beam of a torch. He must have pushed his way through into the field beyond. Viv lowered herself onto hands and knees and crawled forwards until she was almost level with him and had a clear view through the roots of the hedge. The torch was masked and let out a feeble glow, just enough for her to see his outline.

The suitcase was resting on the ground, the torch propped up next to it so the beam illuminated what appeared to be a small notebook. He sat cross-legged and was writing awkwardly on a piece of paper, using the top of the suitcase as a makeshift table. He continued for several minutes, consulting the notebook and making precise additions on the paper.

Viv stretched her legs to combat an attack of pins and needles. One of her feet brushed against the hedgerow and snapped off a twig.

Von Osten stopped dead, listening intently for a moment, then he stood up with the torch and shone it through the hedgerow. The beam was too weak to penetrate its thickness entirely. He walked towards it and listened again.

"Viv, is that you?"

She lay flat on the ground, as lifeless as a corpse, holding her breath until it hurt. He was only feet away. He walked along the other side to a point just beyond where she lay, then turned again, walked back to the suitcase and sat down.

You're imagining things, Otto, he told himself. *Send this message to* Hamburg, *silence the girl* – it really was the only way to protect himself, he had decided – *and clear out triple fast.* With luck he would be in London by mid-morning where he could call up a few favours from old business associates. If he couldn't get out of the country he would lie low until Hitler arrived or peace was agreed. He glanced down at the message he had prepared:

Mechanic transmitting for last time. I am blown. So is Quaver. Repeat Mechanic and Quaver blown. Discard all messages since arrival at targets. MI5 supplied content. They knew about us all along. Have escaped and attempting return to Fatherland. See you on the Reeperbahn.

Underneath it was a string of meaningless letters, set out in small groups; the message in code.

Beyond the hedgerow, Viv was confused. Ted was obviously not trying to hide the suitcase or its contents. So much for that theory. There was some kind of machine inside, but she couldn't make out what it was; at least not until he uncoiled the thin wire of the headset and placed it on his head. She had seen her younger brother do the same, seated at the dining room table, playing with the crystal set their parents had bought him one Christmas. She had tried it herself a couple of times, but didn't enjoy it much; the headset spoilt her hair.

A wireless set! She tensed at the sudden revelation. And as confirmation, the torch flickered across a telescopic aerial as he fed it out from the back of the case.

Von Osten connected the headset and key and switched on. With his awkward left hand, he tapped out his call sign and waited for a response. There was a mass of static and interference, probably due to aircraft activity, he assumed. He listened intently, awaiting the familiar response from *Abwehrstelle Hamburg* hundreds of miles to the north-east. There was none.

Viv knew now. It all fitted into place. This man Ted was a fifth columnist, just like the ones they had been warning about in the newspapers and on the wireless for weeks. There was talk of them being parachuted in all over the country, causing havoc and passing information back to Hitler to help the invasion. Ted must have been caught and was being held prisoner. But why in a house and not in prison, or a police station? That didn't make sense. He had a slight accent, but said he was Dutch, not German. Perhaps he was a Nazi sympathiser. Whatever he was, he had escaped and was reporting back – to Germany! She wanted to get up and run . . . run to find someone to tell. But there might not be anyone for miles. In any case, he would hear her, run after her, catch her, and then what? If he was a Nazi he'd probably kill her; there were terrible stories going around about what they did, especially to women. And she'd just had sex with him! She felt sick.

Von Osten tried his call sign again, tapping as accurately as he could with his unsteady left hand. Nothing. He waited precisely one minute, counting the seconds to himself, then tried a third time.

Viv was on the edge of panic. She could hear the click, click, click of the key. He was sending a message right now. It could be something of vital importance. She had to stop him, before he could go any further. Or maybe just distract him to get him away from the wireless.

At last, the faint signal of *Abwehrstelle Hamburg* found its way through the crackling and whirring in von Osten's ears. They were ready to receive his message. He looked down at the piece of paper that glowed yellow in the torchlight and set his eyes on the columns of coded letters. "Right," he said out loud. "Here goes."

He was tapping again.

Do something! screamed Viv to herself. *Do something!* She stood up and felt along the hedgerow, trying to find a gap. Ted had got into the field somehow; there must be a gap further on. She made her way forward, feeling with both hands as she went. Her eyes were accustomed to the dark now and she could see her way quite well. No gap. She had gone past his position. He must have got through further back. She retraced her steps until the torch light was next to her, still testing the hedgerow, looking for an opening. Eventually she found a place where the branches were thinner, hardly an opening at all. Ted had obviously pushed his way through with brute force. No wonder he had sworn. She did the same, leaning against the branches, letting the weight of her body do the work. Twigs and branches scratched her bare arms and face. Suddenly there was no more resistance and she plopped through and fell to the ground.

Ted was only about ten feet away, but his back was to her and he could hear nothing with the headset on.

Viv struggled to her feet. Now what! She couldn't attack him, she didn't have a weapon of any kind. If she didn't do something drastic she might only interrupt him, get hurt in the process and when he had dealt with her he might go back to the wireless.

Get the wireless. Damage it.

She moved forward until she was right behind him. He didn't move, but stayed in position, squatting over the suitcase, tapping away. She moved to his right side and, with both hands together, pushed him as hard as she was able, feeling the strangeness of the stump below the shoulder as he toppled over onto his good arm. The head set stretched tight, came loose from the connections on the transmitter and fell limply away.

Von Osten was taken completely unawares. He caught the slightest glance of a figure as he floundered on the floor, his only hand trapped awkwardly beneath his body. It took him precious seconds to recover and to roll into a kneeling position. He could hear the high-pitched panting of his attacker.

271

Viv used these seconds fruitfully. She grabbed the torch and shone it at the suitcase. The dark metal inside had several small black dials, and a larger one to the right surrounded by a ring of numbers. It meant nothing to her; she spun the large dial frantically in the hope that it would do some harm. Then she saw two rectangular boxes squeezed in below the dials. They had circular labels on the side and terminals at one end. Batteries! She wrenched one from its place and hurled it into the darkness. Then she dislodged the other and threw it in the opposite direction.

As she let go, an arm whipped around her neck and she felt herself being lifted into the air. With the shock, she dropped the torch, but her other hand managed to grasp the aerial attached to the transmitter next to the battery compartments. As she was jerked upwards, the grip around her throat tightened and she clutched at the thin metal antenna with all her strength. It dragged the suitcase with it, until the metal snapped away at its root.

"You stupid fucking whore!" shouted von Osten.

She was choking. Her feet found the ground again and she pushed hard against the earth, pressing her weight into the man behind her. It was enough to make him lose his balance and to send him tottering backwards. He fell heavily on his back with the girl on top of him. He groaned as the wind rushed out of his lungs. His grip on her loosened enough for her to twist round onto her front; and that was all she needed. One thing she had learnt on the game was to deal with the unwanted advances of men who had no money and wouldn't take no for an answer. As one girl had said to her in the early days, it was the best way in the world for a working girl to win an argument. She positioned herself with her right leg in between his and brought her knee sharply up into his groin. He yelped with the pain. Then the follow through . . . a harsh grinding of the kneecap against soft, unprotected genitals.

Von Osten's grip relaxed and Viv rolled free as he doubled up, clutching his one hand between his legs. She was still holding the aerial, so for good measure she raked it across his face and poked the end into one of his eyes. He screamed again.

Enough is enough. Now get away fast, before he recovers!

She stood up, fumbled around for the torch and ran towards the black mass of the hedgerow. She found the little gap and squeezed through, ignoring the inevitable scratches. Going back down the lane was easier because she was walking towards the glow of Southampton. It would have been even easier with shoes on, but they were still beside the hedgerow somewhere.

Back at the car, she fell against the side, panting heavily from the exertion. She looked at the aerial in her hand; without that he could not transmit, she was fairly certain, even if he did manage to find the batteries in the dark, and recovered enough from the kneeing to concentrate.

Or could he? Had she done enough? Would he be able to improvise something, somehow? The more she thought about it the more she began to panic. She needed help.

The hillside sloped downwards before her. Somewhere below was the road block through which they had passed earlier. The Home Guard might be back in position by now. She started walking down the road. As she went, she stripped the masking tape from the torch until it was clear. She pointed it in front of her and began to switch it on and off; three short flashes followed by three long ones, then three short again. SOS.

Like most civilians, it was the only Morse code she knew.

Chapter 69

(Thursday 1ˢᵗ August 1940)

Major Trautmann arrived at the *Abwehr* receiving station near Hamburg barely minutes after the telephone call had aroused him from a deep sleep. He hurried inside and was met by an anxious-looking duty officer.

"It's Mechanic, sir. He went off the air in mid-transmission. Just stopped dead. We haven't been able to raise him again."

"When was this?"

"About an hour ago. We tried to re-establish contact numerous times, then I phoned you."

Trautmann was annoyed. "God in heaven, we've lost contact with agents like that before, and it's been nothing. Atmospherics probably. Why drag me out of bed for Christ's sake!"

The duty office handed him a piece of paper.

"With respect, sir, you ought to see this, it's the part of the message we did manage to receive."

The major read the short message twice, then nodded understandingly.

"I apologise. You were right to call me. Let me know if anything occurs. I'll be in my office."

Trautmann dialed a Hamburg number and heard it ring ten times before a croak of a voice answered. Wichmann too had been sleeping soundly. Half an hour later they sat together, drinking strong coffee.

"Canaris needs to know about this. I will phone him first thing in the morning. Then it is up to him." Wichmann sipped the steaming hot liquid in his mug. "I know he told me to handle it myself, but this is different. I must keep him informed."

Trautmann said: "I think so. You never know how Göring will react – if he's at all interested any longer."

"Ha! *Luftwaffe* losses – have you heard the latest figures? He *should* be interested."

"He's brimming with confidence about *Adlertag*, the offensive which the Führer's new directive will launch, tomorrow I believe. He thinks this will crush the Royal Air Force once and for all. If he's right, then who cares about Spitfire production anymore."

Wichmann slammed a fist onto the desk. "He *should* care! Spitfires are outmanoeuvring our fighters. They're faster, more agile, and shooting down half the bombers we send over."

"Not according to the figures in the newspapers."

"I'm talking about the real figures, not the shit that Goebbels dreams up. Come on, Trautmann, you know that as much as anyone – you see the intelligence reports."

The major glanced at the piece of paper.

"It's a pity. Agents are hard to come by." He read the truncated message out loud. *"Mechanic transmitting for the last time. I am blown. So . . ."*

"So . . . I wonder what came next."

"So cheerio for now?" As soon as he had said it, Trautmann regretted his flippancy, and hastily added: "Do you think he is dead?"

Wichmann shrugged. "Impossible to say. He may have been captured. If he has, do you think he will talk?"

"Difficult to say. My impression was that he's a tough character. Depends what pressure they use. Ritter would have a better opinion."

Wichmann downed the last of his coffee. "Dead, captured . . . for us it amounts to the same thing. We've lost an agent. At least we still have Quaver."

This was cold comfort to Trautmann. "Yes," he sighed. "We still have Quaver. For what it's worth."

Chapter 70

Viv also finished drinking from a mug. Hers contained tea with three spoonfuls of sugar. She sat with a blanket wrapped around her shoulders, for comfort as much as warmth. The room was small, with walls shelved from floor to ceiling and crammed with books, as you might expect in the office of a librarian. The only furniture was a desk, two chairs and a filing cabinet. She had been sitting there alone for about forty minutes when the door burst open and in strode a Home Guard officer.

"Got him, my dear – caught the blighter!" Colonel Ernest Godby (retired) was fat, unfit and very red in the face. The excitement was creating havoc with his blood pressure. "Nabbed him near his car . . . top of the hill, where you said he'd be. He's in a cell at the police station now. I tell you, my dear, you have done extraordinarily well."

"Thank you," said Viv, smiling awkwardly as he put an arm round her and gave her a paternal squeeze. "Is he alright? I did hit him rather hard."

"Oh, I shouldn't worry about that, he's a bloody fifth columnist. Probably a Jerry to boot. Mind you," the colonel chuckled, "he did seem to have a spot of difficulty sitting comfortably in the car."

"Did he have that wireless suitcase with him?"

"Yes, except for the parts you removed. The batteries were nowhere to be seen. I'll have a couple of men up there at first light. We'll find them."

"So he couldn't have sent anymore messages?"

"Certainly not." He picked up the aerial which had been lying on the desk. "Not without batteries – and this vital piece of kit."

"Thank goodness," sighed Viv. "I was worried I might not have done enough."

"You did more than enough, young lady. In fact, you've done a splendid job. That SOS with the torch did the trick. If we hadn't spotted it and got over to you pronto he might have had time to clear orf."

Viv yawned. "I'm so tired. May I go home now?"

"Of course!" blustered Godby. "Allow me to drive you personally."

"Will the police need to interview me?"

"Oh I don't think so. We've managed to explain it all to them. If they do they can talk to you in the morning. I'll stall 'em until then, tell 'em you're too upset – shock and all that." He lowered his voice and adopted a distinctly unctuous tone. "Frankly, my dear, I hope you don't mind but I haven't actually told them about you yet. Thought I'd bag him ourselves first, then perhaps give them the whole story tomorrow . . . but only if absolutely necessary. Strictly non-kosher of course, but these are rum times we live in. Rum times."

"I understand." Viv stood up. She understood only too well. He hadn't believed her story when she had first told it, she could tell from his condescending manner. Only catching Ted red-handed had convinced him. Now he was going for as much personal glory as he could squeeze out of it.

"If the police want me," she said, "you can give them my address. You've been so kind to me, I'm awfully grateful. I'd much rather be driven home by you than the police."

"Be delighted." They walked out of the library, which had been commandeered as Home Guard headquarters, and Godby helped Viv into the passenger seat of his car.

As they drove off she said: "I hope the bombing hasn't done too much damage tonight."

"Too early to say," said the colonel. "The docks got the worst of it."

"I'll write down my address for you too if you like. Perhaps you might need to question me about something. I'm usually at home during the day. You are welcome to come and see me if you like."

The colonel felt a soft hand brush momentarily across his leg. The accelerator raced and the gears crunched.

"Good Lord! Jolly decent of you . . . I might just take you up on that!"

Chapter 71

(Friday 2nd August 1940)

The RAF's Central Flying School was located at a small hilltop aerodrome just east of the village of Upavon, in Wiltshire, about twenty miles north of Salisbury. Alison Webb arrived there one clear, warm morning for 'conversion'; training that would enable her to ferry all single-engine plus smaller twin-engine aircraft. Two months of flying nothing but Tiger Moths had made her restless, and a spin in Dan Rodigan's Spitfire had whetted her appetite for more powerful machines. She knew it was only a matter of time before her turn came to take the training. The air battle was becoming fierce and Fighter Command needed every male pilot they could get their hands on to replace losses. ATA was constantly under pressure to release them for combat training. Which meant more opportunities for women.

She was only too painfully aware of Fighter Command's losses and prayed every night that Dan would not be among them. Since their night together at The Bush they had seen each other once only, for a few hours. Dan had been released for a morning that had coincided with a lull in ATA work, so she had taken the train down to West Malling. His spirits had been better than before; they were still losing men, but nothing like that dreadful day the Defiants had been massacred. He was hardened to it now and, more importantly, they were making kills.

"My score so far . . . two Junkers Ju 88s, one Bf 110 and three 109s," he announced proudly. "Actually quite a few more than that, but not confirmed." That night Alison added to her prayers the hope that Dan wouldn't become part of a German pilot's 'score so far' one day.

She had hardly seen Heather, who had preceded her down to Upavon by a week and was now ferrying Airspeed Oxfords and Dominoes, both twin-engine planes manufactured by de Havilland at Hatfield. Their duties rarely coincided any longer. Alison knew she too had been down to see Stuart at West Malling. They were madly in love. Heather, too, prayed every night.

278

The course at Upavon was tough, even for someone with Alison's experience. Flying speeds were much faster in more powerful planes, making takeoffs and landings more hazardous, as she had discovered with Dan's Spitfire. Then there were novelties such as constant-speed propellers, and retractable undercarriage, plus dozens of new things to learn . . . not to mention two engines to consider.

Each morning they strolled from their digs in the village up the hill to the aerodrome. There were two other women and four men in the group. Then they would go off to their individual instructors for intense tuition, dual flight practice, including three or four takeoffs and landings, some aerobatics (to Alison's delight), and solo flights that followed with alarming haste. No longer dealing with novices, instructors always seemed to want to teach aerobatics first and basic control second, or so it seemed. This scared most of the others in the group, but for Alison it was routine stuff, looping, spinning and stall turning. Her instructor sensed her ease at handling these manoeuvres and spent more time with her than was strictly necessary. He could tell he had an exceptional pilot on his hands.

It was hard work, and there was a great deal to remember. But she loved every minute.

Chapter 72

On the same day that Alison arrived in Upavon, *Reichsmarschall* Hermann Göring informed his *Luftwaffe* commanders at a conference in The Hague of the Führer's Directive 17, *Adlerangriff* – Operation Eagle Attack. Göring was authorised to launch a major assault on Britain at a convenient date after 5th August.

It was a warm, sunny day in Holland, so the meeting took place outdoors. Göring appeared resplendent in a new all-white uniform. He talked of the heavy blows the *Luftwaffe* would inflict upon the enemy, whose morale was already low. The *Kanalkampf* – the fight for the English Channel – was over; the true invasion push was beginning. This was the prelude to *Seelöwe* – Operation Sea Lion – the Führer's next and possibly greatest success.

Major Schmid made a report on the RAF's radio warning system. "They call it Radio Detection Finding, or RDF," he began. He went on to explain that the location of most of the major stations were known and would be eliminated in raids in the twenty-four hours prior to the first day of the attack. Radio-telephone dialogue between Fighter Command pilots and their ground controllers had been intercepted for weeks now. "The great disadvantage of this system is that British fighters are tied to their respective stations, thus restricting their range considerably. Consequently there is no danger of strong fighter forces assembling at short notice."

A senior *Luftwaffe* staff officer said: "Forgive me, that is all very well, but surely attracting large numbers of British fighters in the sky is precisely what we want. Our task is to destroy the Royal Air Force. How can we do that if we cannot engage them in combat in large numbers?"

Göring himself intervened. "An academic question. Fighter Command doesn't have large numbers of machines to deploy. We have already reduced their resources to a minimum. The intention of *Adlerangriff* is to mop up the few that remain. Osterkamp, kindly tell them how we intend doing this."

A slim man with angular features and a bulging forehead leaned forward in his seat. 'Uncle' Theo Osterkamp was something of a guru within the *Luftwaffe* hierarchy; a commander who had been a First World War ace and was again fighting in combat and notching up kills; the most senior fighter specialist they had. He reported, reading somewhat woodenly from papers in front of him, that intelligence indicated Britain had between four and five hundred fighters dispersed around its southern sector, the only sector of interest in the forthcoming battle. Their destruction both in combat and on the ground would take thirteen days; five to clear a radius within 100 and 150 kilometres south and south-east of London, three within 50 to 100 kilometres, and finally five to clear a circle around the capital with a radius of 50 kilometres.

Osterkamp grimaced.

"So," remarked Göring, "is something wrong?"

"*Reichsmarschall*, from my own experience in combat over England, it seems that the number of British fighters is increasing, not decreasing. I estimate that last month there must have been at least five hundred concentrated on defending south-east of London alone. Surely thirteen days to complete the whole operation is overly ambitious."

Göring waved his field marshal's baton with a flourish. "Nonsense! Our intelligence is excellent. The British do not have that many machines spread across the entire country. Thirteen days maximum – and quite probably less."

"In addition," continued Osterkamp, "I am told that eleven new units have now been equipped with Spitfires, which I consider a match for any of our own fighters."

"Not that shit again!" Göring was now flustered. "The Messerschmitt is infinitely superior to the Spitfire." Beppo Schmid stirred uncomfortably in his chair. He doubted Göring truly believed this. "Osterkamp, you yourself have reported evidence that the British are too cowardly to engage our fighters. So what does the Spitfire matter?"

"Not exactly. I reported that British fighters are sometimes avoiding combat with us . . ."

"That is the same thing."

"Not necessarily." Osterkamp continued to try and balance the plans for *Adlerangriff* with some semblance of practicality. He queried their own figures for available aircraft, both fighters and bombers, and at least managed to convince Göring there were fewer than he imagined. Cowardly or not, avoiding combat or not, the RAF were shooting down large numbers of German aircraft. But it was a temporary dent in the *Reichsmarschall*'s rhinoceros-like hide.

The next day Göring outlined his target for *Adlerangriff* to the German High Command. His intention was to destroy the Royal Air Force just as easily as the Polish and French air forces had recently been annihilated.

Major Schmid had cause to visit *Asia*, Göring's mobile headquarters, that day to deliver a report. He spoke briefly with Christa Gormanns,

Göring's personal nurse, whom Schmid knew quite well. She shook her head with a hint of despair.

"The pills are getting out of control," she sighed. "He's ignoring his diet also, and it's making his behaviour very erratic. He simply will not listen to my advice."

"You're not alone, Christa," he said. "He won't listen to advice from anyone. Apart from his Führer."

Chapter 73

(Sunday 4th August 1940)

Alison arrived back at Hatfield with a piece of paper confirming that her 'conversion' was complete. When she popped her head into the office and waved it gleefully in the air, Pauline Gower smiled approvingly.

"Well done, I should imagine it was a walkover for you."

Alison grinned. "Now I'm officially on *all* single-engine planes and not just light aircraft, so how about a ferry chit for some of those Hurricanes being brought in for repair . . . or a Spitfire even!"

Pauline chuckled. "Not just yet. I'd get used to Oxfords and the like first if I were you. Your turn will come, if I have anything to do with it." She picked up a flimsy sheet of paper and handed it to Alison. "Here, this will take your mind off Spitfires and Hurricanes. It fell out of a Heinkel a few nights ago."

It was a leaflet, crumpled and slightly torn. The bold header read:

A LAST APPEAL TO REASON
BY
ADOLF HITLER

Alison read with growing amusement the text of the speech Hitler had made in the *Reichstag* two weeks earlier. By the end she was laughing out loud. "Oh dear, Adolf thinks we have '*no sensible alternative but to reach a peace agreement*' with him. Who has he been talking to?"

"Thought you'd appreciate that," said Pauline. "They dropped millions all over the country. Makes a change from bombs, but such a waste of paper."

Alison handed the leaflet back. "Thanks. Any sign of Heather?"

"Yes she's back. I think she's gone home already."

Heather was chatting to Mrs Elliott over a cup of tea when Alison arrived at the flat. To be accurate, Mrs Elliott was doing the chatting and Heather was doing the listening.

"Oh hello, my dear. Come and have a nice cuppa. Heather here has been telling me all about everything. Have you been away again? Goodness, I can't keep up with your comings and goings. Such brave young girls."

The old lady chattered on with barely a rest for breath. The 'brave young girls' had learnt that it was quite impossible to interrupt her flow, so they sat and smiled and waited. Heather was restless; she kept standing up and sitting down, playing constantly with her fingers. It was clear to Alison she had something on her mind. Eventually they heard the magic words, "Well I won't keep you any longer." The old lady was barely out of the door when Heather grabbed Alison by the arm and said: "Lord I thought she'd never go! Ally, I've got something to tell you."

"I can see that. Is everything alright?" It was clear from the huge grin that broke out across Heather's face that it was good news.

"Everything is fine, in fact everything is wonderful. Stuart and I are engaged. We're going to be married!"

Alison was shocked. She tried desperately hard not to show it, but if her face succeeded, the shake in her voice did not.

"That's . . . wonderful news. Con – congratulations."

"He rang me last night and proposed over the phone. He's promised to do it properly as soon as he gets the chance – you know, down on one knee. He will too. He's awfully romantic."

"I'm really very pleased for you."

Heather touched her on the arm. "Is anything wrong, Ally? You don't sound exactly thrilled. Stuart says Dan sends his love, by the way."

A tear formed in the corner of Alison's eye and she pulled a handkerchief from her bag. "No, really, it's wonderful news," she sniffled. "I'm sorry, it was such a shock, that's all."

"Don't worry, your turn will come," said Heather, misinterpreting entirely. "Dan is the right man for you, Stuart and I both agree on that – we know it's just a matter of time. Isn't it amazing how we both found someone to love in the same batch . . . on the same day even! Everything happens for a reason, so they say, and we were meant to ferry those Tiger Moths via Catterick!"

"It's not that." Alison shook her head gently. "It's not that at all, far from it. I could never commit myself to Dan, or anyone, at a time like this. He's risking his life, day in and day out, and each time I kiss him goodbye I don't know if I'll ever see him again. It's no time for planning a future. I'm worried for you, Heather, in case . . . in case . . ."

"We talked about that, but you know me, Ally, I live for the moment, always have done. That's why I've always been so forward with men, I suppose. If I see one I like, I go for him. Shocks some people, and I know I have a bit of a reputation, but actually I think mostly they're jealous."

Alison doubted this but said nothing. "I never was a shrinking violet. That's why I learnt to fly I suppose, because it was out of the ordinary. Girls don't do that sort of thing as a rule. So I had to do it. I love the freedom if gives me – and the spontaneity."

"But getting engaged shouldn't be a spontaneous act," said Alison. "It's a decision for life, one that ought to be thought through to make sure you're doing the right thing, and one that you won't regret."

"I won't regret it. I love Stuart, and he adores me."

"Are you sure? After all, you've only known each other a few weeks – and barely spent any time together."

"I'm sure."

"And in a few years from now?"

"We'll cross that bridge when we come to it. I appreciate your concern, Ally my love. Yes, I may be foolish to commit myself to a man who could be killed tomorrow, and if not tomorrow next week, or a month or a year from now. Who knows how long this bloody war will last."

"I don't think you're foolish – I can't put myself in the same situation, that's all. If I were to get engaged to Dan, for the sake of argument, and he was shot down and killed, I'd feel cheated. I'd feel a far deeper sense of loss than I would if I were just his girlfriend."

"Isn't that rather selfish? So if Dan proposed would you turn him down to avoid feeling cheated if he was killed?"

"Well, yes . . . no . . . I didn't mean it like that."

Heather put her hands firmly on her knees and mimicked Alison's voice. "Sorry, Dan, I can't marry you in case you die tomorrow."

"That's not fair!"

"Ally," said Heather affectionately. "Whatever the circumstances, whatever the dangers, if you love someone, truly love someone, then nothing else matters. You should do what your heart tells you. Besides, I couldn't say no to him. Think of the rejection he would feel. And imagine if I turned him down and then one day he didn't return from a sortie. If Stuart does get killed, at least he'll die knowing that I loved him enough to marry him." She took out a cigarette and lit it. "Now we're engaged, Stuart has got something extra to fight for. He said that actually, that he has a future now, one that stretches ahead of him beyond merely surviving from one day to the next . . . and that I'll be with him every time he's in the air."

Alison felt confused. She was very fond of Dan, and very possibly loved him; she was almost certain. But it had never occurred to her that he might broach the subject of marriage. They had made love, but they had only known each other for a matter of weeks. Now Heather and Stuart had done it, would Dan follow suit? Like Heather, she would follow her heart, but her response would almost certainly be no.

285

"When do you plan to get married?"

"As soon as possible. The moment Hitler orders his pilots to hold off for a while."

And when might that be! wondered Alison. *Oh Lord, Dan, please don't ask me to marry you. Not yet.*

Chapter 74

(Wednesday 7th August 1940)

Reinhard Heydrich and Walther Schellenberg stood together in the Tiergarten, having walked there from Prinz Albrechstrasse. It amused Heydrich to be able to stroll past the Chief of the *Abwehr*'s headquarters as they discussed his treachery. If they glanced up, they could even see his office window.

"I'm convinced," said Heydrich. "What Canaris sanctioned the Black Chapel to do before we invaded the Low Countries is happening again at this precise moment, albeit with a different emphasis. Operation *Weser* had a surprise element – or rather shock for them – whereas for Britain it's a matter of *when* the invasion comes, not *if*. Canaris is in contact with Churchill's government, I am certain, feeding them intelligence through his agents – in Spain and Portugal mainly, but also those in England. Look how the RAF is standing up to the *Luftwaffe* so far! You cannot tell me they are not receiving valuable intelligence from somewhere."

"That is possible," agreed Schellenberg. "Although I would not overestimate the agents in England. From what I gather, they are thin on the ground. A handful at most."

"He doesn't need many, only one even – a well-placed agent to link him with British Military Intelligence. Are there any likely candidates in the handful?"

"Possibly. There are two 'Spitfire spies', as the *Abwehr* have dubbed them, whose specific task is to report on aircraft production. Or rather there were. I believe one was blown last week. I don't have details as to how. There's something not ringing true there."

"I know something about this," said Heydrich. "I gather he was cut off in mid-transmission."

"I heard the same." Schellenberg had heard something else too. The blown agent's name was von Osten, which happened to be Heydrich's wife's family name. He was very tempted to mention the fact, but decided against it. A useful piece of information for future reference, especially if

Canaris's agents were proven at some stage to be traitors . . . and one of them was related to Lina Heydrich. Instead he said: "Has the *Reichsmarschall* been informed? I gather he sanctioned the mission."

"He has, but he is no longer interested in such trifles. He is too wrapped up in *Adlertag*. The only intelligence of interest to him is the grossly over inflated claims of enemy losses that his Fifth Branch is feeding him."

"The other agent is still active. He has infiltrated the Spitfire factory in the English Midlands and is providing useful information."

Heydrich turned sharply and stared Schellenberg in the eyes. It was a stare that seemed to bore right through the SD man's head.

"This is beginning to smell – I have the stench of deception in my nostrils." He transferred his gaze to a high window in the Turpitzufer building. "And it emanates from up there."

Schellenberg agreed, but did not want to condemn the old admiral, not without proof. And they had none.

"Time to play our trump card," said Heydrich. Let us find out what is going on once and for all. If this Spitfire factory agent is playing a double game, then it is time we knew about it. If we're lucky, it might give us the evidence we need."

"You mean Moss?"

"Precisely. He has been dormant for long enough. Contact him."

"What about the *Reichsführer*? He should be consulted."

"I have spoken to Himmler already. He has approved the idea."

"Very well. Shall we contact him through Triangle?"

"We have no choice. But Schellenberg . . ." Heydrich held up a warning finger; it wavered threateningly in the space between them. "Tell Triangle only what he needs to know – not a word more. He is a courier, nothing more as far as I am concerned, and he bends with the wind. The *Abwehr* use him too, so he is the weak link. Tread carefully when dealing with Triangle."

They walked together in silence for some time. Schellenberg assumed the meeting was at an end, but did not presume to depart without sanction. Then Heydrich suddenly snapped his fingers, as if to punctuate a thought.

"This is all about aircraft, is it not?"

"How do you mean?"

"These 'Spitfire spies', their mission is to supply information about British aircraft production . . . or the remaining one I should say. Göring wants specific intelligence about the Spitfire. Why?"

"I don't know much about aircraft . . ."

"Nor do I. But I hear enough to understand that the Spitfire is a match for anything we have. I am told it is the perfect fighter plane. It could tip the balance between success and failure in the air war over England. I also know that it is something of an unknown commodity – no Spitfire has so far been captured intact for evaluation. The RAF did not use them in France, they kept them on home turf. Göring must have realised its significance months ago, though he would never admit such a thing. Why else would he sanction such a mission personally?"

"I don't follow," said Schellenberg. "Surely we are more concerned about the prospect of Admiral Canaris using them as double agents."

Heydrich's eyes narrowed to fine slits. "You miss the point, Schellenberg. We have an opportunity here not only to compromise Canaris, if he is the traitor I believe he is, but also to thoroughly embarrass the old bastard. Think about Moss. You are familiar with his file. What skills does he have?"

"Well, he's a cold-blooded killer – totally ruthless. He has boyish looks. An attractive man. The most unlikely-looking spy."

"What else?"

"He has lived in Britain for years."

"And what else?"

"I'm sorry, I don't understand what you are driving at . . ."

"He's a pilot!" Heydrich hissed the words from between clenched teeth. "I know him better than you. He has a British pilot's licence."

"I don't quite see . . ."

"If he can fly, then he can do us a double service. Not only can he find out the truth about these agents, but he can steal us a Spitfire and fly it back to Germany. Fly it to Berlin and land the fucking thing right outside Canaris's window!"

The idea sounded totally improbable to Schellenberg, and a huge waste of a precious asset. "We would lose our only deep cover man in the whole of Great Britain."

Reinhard Heydrich shook his head slowly and indicated the Tirpitzufer building. "It would be worth it to rub that old goat's face in the shit. Instruct Moss accordingly. His brief is to investigate the remaining Spitfire spy, eliminate him if he is a double, then steal a Spitfire and fly it here. Tell him if he succeeds there will be great honour awaiting him in the Fatherland."

Schellenberg said he would, but he thought it would be a Pyrrhic victory – the prize hardly worth the sacrifice. Of course there was more to it than that.

This was revenge.

Chapter 75

(Saturday 10th August 1940)

"Henry Mansell, meet Ruby Russell. She's your new girlfriend." Ballard Ruskin grinned as he made the introduction. "No kissing mind, just shake hands. After all, you barely know each other."

Ruby was in her mid-twenties. She wore a pleated skirt, blouse and jacket, with her hair pulled up into a bun. She was very pretty.

"Hello," she said warmly. "In truth, we don't know each other at all."

"No indeed." Schneider was slightly embarrassed, just as Ruskin had hoped. The intelligence officer was not going to make it easy for either of the supposed lovebirds, and it was a game he intended to enjoy to the full.

"Right, now let's get down to business, shall we? Any chance of a cuppa?" Laurel and Hardy glanced at each other as they stood in the doorway, then disappeared together, a look of mutual distaste on their faces at being treated like tea boys. Ruskin sat at the dining room table and indicated that Schneider and the girl should sit on either side of him. "Ruby here is in the WAAFs. Lucky WAAFs, eh, Henry?"

Schneider ignored the remark. "What's this all about? Why do I need a girlfriend?"

"Shame on you!" scolded Ruskin. "Don't you like our Ruby? I think she's rather lovely."

"And as much a WAAF as I am." Schneider pulled his trumpet mouthpiece from his pocket and rolled it between his fingers, a habit he had developed during schooldays whenever confronted with an awkward or embarrassing situation. No doubt a psychologist would have something to say about it. "Don't you trust me anymore on my own?"

"We trust you – we want to make sure the Germans still do."

"So what has changed?"

"Disappearing for nigh on a week, that's what. Gaps in transmission for no reason are bound to raise suspicions."

"Surely you got the VI to transmit in my absence. He can imitate my style perfectly. *Hamburg* can't tell the difference."

Ruskin wasn't about to disclose what had transpired with von Osten in Southampton. "Suffice to say, circumstances require us to ensure your continued credibility. Ruby here should do the trick nicely."

Ruby smiled. "I'll do my best."

"You really don't have to do anything at all, my dear. You're here to add substance to the myth that agent Quaver has found himself a girl – flesh on the imaginary bones, as it were. Help us to realize her, so to speak. All you have to do is . . . well, you've been briefed, so you know what is required." Ruskin turned to Schneider. "Ruby's one of our most talented new recruits."

"What circumstances?" Schneider licked the mouthpiece and pursed his lips inside the cupped end.

"I beg your pardon?"

"What circumstances demand that you ensure my continued credibility? Clearly something more than my being away for a week."

"That doesn't concern you."

"I'm here, aren't I? So it concerns me."

"I decide what concerns you." Ruskin stifled his irritation. "We're playing a very delicate game here, Henry," he added, using Schneider's work name in the girl's presence. "Your friend Dr Rantzau is a shrewd chap, so are the majority of the *Abwehr* whether we like to admit it or not – and we know most of them. They're not easily fooled, and if our deception is going to succeed we have to keep things moving in the right direction. If something occurs that might jeopardise your credibility then we must make something happen to even the score."

"So something *has* happened. It's Otto, isn't it?"

"It doesn't matter what."

"Come on, Uncle Mac. The *Abwehr* aren't the only ones with brains in their heads. I can put two and two together." Schneider was sure he was right, and equally sure Ruskin would not admit it. "You've been playing the same game with Otto, of course you have. Something has gone wrong. My guess is his cover has been blown. Am I right?" No response from Ruskin. "If so, that could put the finger of suspicion firmly on me. *Hamburg* might be wondering if I shopped him."

"I can assure you there is nothing to worry about. Ruby here is insurance, that's all – or her brother is, which is more to the point."

"Her brother?"

"Warrant Officer Clive Russell."

"Sorry, I'm afraid you've lost me now." Schneider blew into the mouthpiece, pitching a series of harmonics in rapid succession. He was curious but it suited him not to show it.

"It's very simple really. You've found yourself a girlfriend, a pretty thing called Ruby." The girl smiled on cue. "I don't imagine *Hamburg* expect you to live the life of a monk on this mission. As I explained, Ruby's a WAAF. You met her in a local pub and now you're taking her out of an evening, to the pictures, or a dance on Saturday night. You tell her all about yourself – sticking to your cover story of course – and she tells you all about *her* self. In the course of your romantic little chats, brother Clive crops up more often than not. Ruby is inordinately proud of her big brother. He's in the RAF."

"So are hundreds of young men. Thousands."

"Certainly. Only in our scenario Ruby and Clive are devoted brother and sister. You know, the sort who tell each other everything. And Clive writes to Ruby every week without fail, from his station."

Schneider was not impressed. "Tittle-tattle from an aerodrome somewhere in England? Hardly the scoop of the century. I can't see *Hamburg* wetting their pants over it."

"Mind your language, lady present. Ruby, my dear, tell Henry about your brother."

"Oh Clive's wonderful," gushed Ruby with alacrity. "We're so proud of him. He's non-operational, having been wounded soon after the war began . . . crash-landed his Hurricane on takeoff. Not his fault, some sort of engine failure. Anyway, he's terribly bright and once he had recuperated his wing commander recommended him for special administrative duties. He's done very well for himself."

"Tell us how well he's done for himself, Ruby," said Ruskin, grinning in anticipation.

"He is a personal assistant based at Bentley Priory in Stanmore. Fighter Command Headquarters."

Schneider stopped playing with his mouthpiece. The light had dawned, and he could see where this was leading. Now he was impressed.

Ruskin couldn't resist adding a cherry to the icing on his cake.

"Apparently, Air Chief Marshal Dowding says good morning to him most days."

Chapter 76

(Tuesday 13th August 1940)

Adlertag began in a muddle. Hardly the well-oiled operation that *Reichsmarschall* Göring had anticipated.

After two postponements due to poor weather conditions, a good forecast was finally predicted for Tuesday 13th August. So on the Monday, in preparation, the *Luftwaffe* concentrated its attacks on the Chain Home RDF stations that ringed the south-east of England in an attempt to deny Fighter Command the technological advantage of radar. Despite several direct hits and close calls, notably at Dover, Rye, Dunkirk (the one in Kent) and Pevensey, only one station, Ventnor, remained off the air for any length of time.

Then *Adlertag* dawned in a shroud of low cloud, mist and steady drizzle that prompted Göring to order yet another postponement. Unfortunately, the message did not reach all *Geschwaders* (wings) and more than seventy Dorniers of *Kampfgruppe* 2 took off as planned. A recall message was sent out but the bombers had faulty radios and did not receive it. Their Bf 110 escort dipped their wings in an attempt to alert them before returning to base. The Dorniers ploughed on, only to receive a savage mauling at the hands of Spitfire and Hurricane squadrons.

By mid-afternoon, with weather improving, *Adlerangriff* was declared back on again, and a series of dog fights ensued across the whole of Southern England. Fighter Command refused to be drawn wholeheartedly into the conflict and used its planes frugally. By the end of the day they had lost thirteen fighters but destroyed thirty-four German aircraft.

As darkness fell, Field Marshal Hugo Sperrle, commander of *Luftflotten* 3, sent nine Heinkel IIIs from *Kampfgruppen* 100 on a mission with a target of special significance. Major Schmid's Intelligence Branch had supplied more detailed information than usual; the grey index card was precise in every aspect of its location, approach routes and distinguishing landmarks. Even so only four of the nine crews managed to pinpoint their target.

Eleven 250-kilo bombs fell on the Castle Bromwich factory. The damage was mostly superficial, and by the next day Spitfire production was virtually back to normal. The air raid was completely unexpected. Not the first on Castle Bromwich, but the heaviest and a baptism of fire into the harsh reality of being a prime *Luftwaffe* target.

Schneider heard the bombs fall. He could hardly miss them; a strong wind caused some of the bombs to drift north, in the direction of the safe house. He heard them, and felt some, as he sat hunched within the cramped confines of the Anderson shelter alongside Laurel, Hardy and the Voluntary Interceptor. The latter was there to supervise the sending of the first message to feature the new woman in Schneider's life.

In the early hours of the next morning, Schneider tapped out a message to *Abwehrstelle Hamburg*, berating them for not warning him about the raid which had nearly blown him to blazes, having been working on a night shift at the factory. His message was acknowledged but no apology made. Then he sent the message handed to him by the Voluntary Interceptor.

Damage to factory extensive. Production at a standstill and will remain so for some time. Congratulations for that and for not killing me. Give me warning next time. No benefit in blowing up your greatest asset. More good news. Have met useful contact. WAAF girl with brother in RAF administration. Should lead to great things.

Chapter 77

Justice moved swiftly in wartime. Once captured, enemy agents were treated with little sympathy unless they were of use to their captors. Otto von Osten's escape attempt marked him as of no further interest to the British Security Service. He had tried to warn Germany that he had been compromised, and MI5 had no way of knowing just how much information, if any, he had been able to transmit before the girl stopped him. Several tough sessions back at Camp 020, far less civilised than before, had failed to enlighten them.

The military court-martial was held *in camera* and he was charged under section one of the recently passed Treachery Act. The outcome was inevitable, especially considering the violence used by von Osten against his minders. Windrow had no more than a bad cut to his forehead, but Nicholson was still deeply unconscious and had almost certainly sustained permanent injury, probably brain damage, if he pulled through at all.

As soon as the guilty verdict was announced, von Osten was transported to the Tower of London. It had been a military court so he was to be shot; if it had been a civilian court he would have been hanged. At seven o'clock on the morning of *Adlertag* itself, as the first wave of Dorniers broke through cloud over the English coast, he stood before a firing squad in the miniature rifle range located within the walls of the tower. His last request, for a one-way plane ticket to Berlin, was refused, so he settled for a cigarette, which he smoked calmly before being blindfolded. A white lint target was pinned to his chest.

The eight men in the squad from the Scots Guards fired as one. Every man hit his target.

Chapter 78

(Wednesday 14th August 1940)

The contact procedure was simple. A classified advertisement in the London *Evening Standard*, Lost and Found section: *Found, 6pm, Piccadilly Circus Station, a gold cigarette lighter initialed W.C.* Then a telephone number. Ritter had devised the wording. The initials were his own touch of humour and stood not for Winston Churchill, which might have been many people's first guess, but for Wilhelm Canaris.

Two evenings later, at 6pm, Triangle stood outside the entrance to Piccadilly Circus Underground Station with the *Evening Standard* open at the Lost and Found page. As he stood waiting, he wondered how many W.C.s, genuine or otherwise, had wasted their time trying to call the number during the past forty-eight hours. It belonged to a telephone box in the Mile End Road.

Half an hour later Triangle was becoming impatient. If nothing happened within the next few minutes he'd have to come back the next evening, and the one after that if necessary. And that would be a bore.

He watched people as they passed by. It was early evening, and warm still with everyone wearing light summer clothes; some men were in shirtsleeves with their jackets over their arms. There were quite a number of cardboard gas mask cases strung over shoulders. The threat of invasion had revived fears of a gas attack, and people had started carrying them again. They were disappearing into the tube station on their way home, or killing time before a show or dance.

Five more minutes passed and he folded up his newspaper in disgust. As he did so, a man approached him from across the street and said: "Excuse me, do you have a light? I appear to have mislaid my Ronson." He was younger than expected, no more than thirty, handsome too. His English was excellent, with no discernible accent.

"Yes certainly. Was it valuable?"

"Quite valuable. A gift from my Uncle Willie."

"What a coincidence, I too have an uncle of that name."

The man bent forward as Triangle lit the cigarette. "Thanks, old chap." He walked away, heading up Charing Cross Road towards Cambridge Circus. Triangle lit a cigarette for himself and followed.

At Cambridge Circus, the man turned left into Shaftesbury Avenue, then right into one of the side streets leading into Soho. They walked for some time, until the man turned into an alleyway, through an arched entrance and up some stairs, followed moments later by Triangle. A narrow, dimly-lit staircase led to a first-floor landing. The man unlocked a door and they both went inside. It was a tiny bedsit, sparsely furnished and messy.

"Nice place," said Triangle sarcastically. "Is this where you live?"

"Of course not. But it serves its purpose."

"So you're Moss," I've known about you for a while – thought you'd surface sooner or later. These are fascinating times."

"What is your accent, Welsh?"

"That's right . . . boyo."

"Fascinating times indeed. Things are moving at quite a pace, that's for sure. Great Britain hasn't long to go."

"The British don't seem to see it that way. They're worried, certainly, but I don't think they really believe it will happen. An invasion I mean."

Moss was not interested in pursuing chit-chat any further and came to the point. "You have something for me."

Triangle slipped a hand inside his jacket to reveal a buff-coloured envelope. "Courtesy of a friendly diplomatic bag." Moss stretched out a hand to take it, but Triangle pulled back. "There's the small matter of expenses first. A courier charge, you know. Five pounds."

Moss felt inside his jacket and stepped forward as if to pay. In a split second Triangle was stretched helplessly across the bed with the barrel of a gun pressed firmly under his chin and blood trickling from the corner of his mouth. Moss took the envelope, folded it with his free hand and slid it into his trouser pocket.

"We're on the same side – no need for money to change hands. I'm sure you're paid well enough by our mutual friends."

Triangle stared up and into his eyes; he hadn't noticed them before. They were blank, devoid of any sensitivity. They reminded him of a doll's eyes; as lifeless as buttons. If the eyes are the windows to the soul, he thought, this man doesn't have one.

"Keep calm, boyo," said Triangle, struggling to speak through clenched teeth. "Worth a try, no offence taken I hope. As you say, we are on the same side."

The gun pushed harder into his chin. "That is what I am assuming. We *are* on the same side, aren't we?"

"Would I be here if we weren't?"

"I wouldn't be at all surprised."

"Well you needn't worry. Got to reap the benefit while I can. An invasion could bugger up my livelihood."

Moss backed away and let him loose. He put the gun back in his pocket. "If the RAF do their job properly there won't be an invasion."

Triangle rubbed his sore face. "It's up to the likes of us to help stop them then. Put a few spanners in the works, eh? That's why you've come to life presumably?"

"None of your business. You're just a courier. It's not your place to speculate, and it could be bad for your health."

"I'm a damn site more than a courier, if only you knew!" bleated Triangle peevishly.

Moss tapped the pocket containing the envelope. "I don't suppose you've been reading things you shouldn't by any chance?"

"Of course not . . . I'm not daft. None of my business, as you said."

Moss seemed to accept this. "Now listen, as you're my only means of contacting our friends abroad, I'm almost certainly going to need a crash meeting at some stage. I would imagine within the next week or so, possibly less. How do we go about it?"

"Simple." Triangle placed a card on the bed between them. "Phone this number – memorise it please. When you call, say your name is . . . well let's think, how about Mr Mossman? Say you're enquiring about some supplies for premises in Soho. Then I'll understand. The next day, at twelve noon, I'll be outside an Underground station, waiting. Green Park this time. No contact procedure. I'll spot you and follow. You choose where we go."

"What about security?"

Triangle picked up his *Evening Standard*. "This. If I'm carrying a newspaper, all is well. If I'm standing with my hands in my pockets, walk on. Fallback – same again the next day."

Moss nodded. "Good apart from the fallback. Time might be critical so it needs to be sooner. I suggest two hours later back at Piccadilly Circus again – where we just met. Then Green Park again two hours after that if necessary. Agreed?"

"Agreed."

"Now let's get out of here," said Moss. He moved towards the door. "You first . . . boyo."

Chapter 79

(Thursday 15th August 1940)

The day dawned over England with a sky that was dull and overcast. *Reichsmarschall* Göring recalled his commanders to Carinhall for a conference. He was angry.

Losses were high, especially Stukas and Bf 110s, and there seemed to be no end to the resources of British Fighter Command. He stressed to all present the importance of concentrating attacks exclusively on Royal Air Force bases and nowhere else, not even RDF stations . . . "in view of the fact that *not one* of those attacked has been put out of action!" he complained. It was of vital importance to crush Fighter Command for the sake of Operation Sea Lion, which might otherwise be put in jeopardy.

By midday, the weather over the English Channel was clearing. Göring had left strict instructions that his conference was not to be interrupted, so an urgent telephone report did not reach him. One *Oberst* Paul Diechmann, Chief of Staff of II *Fliegerkorps*, used his initiative and gave the signal for an attack to begin. For the rest of the day, all three *Luftflotten* made a series of massed daylight raids on airfields stretching from Portsmouth to Tyneside.

For Fighter Command it was a successful day, and whilst Göring and his commanders enjoyed the sunshine on the terrace at Carinhall, the *Luftwaffe* received another drubbing.

*

The poor weather had not hindered Alison, and by mid-morning she was well on her way, ferrying an Oxford to the north of England. By the time the Home Counties were behind her, the cloud base was already lifting. Her destination was Sherburn-in-Elmet, a small factory airfield to the east of Leeds that was now home to a small ATA pool from where planes were flown on to Scotland by pilots permanently based there. It was a more efficient system, with pilots based in the south able to return much quicker, and thus make several deliveries in a day. Things were also more relaxed now about flying up the eastern side of England as pressure mounted to become more efficient.

The Oxford was usually made by author Nevil Shute's Airspeed Ltd., who designed it, but production had been taken on by de Havilland the year before to augment output of the smaller company. Now Hatfield was concentrating on producing nothing but Oxfords – plus a few Dominoes – and the repair of Hurricanes and Merlin engines. Manufacture of Tiger Moths had been transferred entirely to other locations.

She made good time; by lunchtime she was almost there. To avoid the belt of heavily populated towns and cities running from Leicester to Huddersfield like a backbone, she flew east over Cambridgeshire and Lincolnshire, clipping the edge of The Wash and turning west again when the Humber estuary was in sight.

It was there that she saw them.

High above her starboard side, so high they were nothing more than tiny black specks, were bombers, dozens of them, with even tinier specks above and behind. The fighter escort. They were heading north-west.

For a few seconds she gazed open-mouthed, not from fear but from the unexpected. Never before had she seen such a sight – a huge formation, seventy, maybe eighty planes in all. ATA pilots were under strict instructions to avoid the enemy, should they inadvertently come into contact with them. Fortunately for Alison she was close to her destination. She followed the line of the Humber due west, past Hull, and landed at Sherburn-in-Elmet ten minutes later.

There was organised chaos. Pilots were anxiously awaiting orders to disperse planes, should the threat of an attack become apparent. Alison was told to refuel her Oxford immediately and be ready to take off again.

There wasn't time. When the order came, her plane still had the fuel hose from the petrol bowser attached. Someone shouted at her to run for the shelter. She was halfway there when two Bf 110s came into view, appearing from nowhere and flying very low. Ack-ack guns started firing. Alison kept running and was only feet away from the entrance to the slit trench when the first cannon shells struck the ground behind her. Two aircraftmen reached it at the same time and all three dived in together as the Messerschmitt roared overhead.

"Where the hell did they come from!" said one. "I didn't think 110s had the range to get this far."

"Auxiliary fuel tanks," said the other. "I caught a glimpse of them underneath. No way they'd make it otherwise."

He had barely finished his sentence when more cannon shells raked past them. They crouched low as a shower of earth and clumps of grass sprayed across them. Gradually the noise of planes died away and the guns stopped firing. A hangar was on fire; two aircraftmen had been injured – one badly. Only one plane had been badly damaged as it tried to take off. The pilot was lucky, he walked away with a gash to his forehead and a bloody nose.

As Alison and the aircraftmen stepped gingerly out of the slit trench and surveyed the scene, one said: "Lucky we're only small fry here. The big buggers would really do some damage."

"The big buggers are up there somewhere," said Alison. "I've seen them."

*

Flight Lieutenant Dan Rodigan had also seen the enemy, over the Kent countryside and at very close range. Midas squadron was flying its fourth sortie of the day.

Shortly after eleven in the morning, they had scrambled to ward off Stukas attacking Hawkinge aerodrome, near Folkestone, but not before considerable damage had been done. By the time they reached the area, some Hurricanes had already engaged the enemy and there was nothing more to do other than chase them out over the English Channel.

Then in the afternoon, all hell broke loose. The sky filled with aircraft of every description; Dorniers, Heinkels, Junkers and Messerschmitts. Rodigan had been in the thick of it. At one stage a formation of Bf 110s lost its fighter escort whilst bombing Croydon Airport – mistaking it for Kenley – and he bagged one of seven that never returned home.

Now he was over Romney Marsh, having intercepted a formation of Junkers Ju 88s approaching Hawkinge from the south. The fighter escort was strong; almost immediately it broke up and a series of dogfights developed, with Bf 109s trying to keep the Spitfires away from the vulnerable bombers. Squadron Leader Innes led the attack. Within minutes he had shot down a Bf 109 and sent a Ju 88 homeward bound, bombs jettisoned, smoke billowing from the port wing.

Rodigan was less fortunate. He soon found himself with two Bf 109s on his tail. He managed to take evasive action before they were within firing range, banking sharply to port, and round in a tight arc, climbing and swerving as only a Spitfire could. By the time he levelled out he was five miles away. But the Messerschmitts were still with him, still out of range, though keeping pace. He had no intention of being squeezed out of the main battle, so he banked again, wider this time, losing height rapidly. The German planes were visible in his rear view mirror. Having turned one hundred and eighty degrees, he brought the Spitfire down even lower, until he was hedge-hopping, skimming over trees and hedgerows. Before long he was approaching the coast. He knew he was north of Folkestone now, smoke from Hawkinge was visible to the south and surrounded by a criss-cross of vapour trails. The cliffs were directly ahead, with a sheer drop of several hundred feet to the sea beyond.

The Spitfire shot over the edge at full throttle, the Messerschmitts in hot pursuit. As soon as he was over the sea, Rodigan pulled the control column back as hard as he could, whipping the plane upwards into a tight loop. His stomach felt as if it had slipped into his boots and back as he soared upwards and over to complete the full three hundred and sixty degrees. "Bloody marvellous!" he heard himself gasping, his lungs aching from the g-force. It was risky and dangerous, but so was having two enemy fighters on your tail intent on blasting you to Kingdom come.

It worked. The Messerschmitt pilots were momentarily disorientated by the sudden drop to the sea . . . and the Spitfire appeared to have vanished.

Rodigan levelled out barely eighty feet above the sparkling surface of the sea and immediately pulled back to gain height. The Bf 109s were ahead of him and slightly to starboard. For a few seconds he shadowed them, hoping they had lost him. Then one banked to port, turning to look for their lost prey. It was a disastrous mistake, taking him right across the trajectory of the Spitfire's machine guns. The eight wing-mounted Brownings spat out a noisy hale of fire; a three second burst was all it needed. Smoke, then flames, billowed from the Messerschmitt's engine, chunks of fuselage spun through the air, and the fighter plunged the few hundred feet into the English Channel. Just before impact, it exploded and disintegrated into a thousand pieces.

Rodigan caught a glimpse of a vaguely human shape spinning through the air as the German pilot met his death. There couldn't be a more definite kill. He continued flying straight for a while, gaining height as he took in the glory of the moment. Then he remembered the other Bf 109. Where the hell had it gone? He panned the horizon but could see nothing. He was heading out to sea and well on his way to Cap Gris Nez, so he banked to port and started heading back, still looking in all directions, hoping for a stab at the other bandit. He wondered how Stuart was faring. His mind was elsewhere for a few moments.

He never saw the Messerschmitt that had been shadowing him ever since the kill.

Twenty millimetre cannon shells tore savagely through the Spitfire's aluminum sheeting. Miraculously Rodigan was not hit, but the suddenness of the attack shook him to the core. For a few seconds he wasn't even sure what had happened. Thick black smoke began spewing from the Merlin engine, choking him and obscuring his view. He swung hard to port and sloped into a dive, glancing around for any sight of the enemy. Through the smoke, he saw three Hurricanes bearing down on the German, the leader's guns blazing; it was a beam attack, and he managed a hit on the upper fuselage. The Messerschmitt turned tail and headed back towards France. The Hurricanes chased briefly then let it go.

The Merlin was coughing and spluttering. Rodigan was losing height rapidly and couldn't keep his Spitfire level. He had drifted to starboard; the coast was ahead, the chalk cliffs north of Dover indicating his position. A string of barrage balloons protected the RDF station there. He knew he'd never gain the height needed to avoid them; at his present rate of descent he'd smash straight into the chalk face. And his feet were getting extremely hot from the burning engine.

He released the canopy and tore away his radio lead and oxygen hose. The force of the slipstream was like a punch in the face as air rushed into the cockpit. With fumbling hands, he opened the access door, undid his harness straps and eased himself upwards until he was crouching on the seat. Then he fell out and away from the cockpit, pulled the ripcord immediately and felt the parachute tug him like a rag doll as it braked his descent. Thirty seconds later he was in the sea. He saw the Spitfire ditch ahead of him, nose-diving upside down and disappearing in a plume of spray.

As he bobbed about in the water the white cliffs of Dover seemed much further away than they had from the air. Rodigan now discovered for himself what he had heard from others who had ditched in the drink.

The water was bloody cold.

*

Heather Norbury's deliveries took her well away from the air battles that day. Her two return trips ferrying Miles Master two-seater trainers from the Phillips and Powers factory at Woodley to the RAF storage unit at Kemble, south of Cirencester, were both uneventful.

Back at Woodley she managed to cadge a lift with another ATA girl, Chris Sheldon, back to Hatfield in a Fox Moth, a cramped four-passenger transport used for shorter taxi hops than the Anson, and arrived back at the airfield shortly after five thirty. The pilot dropped them off then flew back to White Waltham. The two girls made straight for the ATA office. Pauline Gower was the only person around. She sat at her desk, an unbecoming tin hat perched on her head.

"Straight to the shelters, ladies," she called. "We're in the middle of an alert. It's been on for a while – no sign of the enemy so it shouldn't be for much longer." They turned to leave. "Heather, when it's over, could you come back and see me? I won't keep you long."

The shelter was full mainly of workers from the factory. The raid had delayed the day shift from getting home, and they were impatient and moody. Those on the night shift were more cheerful, having barely started work. Heather peered round to see if she recognised anyone. There were some ferry pilots further along the narrow concrete passage; she squeezed her way in their direction, hoping to find Alison. One of them, Victoria Gregory, told her that Alison had been sent north and there had been raids up there, so she was probably delayed as a result.

The all-clear sounded and they made their way up the steps into daylight. The night shift returned to their workshops and hangars, others filed away to the changing rooms. Pauline was still in her office, where she had stayed throughout the alert. She closed the door behind Heather and motioned for her to take a seat.

"I've had a telephone call from West Malling, Heather . . . about an hour ago."

Heather's stomach suddenly tightened into a huge knot. She guessed what was to come. Stuart, it must be Stuart . . .

"I spoke with Squadron Leader Innes – your fiancé I believe."

"Oh thank the Lord! I thought you were going to say something terrible had happened to him."

"No. He's alright, he's fine."

"So then what? Who? Not Dan surely . . ."

"Flight Lieutenant Rodigan? Yes. It's probably nothing to worry about. Apparently his plane was hit and he had to ditch into the sea, but he wasn't far out from Dover and there's a very good chance he's been picked up already."

"I see."

"He and Alison are very close, I gather. She isn't back yet and doesn't know. He's only missing after all, and close to home. Frankly I think it was premature of the squadron leader to phone at all."

"That's his way. Rather impetuous. When might they know more, did Stuart say?"

"No, he didn't," said Pauline impassively. "But I'm sure he'll be in touch as soon as there is some news. I expect he'll phone you at your flat. He tried that number before ringing me. If you haven't heard anything by morning, tell Alison to come in for duty as usual. I'll see what I can find out for her."

"Thank you, that's awfully kind."

With a mug of tea in her hand, she sat in a wicker chair on the edge of the aerodrome, and waited. She lit a cigarette and puffed at it occasionally, mulling over the situation. Her heart ached for her friend, and in a way for herself. Dan was missing, but it could as easily have been Stuart. During their rare moments together, Stuart spoke often of the friends he had lost in the past month or so. The chums he had flown with were being picked off one by one.

He never said the words, but they hung over their relationship like a shrouded sign: *It's only a matter of time before my turn comes.*

It seemed that Dan's time might have come already.

And it could be Stuart's tomorrow.

They were to be married in nine days' time, on the Saturday after next, at a church in Maidstone. Stuart had been reticent at first, fearing the commitment at a time when life was so uncertain. Better to wait until the invasion scare was over and this awful battle for survival in the skies had been won, he suggested. In that respect, he and Alison were of a similar view. But Heather had wanted it. She told him that living for the moment was all that mattered. What was the point in waiting until it was safe? You could wait all your life for things to be just right, and miss every opportunity that ever came your way. She had convinced him.

Everything was arranged; no parents, no family, just the four of them and a special licence. Pauline Gower had agreed that she and Alison could have the Saturday off together. Alison would be the only bridesmaid and, *Luftwaffe* permitting, there would be a groom and a best man.

Only the best man was currently missing somewhere off Dover.

Suddenly the Saturday after next seemed like a hundred years away. Anything could happen between now and then. Suppose Dan was dead. What should they do – go ahead, or postpone? Heather knew her own mind; go ahead, come what may. But would Alison feel the same? She hoped so. Dan would be alright; he was probably on his way back to West Malling by now.

She sipped her tea and smoked her cigarette. It was a pleasant evening, with nothing to indicate there was a war on apart from a string of barrage balloons floating above the aerodrome. She looked up at them, their size reassuring, like giant kites above a park where children play, oblivious to the complexities and stresses of adult life to come.

When her mug was empty and several cigarette butts lay on the ground, a speck appeared high above the main hangar, approaching from the north-west and circling wide to make the correct approach to the aerodrome. The faint hum of an aircraft engine became audible above the background of distant factory noise.

A Tiger Moth. It was Alison, she knew instinctively. In a Moth! No wonder it had taken her an age to return south. The plane made a faultless landing before taxiing close to where Heather sat. A gloved hand waved eagerly from the cockpit. The engine faltered and died, and Alison climbed out. She hurried over and pulled a face of exasperation.

"It's all I could get! Either that or a lumpy bed up north, so no contest. What a day – nearly had a close encounter with the *Luftwaffe*, I've never seen so many planes. Good of you to wait for me, old thing. Have you been back long?"

"No not really. Come on, fancy a drink on the way home? We could pop into The New Fiddle if you like." It was their local pub. Heather's voice sounded hollow, despite her attempt to appear normal. Alison sensed immediately that something was not right.

"Alright, what's happened? Come on, Heather, you have something to say, I can tell."

Heather knew honesty was best.

"It's about Dan . . ."

Chapter 80

"This is excellent material!" exclaimed Herbert Wichmann. "First rate."
He held a sheet of paper in his hand, an agent's report, freshly decoded
and marked: *AGENT NO: 3549 – CODENAME* 'QUAVER'

Nicklaus Ritter was more reserved. "It would appear so."

Wichmann laughed loudly. "Perhaps we have underestimated young
Quaver all along."

"On the surface, it certainly seems impressive."

"Look at it – details from confidential reports on the effects of
Luftwaffe raids; an evaluation of morale amongst Fighter Command
pilots; bomb damage estimates. It's a gold mine, an absolute gold mine!"

"If it's genuine."

"Well that can easily be checked. Reconnaissance flights can verify
the bomb damage report. Not much we can do about the morale appraisal
though."

"Precisely my point!" said Ritter. "It can be verified by flying an
aircraft overhead and seeing for ourselves. As an intelligence report that
makes it considerably less than a gold mine. As for morale, it's reported
here as low. A fairly predictable observation when you consider that the
combined forces of three *Luftflotten* are currently bombing the shit out of
them, and reducing their life expectancy to a matter of days."

"Nikolaus, this is the best piece of intelligence to come out of Britain
in over a year. Quaver has stumbled across a gem, a gold mine – call it
what you will. He's found himself a girlfriend whose brother has access to
confidential RAF information. How can you possibly do anything but
applaud the fellow!"

"Because it is *too* good, and that to me immediately makes it suspect.
I find it hard to imagine Schneider being so resourceful, irrespective of
whether luck or judgement had anything to do with it. His reports from
Castle Bromwich have so far been beneficial, but hardly of great
significance. As I said, there is nothing new here. Are we perhaps more
impressed with the source than the content?"

"Come now," said Wichmann. "We must be grateful for what we can
get. Hermann Görtz has failed us – again. He's probably lounging in an
Irish prison, and Tributh and Gaertner are probably his cell mates. What a

waste of time and resources they were! Now Mechanic has gone too. We're getting a bit thin on the ground over there."

"Not for long," said Ritter. "We have several new agents in training. At least two should be ready to be parachuted in soon."

"Indeed. Meanwhile Quaver is currently our best agent in the field and coming up with high quality intelligence. Let's allow him the benefit of the doubt and enjoy some success for once, eh?"

"Don't forget Johnny."

"Granted, he has his uses. But sometimes I think we overestimate his worth. I cannot recall the last time he gave us anything I would consider really worthwhile . . ."

Ritter had to concede. "I take your point."

Chapter 81

(Friday 16ᵗʰ August 1940)

Schneider lay on his bed, smoking and listening to the faint murmur of voices permeating from the next room, where the night's events were being chewed over again and again.

The mood amongst MI5 operatives was almost euphoric. Ruby Russell was a great success, and *Hamburg* had swallowed her – hook, line and sinker. Incredibly, the transmission had gone on for almost an hour, dangerously long, and way beyond recommended safety margins. Eventually *Hamburg* had told him to get off the air and to save the rest until tomorrow. Yet it was they who had prolonged the session by asking question after question in their eagerness to know more about this extraordinary source. And the quality of the information had been moderate, nothing more; not until the big brass had been consulted could the 'juicy stuff', as Ruskin called it, be considered for disclosure. Schneider never knew the precise nature of the material, but it was clearly what *Hamburg* had wanted, judging by the reaction.

Quaver was their blue-eyed boy.

A bottle was being passed round. Laurel and Hardy were in high spirits and celebrating with the VI, Schneider assumed. He wasn't sure. He'd been invited, but Ruskin and Ruby had left and he didn't relish the remaining company. He preferred his own. He was pining for Marion, and hoping she was missing him too. He wanted her badly.

Another escape was out of the question. His minders were ever vigilant now, watching him like hawks. They would never let him embarrass them a second time; and even if he did evade them, this time they knew exactly where to find him. He felt trapped, and very lonely. He knew he could not put up with this unreal existence for much longer, it would drive him insane. The only solace he had was the trumpet, which he practiced for hours at a time.

A poor substitute for love.

*

Alison did not sleep at all that night. She sat silently in the flat, with Heather making comforting noises at her side, until her friend fell asleep. There were no tears. Nothing was known for certain, and Alison knew that Dan was safe, she had no doubt in her mind. It was only a matter of waiting for him to turn up; waiting for the phone to ring.

At five in the morning she was still waiting, and the ashtray on the table in front of her was piled high with cigarette ends. At one stage during the evening, Heather cautiously broached the subject of the wedding, explaining that she planned to go ahead come what may. She knew it might sound selfish.

"Don't worry, you carry on," said Alison. "Dan and I will be there, he'll be fine. Stuart will be calling soon to let us know – or it might be Dan himself. You wait and see."

So they had waited. Shortly before dawn, Alison switched off the light and opened the blackout curtains. She saw the world gradually taking shape as the sun rose imperceptibly in the east. She stood there for a whole hour without moving. The weather looked promising. There would be raids today.

She wandered into the kitchen and boiled the kettle. She took great care in making her tea, warming the pot thoroughly, measuring out two generous spoonfuls of leaves, adding the water. She let it brew for some minutes before pouring, then milk in the cup first. She had plenty of time, and the attention to detail seemed important to her. She picked up the cup and saucer and walked back towards the lounge. She glanced down at the finished product; it was the most precisely prepared cup of tea she had ever made.

And all for nothing.

The shrillness of the telephone bell shattered the early morning silence like an explosion. Alison started, and the cup and saucer went crashing to the ground. Hot tea spilled down the front of her dress, but she felt nothing more than a mild discomfort as it soaked into her dress. She wanted to rush across the room and pick up the receiver. She tried to move but she couldn't. Her legs had turned to lead.

Heather woke up with a start and peered around, bleary-eyed. She clambered off the settee and picked up the receiver. "Hello? Oh hello, yes she is – just a moment." She held out the receiver. "It's for you. West Malling."

Alison could just reach it from where she was rooted to the spot. The mouthpiece felt cool against her chin.

"Hello, Alison Webb speaking."

The voice that she heard sounded tired, flat and devoid of emotion. "Hello, Ally. It's me."

The loveliest voice in the world.

"Dan! Oh thank the Lord. Are you alright?"

"I'm fine. Been for a bit of a swim, that's all. Rather a long swim actually. It's bloody cold in the Channel."

"You're safe, that's all that matters."

"Always was. I say, I could throttle Stuart for worrying you like that. Fancy telling you I was missing! I've torn him off a strip."

Alison felt a tightness building in her throat. She wanted to say something but couldn't. A wave of emotion overwhelmed her and she collapsed into a chair. Heather took the receiver, said a few words, then placed it back on the cradle. She put an arm round Alison's shoulder and led her to her room. "Come on, you need some sleep, lots of it."

Alison buried her head in Heather's shoulder and wept. "I knew he was safe," she sobbed. "I knew all along."

Heather said nothing; she knew the words were not intended for her. Alison was trying to convince herself.

Chapter 82

(Wednesday 21st August 1940)

". . . The gratitude of every home in our island, in our empire, and indeed throughout the world, except in the abodes of the guilty, goes out to the British airmen who, undaunted by odds, unwearied in their constant challenge and mortal danger, are turning the tide of the world war by their prowess and by their devotion. Never in the field of human conflict was so much owed by so many to so few."

"And they're getting fewer by the day," remarked Air Commodore Archie Boyle as he folded his newspaper and looked across the room. "Winston omitted to mention that in the Commons yesterday. We have the planes – Beaverbrook is seeing to that – but they're no good without pilots to fly them."

One of the men seated across the desk stirred slightly and said: "Nor are they any good without airfields from which to operate."

"That's our major concern at present," agreed the air commodore. "This spell of bad weather over the last few days has been a blessing, it's kept Jerry away and allowed us to patch up the worst hit. All the front line airfields are in a mess – Biggin Hill, Hawkinge, West Malling, Manston. If the hammering they've taken recently persists much longer . . . well, it doesn't bear thinking about. Dowding is greatly concerned about it."

Lt.-Col. Ruskin sat forward. "We may be able to help there, sir. We're in a strong position to be able to influence German Intelligence and, through them, *Luftwaffe* strategy. Göring himself, quite probably."

The Air Ministry's Director of Intelligence appeared ambivalent, his face registering a mixture of interest and doubt that mirrored precisely his feelings.

"I have faith in your intelligence boys, you know that – I've supported you all along. The fake Spitfire production figures, for example. Time alone will tell whether it was effective – but worth a try in my view. German Intelligence certainly seem to have swallowed everything we've fed them so far."

"And will continue to do so," interjected Ruskin, "I can assure you."

Brigadier Harker looked disparagingly at his colleague.

"Let's not be overconfident," he said. Assurances are a dangerous thing in wartime, although I must say that the Ruby Russell ploy appears to have passed muster. From the noises the *Abwehr* are making they seem to think they've hit the jackpot. But you're right of course, Ruskin, we are certainly in the strongest position yet to be able to deceive the Germans, and hopefully we might be able to influence decision making at the highest level."

"So let's use our advantage. Feed back to Göring that bombing the airfields is a waste of time."

Harker shook his head. "That won't stop the bombing, it will simply encourage him to drop them elsewhere."

"Isn't that precisely what we need – relief for Fighter Command?"

"What do you suggest he bombs instead – heavily populated areas? Kill civilians . . . women and children?"

The air commodore looked grim. "Of course not. Gentlemen, there is the crux of the matter. Whilst the *Luftwaffe* attacks Fighter Command airfields, other targets are being ignored – towns, cities, factories, a thousand places of strategic importance to the enemy. Our problem is that at this precise moment, Fighter Command stands alone between all those things and a German invasion. If Göring succeeds in destroying our air defences, the whole of Britain may well be lost. I discussed this with Dowding. He more than anyone has no illusions about that. The survival of Fighter Command is tantamount to the survival of Great Britain. Under such circumstances, *anything* we can do to prevent that from happening *must* be done."

Harker and Ruskin relaxed. It was a green light, Ruskin was almost certain.

"Now, how do we go about it?" Boyle spoke so softly that his words were barely audible.

"We need information . . . and permission to use it," said Ruskin. "So we can patch together scenarios that Jerry will believe in."

"Such as?"

Ruskin opened a notepad and leaned forward in anticipation. This was his field.

"Snippets of conversations . . . the kind of things Clive Russell might get to hear at Bentley Priory. Dowding overheard saying *Let's pray they keep wasting their bombs on the aerodromes and away from the important targets* – that sort of thing. Indirect, it's more believable that way."

"Hmmm," pondered Boyle. "Sounds as though you can do that sort of thing without us. You're better at it."

"But we need to pepper it with facts and figures – some names, locations, and a few credible statistics. Without them the whole thing will sound . . . well, bland. Unconvincing. And only the Air Ministry can help there."

The air commodore picked up a telephone and dialed.

"Alright, let's get what you need. Some files will be required. I think this may take a while. Tea, gentlemen?"

Chapter 83

(Friday 23rd August 1940)

Ballard Ruskin arrived at the safe house in the early evening. It had been quiet all week, with little to report to *Hamburg* apart from details of the poor weather conditions, which was hardly news to them. Quaver hadn't transmitted for days, allowing Ruskin to spend time in London, at the Air Ministry and at his office in the Scrubs.

Schneider watched his case officer impatiently. Almost a week had passed since they had spoken about a visit to Coventry. Ruskin had said that he couldn't promise anything, but he'd see what he could do. Nourished by that glimmer of hope, Schneider had survived. Now he had to know if his request would be granted, even for a few hours. Ruskin suggested that he and Schneider should take a walk in the garden together. As soon as they were alone, he came straight to the point.

"Alright, Eric," he said warmly, "you can see Marion."

"I say, Mac, that's terrific news!" Dare he ask when? He found himself asking anyway.

"Tonight if you wish."

"Even better!"

"It's pretty quiet at the moment, so I don't see any reason why not. We can manage without you for a few days. Your VI can make a transmission for you this evening, as it's a 'nothing to report' report." Ruskin leaned against the entrance to the Anderson shelter. "As you know, we had a chat with Mrs Wakeley – a few questions, nothing more. She's been given a clean bill of health."

"I told you all along she knows nothing. How long can I stay?"

"Until Sunday. But there are three conditions."

"Anything, just name them."

"Firstly, we trust you, Eric, despite the fact that you ran away from us once before. If you break that trust there will be grave consequences. You will either spend the rest of the war incarcerated somewhere – or worse.

There will be no more chances. So you be there on Sunday when we come to collect you."

"You have my word."

"Secondly, if anything materialises in the interim you must be ready to come back at a moment's notice, day or night. Do you understand?"

"Absolutely. You needn't worry on either count. I won't let you down."

"Good. And it goes without saying that you say absolutely nothing about what you are doing for us. You stick to your cover story to the letter. Come on, there's a driver waiting for you."

"I'll get my things." Schneider turned towards the house, then hesitated. "You said there are three conditions. What's the third?"

"Ah yes, the third condition," said Ruskin. "It's the most important of them all . . . and it applies to me as well as you. We really must keep this from Ruby. She's the jealous type, and if she finds out you've got another woman, we're stuffed."

*

When she opened the door, Marion wrapped her arms around Schneider and hugged him tight. She was wearing a skirt and blouse, and her hair was neater than usual.

"Thank heavens," she gasped. "I almost wasn't in. I got ready to go out to the pictures with my friend Helen from up the road, but one of her dogs got ill and she had to cancel. I'd have missed you."

"I'd have waited for you on the doorstep."

Marion eyed her lover with suspicion. "Henry, I do hope you're not AWOL again!"

"Not this time. I'm here with official blessing."

They kissed and held each other for a long time, then celebrated with a tot of brandy, sitting close to each other on the sofa and talking. Marion told of her interview with the man who had been waiting outside her house; the man called Jones. He had taken her to the police station where another man, older and more senior, had asked her many questions. She had been there for hours. She hadn't been frightened, but it had unsettled her. Schneider wanted to know what kind of questions.

"About me, about you . . . about Bernard. The older one asked the questions, and Jones made notes. He had some papers in front of him, a sort of report it looked like. Every now and again he'd nod, as if what I said tallied with what he had written down in front of him."

"And did anything you say *not* tally?"

"I don't think so – they seemed quite satisfied. Actually there weren't that many questions, but they kept asking the same ones over and over. It

316

got really boring after a while. Then they thanked me and drove me home – and that was that." She waved a hand as if to indicate the incident was forgotten about. Schneider was relieved. He had expected something more rigorous. Marion seemed not to care anymore about it. Then she said bluntly: "You're not a soldier at all, are you?"

It seemed the most natural thing to reply in all honesty.

"No."

"They wouldn't have bothered with me like that for a soldier whose gone AWOL. Not for just a private in the Royal Essex."

"No they wouldn't, you're quite right."

"Then what are you? Who are you?"

Schneider knew he should not tell her, he had given an assurance to Uncle Mac. But he wanted to be honest with Marion. What harm could it do, to tell her the truth? Who could she possibly tell that might be a risk?

"Do you really want to know?"

Marion looked him in the eyes, and saw her own feelings reflected back at her; feelings of need, and desire, and love. It was too precious to risk losing.

"Not if you don't want to tell me . . . or can't. But can you please answer just one question for me?"

"You can ask me anything." He meant what he said.

"Are you a fifth columnist?"

Schneider smiled and took her hand. He kissed her fingers, barely touching them with his lips.

"No, I am not. You couldn't be further from the truth. My work is secret, but I am most definitely on your side in this war. Shall we leave it at that?"

"Yes, let's leave it at that."

He felt a huge sense of relief. He didn't want to break his word to Uncle Mac, but if asked he would have told Marion anything at that moment. They lost themselves in a deep, tender kiss. Soon they were undressing, tugging at each other's clothes until they were naked. They made love on the rug; long, slow love that seemed to last forever.

Chapter 84

(Saturday 24ᵗʰ August 1940)

.

Heather had been praying for bad weather all week so that her marriage ceremony could go ahead. But it wasn't to be, and the *Luftwaffe* began their attacks on airfields early. RAF pilots had a rude awakening, with their first serious 'scramble' in three days. West Malling was in the thick of it. At Hatfield, Heather stumbled out of bed to answer the telephone and heard a pleasant-sounding WAAF tell her that Squadron Leader Innes was awfully sorry but he couldn't make their appointment, and he hoped that the same time next Saturday would be convenient for her.

"Oh well, Ally," she sighed, "looks as though I'm not getting married today after all."

The sound of Alison's sleepy voice drifted from the bedroom. "Fancy a cuppa?"

"Yes please."

Heather sat on the edge of Alison's bed as they drank their tea.

"You poor thing," said Alison. "Are you terribly disappointed?"

"Not really, I half expected this to happen. We'll just have to try again next weekend."

"I think you're taking it remarkably well. If it was me, I'd be in floods of tears."

"What good would that do? Another week won't make any difference, not when we'll have the rest of our lives together."

"Hmm, do you think we'll be able to get next Saturday off?"

"That depends."

"On what?"

"Whether or not we can earn it. A phone call to the office might be in order – see if we can get some ferry chits for today."

"Shouldn't be difficult, there are plenty of Ox-boxes coming off the production line." Alison finished her tea and swung her legs out of bed. "Come on, let's not sit around moping all day. Let's get cracking!"

Instead of saying her marriage vows in Maidstone, Heather found herself flying to Brize Norton in a Dominoe – a twin-engine biplane used for navigational training purposes. From there she transferred by taxi Anson to Woodley, picked up a chit for a Master and delivered it to Little Rissington. After an hour's wait, she picked up the Anson again which returned her, via most of the airfields in the Home Counties so it seemed, to Hatfield. She didn't see any enemy aircraft, but at Woodley there were faint, snake-like vapour trails visible in the sky to the south-east; evidence that dog fights were taking place, a fact confirmed when she heard the one o'clock news in the mess.

"Kent's being hit badly again," mumbled one of the male ATA pilots from behind a badly rolled cigarette. "Expect it's the airfields again, the poor sods."

Heather took a final bite from a ham sandwich, picked up her bag and walked out. The last thing she wanted to hear was how the poor sods in Kent were being hit badly. She sought solace in the open air with a cigarette.

Alison had not fared as well. A single delivery of an Oxford to Kemble had been followed by a long wait for a flight back anywhere. There was nothing to move on, so she bided her time and prayed for the Anson to turn up. Eventually it did, four hours later, and she returned to Hatfield tired and frustrated.

They spent the evening together in the flat, talking very little, thinking about West Malling and Midas Squadron, and listening to the wireless. The news said there had been heavy raids on aerodromes across the whole of south-east England, but damage and casualties were light. There had been engagements between the RAF and the enemy all day long, as British fighters attempted to break up the attacking formations, and a large number of German planes were reported to have been shot down.

Stuart Innes telephoned just before ten. He and Dan were both fine. He sounded extremely tired, and a little drunk. When he tried to apologise, Heather told him not to be so silly. "Same time, same place, next week?"

"Of course, darling. We'll get hitched one way or the other, that's if Hermann bloody Göring allows us to."

"And the vicar."

"Ah yes, better keep him sweet. I'll get someone here to phone him. Do you think bunging him a few quid might help?"

Chapter 85

The concourse of Euston Station was crowded, even though the rush hour had finished long ago. It was warm, dark and smoky, and there were men in uniform everywhere, some with girls, others standing around in groups talking. Above the hubbub of chatter the steady hissing of steam was ever-present as engines simmered beyond the barriers, recovering from journeys or building up power in readiness to depart.

Moss made his way purposefully towards the departure board and scanned the lists of towns and cities. He soon found Birmingham. He scanned the columns of numbers and noted some down in a small pocket diary, then wandered into the buffet and ordered a double whisky. As he stood at the bar, the whine of a siren filled the air. There were groans, and several expletives. Some people stood up immediately and hurried towards the Underground, others casually finished their drinks. An ARP warden appeared and started shouting orders. Moss knocked back the last of his whisky and went out into the street.

He decided to walk back to his house in Islington; it was only twenty minutes away and the raid was bound to be another false alarm. The bombers never seemed to reach the centre of London. There were quite a few people about, all walking cautiously in the blackout, keeping their torches trained on the ground and using the white stripes on the curbs as a guide. It was a curious feeling, wandering about in the dark, occasionally bumping into someone and apologising with mild embarrassment. He passed Kings Cross and was on the Pentonville Road when he heard the first rumbling of aircraft engines. Searchlights sprang into life some distance away, traversing the sky, like powerful versions of the torch signals that were part of his boyhood games.

The droning increased in volume, the broad, fat sound of multiple engines undulating widely as they strained under the weight of their deadly cargo. By the time Moss reached the Angel in Islington High Street, the muffled crump of bombs exploding could be heard from the direction of the East End. Ten minutes later he reached his building and ran up the stairs to his flat. Once inside, he didn't switch on the light but pulled back the blackout curtains and opened the sash window as wide as it would go. The bombs sounded as if they were landing much closer now; not far off the City, he estimated.

So, it had begun. Hitler had at last decided to target the heart of the British nation. In a way Moss was surprised. He had imagined the Führer might have wanted to leave the capital intact, like Paris, in order to be able to enjoy its treasures to the full once the invasion was complete and he had taken up residence . . . in Buckingham Palace presumably. Was this an admission of defeat, an acceptance that this whole objective was not going to be so easy after all? The *Luftwaffe* had so far failed to pave the way, and if the figures for German losses quoted in the newspapers were to be believed, it seemed as though the RAF were winning Churchill's Battle of Britain.

Hence his mission. Hence his being woken from hibernation. Hence the bombs now falling on London. He thought about his mission as he watched the orange glow in the sky. A mission in two distinct parts. The first should be easy enough.

The second, he predicted, he would either complete with total success, or die in the process.

*

It had been a mistake, and Göring was furious.

German planes seeking out aircraft factories and an oil refinery around the Rochester and Thameshaven areas had become confused, lost their way and decided to jettison their bombs on whatever happened to be below.

London happened to be below.

As soon as he heard the news, Göring dispatched a signal to the operations officer of the offending *Kampfgeschwader* (bomber wing) of Kesselring's *Luftflotte 2*. The signal read: *Report immediately which crews bombed in London prohibited zone. The Supreme Commander reserves the right to punish those commanders concerned by transferring to infantry.*

The attack on London incensed Winston Churchill's War Cabinet, and they were not prepared to let it pass without a suitable punishment to fit such an audacious crime. That night, Bomber Command turned its attention from the German industrial heartland, around the Ruhr, to Berlin. Eighty-one planes – Wellington, Whitley and Hampden bombers – set off from English airfields with reduced loads, the only way they could make the round trip without running out of fuel.

Ironically a similar fate befell the British planes. Thick cloud made navigation difficult, and many of the planes missed their legitimate military targets. Amongst the areas hit was Dahlem, a purely residential suburb of the German capital, where a school and a dairy farm were badly damaged.

The citizens of Berlin were not only angered, but thoroughly shocked. Hitler had promised them that enemy bombs would never fall on the capital; Göring had boasted as much. The raid embarrassed the two most senior men in the Reich's hierarchy. Their people felt a wave of disillusionment.

And more raids were to follow.

Chapter 86

(Friday 30th August 1940)

Heather was incurably optimistic that morning as she climbed into yet another Dominoe and prepared to take off. Pauline Gower had agreed that she and Alison could be released together the next day, and the knowledge that German raids had escalated considerably during the last week was not going to discourage her. She had a feeling that somehow everything would all fall neatly into place; the weather over France would be poor tomorrow, Stuart would be released, and by the end of the day (after a swift and energetic consummation somewhere) she would return to Hatfield as Mrs Stuart Innes. She knew some people thought she was being foolish to go ahead – Alison for one, Pauline Gower for another – and she sensed that some of the other girls were talking about her in a disapproving fashion. But wagging tongues had never bothered Heather. They merely strengthened her resolve.

Her task for the day was straightforward; deliver the Dominoe to Cosford in Shropshire, the other side of Wolverhampton, then return to Hatfield in another. She had never flown to Cosford before, and it was always fun to visit somewhere new. The same old RAF storage units were becoming rather tedious.

The weather was bright, with only a few patches of cloud here and there. Heather made good progress, heading north-west with a mild tail wind. Before long the distinctive outline of Oxford came into view off her port wing and shortly afterwards she passed directly over Banbury.

It was only then that the significance of her route sank home. She would be flying over her home town, Warwick, and very close to her parents, who were oblivious to the fact that their daughter was getting married the next day. She felt a pang of conscience.

Perhaps she should have told them. No, they would have insisted on making the journey down, and as last week had proved, there were no guarantees that it would actually take place. Better they didn't know and to tell them after the event.

Banbury to Warwick was easy flying, just follow the ribbon of the main A41, often in long straight stretches. She knew the road well and recognised more and more of the countryside the nearer to Warwick she flew. Her parents' house was on the southern edge of town.

Several miles away, she lowered her altitude and throttled back to reduce air speed. She had flown over the house before, but never in anything as large as a Dominoe; she just hoped someone was at home to appreciate it. As she approached the town, the countryside made way for houses and streets, and she concentrated hard. There was the turning off the main road, the lane leading to their drive entrance, and the house a hundred yards beyond. There was no one in sight. She pushed the stick forward and allowed the Dominoe to ease into a gentle dive. The house rushed by a hundred feet below and she banked round to see if the explosion of noise had had the desired effect.

It had. She caught a brief glimpse of her mother standing at the French windows, peering upwards. A second run had her mother standing in the centre of the lawn vigorously waving what appeared to be a white tea-towel. Heather waved an acknowledgment before climbing away and steering back on to her north-westerly course. Having skirted to the south of Birmingham, she located Cosford without difficulty and landed half an hour later.

The return journey was, as it turned out, in two parts; a lift in a Fox Moth to Cowley, then ferrying a brand new Tiger Moth back to Hatfield for training purposes. Funny, she thought, to be flying a Tiger hot off the production line back to the factory where they had been produced for so long.

"They're not tooled up to make 'em anymore at Hatfield," explained the dispatch manager. "Whereas we're churning 'em out up 'ere now."

Heather set off after lunch. She hadn't flown a Tiger Moth for ages and it seemed painfully slow compared with the Dominoes and Oxfords to which she had become accustomed. Thankfully Cowley to Hatfield was only a short hop of fifty miles or so.

She flew due east, and low, passing over the county border into Buckinghamshire and on into Hertfordshire. Shortly afterwards she caught sight of black smoke in the distance, plumes of it rising into the air; not from Hatfield, she judged, but further north. Probably Luton. A raid there would make sense, with quite a number of factories around that area.

As she flew nearer, keeping the smoke well to port, tiny black dots appeared, punctuating the sky ahead and above. They were interweaving, smaller dots ducking and diving around larger, slower ones. A full-scale dog fight was in progress, with German bombers intent on dropping their loads and British fighters trying to blast them out of the sky before they did. She stared in shocked fascination at the battle spreading out in front

324

of her. A fighter – Spitfire, Hurricane, Messerschmitt, she couldn't tell – plummeted earthward in a trail of smoke. Then a bomber exploded and that too fell to earth.

She was scared. The de Havilland factory was only a few miles away now, and rather than abandon her course she decided to stick to it and land as quickly as possible. On the ground was the safest place to be.

As she approached, the airfield appeared undamaged, so she made her usual approach, keeping an eye on the barrage balloons and coming in as straight as possible. The battle was forgotten as she concentrated fully on bringing the Tiger Moth down safely.

"Don't worry about elegance, Heather my girl," she said out loud as she reached the perimeter of the airfield. "Just put her down in one piece and get in that bloody shelter as fast as you can."

The landing felt good as the grass seemed to rise up and meet the undercarriage. A slight bounce, a slight loss of line, immediately corrected, and she was down.

It was sheer chance that the Messerschmitt Bf 110 witnessed her landing. The pilot had spent several minutes trying to shake off a Hurricane that had stuck to his tail as if it was glued there. Eventually he had succeeded in outrunning the British fighter. In the process, however, he had missed much of the battle. He had lost altitude and, quite unexpectedly, there was an aerodrome straight ahead of him and a biplane bumping to a halt along the grass. He adjusted his course slightly. As targets went, it was a sitting duck.

The cannon shells spat out from the nose, raking across the grass and straight through the fuselage, chunks of debris splintering in all directions. Glancing backwards he saw the nose tip forward and the propeller shatter in a hail of earth. His gunner added to the damage as they zoomed overhead. No great achievement to boast about back home, but one more enemy plane destroyed.

He considered going round for another run, but fuel was getting low and they needed to catch up with the bomber formation to offer any protection they could on the return journey.

Heather was unconscious when they lifted her carefully out of the cockpit. There was a great deal of blood. A tourniquet was hurriedly applied to her left leg, which was badly broken and almost severed at a point just below the knee. But there was little that could be done about the gaping wound in her side.

By the time the ambulance arrived, the all-clear was sounding, and a crowd gathered to watch the limp body being lifted onto a stretcher, loaded into the back, and driven off at speed through the gates. It was the first time anyone had been injured at Hatfield, and the shock was palpable.

*

The taxi Anson arrived two hours later. By then the damaged Tiger Moth had been towed away, and Alison saw nothing of the ripped fuselage and bloodstained cockpit. Pauline Gower called her in to the office and, with a choke in her voice, explained what had happened. The hospital had just telephoned.

Heather had been dead on arrival.

Chapter 87

(Saturday 31ˢᵗ August 1940)

As it turned out, the weather was clear over France, and Squadron leader Stuart Innes was not released. The men of Midas Squadron were dog tired; the previous day had been long and arduous, and they had almost certainly lost another pilot – Flying Officer George Mathews. His Spitfire had crashed in flames at low altitude and no one had seen him bail out. The order to scramble came early. Then, within minutes of being airborne, they were instructed to return to base.

"Wish they'd bloody well make up their minds," groaned Dan Rodigan as he flopped into a chair inside the ready room.

"Park's orders," explained Innes. "Just 109s and we're not to waste our time with small fry. Got to wait for the big boys."

"They're all E/As aren't they – all enemy aircraft?" said a fresh-faced beanpole of a lad called John Goodwin who had recently joined the squadron. "What difference does it make?"

Innes thought it was obvious, but this boy had a lot to learn.

"It's a deliberate ploy to squander our resources. Jerry sends over his fighters first to tempt us up to meet them and have a scrap. Then the bombers come along to hammer our airfields and we've got nothing in reserve to stop them. Worse still, we come home to an airfield full of craters and have nowhere to land. Park knows what he's doing."

"Well I hope they leave poor old West Malling alone for a while," said Rodigan. "She's looking decidedly sorry for herself at the moment. More craters around here than on the moon."

"I hope so too," said Innes. "Come on, we're released for the time being while those bandits stooge around looking for us. We'd better try and phone the girls and stop them coming down. This idea of getting married between sorties is becoming a bit ridiculous. The vicar's going to be very cheesed off with us too, messing him around like this."

"I'm sure he'll understand," said Rodigan encouragingly.

"Another contribution to church funds might swing it," said Innes with a grin.

There was no reply from the flat. Innes assumed they had already left and slammed the receiver down angrily.

They scrambled again mid-morning; a large bomber formation with fighter escort was heading up the Thames Estuary. German fighter pilots had changed their tactics recently, flying high above the bombers rather than alongside them, stacked in readiness to dive, thus giving them the advantage of height. They had also learnt that at higher altitudes, where the air was thinner, Bf 109s performed better and were more of a match for Spitfires.

The fighting was fierce, and the toll on German bombers high. Two were shot down. Stuart Innes was responsible for one of them, plus a Bf 109, though not without cost. When he returned to base, shell holes stretched obscenely across his starboard wing and fuselage.

"Damaged my kite, the bastards," he explained to his rigger. "But I got him. Went down like a stone."

"That's alright, sir," grinned the rigger. "I was a bit bored with nothing to do. We'll fix it for you. Might take a while though."

"How long?"

The young man scratched his head. "If there's no structural damage, a couple of hours maybe."

"See what you can do. Thanks. Have you seen Flight Lieutenant Rodigan?"

"He's back, sir, I saw him heading towards the officers' mess."

"Perhaps the girls have arrived." He marched across to the debriefing room and made his report, then to his room for a quick wash, and over to the mess. He saw Dan and Alison as soon as he walked in; they were sitting close together looking very serious. No sign of Heather.

"Hello, Ally," he called. "Good to see you. Look I tried to call but I must have just missed you. Sorry you've had a wasted journey, only there's no way it's going to be today. I really think we need to forget the whole thing for a while." He looked towards the lavatory door. "Heather powdering her nose?"

Alison stood up and took his hand. "No, Stuart, she isn't."

"Where is she then?"

The blank expression on Alison's face pre-empted her words. In a split second Innes sensed that something was wrong.

"Listen," he said. "If you've got bad news for me, shall we go outside? I think the fresh air might be beneficial." He lit a cigarette, and they walked out to the edge of the airfield, where thick woodland bordered the perimeter. Rodigan tagged on behind, keeping a respectable distance, as Alison told Innes what had happened and how Heather had

328

died. He listened as she spoke, then asked a lot of questions, absorbing every detail; like a debriefing. When she had told him all she knew, he gave her a huge bear hug.

"Thank you, Ally, you're a brave girl. Coming here to tell me this in person must have been a very difficult task for you. Now, if you'll excuse me, I'd like some time to myself. I'm sure you appreciate . . . under the circumstances." He turned and walked back towards the mess. "Don't go far, Dan," he called. "We're still 'available' officially."

'Available' meant ready to take off for combat in no more than fifteen minutes.

"Do you think he'll be alright?" asked Alison, with genuine concern.

"He's made of strong stuff, he'll be okay. There's plenty going on around here to take his mind off things."

"You'd better get back."

"I know. Is there any chance you could wait around until this evening? I've barely seen you."

"No, I need to be heading off. I'm glad I came to tell him the news in person, but I ought to go. There are things to do – the flat to sort out. Heather's parents don't know yet. I may need to help out there."

"Yes of course." Rodigan gripped her hand reassuringly. "Are *you* alright, Ally?"

"I'm fine. I did all my crying last night. I'll be alright. I need to sort out a way back to Hatfield."

As they kissed goodbye, Rodigan whispered: "Please take care. I couldn't bear it if . . ."

Alison hushed him with her mouth. "That's *my* line."

Chapter 88

As the *Luftwaffe* busied itself with its greatest assault yet on Fighter Command airfields yet, Christa Gormanns noticed a marked deterioration in her only patient's condition. *Reichsmarschall* Hermann Göring, she diagnosed, was suffering from early symptoms of nervous exhaustion. In public he put on a show of being a confident man in control of his position of power, but in private, behind the facade, he seemed to find decision making virtually impossible and was in a constant state of anxiety.

She mentioned this to Major Schmid when he came on board *Asia* at Göring's command. He shrugged his shoulders.

"It's hardly surprising. He keeps promising the Führer 'another three days of good weather and there will be no more RAF' – but it's not working out that way."

The meeting was brief. Göring wanted to forewarn Schmid of the instructions he intended issuing later the same day. With Hitler's blessing, the *Luftwaffe* was to prepare itself for a campaign of reprisal raids on London. And he wanted to know how this change of emphasis would fit in with the latest intelligence.

"By the end of the day, *Reichsmarschall*, most of Fighter Command's airfields in their Eleven Sector, that is the south-east of England, will be inoperable. Any further resources spent on them would be wasted. The *Abwehr* have provided us with some remarkable information recently. They have an agent with contacts at Fighter Command headquarters who has informed us that the British are hoping we will continue targeting their airfields to avoid the devastating blow to morale that attacks on London would bring. The mistaken raid a week ago has had stunning consequences."

"So the timing is right?"

"Intelligence supports it, certainly."

"And the Führer wishes it."

"Quite so."

Göring picked up a document and glanced at its content.

"Your report compares the numbers of British fighter planes we are destroying with production figures of new machines. They can't keep up. Barely fifty Spitfires left in the whole of England!"

"Perhaps less, *Reichsmarshall*. As for the Hurricanes . . ."

"They don't count. Inferior machines – our 109s can pick them off like flies."

Hurricanes did for your nephew, Schmid thought, having been party to the report on how Hans-Joachim Göring had met his end back in July. His body now lay at the bottom of Portland Harbour, courtesy of a squadron of inferior machines.

"It's the Spitfires that matter," said Göring, rapping his fingers nervously against the edge of his desk. "That is all, Schmid."

As Schmid left the carriage he heard the same word muttered over and over, drifting out from behind him.

"London . . . London . . . London." As if Hermann Göring was trying to convince himself he was doing the right thing.

Chapter 89

Midas Squadron was flying its fourth sortie of the day. They had scrambled again in the early afternoon, despite being a plane down, to help counter another attack on Croydon. Stuart Innes's Spitfire had not been ready and no spare was available, so he had bounced young Goodwin out of his and told him to sit this one out. Miraculously all had returned, and this time he was back in his own plane and heading for Biggin Hill to give protection from yet another raid.

Behind him in the formation, Dan Rodigan could tell from the tautness of his squadron leader's movements and the staccato commands over the radio that he was uncharacteristically tense. Who could blame him; his fiancée had been killed the day before what was supposed to be their wedding day. The tension was having a knock-on effect, and for the first time in weeks Rodigan felt scared again. But there was nothing anyone could do about it, and this was no time for being stood down for personal reasons. He just prayed that Stuart would keep his head and not make mistakes, or take unnecessary risks.

They battle-climbed to 17,000 feet, heading west into the sun, to gain the joint advantages of height and visibility. Once there, they banked in formation and immediately saw below what they had hoped for. Row upon row of German bombers, Dorniers mainly, riding above a thin cloud base and escorted by Bf 109s and 110s.

Innes's voice crackled in Rodigan's earpiece. "Bandits at three o'clock low. The bastards are beneath us for once . . . and it looks like we're not the only ones here to greet them." A flight of Hurricanes could be seen between themselves and the enemy formation, already making their attack. The Bf 109s were starting to break out to ward them off, whilst the 110s stayed tight in a defensive barrier.

"Good show," bellowed Innes. "They won't notice us until we're on top of them. Good hunting, all. Tally-ho!"

The Spitfires peeled off with exact precision and dived into the mass of vapour trails and tracer. Innes aimed directly at the Bf 110s, approaching with the sun behind him now. He chose his target in advance and focused on the Messerschmitt as it joggled and shook in his gun sights. His thumb was tense above the firing button as he dived nearer, waiting until the last possible moment before squeezing 'the tit'. The Browning machine guns spattered for several seconds and trails of bullets hurtled around and into the enemy plane. Suddenly it vanished from view as the Spitfire overshot. He glanced backwards but could see nothing. He knew it was a hit, but was it a kill?

Rodigan had followed him in, targeting another Bf 110. In his peripheral vision he glimpsed Innes's target ripping apart.

"You got him, Stu!"

"Thanks, Dan, first of several. I feel it in my bones."

They turned sharply, this time with the intention of attacking from below and behind. They were in the thick of the dogfight now, and without warning several Bf 109s were upon them. Rodigan twisted and turned to lose one on his tail. Suddenly it was gone, and another was ahead of him, and he managed to do some damage with a short burst as it crossed his path. He then climbed at full throttle to regain the height advantage.

Innes was fighting like a madman, taking on anything that came his way. He quickly dispatched a Bf 109, firing straight at it head on and only banking away at the very last moment. As he glanced below and behind, he saw the plane's propeller spinning through the air like a duff firework. A kill for sure. He stalked another for several minutes in a cat-and-mouse chase until he had closed in as far as he dared before firing. He knew from experience he had to be able to read the plane's markings to ensure that at least some of the bullets would hit home. He must have got the fuel tank, for the plane exploded in a huge fireball and fell in chunks, landing partly in a field and partly across a railway line.

He was at low altitude again. Plumes of black smoke were rising upwards several miles away. They hadn't been able to prevent the bombers from reaching Biggin Hill. Innes stared at the sight, and felt a great rage building up inside him.

"We should have stopped it!" he yelled, to no one but himself. "The bloody Hurricanes should have knocked out the Dorniers!" But he knew it was useless, they were outnumbered and the odds stacked against them.

Heather flashed into his mind, shot to pieces in her Tiger Moth, possibly by one of the Jerry bastards up there right now. If he could he would shoot down the lot of them. But he was too tired, too exhausted. Let someone else take a turn.

No! You're the squadron leader – so lead!

And get out of this straight line – you *never* fly straight when there are bandits about.

CRACK! A cannon shell pierced the engine cowling with a deafening explosion. A Bf 109 was attacking from above and behind, firing a long burst at him. Miraculously only one shell found its mark. A wisp of smoke trailed from the Merlin engine, and there was an immediate loss of power. With the shock of the attack, Innes momentarily lost control of the Spitfire and it twisted into a dive. It was unintentional, but it saved him from another burst of cannon fire from a second Messerschmitt. By the time he had regained control, the first German pilot was back on his tail. A third burst ripped into the fuselage, and Innes felt a sharp tugging at his thigh followed by a burning sensation as if he'd been branded with a red-hot poker. His brain acknowledged the pain but kept him focused on the task in hand. Survival.

He was very low now, flying over a farmyard. The Bf 109 was still with him. He weaved to left and right, denying the German his final kill, but no longer with the power to escape. If he drew his pursuer west as far as he could, there was a chance he might turn back for fear of running out of fuel.

His engine was overheating badly, and the smoke from the cowling was getting worse. Glycol was spewing everywhere and he could barely see ahead; dangerous enough at the best of times, but critically so when flying low with a Jerry on your tail.

Innes banked sharply to port, straining the throttle for every ounce of thrust. The choking Merlin responded surprisingly well, and the unexpected manoeuvre put some distance between him and the Bf 109. But he was now heading due east. Not good.

*

Dan Rodigan was out of ammunition.

His last burst, just three seconds, had made contact with a Dornier's starboard engine, not enough to down it but enough to send it limping back towards France with the hope it might ditch in the sea before reaching French soil.

The scrap was all but over. He gained height to survey the scene and glimpsed a Spitfire below being chased by a Bf 109. They were heading towards him. Rodigan tipped his plane into a dive and met the two planes head on, overshooting the Spit, and aiming at the Messerschmitt. He had no ammunition, but the German pilot wasn't to know that.

The bluff worked. The 109 swerved to starboard to avoid incoming fire, and pulled away southwards.

*

Innes banked to port. He had no idea who was in the other Spitfire, but he was bloody grateful to him.

His engine spluttered and coughed. Thick smoke gushed out in an acrid cloud, obscuring his view on all but the starboard side. His left foot was getting very hot indeed on the rudder pedal; he couldn't feel the right one at all. There was no way he could make it back to base, and he was too low to bail out. A crash-landing was his only option. Bad show, the squadron leader losing his kite like this.

With one hand he pushed back the Perspex hood to try and see better, but smoke billowed into the cockpit and engulfed him. Coughing and choking, he pulled it shut again.

Visibility was nil. He felt awfully tired, his brain numb, his body drained. There was nothing he could do other than stare at the altimeter, and that told him that the ground was very close. Instinctively he operated the flap lever and throttled back. The impact was bound to happen any second now. He thought of Heather again, and smiled.

*

Rodigan watched from above as the Spitfire pancaked into a hop field. It had slowed almost to stalling speed by the time it crashed and the impact was softened by the rows of canes that snapped like matchsticks and dragged along until everything settled in a mass of hop plants and dust. The pilot might have broken limbs, he guessed; smashed teeth, perhaps, and a messed up face. But there was a good chance he would survive the impact.

Then, as the Perspex canopy was pushed back, he glimpsed flames inside the cockpit, and the pilot writhing frantically as he fought to escape being burnt alive. The last image Rodigan had was of some men running through the field towards the tangled mess.

Chapter 90

(Monday 2nd September 1940)

Like Schneider before him, Moss spoke to the policeman at the gates of the Castle Bromwich factory, inquiring about the location of the personnel office, and was directed into the heart of the complex. He walked purposefully down the main roadway, mentally absorbing everything as he went.

The sheer size of the place took him by surprise, as it had Schneider. It was hard to envisage that this had all been built specifically to produce fighter aircraft. He was under the impression that Britain had not prepared for war, but this must have been planned years ago. Heydrich's briefing had been detailed enough to explain that Castle Bromwich had not converted to war work, it was purpose-built for making Spitfires.

Moss remembered driving past the site before the war; he had even landed at the aero club across the road a few times. In those days he had never really absorbed what was going on on the other side of the Chester Road. He couldn't remember what had stood there before, if anything. He strolled confidently along, diverging from the route the policemen had indicated. He wanted to see as much as possible whilst the opportunity presented itself. Part one of his mission was to locate and evaluate a man, an agent; the *Abwehr*'s spy in the factory. The more he knew about the place the easier his task would be.

It was lunchtime, and he was able to merge in with the crowds of workers taking a break. His luck held for nigh on half an hour, by which time he had gained a basic knowledge of the layout of the place; enough at least to sketch a rough plan from memory.

"Looking for something, pal?" A works policeman had pulled up behind him on a bicycle.

Moss put on a puzzled expression. "Indeed I am. Your colleague at the gate kindly directed me to the personnel office, but I seem to have taken a wrong turning somewhere."

"I should say so," said the policeman. "You're way off." He proceeded to direct Moss with patronising simplicity. Moss thanked him and walked on. He could sense that he was being watched and so followed the directions precisely.

At the personnel office, he explained to a dowdy-looking clerk with discoloured teeth and serious halitosis that he was trying to track down a relative who worked at the factory. The clerk had better things to do and leaned forward with his hand firmly on the counter between them.

"What for?"

"I beg your pardon?"

"What do you want to track him down for?"

"It's a personal matter."

"Can't give out information for personal reasons – against the rules." A request refused was a point scored for the clerk. He celebrated by picking his nose.

"But it's rather important."

"So's my work. Anything else I can help you with?"

"Please, his name is Mansell – Henry Mansell."

"I'm sorry, we can't give out information concerning employees without a good reason. Rules is rules. There's a war on, you know."

"Yes I know there's a war on, and that's why I'm here. I do have good reason. He's my cousin, and I've come all the way from London to try and find him, with some news."

"Sorry, unless I have a proper reason, I cannot divulge information."

"To be frank, I'm not entirely sure he works here at all. Could you just tell me that? A yes or a no would suffice. It it's no then I will look elsewhere."

"If he's your cousin, how come you don't know where he works?"

Moss hadn't expected such bureaucratic stubbornness. He wanted to climb over the counter and stamp on this little runt's head, which he would have gladly done without compassion. But he kept his cool and improvised. "We're not very close. I was told by my aunt, his mother, that he worked at one of the factories in Castle Bromwich but I can't remember which one exactly."

"Why don't you ask your aunt?"

"Because she's dead. That's the news I have for him. Henry's mother was killed in an air raid last week. House blown to pieces, in Canterbury. That's in Kent."

The clerk eyed him suspiciously for a moment. "Wait a mo," he said and moved away from the counter to confer with a man sitting at a desk. They spoke in low voices and looked across at him a couple of times. Moss was getting worried. This could go horribly wrong, he realised, if they chose to start asking him for more details. He hadn't thought his

337

story through as thoroughly as he should and any further questions might trip him up. Names, dates, addresses, family connections. He was angry with himself for not having prepared better for such sticklerism.

The clerk finished talking with his boss who had agreed that they may be able to help this man but would require further clarification before doing so. He returned to the counter. The man had gone. Strange, he thought. Very strange. He shrugged his shoulders and returned to more important clerical duties.

Later that afternoon, out of curiosity, he flicked through the card index of current employees. *Mansell, H* – yes there he was. But hang on, no, this was Howard, not Henry, and he was in his sixties; too old to be that chap's nephew. There was one other card with the same surname – Barbara – also in her sixties. Probably Howard's wife.

"Must be the wrong factory altogether," he mumbled as he closed the card index drawer.

But he couldn't stop thinking about the man, wondering why he had just disappeared like that. He mentioned it to his boss, who shared his puzzlement and told him to report it to the works police. The works police were grateful, thanked him for his vigilance and wanted to know everything he could remember about the man.

The description fitted the man who had been seen earlier trying to find the personnel office.

*

The Tyburn House was busy for a Monday. It was a warm and pleasant evening, and many of the customers had taken their drinks outside and were standing in groups chewing the fat. The pub was situated on high ground at a crossroads where the Chester Road crossed the Kingsbury Road; beyond the latter was Castle Bromwich Aerodrome, and to the right, on the far side of the Chester Road, the camouflaged, wedge-shaped roofs of the Spitfire factory stretched almost as far as the eye could see.

Moss ordered a pint of Ansells bitter and wandered out into the open. He took a sip and winced at the sour taste. He stood for a few moments gazing in the direction of the aerodrome. The faint throbbing of a distant aircraft engine could be heard above the occasional passing car or van. Shortly the revs increased and, between the rows of poplar trees, a Spitfire could be seen taxiing for takeoff. As it rose into the air, there were cheers from some of the men around him, a swell of pride from those who had spent their working lives putting the machine together.

"Bloody marvellous!" shouted one.

"We med that!" yelled another.

Moss noted which of the men spoke. Some leg pulling followed which brought responses from others.

"'Ere Terry, you're on wings, ain't yer?"

"So what?"

"Port bugger just fell off!"

"Ha bloody ha."

"You can talk, Ron. That'd be an assembly cock-up."

They laughed and joked, but never once did they take their eyes off the fighter as it circuited the aerodrome. They seemed mesmerised by the beauty of what they had helped to create, like fathers who have not yet come to terms with the sight of a newborn baby. The Spitfire disappeared into a bank of cloud, climbing away in the direction of a huge power station in the distance. Minutes later it reappeared, barely a speck in the sky at first, then gradually taking on the familiar shape. When it flew over the aerodrome and banked smoothly over their heads, another cheer went up, drowned out by the roar of the throaty Merlin engine. There followed a brief aerobatic display as the test pilot put the Spitfire through its paces before coming smoothly in to land.

"That's a sight I'll never get tired of," said one of the men.

Moss too was impressed. His instincts as a pilot had been heightened as he watched the impromptu show. He had never seen anything quite as smooth and powerful before – or as beautiful – and had certainly never flown anything like it. The idea of doing so excited him; the opportunity to take control of one would come soon as part two of his mission.

A couple of older men had caught his attention during the test flight, one was grey-haired and the other almost entirely bald. It was clear from their faces and the way they watched that they took more than an impartial interest in the show. He edged closer to them.

"That was quite something, I must say! I have never seen a Spitfire that close up before."

"You haven't lived then, mate," replied the grey-haired man. "She's an absolute beauty."

"Did you make her?"

"We did our bit."

"I really envy you, being involved in producing a magnificent plane like that."

The bald man found this amusing. "It's only a factory, mate. We just mekk 'em . . . we didn't design it. Any road, what do you do that makes a production line look glamorous?"

"I'm a pen pusher, in London. Very dull."

"What you doing up here then? That's a bloody long way to push a pen . . . London to Brum."

Moss looked down to the ground. "I came to try and find someone who works here – to tell him his mother has been killed." He gave them the air raid story.

"Sorry to hear that, mate, rather you than me."

"Quite." Moss tried to keep as mournful an attitude as possible. "I tried the personnel office over there but they wouldn't help me."

"Officious buggers. Surely under the circumstances . . ."

"The thing is, I can't be sure he works at this particular factory. He left London a while ago and no one has heard from him. The only person who knew for sure was his mother, and she's gone."

"What's his name, this bloke?"

"Henry Mansell."

They shook their heads in unison.

"Never heard of 'im."

"It's hardly surprising, this factory is a huge place." It had been a long shot; nevertheless, Moss was disappointed.

"Mark you," added the grey-haired man, "Charlie the Checker might know. He's an inspector – knows everyone, does Charlie."

"Do you know where I might find him?"

"The Bagot Arms probably. Next pub along the main road here. He usually pops in on his way home. To be frank, him at the Bagot and us here is about how we like it."

"Oh, why is that?"

"Can't stick the man. Mean sort of bloke, don't care about anyone but hisself. Never crossed him personally, but best not to have too much to do with him. Any road, he knows everyone. He's your best bet."

Moss took another sip of beer and pulled a face.

"Not keen on the local brew then?" said the bald man.

"I've tasted better. Actually it doesn't really taste of much at all to be honest," replied Moss.

"Agreed. 'Ere, what's the difference between a pint of Ansells and mekkin love in a boat?"

Moss shook his head.

"Nowt. They're both fucking close to water!"

Someone chuckled but most had clearly heard it a dozen times before.

Moss placed his half-full glass on the window ledge. "Thank you for your help, I'll see if I can find this Charlie right now."

It wasn't difficult. Everyone seemed to know Charlie Rix. Moss found him within minutes of entering the Bagot Arms, leaning against the bar with a pint glass in his hand. The inspector eyed the stranger suspiciously at first, but the offer of a drink instantly broke down any barriers and Moss soon had him answering questions as if the two were old school mates.

"Mansell – arr I know him. Oldish bloke with specs. Werked for Morris at Cowley for donkey's years, if I remember right."

"This man is in his twenties," explained Moss. "And he only came up here to work this year. I doubt it's the same person."

"Howard's getting' on a bit. He's got a lovely wife mind . . . Barb."

"My cousin is Henry, not Howard."

Rix thought for a moment. "'Enry Mansell . . . that name rings a bell for some reason, but can't think why. Can't place him at the fact'ry. But it's a big place – I don't know everyone." He took a long draught of beer. "Mind you, they're tekkin on at a fair old rate these days. Could be new. Could be one of the Supermarine boys."

"Is there any way you could find out for me? It's rather important." Once again he told the mother-killed-in-an-air-raid story.

"Who did yow speak to up in personnel?" Moss described the officious clerk as best he could. "Oh, Cooper."

"You know him?"

"Arr, I know him. He's a miserable cunt at the best of times."

"Do you think you might be able to . . ."

Rix pursed his lips. "I'll see warra can do, but he ain't easy to get round. The only thing interests him is notes – banknotes like. He collects them as an 'obby."

Moss needed no further hint. He took his wallet from his pocket, keeping it at waist level between the two of them, and handed over two pound notes.

"Here's one for his collection, and one for yours. I don't mind paying if it helps find Henry. To be honest, Mr Rix, I just want to get this over with and back to London. I have a wife and children there and I want to be with them. This bombing is very worrying."

"Arr, we gerrem up here an' all, in case yow ain't 'eard." He pocketed the money and drained his glass. "I can afford to buy another pint now. Same again?" When the drinks arrived, he said: "I'll ask around . . . see what I can find out. Sorry, I didn't catch yowr name."

"David Green."

"Alright, Dave, I'll be in here same time tomorrow. If this 'Enry Mansell works over the road I'll know it by then. Might even bring him with me if he fancies a pint."

"That would be splendid, thank you."

Moss left the pub and caught a bus into the centre of Birmingham. In a cheap hotel close to New Street Station, he lay on his bed with a glass of vodka in his hand and thought how he would approach agent Quaver when they met. Somehow he had to assess him without generating suspicion. Heydrich's brief had offered little guidance on how to carry out this part of the operation. It might take time, and he didn't have much, that much Heydrich had stressed.

He hoped that the man Rix would come up with either Quaver in person, or at least an address for him. He also doubted Cooper, the clerk, would ever see his pound note. He didn't care. He was a step closer to Quaver now, and that was all that mattered. Not a bad day's work. He felt relaxed and was enjoying the soporific effects of the vodka. It also helped to take away the lingering taste of the Ansells beer.

He would have dozed off had the air raid siren not sounded. His stomach was grumbling furiously, so instead of finding a shelter he went in search of a restaurant that placed business before safety.

Chapter 91

(Tuesday 3rd September 1940)

The remaining pilots of Midas Squadron had reached a point of physical weariness beyond exhaustion. They were waking at dawn, flying four or five sorties a day, then slumping into bed for a few hours of delicious oblivion from their nightmare existence. They were too tired to eat, too tired to get drunk, too tired even to think.

Dan Rodigan's feelings were frozen. Emotions wouldn't come, and when he heard that Stuart Innes was in a hospital in East Grinstead with multiple injuries and severe burns, he felt neither sadness for his friend's predicament nor relief that he had cheated death. He imagined it would happen later, when this was all over.

A group captain came to congratulate him on his promotion to the rank of squadron leader. Rodigan shook his hand without the words fully registering. He was now in charge of Midas. *That's good,* he thought, *shame Stuart isn't around to hear the news*. Then it occurred to him that if Stuart was around he would not have the promotion. Muddled thinking.

Losses were high, and the airfields were being pounded on a daily basis. As soon as bomb craters had been filled, telephone wires reconnected and buildings repaired into some sort of working condition, another raid smashed them up again. Any longer and Fighter Command would cease to exist.

West Malling was eventually hit so badly and so often that the decision was made to class it as inoperable for the time being. When Midas Squadron returned from one sortie, they were unable to land and had to divert to Biggin Hill and Kenley; even then it was amidst a maze of flag-marked craters and burnt-out aircraft. Once they had re-grouped Squadron Leader Rodigan announced that they had been transferred to a new base, Tangmere, near Chichester in Sussex, which had so far avoided the worst of the bombing.

They flew down early the next morning.

Opposite the Bagot Arms was Pype Hayes Park, a large stretch of undulating grassland dotted with occasional trees that gradually sloped down to a small lake. The wider expanses of grass were covered with debris to discourage enemy aircraft and to give parachutists an uncomfortable landing should they be foolish enough to try. Fear of invasion was as high as it had ever been, and the mass of concrete blocks, old prams, bicycle frames and tyres was added to daily.

On the edge of the park, directly facing the pub across the Eachelhurst Road, was a public convenience. From behind a metal grill in the only male cubicle, Moss watched as the first trickle of workers turned up outside the doors, waiting for opening time. He was close enough to be able to recognise faces, and Charlie Rix's arrival would not go unnoticed. He had spent most of the day walking around the perimeter of Castle Bromwich Aerodrome, learning its layout from all angles and observing the activity of the ground staff. He avoided the border along the Chester Road facing the main entrance to the factory, where the barrier was permanently manned. For all he knew, the site policeman who had confronted him might be on duty and spot him.

Tucked out of sight behind some trees, he had trained his binoculars on the ground staff, identifying their various functions and trying to memorise faces. There had only been a couple of test flights all day. He had expected more. He had assumed that the flight he witnessed the day before had been the last of several; but perhaps it had been one of just a few. If so, they could not be producing more than about fifty or so Spitfires a month, in which case they were either incredibly inefficient or they had serious production problems. Whichever, it was good news for the *Luftwaffe*, and presumably agent Quaver was keeping them informed of the fact.

The test pilot looked familiar. He was tall, with grizzled hair and boyish features. Through the binoculars Moss watched him complete his test procedure then sit in a car at the edge of the aerodrome to fill out some paperwork. The low production levels didn't justify office space for such things, so it seemed. Moss wasn't certain, but he thought the pilot might be the chap who had flown to Cape Town and back virtually non-stop just before the war. Everyone at his flying club had been talking about it at the time. What was his name . . . Henshall? No, Henshaw, that was it. Alex Henshaw.

The doors of the Bagot Arms opened at precisely six thirty. Moss stood on the toilet seat and watched and waited. He wanted to make his appearance after Charlie the Checker, to see whether or not he had Mansell with him. He had been given a rough description in Heydrich's instructions, enough to make an identification. This precaution was also in case Rix had decided to report him instead of help him. Unlikely, he thought, but not out of the question.

After a while his legs began to ache, so he stepped down and walked around in the confined space, bending his knees. He heard several people come in to use the urinal, then someone tried the cubicle door, shaking the handle.

"How long are you gonna be in there, pal?"

"As long as it takes to have a shit in peace!"

"Sod you then, I'll hold it 'til I get home."

Back on the seat, Moss continued his vigil. It wasn't long before he saw something that made his caution worthwhile.

Along the Chester Road came Charlie Rix, wheeling a bicycle on the pavement. On either side of him were two policemen, also with cycles. As they approached the pub, they leaned their bikes against a wall, then one of them pointed to the side entrance, which led to a beer garden, and positioned himself next to it. The other, accompanied by Rix, walked towards the main entrance. All three entered the pub at the same time.

The bastard, thought Moss. He was surprised; he had half expected Rix not to turn up at all, or without Mansell and to try and squeeze him for more money in exchange for an address. But not this. He jumped down from the toilet and went to unbolt the door. Then he stopped. This was a safe place to be, and he needed to know the outcome of his non-appearance. Better to stay put.

He stepped up again and lit a cigarette. Rix had clearly expected him to be waiting inside the pub because they soon came out again and stood together in conversation. Rix looked puzzled, and the policemen unimpressed. After a few minutes they went back in again, presumably to give it a while longer for David Green to turn up. But soon they were out again. The policemen pedalled off down the main road.

Charlie Rix went back inside. He would be out at some stage, and Moss was intent on following him, although he had no idea whether it might be in five minutes or several hours. He needed to be able to keep up with him, so he left his vantage point and hurriedly went in search of a bicycle. Fifteen minutes later he was back with one, freshly stolen, which he propped up against the side of the toilet block.

Just before eight, Charlie Rix came out of the pub, grabbed his bike and started cycling away down the side of the park, along Eachelhurst Road. Moss climbed onto the saddle of his bike and followed, keeping on the grass, parallel with Rix but a good fifty yards behind. He wasn't familiar with cycles, made a hash of the gears, and the distance between them increased. Fortunately, the road was long and curved to the left, and by cycling in a straight line Moss managed to make up the loss. A stream forced him to veer towards the road, and shortly afterwards he saw Rix turning off into a side road. Ahead of him Rix had turned left. Several more turnings later, Rix dismounted outside a small house halfway along a quiet cul-de-sac.

Moss cycled past the end of the road, glanced across to see Rix wheeling his bike through a green gate, and rode on.

*

The bombs started falling at about eleven that evening. The raid was small-scale, but enough to worry people into their shelters, there to listen with trepidation as sporadic explosions brought death and destruction to the unlucky ones.

The ditch in which Moss lay ran along the edge of a narrow stretch of waste land that bordered on to Charlie Rix's back garden, with only a low wicker fence separating them. At the rear of the garden was a mound of earth, beneath which was an Anderson shelter. Inside the shelter, alone, was Charlie Rix.

Moss was cold and stiff; he was hungry too, not having wanted to let the house out of his sight to go in search of food. Arms and legs had turned numb long ago, and when he eventually crept forward he had to stop and rub feeling back into them.

Until darkness fell, he had watched the house from a distance, cycling past the end of the road, or tramping purposefully across the waste land as if taking a short cut. There were people about, but they paid him no attention. Then, when it was safe to do so, he settled in the ditch . . . and waited.

The front door of Rix's house was at the side of the building and could be seen clearly from where he crouched. At around nine thirty, a woman, a mere silhouette in the twilight, had come out of the house, a bag under her arm, and walked down the path to the road where she turned right and disappeared from view. Mrs Rix? So was he alone now, or were there young or old Rixes living there? Moss had no idea and no way of finding out; the blackout regulations made the chances of peeping through windows out of the question. He decided not to risk anything.

Eventually the air raid siren sounded. Two minutes later he watched as Charlie stumbled across the back garden by the feeble light of a torch, wearing pyjamas under a dressing gown. Even against the wailing Moss could hear him cursing as he bent low to get inside the Anderson shelter. He heard back doors banging shut and snippets of conversations as others in the street did the same.

Two more minutes. No one else emerged from the house.

Five more minutes. Still no one.

Rubbing his legs to restore circulation, Moss crawled gingerly forward out of the ditch towards the wicker fence. A gate at one end was slightly ajar, the lower hinge broken long ago and never mended. It creaked loudly as he moved it. He stopped dead in his tracks, waiting for a reaction. But there were other sounds to smother it; anti-aircraft guns firing, bombs dropping. Brilliant against the darkness, several searchlight batteries pierced the ink-black sky in the distance. He pulled out a torch, smothering the beam with his hand as he switched it on, and approached the side of the shelter.

As he peered round to the front, he saw the bright orange glow of a cigarette. Rix was standing in the entrance, watching the searchlights. Moss heard a throaty cough, followed by a spitting sound.

Rix heard nothing and saw only the brilliant, blinding glare of a torch beam full in his eyes as Moss struck.

"What the f . . . !" was all he could manage before the air was crushed out of his lungs, and he was sprawling on the floor of the shelter with the full weight of someone on top of him. Both legs were pinned firmly down, and his arms had contrived to end up underneath his body. One of them, his left, hurt like hell. He couldn't move an inch.

"Keep your mouth shut!" hissed Moss. "If you say a word, you're a dead man." He shone the torch momentarily into his own face until he was sure Rix had recognised him. "Remember me?" He turned the beam back on to Rix; it was obvious from his expression that he did.

"That woman who left – your wife?" Rix nodded. "When will she be back?"

"Gone to her mother's."

"When will she be back!"

"Late. . . not when there's a raid on. My arm, I think it's broke!"

"I should break your neck," said Moss. The noise of aircraft engines was getting louder; the sound of an explosion came from a few streets away. He hardly noticed. "You brought policemen with you. Why?" There was venom in his voice, partly adrenalin, partly deliberate to scare Rix. "*Why!*"

"What's goin' on? What d'yow want from me? I didn't dob on you, honest!"

"Then why the police?"

"Cooper called them . . . he'd already reported yow."

"Liar!" Moss shook him violently.

"It's true, honest! When I went up to ask about this bloke, Cooper's boss 'ad me in his office like a shot. He called the police, an they asked me loads of questions. They were a man in civvies with 'em an all. What did I know about 'Enry Mansell, 'ow did I know him, why was I asking after him, what yow looked like . . . all that bollocks."

"And I suppose you told them."

"Why not! It's only to 'elp some poor bugger find out 'is mum's died. What's wrong with that?"

"What did the police say at the pub – when I didn't show?"

"To wait an hour. If yow 'adn't turned up by then to go 'ome."

"And if I did?"

"To nip outside to the phone box an ring 'em." Rix tried to stare past the torch beam. "What's this all about any road?"

"None of your concern. What about Mansell, do you have his address?"

"Ha bloody ha!"

Moss bore down on the body beneath him. Rix screamed, but any sound was swamped outside by the sounds of the raid.

"There is nothing amusing about your situation, my friend. How do I get hold of Mansell . . . speak!"

"Look I don't know what's going on, nor do I fucking care. All I know is there's no one called 'Enry Mansell workin' at the fact'ry. Cooper let it slip."

"What! Are you certain?"

"Yes! *There's no 'Enry Mansell workin' at Castle Bromwich!* Either yow've got the wrong name or the wrong bloody fact'ry."

Moss relaxed his grip. He knew he hadn't got the wrong name . . . or the wrong factory. But the name obviously had some significance, enough to warrant his being sought after by the police. Something was seriously wrong with this whole situation. If there was no Henry Mansell working at the factory, who then was feeding intelligence back to the *Abwehr*?

The whine of a bomb plummeting to earth too close for comfort broke into their world. The ground shook as it exploded nearby. Moss's priority now was to get away fast and make his report.

"Will yow let me go now?" Charlie Rix's voice was tight with panic.

Moss made no reply but moved away towards the entrance and watched Rix pick himself up very sluggishly off the ground.

"Listen, pal, I've remembered summat. I thought that name rang a bell – 'Enry Mansell. I got chatting to a bloke in the Bagot, ooh a couple of months ago now, and I'm pretty sure his name were . . ."

But Moss's mind was elsewhere and he was no longer listening. As Rix reached a kneeling position, wincing with the pain in his arm, Moss sprang at him and wrapped an arm round his neck. With a knee in the small of his back, he twisted Rix's head violently to one side until there was a loud crack.

Charlie the Checker slumped to the floor – dead.

Chapter 92

(Wednesday 4th September 1940)

Early the next morning, a telephone rang in a house in a road not far from the summit of Richmond Hill. The man who answered was slurred in his speech, due partly to being still half asleep and partly to an excess of whisky the night before. He heard a Mr Mossman asking him for an appointment to discuss some important supplies needed for a house in Soho. He felt it imperative to meet at once, by which he meant that very day.

Without asking when or where, the man agreed, slammed the receiver back onto its cradle and went back to sleep. When he woke again an hour later, the woman lying next to him was smoking her first of the day.

If she hadn't asked who it was calling earlier, he would probably have forgotten all about it.

*

As Moss walked past the Ritz, a doorman was opening a car door for a lady wearing a fur stole and a very expensive evening dress. Round her shoulder hung a morocco-covered box containing her gas mask. She swept in through the entrance with an air of indifference to her surroundings that made him cringe. War to her, he thought, is a game played by other, lesser beings who make the sacrifices; and no doubt she'd be one of the first to pamper to the new lions of London society in a few months from now. Moss hated her.

A hundred yards or so further on he saw Triangle's diminutive figure standing outside Green Park Station, a newspaper under his arm. No routine of recognition was necessary this time. As soon as they had noticed each other, Moss turned in to the park and strolled along Queen's Walk, slowing his pace as an indication that Triangle should catch up with him. Soon he sensed rather than saw the little man by his side.

"This is a bit risky." The Welsh accent seemed more pronounced than the last time they had met.

"It's as good as anywhere. I wasn't followed, so if you weren't either then we should be safe." Moss never once looked at him, keeping his eyes firmly on the pathway ahead. "I have an urgent task for you."

"Oh yes, and what's that?"

"To send a priority message to our mutual friends – by the fastest means possible."

"Dear me, that does sound serious." Triangle sounded almost flippant which annoyed Moss.

"Tell them agent Quaver is blown. He is not working at the Castle Bromwich factory. I suspect he is being run as a double agent by British Intelligence. Tell them not to believe anything he sends them."

Triangle whistled in a long downward glissando. "My word, you have been a busy boy. Is that true then?"

"Of course it's true, you fool. Would I be wasting my time telling you if it wasn't?"

"Well in that case I think I had better do as you say. That is a priority message if ever I heard one. *Agent Quaver blown, not working at Castle Bromwich, possible double agent, ignore all his messages.*"

"Can you remember that?"

"Of course."

"Then do it."

"Why can't you do it yourself if it's that urgent?"

"Because I do not have the means, you ignoramus. I have no access to a transmitter."

"There's rude."

"Nor can it wait to be couriered. This message is extremely important. You must promise me you will send it by radio immediately."

"I promise." They had reached the far side of the park. Buckingham Palace stood majestically to their right, not a sign of bomb damage visible. The Mall stretched to their left.

"What are you going to do now?" asked Triangle.

"I have another task to perform, then I am leaving Britain."

"And what about Quaver?"

"If I knew where to find him, I would very much like to kill him. But I don't, so it is up to our betters to decide how to deal with him – and to discover if the rot has spread any further." He turned his back on Triangle and started to walk away. Over his shoulder he said: "Fail to send the message and I will track you down and kill *you*. Goodbye, it has been a pleasure."

"Wait a moment!" Triangle pulled a notepad out of his pocket and flicked through it. Then he tore out a blank page and hurriedly scribbled something on it in pencil. "Here, this might be of interest to you." He pressed the paper into Moss's hand.

"What is this?"

"The name and address of a woman in Coventry. Quaver's woman. I think you might find him there."

Moss glanced at the piece of paper. "Thank you. But how . . ."

It was Triangle's turn to walk away. "Just some insurance I took out a while ago," he called. "Goodbye and good luck." He crossed the road and passed Buckingham Palace, heading towards Victoria.

As Moss walked in the opposite direction along The Mall towards Trafalgar Square, wending his way back towards Euston Station, he remained deep in thought. The idea of tracking down and eliminating Quaver was very tempting. It was part of his instructions, but it might be dangerous. His priority lay firmly in another direction now. Steal a Spitfire and fly it to France. Nevertheless, the Coventry address was a gift, and very difficult to ignore, especially as he was returning to the Midlands anyway. He had decided Castle Bromwich was where he would take the plane. There were plenty of aerodromes in the south much nearer to France, but his chances of getting away with it were much slimmer there. Castle Bromwich was a better option.

The address was a gift indeed. Where the hell did Triangle get it from?

*

Less than an hour later, Major Joseph Atkins was sitting on a bench in St James's Park. He watched as agent Snow approached. What would it be this time, he wondered; another handout in exchange for information? It usually was with Snow.

"Hello," said the Welshman, as he sat down. "Decent of you to see me at such short notice."

"What do you want? I'm a busy man." Atkins disliked Snow and didn't care if it showed.

"I have something rather special for you, at a special price of course."

"Really, and just how special is that?"

"It concerns details of a German agent – one you know nothing about."

"I very much doubt that. We have the *Abwehr* sown up, as you very well know."

Snow adopted a supercilious tone as he played his trump card. "He's nothing to do with the *Abwehr*. He works for the Nazi Security Service direct – the SD – *Sicher* something or other . . ."

"*Sicherheitsdienst?*"

"That's the one. So the *Abwehr* know nothing about him. They don't even know he exists!"

"So how do you know about him?"

"I'm his contact. I was talking to him earlier, not a quarter of mile from where we're sitting."

"And you are prepared to give him to us, but at a price, is that right?"

"That's right."

"How much?"

"A thousand pounds."

"A thousand pounds! That's outrageous." Atkins stood up to leave. "You're mad, and what's more you're wasting my valuable time . . ." He began to walk away, knowing full well that Snow would not allow him to do so.

"I tell you it's true . . . one hundred percent!" said Snow, hurrying alongside him. "I have information, urgent information which he has given me to pass on to the SD. I'm offering it to you instead. He knows Quaver has been turned and is working for you as a double agent. And that's going to make them wonder about the others, isn't it? Myself included. This could blow your entire network." He paused for effect. "And I can save it for you."

"You're bluffing." Atkins knew he wasn't. He felt a shiver around the back of his scalp, and was suddenly taking Snow very seriously.

"I'm not bluffing! If I was I wouldn't be asking such a price, would I? And there's more. I'm offering you the chance to intercept this agent. I know where you can find him before he disappears back to Germany to report in person what he has told me, in case I let him down . . . which I might well do."

"For a thousand pounds?"

"For a thousand pounds."

The MI5 man stopped walking and stared down at Snow. "You nasty, conniving, treacherous . . ." He stopped himself in mid flow. "Come on, it's time you spoke to the big boys, right now." He hailed a taxi and gave an address in Shepherds Bush. As they sat and watched London go by outside the window, Atkins shook his head in wonderment.

"So you're working for the SD as well, eh? You really are a totally amoral bastard, you know that don't you? You're our agent Snow, you're the *Abwehr*'s agent Johnny. What the hell do the SD call you – Triple?"

The Welshman grinned smugly.

"Not quite, boyo. But you're on the right lines."

Chapter 93

(Thursday 5th September 1940)

The Norburys were not particularly religious and agreed to have Heather's funeral at Hatfield rather than arrange for her to be brought all the way up to Warwick. They travelled down by train and Alison met them at the station. The funeral party was small. There were no other relatives, just Pauline Gower, her adjutant and two other women from the ferry pool who had not been given chits for the day.

Afterwards, Alison took the Norburys to a hotel for tea. They talked somberly about the war, and rationing, and the weather; anything to avoid the thought that they had just seen Heather's remains being lowered into the ground and buried forever. Then they walked back to the station together and said their goodbyes. It all seemed like a dream. Alison felt she was watching herself doing these things, that she was not personally involved. It was very strange. And people kept popping into her mind, pretty much at random – Lucas Kelly, Jan-Arne Krobol, even Margery Ashford-Hope – then disappearing again, like a slide show of her own personal history.

Back at the flat she felt thoroughly depressed. Heather's clothes, her handbag, cigarette case and lighter were still lying around, as if she might pop out of her bedroom at any moment and say, "Fancy a bloody big gin, Ally?" Mrs Norbury hadn't felt up to sorting out her daughter's things. She said she would come down another time; and Alison had avoided the finality of putting them all away somewhere.

Tears welled up in her eyes. She lay down on the sofa and let her emotions loose. When the crying was over, she made two telephone calls, one to Pauline Gower asking if she could be relieved for a couple of days to come to terms with Heather's loss, which Pauline readily agreed, and the other to her parents asking if they would pick her up from Castle Bromwich Aerodrome. She would try and cadge a lift up there and phone from the Midlands Aero Club office once she arrived; if Arthur, the secretary, was around and didn't mind. Nothing was wrong, she assured them. She just wanted to see them.

Pauline was sympathetic as ever and arranged a lift for her in an Oxford. That would take her to Cowley; from there it should be easy to pick up a taxi plane to the Birmingham area. Alison offered to fly herself, but Pauline would have none of it. At a time like this, she said, it would be better for both the plane and Alison to let someone else take the controls.

At Cowley she didn't have to wait long. An Anson was doing the rounds and, although not scheduled to land at Castle Bromwich, the pilot was happy to make a diversion for her. The duty officer wore a mock frown, but said nothing.

The Anson touched down on the far side of the aerodrome, away from the clubhouse, where it was least likely to be an obstruction to other aircraft. Alison shouted thanks to the pilot and waved as she stepped out onto the grass clutching her overnight bag. The plane had been stationary for barely thirty seconds before it was taxiing away again. She watched as it rose into the air, banked towards the east and disappeared beyond a wedge of low cloud. She slung the bag over her shoulder and walked round the aerodrome, cutting the corner near the Tyburn House on the Chester Road perimeter, behind the control tower and to the clubhouse.

*

Moss saw the Anson land through his binoculars. Its purpose baffled him at first, then when a woman in blue uniform climbed out and the plane took off immediately, he guessed it was a transport plane. The woman was about two hundred yards away from where he lay. Her back was to him as she watched it take off. He did not recognise the uniform – an RAF unit of some description, but he had no idea what. She had a good figure. He wished she would turn round so he could see if she was pretty.

He was hidden in a tiny copse in the deep undergrowth that ran along the Kingsbury Road. From there he could not be seen, and from the aerodrome someone would have to be standing only feet away to notice that some of the tall grass had been flattened. If anything was to give him away it would be the reflection of the sun off his binoculars, and that was unlikely as there had barely been any sunshine all day. Beside him lay an empty coffee flask and the remains of a packed lunch, prepared for him reluctantly by a miserable night porter at his hotel.

The day had been devoted to this uncomfortable vigil for good reason; to find a means of infiltrating the airfield. He was focusing on ground crew, someone he could get to know, then coerce into helping him achieve his aim of getting into a Spitfire with a full tank of fuel. The controls he felt sure he could learn in a few minutes; and a few minutes was all he would have.

There were few candidates. He ruled out approaching a test pilot. The only one he had seen all day was the one who had given the show two days earlier. It was definitely Alex Henshaw, Moss realised, now he had had a chance to observe him through binoculars. He had never met him but pictures of him had been in all the papers when he'd flown to Cape Town and back. Moss remembered one of him being lifted out of the cockpit of his plane when he landed back in England, too exhausted to climb out himself. And if there had been any doubts they were soon expelled when he witnessed again the remarkable Henshaw skills as he put a new Spitfire through its paces. The precision with which he controlled the plane was breathtaking.

Henshaw was not his man. Too sharp-witted, too strong-willed by far, he imagined. And his comings and goings were erratic. He had a fast two-seater car that he disappeared in from time to time. Impossible to keep tabs on. A couple of the ground crew were possibles, both young and more likely to be won over. They spent much of their time around the large flight shed at the far end of the field. Both owned bicycles and would be easy enough to track when they left at the end of a shift.

Then the girl arrived in the transport aircraft and his plans changed completely.

He took no real notice of her initially, other than to admire her figure and to wonder if she had looks to match. She stood watching the plane head off to the east. Then she turned round.

Moss's eyebrows rose as high as it was possible for eyebrows to reach. Through his binoculars he followed her across the airfield and into the clubhouse. He saw her come out again and chat with a man as they smoked together. Later a car pulled up and she ran to greet the driver and his female passenger with a hug each. Her bag went into the boot, they all got into the car and it drove off up the Chester Road in the direction of Sutton Coldfield.

Moss threw down the binoculars. Lying back in the grass he stared up at the sky, his mind racing with the possibilities this turn of events presented.

"Well, well. It is a small word we live in," he mused. "A very small world indeed."

Chapter 94

Marion fell back on the bed, exhausted, and ran a hand through her hair. It was matted with perspiration.

"Thank heavens the siren didn't start," she panted. "That was the best yet – by far!"

Schneider chuckled. "We wouldn't have heard it. There are some things even Göring can't interfere with." He pulled Marion back close to him. He was exhausted too. Their lovemaking had been intense, the physical demands on each other greater than anything he had experienced before. With Renate it had always been good; but always the same, never varying in intensity. Predictable. With Marion, each time seemed to be striving for something deeper, more passionate, more fulfilling. And not just in bed. He felt she was a woman whose emotional dam had burst, experiencing many things for the first time, and whose life was being swept forward in a new direction.

Schneider felt the same, and he loved her.

Lying in a haze of post-coital contentment, he wondered again why they had let him come to Coventry, all arranged so hurriedly the night before. They had tried to pretend it was another reward for good behaviour, but there was no hiding the edge of urgency amongst them; Laurel, Hardy, and Uncle Mac who had turned up unexpectedly with the major, Atkins. Before he knew it he found himself being bundled out of the safe house and into a waiting car.

Spend a little time with your lady friend like last time, he was told, *for services rendered*. The VI would take care of the next transmission. There was a flap on for certain. But what the hell . . . if it meant spending time with Marion he wasn't about to complain.

He knew they were out there, watching the house. He had first noticed them when he went out to buy a newspaper at the corner shop that morning. Two of them – one leaning against a wall further up the street, another sitting in a car, smoking. From the front window he had seen them change shifts mid-afternoon. When he had taken the dustbin out into the back alley after dinner for Marion, he'd noticed another, hanging around where it joined the street. Three, possibly more.

Were he and Marion in danger? Surely not. But if not, what was the point of them being there?

His mind mulled over the possibilities as he gradually drifted into sleep, Marion's warm body next to him. Perhaps his cover had been blown. Maybe fifth columnists were onto him. At this precise moment he didn't care. He was happy. He slept.

What seemed like seconds later, the air raid siren wailed.

Chapter 95

(Friday 6th September 1940)

The Voluntary Interceptor sat patiently in the back bedroom of the safe house. He tapped out Quaver's call sign and waited for the acknowledgment. It came almost immediately. A good strong signal tonight. Referring to the columns of coded letters on his notepad, he tapped away, slowly and with the occasional rehearsed error, imitating Schneider's poor technique. When it was finished he felt pleased with how it had gone.

A second acknowledgment came through from *Hamburg*, followed by the beginning of what appeared to be a long transmission, possibly with questions requiring answers. The VI ignored it and packed up the equipment. He wasn't chancing his luck without Quaver present or, more to the point, without a brief from Ruskin. They could always claim a raid had forced the interruption.

*

In Hamburg, Quaver's message was decoded and absorbed.

His girlfriend, Ruby, had let slip that brother Clive had seen new reports detailing the effectiveness of *Luftwaffe* raids on Fighter Command airfields. Although they were causing serious damage to the few they targeted accurately, others were hardly being affected at all and remained operational. But it was irrelevant now as they couldn't replace aircraft quickly enough; aircraft factories couldn't keep up with demand. Fighter Command barely existed any longer.

In other words, Göring was wasting his resources bombing airfields. And the British wanted it to stay that way.

Chapter 96

Moss slept until after noon. He woke with stiff limbs and an aching belly. Having washed, shaved and dressed, he went down to the hotel restaurant and ate as substantial a meal as rationing allowed. Several other tables were occupied; businessmen having lunch mostly it seemed, and a couple in uniform. He would move on to another hotel shortly, as a precaution. It should only be for another night; two at the most. Then he'd be gone.

In the bar he downed a double vodka and soda and picked up a newspaper. It was full of glowing reports of how the RAF boys were shooting down large numbers of German raiders. He wondered just how accurate the claims were. One thing was certain, they weren't shooting them all down. In the same paper were stories of cities and towns being badly hit.

Back in his room, he lay down for a few hours to kill time, then loaded and checked his pistol and placed it in his jacket pocket. From a drawer he took a compass and a sheath containing a long-bladed knife. When they too were hidden in his clothing, he glanced around the room, locked the door, strolled the few hundred yards to New Street Station and bought a return ticket to Coventry.

After a cup of coffee and a whisky chaser at the station buffet, he caught the next train, arriving twenty minutes later. At the kiosk he asked for a street map of the city.

"Sorry, not allowed to sell 'em no more," replied the girl tartly. "In case of invasion."

"Do I look like a Nazi parachutist?"

"No, but you might be a fifth columnist, and rules is rules."

"Quite right. Well could you please direct me to Spencer Street then?"

"Never heard of it. Porter might know." She pointed a finger in a direction that could have been anywhere. He eventually found the porter and an hour later had found Spencer Street and walked along its entire length twice, the first time wearing his coat and hat, the second without either. He pinpointed number twenty-nine, about a quarter of the way along the row of terraced houses. He also noticed two men sitting against a wall, smoking, and in no apparent hurry to go anywhere.

Now why would they be doing that? They were quite obviously there for a reason. Nor did it have the feel of routine surveillance to Moss; this was a welcoming committee.

Triangle! There was no other way they could have known. The little bastard must have shopped him.

He made his way back to the station for more coffee, to wait until darkness and to consider his next move. It would be easy to walk away from this, just hop on a train back to Birmingham. Killing Quaver was part of his brief, but his priority was to get back to Castle Bromwich and steal a Spitfire, a mighty enough task in itself! Assuming now that Triangle had failed to pass on his message to the *Abwehr*, he also had the responsibility of reporting Quaver's duplicity . . . and Triangle's. He must not fail. Men as ruthless as Himmler and Heydrich didn't tolerate it. This was his one and only opportunity to please them. But there was also a need to tie up loose ends, and he'd been given Quaver on a plate, plus the chance, when he reached Germany, to impress above and beyond what was expected of him. Quaver was a traitor to the Reich, and he must be killed.

On his brief reconnaissance trip, he had noticed the entrance to an alley that ran along the back of the terrace. If there were men at the front, there was bound to be at least one at the back. He had also noticed a pub a few streets away. He had a meal in a British restaurant, then killed some time wandering around the narrow streets, passed the cathedral but did not go in, and headed towards the pub. He stepped into the public bar and ordered a double whisky.

*

The gate leading from Marion Wakeley's back yard into the alleyway was open by about two inches; enough to give Sergeant Stanley Mackenzie of Special Branch a clear view to the end of the alley on his right. By standing on a large tree stump used for chopping wood, he could see over the fence in the other direction. He was pleased with his positioning. The big disadvantage was the blackout; it was pitch dark. He had just lit a cigarette when he heard the crunch of footsteps. Instinctively he felt for the revolver in his pocket. The sound came from his right.

Through the gap in the gateway he could see the narrow beam of a torch wavering as someone approached. Then tuneless whistling, a barely tonal rendition of *Scotland the Brave*. Mackenzie relaxed. One of the MI5 chaps on a routine check. Probably Atkins.

"Everything alright, Mackenzie?" said a voice as the torchlight stopped just ahead of him.

"Aye, nothing to report."

"Nothing at the front either. A few passers-by, back from the pub mostly. No sign of chummy."

"All was well here until you turned up and murdered a fine melody. Will there be a raid tonight, do you think?"

"Possibly. Weather's fair enough."

"And our man . . . will he show?"

"Let's hope so. He knows where to come . . . and if he does we're ready for him. Alright for smokes?"

"Yes thanks. Am I relieved at one?"

"That's right, see you then." The torch beam faded and the footsteps diminished. Mackenzie drew on his cigarette and looked skywards. No moon, but at least it was dry. He predicted a raid later for certain. The sirens had already gone off once but it had been a false alarm.

Footsteps again; from the left this time. Erratic, stumbling. He stepped cautiously onto the tree stump and peered over the fence. He saw the faint outline of a figure making its way down the alley, swerving from side to side. The gun came out of his pocket, a practised finger releasing the safety catch.

He heard a loud belch. The footsteps ceased and he saw the figure lean against a fence several houses along. The last of the pub drunks, Mackenzie deduced. He stayed on the tree stump until the figure was on the move again. He waited for the man to pass before stepping down.

The footsteps stopped next to him. Another belch. The gate was pushed open roughly.

Mackenzie was down from the stump in a second. The drunk was halfway through the gateway, so he slammed it shut hard, trapping him between gate and fencepost. There was a loud grunt.

"Who are you – what do you want?"

"Who am I? Who are *you*, standing in my back yard!"

A blast of whisky breath hit Mackenzie. The man was slurring his words badly.

"You've got the wrong house, laddie. What number do you live at?"

"I live here . . . at number thirty-three. So don't tell *me* I've got the wrong place!"

"This is twenty-nine."

". . . And what are you doing in my yard, I'd like to know?"

"This is twenty-nine, not thirty-three. You're two houses out, so clear off." The drunken man seemed puzzled for a moment, then his mistake appeared to sink in.

"I've done it again. I'm really shh . . . shorry. All these houses look alike." He lurched forward and placed a hand on Mackenzie's shoulder, as if to steady himself. "Especially when you've had a skinful! Please accept my apology, and I'll leave you in peace."

"That's alright, now will you . . ."

Moss's hand shot from Mackenzie's shoulder to his mouth and pressed hard onto it. In the same instant, his other hand jerked upwards, the long blade of his knife stabbing deep into the stomach and high up behind the ribcage. When it had penetrated as far as it could, he twisted the handle savagely. His victim gave a muffled groan before slumping backwards onto the ground. Moss was on top of him, stabbing several more times until Mackenzie lay still.

Chapter 97

Schneider switched off the light and parted the curtains. Marion was asleep, her breathing even and deep. He had given up waiting for sleep to come; he felt anxious and restless.

The car was still there, with one man inside and another a few feet away, pacing up and down. Why? What were they expecting to happen, and why hadn't they told him? The glow of their cigarettes made him want to smoke, so he fumbled on the dressing table for his packet. Marion's alarm clock stood next to it. He carried it over to the window and could just make out the hands. Nearly midnight.

He was placing it back on the table when he heard the noise; glass splintering, very faint. It came from downstairs. He picked up the torch from beside the bed and crept onto the landing, listening. Nothing. He made his way into the back bedroom where Simon and Annette normally slept. Pulling back a corner of the curtain, he shone the torch through the glass into the back yard. A man's body lay spread-eagled obscenely on the ground.

A floorboard creaked somewhere below.

Schneider crept out onto the landing and back into the front bedroom, closing the door behind him. He put a hand gently over Marion's mouth and whispered: "Wake up." Her eyes fluttered open, a puzzled look on her face. "Shhh, don't say a word. There's someone in the house, downstairs – I think they broke in through the kitchen window." He took his hand away from her mouth.

"Is it a burglar?"

"No. Someone has come for me. Quick, you must hide." He steered her out of bed and across the room. Next to the door was a wardrobe, beyond which stood a small dressing table squeezed next to the window. He handed Marion the torch, then carefully pulled out the table, lifting it so it didn't scrape across the floor. "Here, get in the corner." He pressed her against the wall and replaced the table in front of her. From the door it was impossible to see her.

"What shall I do? I'm scared."

"Nothing." He thought for a moment, took the torch from her and handed her a ceramic ornament from the dressing table, the figure of an eighteenth century lady. "Here, if anyone comes near you, or I tell you, throw this through the window, as hard as you can – hard enough to smash it for certain. There are men outside who will come and help."

"How do you know that?"

He kissed her hurriedly on the lips. "Keep quiet now."

Schneider crept over to the bed, pulled the pillows down under the blankets to give the impression there were bodies in it, then tiptoed across to the door. He flattened himself against the wall, switched off the torch, and listened.

*

"Did you see that, sir?" said the man standing in Spencer Road, addressing the man in the car.

"Yes," replied Major Atkins. "Someone's got a torch on up there. Funny, those curtains were drawn properly earlier." They watched in silence for a while.

"Might be just going for a piss."

"They're moving about a lot if they are."

"Maybe they can't find the chamber pot. They'd better hurry or they'll have an ARP warden onto them."

The men watched for a while longer. Then the light disappeared.

Atkins opened the car door. "Go round and check on Mackenzie, will you? I'll wait here."

"Sir." The man walked away towards the end of the street.

Probably nothing, thought Atkins.

*

Another creak, this time on the landing, immediately outside the door.

This is insane, thought Schneider. *Alert the watchers, let them deal with it!*

Whoever was on the other side of the door was here to kill him, he knew it. The protection outside wasn't just for show. *Hamburg* must have found out about his treachery and sent someone to silence him. And MI5 bloody well knew he was coming.

He knew he could smash the window and bring them running. But something was holding him back. The need to be a hero? To protect the woman he loved? He didn't know. He heard a soft click. What the hell, it was too late now.

The door knob began to turn. A feeble glimmer appeared around its edge as the door opened a fraction, a thin wedge of yellow light, growing fatter as the door opened wider. Schneider turned his head slightly to hear

364

if Marion was stirring. Nothing. He couldn't even hear her breathing. The door was open about a foot now. A torch beam panned around the room, towards the bed.

Just a little more, he begged. *Just a few more inches.*

The head of the torch was now visible, and part of a hand, the fingers clenched tightly. He raised himself onto tiptoe. *Just an inch more . . .*

The beam of light reached the bed and stopped.

Schneider hurled his entire body weight against the door, slamming it hard onto the intruder, pinning him against the jamb. There was a cry of pain, and the torch fell to the ground. Something else heavy fell . . . a gun, a knife? He grabbed the door knob, pulled the door back about a foot and slammed it once more against the body. He heard a sickening thud, then a grunt, then a rustling sound as the intruder slumped to his knees. Reaching down to pick up the torch, Schneider let go the door and stepped back, shining the beam into the man's face. Blood was streaming down his nose and he appeared stunned, his eyes half closed, arms hanging loose by his sides. He didn't look like a killer; he had an ordinary face, the kind you walked past in the street every day.

Beside him lay the gun. The man looked as though he might lose consciousness any moment. He was beginning to sway slightly. Schneider pushed the door open wider and moved forward to drag the gun towards him with his foot.

The arm lunged out so fast that Schneider had no time to react. Before he knew what was happening, a hand had clasped the back of his ankle and jerked the foot forward with force. He lost his balance instantly and fell flat on his back, cracking his head against the floorboards.

The gun spun out across the landing and clattered down the stairs. The intruder flung himself on top of Schneider and clamped his hands around his neck, but not before Schneider was able to raise a leg in defence, keeping his attacker at a distance, his knee rammed hard against the man's ribs. They stayed like that for a few seconds, their faces only inches apart. Schneider tried to push away with his foot, but the man had a firm grip around his neck and wasn't letting go.

The intruder spat in Schneider's eye. The spittle made him blink uncontrollably, but the distraction was only brief. Lack of oxygen was his main concern; he couldn't breathe and he could feel the blood pulsating in the veins around his neck. He was being throttled.

The panic this generated seemed to give him added strength. He managed to push the man away from him far enough to bring his other knee up. With the strength of both legs now against his attacker, Schneider was able to force him away and to one side. The hands around his neck loosened and the weight on top of him eased.

Air rasped back into Schneider's oxygen-starved lungs as he scrambled to his feet. He lunged downwards with his fist. It made contact with soft flesh – a cheek, he guessed – before slamming into the wall, making him yelp with pain.

*

Marion quivered in her hiding place, listening to the fight taking place in front of her and trying desperately to follow its course. All she could see were vague outlines.

Her hand clutched the figurine tightly. Oh God, what if the intruder killed Henry and then saw her! Would she have the courage to throw the figurine at the window? Maybe she should do it now. She heard a yelp that sounded like Henry.

*

Schneider had the intruder by the throat now. He was on his knees with the man pressed against the wall. He had found the neck by chance and was making the most of his good fortune, squeezing with all his might. At Camp 4 they had been told to use all their strength and to bear down using their entire body weight. He was doing just that.

Moss had been trained too. He managed to slide his hands up in between Schneider's arms and whip them outwards, breaking the grip around his neck. At the same time he lunged forward and cracked his head against Schneider's mouth sending him tumbling backwards. Blood sprayed across them both, and a tooth fell to the ground.

It was a race now to see who could recover the quickest. Moss won. He was standing by the time Schneider had got to his knees. A fierce kick caught Schneider in the side and he keeled over.

"Marion! Now!" he screamed. Moss stopped dead as he was about to kick out again. He looked round. The room was mostly dark, but he caught a glimpse of a shadow in the corner. He did not see but heard the front window smash, followed by a hysterical scream.

"Help! Oh God, help us!"

There was immediate shouting from the street below, and heavy footsteps running.

Moss flashed a wild-eyed glance towards the window and realised what was happening. He kicked out at Schneider once more, stumbled across the landing and ran down the staircase.

Marion pushed the dressing table away from her and hurried over the Schneider who was doubled up on the floor. "Henry, are you alright? Are you hurt?"

366

"I think so . . . I don't know."

There was loud hammering against the front door, shouting and what sounded like furniture being smashed downstairs.

"There are more people trying to get in, Henry. I'm scared!"

"Don't worry, they're policemen. Where is he?"

"Gone. He ran when I broke the window."

"Well done. You saved me from a beating." He tried to move. "Help me up, will you?" She clasped his arm and helped him to sit on the edge of the bed. "You might as well turn the light on, but close the curtains first."

They heard the front door give way, then voices in the hallway, more footsteps and someone shouting: "The back, quick!"

Nothing happened for a while. It was silent below. Presently they heard someone coming up the stairs. Schneider recognised Major Atkins.

"You alright, lad?"

"Kicked about a bit. Did you get him?"

Atkins shook his head. "No. He's killed our man Mackenzie, and I've another injured down there. I've got men scouring the streets, but you can't see your hand in front of your face in the blackout. Hopefully he won't get far."

"Why didn't you tell me someone was after me!" said Schneider angrily. "You put Marion in danger too."

Atkins shrugged. "We needed to try and catch him. If we'd told you, you'd have wanted to protect Mrs Wakeley here – told her to get away. For all we know, you might have cleared off yourself, as you did once before. We needed you to behave as though everything was normal."

"And we played our parts, Marion was terrified, I got beaten up – and he slipped through your fingers!"

"We'll catch him!" Atkins said angrily. "Did either of you get a good look at him?"

"I did," said Schneider.

"Right, get some clothes on, you're coming with me."

"Where to?"

"We think he'll head back to the factory. He has something in mind. We don't know what . . . sabotage possibly."

Schneider shook his head. "Oh no, I'm staying here. I've had enough of all this."

"You're the only person who can recognise him," said Atkins. "You have to come."

"What about Marion? I'm not leaving her alone."

"She can't come, it's too dangerous."

"More dangerous than here? Sorry, my friend, either Marion comes along or you go spy hunting without me."

367

"I can force you. I can have you arrested."

"Arrest me then."

Atkins was boiling over with anger now, but he really did not want to follow that route.

"Alright. But get dressed quickly, both of you. We'll take you to the safe house. Be warned, Mrs Wakeley, it's a mess downstairs. Our man tried his best to stop the bastard – pardon my French – but a few things got broken in the process. He's still down there . . . we're waiting for an ambulance."

"Thank you," said Marion.

"And I'm afraid Mackenzie's in your back yard. He'll be gone soon."

Chapter 98

(Saturday 7ᵗʰ September 1940)

It had been a stroke of luck, if not a minor miracle, coming across the Air Raid Warden; Moss didn't imagine many had motorbikes, let alone the petrol coupons to keep them on the road. This one did. Now he lay dead in a Coventry back street.

He talked his way through the two road blocks that he couldn't avoid en route for Sutton Coldfield. The Home Guard accepted his stolen papers and hurriedly concocted story and let him pass. His bloody nose helped. He told them he had fallen off his bike in the blackout. On a quiet stretch of road, he pulled over and sat smoking for a while. He was very thirsty and extremely tired. He lay back on the grass verge, and despite willing himself not to, fell asleep.

There was the slightest hint of light in the sky when he awoke. He stood up, smoked another cigarette, and set off again.

He drove right past the Castle Bromwich factory, along the Chester Road, then a mile or so further on turned right onto the Lichfield Road. This took him through the centre of Sutton Coldfield, along the main street, The Parade, then up Mill Street, past the Town Hall and on towards the Four Oaks district of the town. At the corner of a quiet side road, he pulled over and turned off the engine.

Apart from the soft ticking as the engine cooled down, there was absolute silence.

Moss felt his nose gingerly. Not broken, he didn't think, but it throbbed painfully. His chest hurt too, badly when he breathed in, agonisingly when he coughed. He was angry with himself. If only he had kept a grip on the gun he could have killed Quaver. And he could have strangled him, or caved his head in with something if that stupid bitch hadn't smashed the window and alerted the minders. After that he had been lucky to get out at all.

The house was completely dark; no lights on anywhere. He crept cautiously up the drive, along the side path and into the back garden. He looked up at the rear bedroom window; the blackout curtain made it look like a dark and empty void. Surely it must be the same room. Her room. He bent down and picked up a handful of gravel from the path. It made a louder noise against the window pane than he had expected, a harsh rattle. He crouched low, defensively.

Nothing.

He threw some more, but not so much this time.

Nothing.

He was reaching down for a third handful when a light appeared at the French windows directly in front of him. A torch beam. It took him by surprise. Of course. The blackout curtains must be permanently fixed in the bedroom; she couldn't open the window without unpinning it all. He had the same problem in the bedroom of his flat in London. He crept forward. One of the French windows opened slightly.

"Who is it?" The soft female voice was so familiar to him.

"Alison?"

"Who's there?"

"Let me in, please." He placed a hand on hers and bent her arm upwards until her torch beam shone into his face. "I need your help. Please let me in."

Alison gasped as she stared at the bloodstained features. Her faced reflected utter bewilderment.

"*You!*"

*

The safe house was full of people.

Marion was upstairs asleep in one room, the VI was asleep in another. Downstairs, Schneider was being debriefed by Ruskin and Atkins, while Laurel made detailed notes and Hardy hovered about, anxious to be of help but with nothing specific to do. Atkins went into the hallway to use the telephone; they had a detailed description of their man now and it needed to be distributed as quickly as possible. He spoke to the local police station, who forwarded the information on to Home Guard units in the area. Then he rang the site police at the Castle Bromwich factory warning them to be extra vigilant.

"He ought to lie low for a while. I would in his shoes," said Ruskin, once the questioning was over. "He has a few cuts and bruises to contend with too. On the other hand I suspect he's in a hurry – he's on a mission and needs to finish it."

"What do you think he will do next?" asked Schneider.

"I don't know. He'll be lucky now to do any major damage at the factory, if that was his objective, especially if he's working alone, which I suspect he is . . . although I could be wrong. We're too much on the alert. But whatever he has in mind we have got to catch him. He's a rogue agent, not *Abwehr*."

"Not *Abwehr*? Then who is he working for?"

"We're not sure." Ruskin knew but wasn't about to share his knowledge. "An independent of some sort, possibly sent to check up on you and to report back on your loyalty. Fortunately for us, he thinks Germany know now that you're a double. Unfortunately for him, we managed to prevent that."

"How did he know about Marion, and where she lives?"

"I don't know." Ruskin was telling the truth this time. "Though I have my suspicions."

"From your people, surely. You must have a leak somewhere."

"We are looking into that."

"So what now?" Schneider slumped back in his chair; he felt drained all of a sudden. He was sick of the whole business.

"We wait." Ruskin paced around the room, thinking out loud. "This chap is in a hurry. He took risks trying to kill you. He's under pressure. Time constraints perhaps – a deadline perhaps. Even if he does lie low I don't think it will be for long."

"Sabotage – at the factory?"

Ruskin shook his head. "As I said, I don't think he could now. He has no way of infiltrating the place, not without help. It may have been his intention to join forces with you and cause some mayhem. But not now."

"What then?"

"I don't know . . . I just don't know."

The telephone rang in the hallway. A moment later there was a knock on the door and Hardy appeared.

"You need to take this call, sir – it's the police. A man fitting our description has just abducted a woman a few miles from here."

Ruskin hurried to the phone. He was back moments later.

"So much for lying low. Come, no time to lose."

Five minutes later, Laurel was driving Ruskin, Schneider and Atkins towards Four Oaks as fast as the meagre light of early dawn would allow.

Chapter 99

Iris Webb sat on the sofa next to her husband. She was wearing a dressing gown and fluffy slippers, and she was sobbing. Leonard Webb had a protective arm around her and muttered sympathetic noises in between telling Ballard Ruskin their story. Schneider and Atkins stood and listened in silence. Laurel took notes.

"I woke up and heard two people talking downstairs. One was Alison, my daughter, and the other a man – a familiar voice but I couldn't make out who it was at first. I looked at the clock. It was half past four. Naturally I wanted to know what was going on at such an unearthly hour, so I came downstairs. They were in the lounge, and as I got nearer I could tell they were arguing. Ally sounded very upset, and frightened. 'No!' I heard her say, several times. 'No I won't!' I opened the door and barged in. As soon as I saw him, his face covered in blood, I kicked myself for not recognising the voice."

"So you know the man?" Ruskin was astonished. "You know his identity?"

"Of course. He was a regular visitor here at one time. You see . . ." He was about to explain when his wife cut in.

"They were engaged once, he and Alison. Jan-Arne Krobol – a Norwegian. A dreadful man. He broke it off two days before the wedding and went off and married someone else. I never liked him, certainly never trusted him. Poor Alison was heartbroken. She had to go to the other side of the world to get over it."

"Australia," added Leonard Webb, for the sake of Laurel who was scribbling in a notebook. "I'm afraid my wife isn't telling it quite the way it was. It was Alison who called off the wedding. Cost me a small fortune."

"He was to blame though, dear. He broke it off by doing . . . well you know, what he did."

"In a sense that is true." Alison's father looked apologetically at Ruskin. "I'm afraid this is not only upsetting for us, but rather embarrassing to relate. All I will say is that my daughter found Krobol . . . in a compromising position with another woman."

"In bed together," interjected Iris Webb.

"As a result, the wedding was impossible to contemplate."

"They were having sex!"

'That'll do, Iris.'

"He was having sex with Margery Ashford-Hope!"

"Iris, leave it . . . and no need to name names! If any further details are required we can give them at a later time. Now please leave this to me."

"When was this?" asked Ruskin.

"April 1938."

"And have you seen this man Krobol since then?"

"Not until tonight. We imagined he went back to Norway when the war started."

"Please tell me more about tonight. When you walked in on your daughter and Krobol, what happened next?"

"They stopped talking. It was a shock to see Jan-Arne. As far I knew he and Alison had had no contact at all. He was the last person I expected to find in my house. He was in a bad way, blood all down his front, it looked as if he'd been punched on the nose. Alison had washed his face but his nose was still bleeding. My very first thought was that *she* might have hit him!"

"I would have done the same," muttered Iris Webb.

"Alison said, 'Well, Daddy, look what the cat dragged in . . . after all this time, Mr Krobol here needs my help.' He rudely told her to be quiet and apologised to me for intruding. He said it was vital that Alison helped him in a matter of national importance." He stopped for a moment. "You know, Alison was dressed. I think she must have agreed to help him initially, got dressed, and then changed her mind. I'm not sure. It's quite likely, he had a great deal of personal charm. A born liar too, as we found out to our cost. Anyway, then he had the cheek to suggest I go back to bed and forget I'd ever seen him. That was too much for me. I told him to get out immediately, otherwise I would call the police."

"And did you?" asked Ruskin.

"Not immediately. He became very aggressive, shouting at Alison that she must do as he said. She told him to . . . well, I won't repeat precisely her words. I imagine she picked up that sort of language in Australia. Needless to say she left him in no doubt as to her feelings. He grabbed her by the arm. I moved forward to protect her, and he pulled out a knife. He demanded I give him my car keys. Ally told me not to, but he put his hand over her mouth. I was frightened for her safety, so did as he asked. Then he dragged her away." He pointed towards the French windows. "Through there."

"Did you try to follow them?"

"I was frightened I might aggravate him and that he'd hurt Alison. I offered to take a look at his injuries, see if I could patch him up a bit to delay him – I'm a doctor – but he would have none of it. It seemed clear to me that he *would* use the knife if provoked."

"He said he needed help in a matter of national importance. Did he explain what he meant by that?"

Leonard Webb shook his head. "No, that's all he said. He didn't explain what he meant."

Iris Webb began to cry again. Her husband spoke gently to her, soothing words from his bedside manner vocabulary.

"Do you know where they have gone?"

"No idea. Alison tried to say something as they left. She struggled, as you can imagine, but she couldn't speak with his hand over her mouth. His hand slipped for a second and she called out something, and that was all. It sounded like *Harbour*, or *Arthur*, or *larder* even. I really couldn't say. Do you think she's in danger? Surely he wouldn't harm her, not really . . ."

"I hope not," said Ruskin. "Arthur. Does your daughter know anyone of that name?"

"I don't think so. There are no harbours around here of course. We do have a larder."

"There's Arthur at the club," said Iris Webb softly, her voice muffled by a handkerchief.

She suddenly had Ruskin's undivided attention. "Which club is that, Mrs Webb?"

"The flying club. Arthur is the club secretary. He has a soft spot for Alison."

"Which flying club is this, please?"

"He's too old for her of course."

"Mrs Webb, please!"

Leonard Webb came to the rescue. "The Midland Aero Club, it's a few miles from here . . . at Castle Bromwich Aerodrome."

"So Alison is a pilot?"

"Why yes, didn't you know? But how could you. She's in the Air Transport Auxiliary. I don't think it's unfair to say she is one of the best female pilots in the country."

"My God!" cried Ruskin. "He's going to get her to fly him out. That's why he needs her."

"I very much doubt that," said Leonard Webb.

"What do you mean?"

"Krobol is also a pilot – quite a good one. So he should be . . . Alison taught him. That's how they met."

"Why then? Why does he need her help?"

Webb shrugged his shoulders. "Alison is a familiar face down there at the club. He wouldn't look suspicious wandering around the airfield with her. But he'd be accosted in no time on his own. That's my guess."

"Thank you," said Ruskin. He moved towards the door, indicating that Schneider, Atkins and Laurel should follow. "Come on, we have no time to lose."

They had to run to keep up with Ruskin, despite his being at least twenty years their senior. Schneider tripped and fell on the gravel drive and the car was already moving as he scrambled into the passenger seat. None of them heard Leonard Webb's disgruntled voice calling out as an afterthought.

"*And* he stole my coat and gloves!"

Chapter 100

From a distance, it appeared as though the couple were walking across the aerodrome arm in arm. Lovers out for an early morning stroll perhaps; albeit a very early morning stroll. The sun had barely risen.

Closer observation would have shown that the couple were anything but lovers. The man's right fist was clenched tightly around the woman's upper arm, so tight that it was hurting her. He was forcing her reluctantly forward. His left arm rested across his chest, a knife concealed in his hand and touching her skin.

Moss was wearing Leonard Webb's coat to hide his bloodstained clothing. The doctor's car lay abandoned at the edge of the Chester Road.

"This is no way to treat your ex-fiancée," hissed Alison through clenched teeth.

"I'm sorry, Alison, but you're too good an opportunity to miss."

"You didn't seem to think that when you were fucking Margery Ashford-Hope two days before our wedding day."

"This is hardly the time to dredge up the past. That was unfortunate. If you hadn't walked in on us you'd never have known. Pity, we could have been happily married otherwise. Instead I ended up shackled to that bitch."

"You deserved each other."

"Shut up!" They walked around the perimeter of the airfield and cut across towards the flight shed. Two Spitfires stood next to each other, their slender noses pointing inquisitively towards the sky. Even unpainted, without green and brown camouflage, RAF roundels or white squadron markings, they looked magnificent.

There was hardly anyone about. A couple of engineers wearing overalls were standing close to the shed doors, stretching, smoking and drinking tea from enamel mugs. A couple of ground crew could be seen over by the RAF hangar, which was situated next to the control tower.

As they approached the flight shed, Krobol brought his arm down and slid it behind Alison so that the knife blade dug into the small of her back. She winced.

"What's all this about?" she said. "What do you want from me?"

"I want to fly a Spitfire, and you're going to help me."

"But why . . . what for?"

"None of your concern."

"How can this be in the national interest? This is madness. The opposite I suspect. Are you a traitor?"

"I didn't say in whose national interest. Now be quiet and listen. Just do as you're told and you won't get hurt. I want you to chat nicely to these two for a few moments. Do you know them?"

"By sight. They'll probably recognise me."

"Good. Turn on your feminine charms and find out if either of these Spitfires is ready to fly. Then I want you to ask if I could have a look at the controls – just take a look, pop my head in the cockpit."

Alison was very confused. "You're mad."

"I can assure you I am not. Just do as I say. And don't try anything foolish. If you do, I'll knife you on the spot." To make his point, he pressed the knife into her back harder and she felt the tip bite into her flesh. Through the fog of confusion the reality of what her ex-fiancé was doing was beginning to dawn on her. They reached the flight shed. The ground crew broke off their conversation and looked towards them.

"Morning," said one. "It's Miss Webb, isn't it? One the ATA girls . . . ladies, beg your pardon."

"That's right. I'm sorry, I don't know your name."

"Pine, miss. Barely recognised you out of uniform. You're up bright and early. Not flying today?"

"No, I've got a couple of days of leave. My friend here . . ."

"How do you do," said Moss, thrusting a hand out. "David Green."

"Good morning, sir. Nasty cut you've got there."

"Ah yes, an accident in the blackout last night. I can assure you it looks far worse than it is." Moss pointed to the Spitfires. "Magnificent machines."

"They certainly are," said Pine. "Finest fighter aircraft ever built. Fresh off the production line, these two. Waiting to be test flown."

"An enviable job. I fly a little myself, but I've never flown anything as advanced as these."

Pine smiled. "You should hang around and watch the test flights later. Mr Henshaw can handle a Spitfire like you wouldn't believe. He'll be pleased to see two ready for him. The factory is really coming together now, working all hours. Might even be a third one along later."

There was a silence. Alison felt her arm being squeezed tighter.

"Umm, actually, I was wondering. Would it be possible for David here to have a quick look in the cockpit? He's so interested."

"To be honest, miss, the gentleman shouldn't even be on the airfield. It's a restricted area. But as he's with you, I can't see no harm. Just for a moment, mind."

"That's very decent of you," said Moss. "This one here?" He moved towards the Spitfire nearest to them, still holding on firmly to Alison.

"That's right, sir. Hop up on the port wing there. You too, miss, if you like. Don't suppose you've flown a Spit before?"

"Actually I have – just the once." She and Moss climbed onto the wing. Pine walked round and climbed on to the starboard wing. He slid back the canopy and leaned over to release the pilot's access door.

"There, that'll give you a better view."

They stared into the narrow cockpit with its control column, pedals, levers and array of switches and dials on the instrument panel.

"Goodness," said Moss, "it looks complicated. "I've never seen so much gadgetry."

"Quite straightforward really," said Pine. He pointed across the panel. "Usual stuff . . . airspeed indicator, artificial horizon, climb and descent, altimeter, giro, turn and slip indicator, revs. Then there's oil pressure, temperature, fuel gauge, and over here are the oxygen controls."

Moss tapped a bulky handle on his side of the cockpit. "The throttle. Now that I do recognise."

"That's it, sir. Next to it's the airscrew control."

Alison knew Krobol was playing the innocent and understood far more than he was letting on.

Pine drew their attention to the other wall of the cockpit. "This is new to the version they're building here at Castle Bromwich – power-operated undercarriage retractor. At the moment on Spits you have to pump away at a handle between your legs to get the wheels up. This is a lot simpler. Of course these don't have any fancy stuff yet, being hot off the press so to speak. No radio, no armament, that's all added at RAF maintenance units once the ATA have delivered them. You'd know all about that, miss."

Alison nodded, then remarked: "Only men get to fly Spitfires and Hurricanes. They don't trust us feeble women with them . . . yet."

"Your turn will come, miss."

Moss absorbed everything with intense concentration, asking questions as casually as he was able bearing in mind that adrenalin was pumping through his body. He was now in a high state of nervous tension.

"Are they ready for their test flights?"

"Pretty much. Fuel tanks are full, and we're just about to start them up for a few checks before Mr Henshaw arrives."

"How do you do that?"

Pine indicated a small black button towards the bottom of the instrument panel, slightly to right of centre. "Push that and it should fire first or second time."

"Sounds simple."

"Of course you need some juice first time." Pine nodded his head towards a trolley on the ground nearby that had a lead stretching back into the flight shed. "Plug that battery accumulator into this socket here and Bob's your uncle."

Alison knew this but kept quiet. She was becoming very anxious. She had it all now; the pieces of last night's jigsaw had fitted into place. Jan-Arne was a fifth columnist. He wanted the Spitfire to make an escape, for some reason she could only guess at. She should warn Pine, risk the knife and the pain and possible death, and scream. Her heart was beating fast, and inside she was in a state of panic. She was also very scared.

A telephone started ringing inside the shed. The man Pine had been talking to when they arrived was calling from the door of the shed.

"Alan! You're wanted."

"Thanks, Brenner. Would you excuse me for a moment?" Pine jumped down to the ground. "I'd be grateful if you wouldn't touch anything." Then as he walked away he called back: "Might be better if you got down now, or I'll get a roasting if someone sees you."

The moment Pine had disappeared from view, Moss jumped down from the wing, ripped off his coat and dragged the starter trolley next to the fuselage of the Spitfire. In seconds he had attached the cable. Then he pulled away the chocks from in front of the wheels and climbed back on to the wing next to Alison. She watched as he eased himself into the cockpit and pulled up the access door. He had the seat straps tied in no time. He felt for the rudder pedals and placed his hands on the control column.

"You haven't got a parachute," she said. "No gloves, no helmet." They seemed inane comments, but it was all that came into her mind. Her stomach was in spasms, and she thought she might be sick at any moment.

"Gloves I have," said Moss, pulling some from beneath his shirt. "Your father's. Now I suggest you hop off the wing, this plane will soon be on its way. Be an angel and pull out that cable once the engine has fired. You've been very helpful, thank you. It was good to see you again."

Alison jumped down to the ground. Suddenly she seemed to snap out of her state of inertia. She had done nothing to try and stop him; and Jan-Arne had just *thanked* her for being so helpful! A deep anger welled up inside her and she screamed: "NO!"

At precisely the same moment, Moss pressed the starter button. The Merlin engine exploded into life, drowning Alison's voice completely. Smoke spewed from the exhaust manifolds on either side of the nose. The engine faltered, but did not stall. Moss pushed the throttle forward and the plane began to move, edging slowly forwards towards the open field.

"Oh Christ, I hope I can get this bloody thing off the ground," Moss said to himself.

Alison ran towards the shed to warn Pine, but there was no need. He and Brenner were already standing at the shed doors, wide-eyed. "What's going on? What's he playing at?"

"He's stealing that Spitfire!" yelled Alison. "We've got to stop him."

"Too bloody right," yelled back Pine. He ran forward. The plane was only about twenty yards ahead of him, but when he was almost within touching distance, the Spitfire lunged forward with a jerk as Moss struggled with the unfamiliar controls. The tail lifted and the nose dipped, bringing the propeller dangerously close to the ground for a moment. The starter trolley was still attached; the lead ran out of slack and was suddenly pulled tight. For a second it dragged the trolley along after it before the cable snapped loose from the fuselage, writhing snake-like along the ground.

Pine sprinted after the plane, keeping up with it long enough to hurl himself onto the port-side wing. Alison stared aghast as the Spitfire pulled away. Then her attention was drawn to a car that had turned off the Chester Road onto the airfield. It was heading across the field and straight into the path of the Spitfire.

The springy grass and the pilot's inexperience were making the task of clinging on to the wing very tough for Pine. As the Spitfire accelerated, approaching takeoff speed, he realised there was nothing he could do and to hang on any longer would be both suicidal and pointless. He loosened his grip and allowed himself to slide backwards until he fell roughly to the ground. He rolled several times and felt pain sear through his shoulder as it dislocated. He saw the Spitfire surging away from him across the field. Then the car came into view, driving at speed on a collision course.

"Christ, they're going to hit!" he gasped.

They would indeed have hit had Moss been more familiar with the Spitfire's controls and not made the most appalling takeoff. He had pushed the throttle lever too far forward too soon and reached full power prematurely. Instead of a gentle lifting into the air, the plane seemed to be forced upwards, wavering perilously as it went. The car shot beneath it, the roof barely missing the tail wheel.

Alison was standing a few feet away from Brenner. "Blimey," she heard him say. "That was really bad."

Wobbling and very uneven, the Spitfire levelled out until it was gaining height at a more reasonable rate, then banked awkwardly round to port, narrowly missing the cables of a barrage balloon and headed away in an approximate south-easterly direction.

The car screeched to a halt in front of the flight shed. Four men Alison had never seen before got out. The eldest hurried over to her.

"Alison Webb?"

"Yes, that's right."

"Are you alright? Was that Krobol taking off – Jan-Arne Krobol?"

"I'm fine. Yes, that was him!"

"Damn and blast, we've missed him! Moss has got away."

"Moss? Did you call him Moss?" asked Alison.

Ruskin did not reply. He was thinking faster than he had ever done before in his life. "He *must* be stopped. We must contact the Air Ministry, tell them to get Fighter Command to shoot him down. He'll be heading for France. Did that plane have a full tank of fuel?"

"Yes, sir," said Brenner. "Ready for test flying."

"Bugger! Atkins, get on to the Ministry immediately. There, in the control tower. Tell them he's heading south-east from here – flying an unmarked Spitfire. Shouldn't be difficult to pick up. Fast!"

Atkins jumped back into the car and sped across the airfield towards the control tower.

Ruskin noticed the other Spitfire for the first time. "Quick, someone get after him. We can shoot him down in this." He looked at Brenner. "Can you fly it?"

"No sir, I'm not a pilot."

"Well who is around here?"

"No one, sir. Not until Mr Henshaw arrives, our test pilot, and that won't be for a while." Then as an afterthought: "Apart from Miss Webb here of course."

Ruskin's brain whirled. He remembered her father's words . . . *one of the best female pilots in the country*. Good or bad, she was here and she could fly a plane.

"Miss Webb, do you think you can fly a Spitfire?"

"I know I can."

"Right, go after him! Do anything necessary to stop him."

"Hang on a minute," interrupted Brenner. "You can't just help yourself to our planes like this. Who do you think you are?"

"Look," replied Ruskin. "I know this is highly irregular, but the man who took off in that plane just now is a German agent . . . a spy if you prefer. He has vital information that must *never* reach the enemy. I'm with military intelligence – a security officer." He waved an identity card as proof.

"Mr Henshaw will be furious . . . and Mr Dunbar . . . and Mr Talamo."

"No idea who they are, but I suggest you refer them to the Air Ministry – Air Commodore Archie Boyle. Or Air Chief Marshal Dowding, if you prefer. Or Winston Churchill himself for that matter!"

Brenner looked stunned. "Blimey."

Ruskin bustled Alison towards the Spitfire. "Hurry," he said. "Shoot him down if necessary."

"This Spitfire has no armament," she explained. "Nor does the other one. The Browning machine guns haven't been fitted yet. I can't shoot him down but I can do other things to stop him."

She was just about to climb into the cockpit when Brenner appeared. "Wait, do this properly." He was carrying an Irvin flying jacket and seat parachute. "Put these on."

"Thanks." Alison pulled on the jacket and stepped into the straps of the parachute pack.

"Hurry, please," pressed Ruskin. "He'll get away."

"Not from me he won't. By the way, did I hear you call him Moss?"

"I did. It's a cover name he uses."

"Do you know why?"

"No, do you?"

Alison nodded. "Moss is a small coastal town in Norway – to the south of Oslo. Jan-Arne was born there."

"Well I'm blowed."

"Goggles and gloves, miss?" asked Brenner.

"No time," said Ruskin impatiently. "Are you sure you can handle this machine, my dear?"

"Oh yes."

Brenner trundled the starter trolley across and plugged it in. He gave a nod and Alison's finger found the starter button. The roar of the Merlin was deafening and was Ruskin's cue to stand aside. Brenner unplugged the trolley then scurried like a ferret into the flight shed and back out onto the plane's wing. He pressed a flying helmet onto Alison's head and positioned the goggles for her, then waited until she had fitted on her gloves before jumping down.

Alison gave a thumbs-up in gratitude and increased the engine revs. The Spitfire eased forward.

"Must have goggles and gloves, sir," shouted Brenner to Ruskin. "That other bloke will be sorry not to have 'em, mark my words, especially the goggles. There's usually swarf lying along the bottom of the fuselage when they come new out of the factory – little chips and shavings of metal and shit like that. If he spins it'll spray everywhere and he'll get an eyeful. And no parachute!" This seemed to Brenner to be more of a sin than stealing the Spitfire.

As he watched the fighter taxiing across the grass, Ruskin felt a sudden pang of guilt. Suppose he was sending this young woman off to her death! He followed the Spitfire's progress as it increased in speed, gradually accelerating the length of the aerodrome. It seemed to take forever and he was suddenly scared she may not make it into the air. Then the plane lifted smoothly from the ground and was airborne. Rays from the newly risen sun glistened off the Perspex of the cockpit canopy as

Alison banked round over the Chester Road and headed off in the direction Moss had taken. He saw the undercarriage retract as she levelled out.

"Well I don't know much about flying," observed Ruskin, "but I'd say hers was a much better takeoff than his."

"She's a better pilot, that's why," said Brennan.

For the first time since he had arrived at the airfield, Ruskin became aware of Schneider. He was walking towards him, propping up Pine who looked pale and was clutching his shoulder.

"Do you know the range of those machines?" asked Ruskin, as they reached him.

"Four hundred miles, on a full tank – if you fly sensibly."

"So they could make it to France from here then."

"France!" spluttered Pine. "Are you joking? Was that Miss Webb in the other Spit? Can somebody please tell me what the hell is going on here?"

Ballard Ruskin put on his most soothing avuncular voice. "Come along with me to the control tower and I'll explain as much as I can. We need to get you some medical attention. I'm sorry about your Spitfires – hopefully you'll get them back in one piece. But you must appreciate just how important it is that that man does not get away."

Pine looked confused and forlorn. "Two Spitfires stolen. What's Mr Henshaw going to say about that?"

Under his breath Ruskin said: "Not half as much as Winston if he ever hears I let a woman fly off in one of them."

Chapter 101

As soon as Alison straightened out of her turn, she eased the stick forward, levelled out and opened up the throttle. The Merlin responded with enormous thrust, pressing her body hard against the seat back. Speed was of the essence. She had to regain visual contact with Jan-Arne's plane as quickly as possible.

She guessed he would not gain much height – two or three thousand feet, no more; he had no flying jacket for warmth and he would be struggling to keep control. Alison had at least flown a Spitfire before whereas Jan-Arne had not, and everything would be unfamiliar to him. As his tutor she knew he was a good pilot, but not outstanding. She was better. She also had a tactical advantage; he would not imagine for a moment he was being pursued.

At fifteen hundred feet the Spitfire sped along above the patchwork countryside at two hundred miles per hour, and still nowhere near full throttle. The controls felt well-balanced and incredibly responsive compared with the Oxfords and Dominoes to which she had grown accustomed in recent weeks. Visibility was excellent; apart from a few puffs of cloud the sky was clear. She kept the sun slightly to port and scoured the sky ahead for signs of the other plane. She was worried the time span between takeoffs had been too long and the other Spitfire was too far ahead. On the other hand, Jan-Arne wouldn't be foolish enough to use too much throttle until he was comfortable with the controls.

Then she saw something. A tiny black dot in a sea of blue, above and to starboard. Higher than she had expected, maybe four thousand feet.

Increase throttle. Air speed two-fifty.

As she sped forward, Alison watched as the dot gradually took on a recognisable shape. It was rocking about all over the place. She eased the control column back and began to climb.

*

It took a lot to scare Moss, but he was scared. The Spitfire was proving difficult to handle; a dream to more experienced pilots perhaps, but to him it was a beast that needed taming. The controls and instruments weren't complex, but the fluidity and speed of response, coupled with the enormous thrust of the engine, were beyond anything he had experienced before. He was used to slow-moving Tiger Moths and Miles Magisters. He couldn't believe the altimeter when it read five thousand feet after what seemed like only moments after takeoff. He pushed the column forward, over compensated, and went into an alarming dive before pulling back again, eventually levelling at four thousand.

It was then that he noticed a green light shining at him on the instrument panel. His mind went back to Pine's summary of the controls; it meant the wheels were still down. He saw the undercarriage selector to his right. To activate it he had to move his left hand from the throttle onto the control column to free up his right hand. He struggled to push the lever from bottom to top, but managed it eventually and heard two bumps as the wheels slotted into place under the wings. The green light turned red.

He then tried to block out everything in the cockpit that had nothing to do with simply flying in a straight line at a steady altitude. He concentrated as never before, and in a short time felt himself relaxing slightly. The plane seemed to sense this, wavering less and settling down, responding more smoothly.

He was aiming to stay on a straight course as much as possible, flying directly over London if necessary, across Kent and out over the English Channel. It occurred to him that an RAF fighter was safest over home territory and the less time spent over coastlines and the sea the better. The last thing he wanted was to be shot down by a marauding Messerschmitt. Mixed with the fear of losing control of the fighter was the adulation of having so far achieved his objective. He had done as he was ordered, stolen a Spitfire from under the noses of the British. All he had to do now was keep flying in the right direction, stay away from trouble, and make a safe landing somewhere in occupied France.

His thoughts flashed back to Alison, and the irony of having used her of all people. He had loved her once. Being caught with Margery Ashford-Hope had messed up his plans. Still, she'd been terrific in bed – better than Alison – and it had been a lively marriage while it lasted. Alison had never really been able to let herself go. She was unadventurous. There were things she wouldn't do, things she wouldn't try.

A glance at the instrument panel showed that everything was as it should be. He felt more comfortable with the Spitfire now.

Yes, Alison was never able to let herself go . . .

Chapter 102

Lt.-Col. Ballard Ruskin stood in the control tower and let the chaos drift over him as best he could. The duty officer was close to panic and had been persuaded against having them all arrested only by a hair's breadth. Half-a-dozen people, including the works manager, had been telephoned and were on their way. He had allowed Ruskin to telephone the Air Ministry in London, but only when Ruskin threatened to have *him* arrested on charges of complicity in the theft of the two Spitfires and high treason if he failed to cooperate. To his relief Ruskin found himself being put through directly to Air Commodore Boyle, who in turn arranged contact with Fighter Command headquarters at Bentley Priory.

Schneider stood in the corner of the control tower, feeling helpless. He had been brought along to identify the German agent, and that was no longer necessary. His mouth was sore and swollen from his fight with Moss, and he was missing a tooth. He saw Ruskin stare out of the window into the sky above Castle Bromwich, as though willing himself to see the two planes as they sped towards London and beyond.

"Do you think he'll make it?" he asked.

Ruskin shook his head. "He can't. It'll be the end of the network."

Schneider looked up at the sky too. It may be the end of the network, he thought, but it would let him off the hook. "Well, Uncle Mac, only time will tell. Or should I call you Ruskin?"

Ruskin turned and stared him in the eyes. Of course! Quaver had been standing next to him, listening to him speak on the telephone. Shameful lapse of security.

"Don't worry," grinned Schneider. "Your secret's safe with me."

*

The underground Operations and Filter Rooms at Bentley Priory were ominously quiet, the great plotting table empty as the weary night shift prepared to hand over to their fresh morning colleagues. So far there had been no sign of enemy aircraft either from the Chain Home Stations or the Observer Corps. But it was still very early. Everyone knew the attacks would come, that this was the calm before the storm, as it had been almost every day since early July.

When the teleprinter message came through from the Air Ministry, it was met at first with confusion, and a good deal of scepticism. There was no precedent for such an extraordinary requirement, no procedure in the book. Then, with reasonable haste, someone took it on themselves to have faith in what was being instructed and to regard it as an orthodox report of an enemy raider, from an unorthodox source. 12 Group and 11 Group headquarters were contacted and they in turn informed the relevant Sector Stations – Wittering, Duxford and Northolt. Inland Observer Corps were notified to be on the lookout for two unmarked Spitfires heading from the Midlands towards the South East – one hostile, one friendly.

Air Chief Marshal Dowding was informed of the situation when he arrived at his office shortly afterwards. The previous day had been strenuous above all others – Fighter Command was struggling for survival like never before, with exhausted pilots battling against overwhelming odds. Not the best moment for entertaining royalty, yet the King and Queen had chosen that day of all days to visit Bentley Priory. Now he started the new day with a fresh problem; ironically his greatest asset, a Spitfire, hurtling across England piloted by a German spy!

Dowding approved the course of action that had been taken and asked to be kept updated, before turning to the reports and analysis of the previous day's activity awaiting his attention.

Chapter 103

At the climb rate of a thousand feet per minute, Alison soon reached the same altitude as Jan-Arne and continued to climb until she was well above him. She was certain he hadn't seen her; he was no doubt too busy keeping control of the plane to be aware of what was behind him.

They were still flying south-east. Alison needed to do something to steer him off course and push him over to the west, away from the direction of France. She peered through the canopy and recognised Northampton below; she had flown over it many times.

Time was moving on. She must act. She had no armament, so trying to shoot him down was not an option. But she could shake him up, confuse him, until he didn't know whether he was flying north, south, east or west. Nudging the column forward, and with increased throttle, she felt the Spitfire sink gently into a dive. She accelerated fast and felt the g-force pushing at her body. The controls responded beautifully and she could sense what others had said; that this was a pilot's machine, designed to take anything an experienced flyer could demand of it.

Jan-Arne's plane loomed larger and larger ahead of and below her. She had lost track of her air speed; all her attention was on the trajectory of her Spitfire. Suddenly the other plane seemed to mushroom in size, filling her windscreen before disappearing beneath as she roared over it from starboard to port with only a matter of feet separating them. She immediately banked and climbed sharply to port to regain the advantage of height.

She glanced back through the Perspex, craning her neck for a better view. Jan-Arne's plane was all over the place, losing height, swinging wildly off course to starboard, and shaking like a wounded bird.

*

Moss didn't know what the hell had happened. The sudden explosion of engine noise and the belly of a plane swooping so close overhead shook him to the core. It happened so fast he barely saw the other plane. One moment it was there, the next it had gone. For a moment his coordination was in pieces and his Spitfire went into a spin, plummeting earthwards.

The screaming of the Merlin engine seemed to blank out everything else, and it was the sight of fields and hedgerows rising to meet him at an alarming rate that shocked him into regaining control.

By the time he had the column back firmly in his grip, and feet in control of the rudder pedals, the plane was levelling out at barely five hundred feet. He could feel the sweat trickling down his temples and his heart pounding inside his chest. He thought he might vomit and felt his muscles begin to retch, but the feeling subsided.

As the Spitfire climbed again, he looked all around but could see no sign of another plane. By the time he levelled out, he had regained his composure and was thinking clearly again. Who the hell had it been? Surely not a German raider at this time of day and so far inland. If it had been he would have been fired at. Some RAF Johnny mucking about? He knew some of them before the war. They used to hang around at the flying clubs; big egos, with a wild streak, and a bizarre sense of humour. Buzzing a lone plane for fun would appeal to them.

The second attack came just as suddenly, another swoop from above, this time from port to starboard. It was marginally less of a shock, but nevertheless the noise and the wash caused by the other plane – it seemed even closer than before – still made him lose control.

He caught a glimpse of the distinctive wing shape. A Spitfire. But it was gone before he could see any markings.

He regained control quicker this time and without losing so much height. He knew now to expect more. If word had got out that he was in a stolen plane there might be machine gun fire third time round. The first two sweeps may have been to let him know of their presence. He had to abandon flying straight, before it was too late. He levelled out and began to sweep around the sky, zigzagging, first to port then to starboard.

Each time he altered course he craned his neck to see behind him and squinted into the sun. It had not yet occurred to him what the sun's position implied.

*

Alison smiled as she watched from a thousand feet above. That's it, try wriggling about a bit. You don't know what the hell is happening, do you?

It was hard to imagine Jan-Arne inside the cockpit below; all she could see was a Spitfire flying through the early morning sky. It was even harder to think of either the plane or its pilot as the enemy. After all, it was only Jan-Arne . . . and a Spitfire. He'd treated her like dirt, but that was a long time ago. Before Australia. And here she was, having to think of him as the enemy, a fifth columnist who must be stopped at all cost. In her mind it was hard to assimilate the two threads. Love and war. For a moment she didn't care anymore and wanted to give up and fly back to Castle Bromwich. She could say she lost him. What did it matter if he stole a plane . . . what was the big deal? Then she thought of Heather, a young life cut short by this nightmare, and the many countless thousands of others who had also died so far in the wake of this madness. How many more would follow? Jan-Arne was part of the madness. He was on the side of evil. She hated him for it, and in doing so forced herself to hate him again for what he had done to her. She *must* stop him.

The scrap of Winston Churchill's speech flashed into her mind. *But let us all strive without failing in faith or in duty, and the dark curse of Hitler will be lifted from our age.*

It was her duty to stop him. She glanced down at the instrument panel, picking out the direction indicator. She smiled again.

They were heading south-west.

*

A dark spot in the rear view mirror caught Moss's eye. He turned sharply to starboard and twisted his head round. Yes, there it was! Above him, and looking as if it was about to dive again.

"Come on, Krobol!" he yelled to himself. "It's time to fly this plane properly." The safest place to be, he decided, was behind the other plane. He straightened up his course and deliberately flew as straight and level as he could, his hands tense on the stick . . . waiting.

Whoosh! The plane swooped across him with the same precision as before. Instantly, Moss pushed the throttle forward to full for the first time. The surge of power stunned him; his control was better now, enough at least to manoeuvre competently, and the rapid acceleration was manageable. He could see the Spitfire ahead clearly as it banked and climbed. He followed. It didn't take long to close the gap between them. The other plane levelled out and seemed to slow down, as though willing him to catch up. It was veering gradually to starboard, and losing altitude. Soon he was close enough to see that the Spitfire was unpainted, with no identification marks, no white letters on the side of the fuselage. Just like his own.

Then the penny dropped. Of course, the other Spitfire from Castle Bromwich! It must have taken off shortly after him and been in pursuit ever since. In which case it was no more armed than his. He sighed with relief. All the pilot could do was try and distract him, which explained the mock attacks. It must be the test pilot flying it. Henshaw. Perhaps he had been in the car that had almost collided with him on takeoff.

Unless . . . surely not! Alison?

A very experienced pilot, there on the spot, able to take off in the other Spitfire at a moment's notice. Would they let her? They must have done.

As he pondered over the identity of the mystery pilot, Moss's focus moved towards the direction indicator. South-west! He was being pulled away from his course . . . away from London, away from the Kent coast and France. That's what these antics were about. The sly bitch.

He altered course immediately.

*

Alison saw Jan-Arne disappear from her rear view mirror as he changed course. Damn! Oh well, it had worked for a while. They had skirted Oxford and were somewhere between there and Reading. She banked hard to port and flew round in a huge arc, peering in all directions, trying to regain visual contact. It would be harder now that he was on to her, much harder. But she still had a few tricks up her sleeve. If she could get behind and above him again she could push him down to low altitude, as low as possible, and try and force him to make a mistake. A fatal one preferably.

But she was worried now. There was only so much she could do. She badly needed some back up. And fast.

*

At Sector Stations, the response from the Observer Corps had been disappointing. A couple of reported sightings had come in, one from Towcester, near Northampton, and another from Wallingford, but neither could make a definite identification.

Then, out of the blue, 11 Group Headquarters at Uxbridge received a curious report from Tangmere Sector, which had not been warned about the two Spitfires. The sector covered a rough square from the south coast, between Bournemouth and Worthing, up to West London and across to Reading, and had been presumed to be too far south and west to be of relevance. The report originated from Odiham, in the north-west corner of Tangmere Sector; an observer there had reported two unmarked Spitfires, in his words, 'acting the goat' as they headed roughly south-west towards the Hampshire / Surrey border.

Minutes later a report from the village of Liphook was followed almost immediately by one from Midhurst. Both said the same; two Spitfires, confirmed without squadron markings, flying dangerously low, as if to try and outdo each other: "A bloody stupid stunt to play at a time like this," said one.

After consultation with Bentley Priory, Uxbridge telephoned Tangmere and ordered one section only (three aircraft) to be scrambled for a special sortie and, once airborne, to fly eastward at low altitude. The station commander at Tangmere thought it sounded rather dull; a patrol of some kind, no doubt. He decided to send some of the new boys who had recently arrived from West Malling. He telephoned the dispersal hut.

"Midas Squadron . . . Red Section, scramble! Angels three!"

*

Alison was desperately trying everything she could to intimidate Jan-Arne into losing height, buzzing him from both sides and above. Each time he had responded by dropping several hundred feet, until eventually they were almost hedgehopping, which she knew was a damn sight more hazardous for him than it was for her. His reflexes had been good, she remembered, but not exceptional.

She imagined he would be relieved to reach the sea and a smooth surface to fly across without obstacles. This part of the country was unfamiliar to her and she didn't know how far they were from the coast. They were flying almost due south now. She saw a large town to starboard, and a cathedral spire. Salisbury, or Chichester? Not Winchester, she knew, which didn't have a spire. Chichester she was fairly sure.

She glanced at the fuel gauge; nearly half empty. They had already taken a roundabout route, but once they reached the coast he could follow it and hop across to France with ease.

Her next ploy was highly dangerous, and she didn't want to attempt it unless absolutely necessary. But there was no sign of help from any quarter, so she started to prepare herself mentally. Ironically she now needed Jan-Arne to gain height.

*

"Golden, this is Shortjack. Your vector, one-four-five."

Squadron Leader Dan Rodigan listened to the ground controller's metallic voice in his headphones. He and the other two Spitfires had climbed to three thousand feet as instructed, and now knew what course to take. He waited for details of their target. When they came it was like a bad April Fool's joke.

"Look out for two Spitfires, approaching from inland – north to north-east. No squadron markings. Lead Spit is the *bandit* and must be intercepted. Repeat – *Bandit is a Spit*. Pursuing aircraft is friendly. Repeat – *pursuing Spit is friendly*."

Another voice crackled over the airwaves.

"Hear that, Red Leader? We're attacking our own now! As if Jerry isn't enough. What's going on?"

Rodigan shared his confusion. "Are you serious, Shortjack? Repeat again please."

"Absolutely serious. Two unmarked Spitfires coming your way – one is your target, the other is friendly and trying to stop him. Your bandit is being flown by Jerry, trying to reach France with a birthday gift for Göring."

"Roger, Shortjack. Alright chaps, let's get on with it shall we? Do as we're told."

"Ours is not to reason why and all that . . ."

They flew in tight Vic formation, scouring the skies all around. The radio went silent as they pondered their curious assignment.

Red Three was first to spot them.

"There they are! Ten o'clock below." The two Spitfires were cutting across their trajectory and almost at the coast.

"Vic in line astern – go!" ordered Rodigan. Red Two and Red Three slotted their planes in a line behind their leader. "Keep with me. Buster!"

Rodigan banked and the others followed, on full throttle.

"Which is which, Red Leader?"

"You heard the man . . . bandit in front, friendly behind."

"I hope he's got that the right way round."

They stared ahead as they descended with increasing speed, just as the two planes ahead of them left land behind and shot over a pebbly beach and out to sea. Red Section were closing rapidly on their strange quarry. When the leading unmarked Spitfire changed course, heading due east, hugging the coastline, they all did likewise.

Red Three said: "Whoever they are, the friendly one is a damn sight better pilot. Our bandit is wobbling all over the place, like a jelly."

"I should say," added Rodigan. "Will you look at that – he nearly pancaked into the water!"

"Keep on like that and we won't need to stop him."

*

As soon as Jan-Arne turned east, Alison made her move, oblivious to the Spitfires behind her. She guessed he would stay straight and level now, all the way to France. She saw him almost pancake, then gain height to compensate. But he was still flying low, no more than three or four hundred feet. His erratic horizontal balance made it more difficult for her, but there lay the challenge, and she felt hugely exhilarated, as if she was back in Australia, stunt flying.

Dropping to a hundred feet below his wake, she pushed the throttle gently forward; just enough to gain some ground. She could see the surface of the sea below. The water looked smooth with just an occasional white horse breaking it up. She gripped the control column rigidly, feeling for the slightest disturbance, correcting immediately. Her position was perfect. She was now no more forty yards behind Jan-Arne, slightly to port of him. And closing.

As she drew even nearer, she gently eased back the stick, smoothly, slowly. The Spitfire's nose rose in front of her and the horizon slipped out of view.

Twenty yards behind him – sixty feet below.

*

Moss felt good. Just follow the coast then south-east and across to France. He recognized Brighton Pier as it flashed past to port, then, further on, the beautiful stretch of undulating cliffs known as the Seven Sisters. He glimpsed the Belle Tout lighthouse above Beachy Head. Then another pier – Eastbourne presumably.

He'd lost visual contact with Alison's plane and frankly he didn't give a shit. There was little she could do now. He just had to focus on keeping straight and steady.

His plane shuddered, rocking to left and right, each wing dipping in turn. But that was fine; he knew how to compensate now.

*

Poor aileron control, Alison diagnosed as she continued to close in. He really should have that sorted by now. On reflection, she had had better pupils.

Twenty yards behind – forty feet below.

He was flying steadily again. She guessed he was trying to concentrate on his controls as much as possible, and not so much on her. He should worry. They were flying at nigh on three hundred miles an hour, the English coastline would soon be running out to port and France was only minutes away.

Ten yards behind – twenty feet below.

"Don't see me now!" she shouted out loud. "And don't lose control. Not now!"

Full throttle!

With a burst of power, Alison's plane thrust forwards and upwards, banking hard to port. As she did so, the top edge of her starboard wing clipped the underside of Jan-Arne's port wing, flicking his plane over to

394

starboard. She straightened up immediately to avoid a turn that would end up as a nose dive into the sea. Through the canopy she caught a fleeting glimpse of Jan-Arne as he fought desperately for control. The plane corkscrewed in one direction, and then the other, but miraculously he managed to level it out.

She couldn't believe it. He had the luck of the Devil!

They were flying almost parallel with each other. What to do now!

Suddenly she was shocked by the staccato rattling of gunfire; machine guns, seemingly from nowhere. She looked to her right and saw, to her astonishment, another Spitfire closing in behind Jan-Arne's and firing at him. The bullets seemed to go everywhere except into their target. The attacker overshot and banked hard to starboard. There was another one immediately behind, again firing straight at Jan-Arne, but with no more success than the first. For a few moments, it seemed Jan-Arne was unable to comprehend what was happening and made no attempt to manoeuvre away from danger. Then as the second attacker overshot him, his plane rose sharply and disappeared from Alison's view.

The RAF boys were on to him! Fearing for her safety, Alison followed suit and started to climb. Then she felt a sudden anger at the thought that she might not be the one to finish him off. He should be hers to destroy, just as he had destroyed her life two years before. Now it was being taken away from her.

Jan-Arne's plane was ahead and to starboard. She knew what to do next and how to do it. Smash his prop with her wing tip. It would almost certainly bring her down, but it would stop him too.

She did not see the Spitfire closing in behind her.

*

How had he missed a sitting target like that!

Rodigan couldn't believe it. It should have been a dead certainty. When Red Two failed to hit the target as well he was equally baffled.

"Sorry, Red Leader. I don't believe I missed!"

"Me neither," replied Rodigan. But he knew inside the reason why. It felt wrong to be pumping bullets into a Spitfire. Deep down he had wanted to miss.

"Your turn, Red Three. It may be a Spit, but there's a bloody Jerry flying it. Go for the kill."

"I hear you, Red Leader. Here goes." The attacking Spitfire's nose dipped as it began to dive.

Out of the corner of his eye, Rodigan saw the second unmarked Spitfire climbing into the line of fire.

"Watch out, Red Three! Beware the other kite!"

"I see him, Red Leader, I see him."

"Make damn sure you hit the right one."

The Browning machine guns rattled again.

*

Alison revised her plan at the last second. Going for the prop, she decided, was too dangerous and would mean almost certain death for them both. Going for his tailplane might bring down his plane without crippling her own. Shattered elevator tabs and a messed-up rudder would be the end for him. She pulled up suddenly so that she was right behind him.

Almost immediately there was a loud bang from somewhere at the rear of her plane, then another from in front a split second later. She went rigid with shock. Black smoke started pouring from the Merlin engine, and glycol gushed from the ruptured coolant tank, covering the canopy.

A kind of automatic logic took over. All thoughts of stopping Jan-Arne vanished from her mind as the survival instinct kicked in. Ironically, her own rudder pedals were now useless, the cables shot away. The Merlin was coughing and spluttering, and vibrating to an alarming degree. As power began to wane, the plane started sinking gradually in a downward curve.

To bail out she needed to release the canopy – but didn't know how. She looked up, saw a wooden ball above her head and pulled it. Nothing happened. She could feel herself panicking. She pushed at the canopy with both hands but still it did not budge. Then she lifted her elbows and rammed them up and outwards, forcing it off the pins it slid on – and suddenly the canopy was gone. She peered down through the smoke. Just enough height to jump. She undid her harness, opened the access door and eased her feet up on to the front of the seat, wriggling into a squatting position. The plane was beginning to slip into a dive that would soon end its very brief flying history.

She turned towards the port side, threw herself forwards . . . and let the slipstream take her.

*

"Sorry, Red Leader, he swerved right across as I attacked . . . there was nothing I could do!"

"Roger, Red Three, I saw." Rodigan watched as the stricken Spitfire began veering off to port and sinking downwards leaving a trail of smoke in its wake.

"He's bailed out!" cried Red Three with relief. "Chute's open, thank Christ for that!"

"We're just off Dungeness – he'll be picked up. There are plenty of boats down there."

Rodigan's attention turned towards the other unmarked Spitfire; their intended target.

"I've got enough ammo to finish off this bastard, whoever he is. He's not getting away."

"With you, Red Leader."

"Me too, Red Leader."

"Very well. Buster!"

*

Moss was heading out to sea, flying due east at five hundred feet and leaving England behind as the coastline curved away north-east towards Folkestone and Dover. He knew Alison had been hit; she had taken the bullets intended for him. The RAF boys seemed to be holding back for some reason. Maybe she was dead. He really didn't care. Serve her right for interfering.

Thirty miles to the French coast, perhaps less, then he'd be home and dry. Just keep the throttle open and stay on course. He glanced in the rear-view mirror and glimpsed three black dots in the shape of a triangle.

Just keep the throttle open.

A minute passed. He looked again. They were nearer, their shapes clearer. It was a sheer race now.

They were bound to turn back at the French coast, Moss guessed. Surely they wouldn't be foolish enough to follow. He knew he must then land as soon as possible for fear of being shot down by anti-aircraft fire, or even a German fighter. He needed to consider where. If he couldn't identify an aerodrome, a field would have to do; a straight stretch of road even. He could see the coast clearly now, a thin wedge of land sandwiched between the varying blues of sea and sky.

Just keep the throttle open.

*

Red Section's engines were more finely tuned than Moss's, and in the hands of more skilled and experienced pilots. The gap was closing. But not rapidly enough.

"It's no good. We're not going to make it." Red Two's voice was dry with tension.

"We bloody well have to," replied Rodigan. "Look, he's gaining height. Maybe we can hit him from below."

The unmarked plane was indeed rising as it approached the French coast.

Red Two's words echoed Rodigan's thoughts. "That could be your big mistake, chummy."

*

Five miles from the French coast – no more.

Moss glanced behind him. The Spitfires on his tail had closed the gap alarmingly, but he felt certain they would turn back at the coast. He was nervous about the land mass ahead and so had started to climb. At a thousand feet now. The RAF boys were staying low, not following him.

Gradually the coastline loomed closer. He could see a beach, waves breaking onto the sand, and some low cliffs. Suddenly the sea was gone and he was over land. France lay spread out as far as the eye could see.

He'd made it . . . he was over German-occupied territory! Moss felt elated.

The Spitfires chasing him hadn't turned back; they were still behind him. What the hell; they would soon turn round. Any second now. He felt joyous. In a moment of utter spontaneity, he decided to perform a roll . . . a victory roll to taunt his pursuers. He'd made the manoeuvre before in other aircraft, and felt confident with the controls of the Spitfire now. Concentrating as hard as he could, and with a fluency that surprised himself as much as the three Spitfires of Red Section behind him, he eased his plane into a cautious three hundred and sixty degree roll.

At the fully inverted position, he heard a strange rattling noise. A small avalanche of swarf filtered down from the well of the plane; slithers of metal from machining and riveting, particles of aluminum from the sheets covering the fuselage, and fragments from a dozen other components and processes. Some of it rested momentarily in the top of the Perspex canopy, then as the plane completed its roll sprinkled down around Moss's head, finding its way into his unprotected eyes.

He screamed, blinking uncontrollably as the particles scratched his eyeballs, sharp needles of pain stabbing into him. His vision became a watery, agonising blur.

*

Red Section watched as their prey began to lose control.

"What's happening?" cried Red Three. "He's going potty!"

As the inverted Spitfire wilted into a shallow dive, it began to spin. The dive became steeper and the spin became faster.

"He's going down!"

The three pilots watched as the dive became a vertical drop – at approaching four hundred miles an hour, Dan Rodigan estimated. It plummeted into a hedgerow on the edge of a meadow. A great cloud of dust rose above a fireball that engulfed the wreckage

There was an eerie silence in the cockpits of Red Section, broken eventually by Rodigan. "Show over, gentlemen. Back to base, before we run out of juice."

"Or we get bounced by Jerry."

They turned, tightened into Vic formation and headed back towards the English coast.

"Where is Jerry anyway? He's late today. Don't normally have to come over to wake him up."

"Perhaps he's buggered off back home to Jerry land, where he belongs."

"Alright," intervened Rodigan. "Cut the cackle. Let's just concentrate on getting home, shall we?"

Silence prevailed for all of thirty seconds.

"Red Leader."

"What is it?"

"I'm glad we didn't have to make the kill. Doesn't seem right – shooting up a Spit."

Rodigan felt exactly the same way. Even if it was a Jerry frying in the wreckage, it didn't seem right to fire on a Spitfire. Whatever had happened to make it lose control and crash like that, he was thankful they hadn't been responsible.

Chapter 104

By midday, Jerry still hadn't come. Back at Tangmere, Dan Rodigan lay fully-clothed on his bed and dozed fitfully, regaining a small fragment of the sleep lost during past weeks. Midas Squadron had been released until fourteen hundred hours, and he was trying to make the most of this brief respite.

There was a firm knock on the door. It was his batman.

"What the bloody hell is it!" yelled Rodigan sharply.

"Very sorry to disturb, sir, but there's a young lady to see you."

Rodigan raised his head from his pillow and tried to focus on the voice. "Lady, what lady?"

"Won't give her name, sir, but she says you know her. Flew in on one of them ATA ferry planes, though she ain't exactly wearing the uniform."

Rodigan sat bolt upright. "It can't be . . . surely not!" He stood up and hurried to the door.

Outside, looking very bedraggled and wearing borrowed clothes several sizes too large, stood Alison.

"Hello, Dan."

"Ally! Good grief, what a wonderful surprise." He took her hand, pulled her inside and closed the door. They kissed. Then he stood back and looked her up and down. "What on earth are you doing here – and why are you dressed like that for heaven's sake? Is something wrong?"

"Nothing's wrong. I've just been for an early morning swim, that's all. Got soaked so had to borrow some dry things. Not ideal."

"Really – a swim? Around here somewhere?"

"No, off Dungeness."

Rodigan stared at her incredulously. "You went for an early morning swim off Dungeness? Surely not!"

"Yes, it was definitely Dungeness. I was flying over actually – until I unexpectedly found myself in the water."

"What an extraordinary coincidence, I flew over there earlier too."

"It's bloody cold in the Channel."

"I know!"

"I was very lucky . . . splashed down almost next to a boat and was picked up immediately. I was only in the water for a couple of minutes."

"And here you are, a few hours later, knocking on my door. That's fast work – how on earth did you manage it?"

"They put me ashore at Dymchurch and a very nice policeman arranged a lift to Hawkinge for me. Only about twenty miles. Then another bit of luck – Howard was there. He flies one of our ATA taxi planes. I managed to persuade him to drop me here on his way back to White Waltham. Not exactly en route, but he's very obliging, our Howard. Poor man is still very cut up about Heather . . . he adored her. I hope you don't mind my turning up like this, only I've had a hell of a time and I just wanted to see you."

"Of course I don't mind. So there *is* something wrong."

"It's a long story, can I tell you over lunch? I'm starving."

"Come on then. We've been released, but that could change any moment. Jerry's late today for some reason."

They strolled towards the mess, hand in hand. There was silence as they mulled over the morning's events, and the coincidence of having both been over Dungeness. Rodigan spoke first.

"Odd place to be ferrying a plane."

"I wasn't ferrying it exactly. Anyway, what were you doing over Dungeness so early in the morning, if Jerry hasn't shown up yet?"

"Hard to believe, but we were chasing a couple of . . ." He stopped in mid-sentence, suddenly mindful that perhaps he ought not to say precisely what they had been chasing.

There was another silence, broken this time by Alison.

"You weren't by any chance chasing a couple of unmarked Spitfires?"

Rodigan's eyes widened as the truth dawned on him. "And I don't suppose that was you – in the friendly Spit that we . . ."

"It was indeed."

"Well of all the things! Unmarked . . . of course, it must have come straight from the factory."

"You shot me down!" said Alison accusingly.

"Now hang on, that isn't strictly true – not guilty. I tried and missed. But I know the man who did."

"Thank you, kind sir, that was jolly decent of you to miss."

"Don't mention it."

"What happened to the other Spit?" asked Alison apprehensively. "Please don't tell me he got away."

"No, not quite, but very nearly. We bagged him – or rather he bagged himself. His flying days are over." He put his hand round her shoulder, pulled her to him and kissed her on the cheek. "Tell me, what was a nice girl like you chasing a bloody awful pilot like him – and who the hell was it up there? They told us he was a Jerry."

401

"A Norwegian actually. But on Jerry's side. He wasn't that bad a pilot – just not used to flying a Spitfire."

"Norwegian did you say?"

"That's right." They had reached the entrance to the mess hall. "I say, do you think they will let me in dressed like this?"

"I don't see why not," said Rodigan. "Look at the building – not exactly at its finest either. Took a direct hit a couple of weeks ago." He opened the door for Alison. "So what *were* you doing chasing that Norwegian?"

"I was giving him a flying lesson."

"A flying lesson!" He nodded patronisingly. "I see."

"Yes, a flying lesson." She kissed him back and stepped inside. "He used to be a pupil of mine."

EPILOGUE

(Tuesday 7th August 1951)

It was a warm and sunny day when Monsieur Viardot arrived in London for a week's holiday with his wife and their three children; an eight-year-old, and two adolescents from Madame Viardot's first marriage.

They stayed in a guest house in Pimlico and spent several days seeing the sites. The Festival of Britain was on and they could see the Skylon pointing towards the heavens on the South Bank as they set out each morning. Inevitably they ended up crossing the river to take a closer look. They rode on the miniature railway and wandered around the Pleasure Gardens and the Dome of Discovery.

Monsieur Viardot limped quite badly, so much so that he always walked with the aid of a stick. But he managed to get around well enough and kept up with the others.

The children wanted to see England, where their father came from. Their mother was less enthusiastic. But it was a refreshing change to be in a city for a while, whether in France or England – very different from the isolated fruit farm at the foot of the Monts d'Auvergne which was their home.

On the fourth day he told the children that he had some business to attend to and he would have to leave them for the day. His wife was in sullen mood; it wasn't business at all. She didn't want him to go and found it impossible to conceal her feelings. She didn't see the point. The past was the past and he had turned his back on it more than ten years ago.

But he had the burn of curiosity inside him, and it would not leave him alone.

They parted without a kiss. He limped the short distance to Victoria and caught a bus to Euston where he boarded a train for the Midlands, arriving at Coventry just over two hours later, his leg aching painfully from having been tucked under a cramped seat.

He knew the city had suffered terribly. News of the *Luftwaffe*'s devastating raid on 14th November 1940 had penetrated even into the depths of the French countryside. The Germans had called it Operation Moonlight Sonata. More than five hundred planes; ten hours of bombing, with pin-point accuracy; a third of the city's buildings destroyed; another third badly damaged; a hundred acres of the city centre decimated.

He had read that the German Minister of Propaganda, Joseph Goebbels, later used the word *coventriert* – 'coventried' – to describe similar mass destruction of enemy towns.

Nearly six hundred people had been killed in Coventry that night, and almost a thousand wounded.

As he limped slowly through the streets, the occasional building struck him as familiar, but mainly there were new buildings, or gaps where buildings had once stood. The cathedral was just a shell, though remarkably the huge tower remained intact. He had never been particularly religious and never once set foot inside it. Now he wished he had, out of curiosity.

The more he walked, the more the pain in his leg decreased as the circulation improved. He walked for a long time, making his way gradually, inevitably, towards the street that he needed to see again. He grew nervous. He knew he was playing with fire, and that the consequences of what he was doing might range from simply satisfying his curiosity to stirring up emotions and causing pain and anxiety. Part of him wanted to know, part of him did not. If he could have written to someone and asked questions, he would have done so. But there was no one. Coming in person was the only way.

And when he reached his destination, most of his questions were answered in a moment, without a word being spoken. The street barely existed anymore.

It had been a long street, and at the far end a small cluster of terraced houses still remained. As for the rest, it was a waste land, bulldozed flat, with corrugated fencing creating a corridor where houses had once stood. He gazed motionless for a good ten minutes, absorbing the nothingness, comparing it with his memory of how the street had once looked. Then he walked the entire length of the corridor, towards the houses at the far end. The side of the nearest house had huge timbers propped against it, shoring it up; the outline of the rooms of the house that had once stood next door could be clearly seen. It was as though a great knife had sliced them apart.

There were about ten in all still standing. He approached the first.

A man in his shirtsleeves answered the door. He was young, no more than twenty-five. No, he'd only lived there for six months and didn't know much about the area. But there was an old woman two doors along who might be of help; she used to live further down the street until she was bombed out.

Before knocking on the door, the man tugged self-consciously at his bushy beard, wandering if he might be recognised. He need not have worried. When the shuffling footsteps reached the front door and it creaked open, the face that appeared had the sunken eyes of the blind. She was probably in her late sixties. He recognised her; he'd helped her across the street a few times. She invited him in.

Over a cup of tea, the old lady reminisced, steered gently by his questions.

Marion Wakeley. Yes, the young woman who lived a few doors down from her . . . number twenty-nine or thereabouts. Her husband was killed at Dunkirk. Nice girl, lovely children too. He had been a bit of a so-and-so, the husband. Used to knock her about, or so she had heard.

Yes, he said, he had heard that too.

She had found herself another man quite soon after. He was much nicer. Henry, his name was – a musician. He played the trumpet down at the local on a couple of occasions. Some said he came on the scene a bit too soon for the sake of decency. But he was good for her and made her happy. The children had been evacuated by then – almost every child in the street went somewhere or other. He and Marion used to pop down to see them at weekends. They adored him. She had been very happy. Pity it had lasted such a short time.

So what happened to them? Presumably they were bombed out. Where did they go?

The old woman stirred in her chair, her sightless eyes seemingly fixed on a point close to infinite. That was the sad part. No sooner had she found happiness than it had been taken away from her. Not just Marion, of course. So many people were killed that night, half the people in the street. She began to cry. She lost a lot of friends – and most of the ones who *had* lived through it had moved away since. How she survived she would never know.

Killed?

Both of them.

And the children?

No idea. They never came back from where they were evacuated. Somewhere in the Cotswolds, she seemed to remember. It was ten years ago, they could be anywhere now. Lovely children. She couldn't remember their names.

Simon and Annette, he reminded her.

She smiled. Of course, that was it. Why did he want to know these things? Was he a relative? His voice sounded vaguely familiar.

He didn't answer. She heard him shuffle across the room. The front door slammed, hard, and she was alone.

He walked back towards the station. *Killed at Dunkirk!* So that was what everyone thought. He never got that far.

He thought back to that afternoon in late May 1940; the day he had been captured, stripped to his underwear and then force-marched across a field, along with the rest of his company. Others had gone before them. He was one of the last to cross the field, having been detained by the men who had taken his clothes. He saw others being herded into an old barn ahead of him, with *Waffen SS* soldiers guarding the outside. It started to rain and he naively assumed the Germans were keeping their prisoners dry. But he sensed danger before he reached the barn door. Something was terribly wrong.

A British officer was complaining vehemently. The barn was too small for so many men. It was inhumane to treat them in such a way. One of the German soldiers yelled, "English pig, there will be plenty of room where you are going!" and pulled a stick grenade out of the side of his jackboot. He saw the officer pleading with the soldier not to throw it. But throw it he did . . . into the crowded barn.

So he had turned and run – faster than he had ever run in his life. The weeks of humiliation in battle, the hunger and thirst seemed to slip away as he hurtled through the rain, zigzagging and ducking, bullets skimming past him on either side. He reached a hedge and tore his way through it, barely noticing the pain from the cuts and scratches on his arms and legs.

There were shouts in German. They chased him. He reached the edge of the next field and had almost scrambled through another hedge when a bullet hit him in the leg. He remembered the worst stabbing pain he had ever known. He screamed, and blacked out.

For some reason the Germans had not pursued him to finish the job, probably ordered back to the barn where there was other work to be done. Only much later did he hear what had happened after the British officer had tried to stop that stick grenade. More grenades thrown into the barn, survivors pulled out and shot, then guns fired into the barn to finish off the others. Eighty dead. Miraculously, not everyone was killed. Fifteen survived, protected by the bodies of their comrades. The injured remained there for two whole days before help arrived.

The Wormhout Massacre.

Hours later, a Frenchman dragged him to a farmhouse and hid him in a cellar. A doctor came and tended to his leg. The bullet had damaged the bone and he had lost a great deal of blood. But he would live. Then a journey in a hay cart, and another farmhouse; the first of a string of hiding places. The French helped him but some clearly found the task distasteful. They hated the British for giving up the fight, escaping back home in their boats, leaving France to be overwhelmed by the *Bosch*.

It took him two months to reach the Auvergne, where he was hidden by a woman, the widow of a farmer who had died recently – nothing to do with the war but in a hunting accident of all things. She was older than him, in her early thirties, with two young children. She was struggling to manage the fruit farm on her own. Her married name was Viardot. They liked each other, and he helped her with the chores as best he could. They seemed to understand each other instinctively, despite the language barrier. She countered his temper with her own Gallic flare, and he respected her for it. Marion had always been too soft with him. In this new woman he found his match. One evening, after too much wine and a heated exchange over something trivial, he hit her. She immediately hit him back, so hard she broke his nose. He never touched her again.

So he stayed. The farm became his home. Until the war ended few people even knew he was there, and by then he spoke French fluently, had fathered a child, and was known to one and all as Monsieur Viardot. The Germans had pretty much left the area alone; he hardly saw one from the time he arrived until the liberation. Apart from the pain in his leg, which never disappeared for long, he was happier and more content than he had ever been in his life.

It had taken more than a decade for curiosity to draw him back to England, to find out what had happened to his other family. Next time, if there was one, he might come looking for the children. But he felt no real urge to do so. He had a new family now.

Bernard Viardot limped his way back to Coventry Station and waited for the London train. As he waited he glanced at a poster on the wall. Next week the City of Birmingham Symphony Orchestra was giving one of a series of reconciliation concerts featuring German music and musicians. Performing Bach's Double Violin Concerto would be guest soloists Bruno and Renate Rolf.

He didn't care much for classical music. It was boring. Nothing could beat a good swing band.

The train hissed and clanked into the station. He swung the carriage door open and slumped into a seat, preparing himself for the discomfort of the next couple of hours back to London.

He wondered what his wife and children had been doing all day.